Benedict Arnold: Legacy Lost
(A Ghost's Story)

*Chris
I hope you
enjoy this journey*

Will Martin

Will Martin

BENEDICT ARNOLD: LEGACY LOST
(A Ghost's Story)

Copyright © 2011 Will Martin

ISBN 978-0-9839307-1-6

1. Benedict Arnold 1741 – 1801. 2. Historical Fiction.
3. American Revolution. 4. George Washington 1732 – 1799.
5 Martin Van Derwerker 1744 – 1841

Library of Congress Catalogue Number: 2011914680

Legacy Lost Publishing
Saratoga Springs, New York 12866-8828
http://www.LegacyLost.net

Cover Design by DJM Graphix

On the cover: Gary Petagine and Bill Wienecke
Members of the 5th New York Regiment
Photograph: Rob Dadekian

Printed in the United States of America

DEDICATION

This work is dedicated to:

<u>My own band of brothers</u>: Sherwood and Raymond, with whom I share the ups and downs of life's journey;

<u>My band of children</u>: Ben, Chris, Danny, Ryan and Renée, each of whom I love more than they can possibly know;

<u>My band of friends</u>: Ralph (Butch) Sparks, George Moore, Frank Dumin, and Rob Dadekian, each of whom provided me friendship, companionship and encouragement during important turning points in my life.

As others can attest, the writing of a novel is a lonely and isolating endeavor. Therefore, I also dedicate this work to my wife, Shelley, who spent many a lonely hour while I sequestered myself at the computer composing thoughts and words into the storyline within this novel. On many an evening, she was to fall asleep before I extinguished the lamp above my desk. On many a morning, she awoke to find me missing, as I tried to squeeze in a few early morning hours of writing during a time of day when I hoped my absence wouldn't be noticed…It was.

ACKNOWLEDGMENTS

There are several individuals to whom I owe a debt of gratitude for inspiration and encouragement as I journeyed down the uncertain path leading to the publication of this work. Although I've read the works of many who have written about the life and times of Benedict Arnold, three authors in particular provided my greatest moments of insight and were responsible for triggering my interest in this controversial man of history. The first was James Kirby Martin (no relation) and his work, _Benedict Arnold Revolutionary Hero._ His telling of Arnold's contribution to the war effort was a refreshing refrain from others who cast a darker cloud over the man often called simply, _"Traitor."_ Then there was Audrey Wallace and her very personal descriptions of Arnold and his life as depicted within her work: _Benedict Arnold – Misunderstood Hero?_ And finally, Kenneth Roberts whose works of historical fiction, _Arundle_ and _Rabble in Arms_, written in the 1930s, breathed life into Benedict Arnold's character – the likes of which I haven't seen since. His works set my imagination in motion. These three individuals sparked my interest and provided me with valued insights into the man, Benedict Arnold and, by their collective descriptions of this man and his life, provided the seeds from which my writing blossomed.

I wish to acknowledge as well the contributions of Dawn Josephson, Master Writing Coach, who taught me the difference between telling a story and writing a novel. And finally, I need to also acknowledge the assistance of Verna Gerrity, Jean Elsroth, Sarah Martin and Deborah Horton. Their collective proofreading skills and attention to detail helped to improve this book beyond measure. Should any mistakes remain, I only have myself to blame because of my "tinkering" after their work was completed. God only knows the number of "suggestions for improvement" they each offered.

PROLOGUE

A review of the literature published within the last 100 years about Benedict Arnold is remarkable. What is even more curious is that, for reasons not so obvious to the casual observer, there appears to be an increasing interest in the subject of Benedict Arnold of late. Fictional stories of his life have been fashioned; biographies have been written; screenplays and documentaries have been produced; and tales of Benedict Arnold's participation in the American Revolution have been well documented. Indeed, some researchers and history buffs have spent lifetimes studying every available facet of Benedict Arnold's life and appear to have become somewhat fascinated with the hope and prospect of understanding and getting to know Benedict Arnold, the man.

Frankly, I am not certain that I can now determine how my own interest with this man of history started, or what causal factors led me to this point of captivation. However, to my family's chagrin, fascinated I have become. Suffice to consider it a "hobby," which became of greater interest to me when I could not escape the conclusion that the whole story regarding Benedict Arnold has not yet been told. *Why did he do it?* This seems to be the focus of most current writings; trying to understand and explain why Benedict Arnold, a Patriot who sacrificed much, became a traitor. Why did this man who, from the very beginning of the Revolution, was separated from his young family for so many years; who fought in so many battles; who was wounded not once, but twice; who became a loyal supporter and, indeed, friend of George Washington; who gave money and blood to the cause of independence, why? Why did he do it? Why did he betray not only his country, but his friends, his family and, indeed, himself?

Some say it was because of the way members of the Continental Congress treated him with respect to pay and promotions. Some say it was due to the influence of his second wife, Peggy Shippen-Arnold, and her family's support of the loyalist position during the early days of the revolution. Others say it was Benedict Arnold's concern about the Roman Catholic-dominated French and their growing involvement in the war; consequently, American affairs after the successful Saratoga campaign. And, finally, some say it was greed and money, pure and simple – he did it for the money. Yes, many theories and explanations have been offered. However, as one reads the work of others, it becomes clear that, like me in the beginning, they essentially ask the same questions and essentially draw the same conclusions based on the writings of others; adding their own personal interpretations and speculations as they do so. The conclusions thus far put forth are, by and large, all based upon the same observations and, indeed, the same writings upon which the history of Benedict Arnold has been cast.

However, as I read more and more, a new focus started to emerge. As I pieced together more facts about this man, and those around him, a different question started to emerge. Soon it became clear to me that authors have, for the most part, been asking the wrong question. The difference between others and me at this point in time is the premise of the question. They ask why he betrayed his country. I ask why the truths about Benedict Arnold's real objectives were never revealed. Could the act of which so much has been written, be something other than betrayal? Might this *"act of betrayal"* be simply that: an act? Might the traitorous actions of Benedict Arnold, of which there has been so much conjecture, be nothing more than another sacrifice?

What the readers and writers on the subject of Benedict Arnold have thus far not done is to peer into his soul and allow the man, in spirit, to join in this quest for understanding. It is by this means that understanding can truly be found. Like others who have studied Benedict Arnold, I, too, have been touched by the man, intellectually and emotionally. This work is driven by the belief that his spirit is reaching out to have the truth become known; to have his family name cleansed and have the legacy of his life righted from that of traitor to that of patriot and hero. In essence, *the spirit ghost of Benedict Arnold writes this story.*

The intention of this account is to present the reader with an opportunity to see a seldom-witnessed side of Benedict Arnold and to also consider a proposition that is rarely, if ever, openly discussed among the serious minded. Although demonized for well over 230 years; hated in life, ridiculed and scorned by generations since his death, Arnold is, nonetheless, a man that historians and readers of history are still attempting to understand and explain. Historians and the readers of history have often asked themselves:

> *How could a man who fought so hard and suffered so many personal pains and losses for the cause of the revolution; how could this man, poised for greatness by his demonstrated battlefield leadership, fall so far from the graces of his countrymen and the nation for generations upon generations?*

This question has perplexed historians who have looked back to study, analyze, and try to explain why this battlefield leader turned his back upon his country, his friends and his family. The writers of history have thus far limited themselves to a review of known early records and accounts of witnesses who professed to possess an understanding and insight into the motives of this man named Arnold.

Nevertheless, the writers and readers of the subject of the American Revolution and Benedict Arnold have not given up the quest for a greater understanding of this man and his actions – they've yet to be satisfied. The cognitive dissonance between the knowledge gained from what one reads, and what one feels in his or her gut, keeps the flame of interest in the subject of Benedict Arnold burning still. The intellect vs. the emotion – the ever-present human condition where what one *knows*, from what one reads does not strike a chord with what one *feels*. The conflict between the intellect and one's intuition is evidence of man's continuing struggle for understanding. As one seeks a greater understanding of Benedict Arnold, one must consider both what one learns from the information taken in and what one feels. Once the balance is struck between the two centers of our being, only then can one arrive at a greater understanding of this man. For me, the struggle for conflict resolution on the subject of Benedict Arnold is ended.

This reading of Benedict Arnold's untold story will undoubtedly ring familiar to some. Although a chronicle on this order has not heretofore been written, I am certain that this accounting of Benedict Arnold has been whispered to historians and readers of American history before – whispered in the minds of those who have, over the years, attempted to explain the inexplicable. Having said this, I am also certain that I am not the only individual who has discovered the yet untold explanation to what the world has almost universally believed to be fact – I am simply the only person who has listened to the whispers. It appears that others have not listened quite so carefully. Quietly at first, the whispers were gentle; even subconscious. Only when I allowed myself to listen; to focus and concentrate on this man called *"traitor"* did the whispers become something more – something persistent, unmistakable and unavoidable.

I call them *"whispers."* But a friend who was much more in tune with the universe and all its mysteries, referred to them as *"agreements."* This was a concept he shared with me from his readings of Carlos Castaneda and his several writings on the subject of Don Juan Matus – a man who Carlos professed knew more than most mortal men about the mysteries of life – and of death. Once I became comfortable with an understanding of alternate realities, I was then able to unlock the secret behind Benedict Arnold's actions. This key to understanding led me to ultimately discover how Benedict Arnold demonstrated his love for country, his friend George Washington, and his family, as well as his commitment to honor his word – even until death. I am now convinced that Benedict Arnold, a man so hated in life as well as in death, was nothing less than an ultimate patriot – a patriot who sacrificed his reputation and lived the remainder of his life in obscurity so that the posterity of the United States of America could be assured.

While acknowledging the gruff and egotistical nature of Benedict Arnold, this writing will provide insights into the previously unseen compassionate and softer side of the man. Although known to the world at large and virtually every American school student today as a traitor, this writing will demonstrate that, even in his darkest hour and when he was hated most, Benedict Arnold was, indeed, nothing less than a patriot willing to sacrifice everything in his personal struggle for what he accurately perceived as the birth of a nation.

Historians have characterized Benedict Arnold as a proud man, who overcame the troubles, trials and tribulations of his youth, while he and his family suffered under the influences of an alcoholic father. History documents that Benedict Arnold was blessed with a loving, caring and proud mother, who struggled somewhat successfully to keep the Arnold family together and meet their daily needs. It was his complicated life as a youth that planted the seeds from which his character and personality blossomed and that, undoubtedly influenced his actions and behavior as an adult. It was during these formative years that the path which Arnold's spirit and soul were to take throughout life and beyond was charted and the sails for his life's journey were set. It was the teachings of his mother that cultivated Arnold's beliefs in God and enabled him to recognize and acknowledge the influences of Providence in his life. This writing will show the side of Benedict Arnold thus far not commonly known. Arnold will be seen as an obsessive and unfaithful, yet loving husband. Readers will witness the depth of Benedict's love for his first and second wives – both of whom shared the common first name of Peggy. Readers will also see that Arnold loved and provided for his children and his sister Hannah, the only sibling of Benedict to survive into adulthood. Readers will learn that Benedict's passion extended also to his friends, his countrymen and, ultimately, to his country. Yes, for Benedict Arnold, it was all about family, friends, and country, as well as self.

This tale of discovery is centered on 15 facts regarding the lives of Benedict Arnold, George Washington, Peggy Shippen-Arnold, as well as British Major John André, and draws upon the lives of other, lesser-known individuals who lived during the time of the Revolution. This writing will document Benedict Arnold's relationship with a patriot and simple farmer, Martin Van Derwerker. As a member of the militia, Van Derwerker lived in a small colonial community near the current day, Saratoga Springs, New York, and fought under Arnold's command at Ticonderoga, Valcour Island and, finally, on the battlefield at Saratoga.

Like Arnold, he, too, was wounded during the Battle at Saratoga and also cared for at the same hospital as Arnold in Albany. Martin Van Derwerker's wife, Martha, traveled to Albany from Saratoga to care for her husband and ended up as well caring for Arnold, who was in much worse condition and near death on more than one occasion during his convalescence. It was during this four-month period of recovery in Albany that Arnold learned the true meaning of sacrifice, the meaning of love, of life and of God. It was also at this place, during this time when Arnold first conceived his *victory plan* that would one day cause others to curse his very birth. Readers will learn that the plan conceived by Arnold during the winter of 1777 and spring of 1778, the plan that took form and shape over the next year and a half, was never fully revealed to the world.

No more than seven others ever knew anything about the full scope of Benedict's actual plot. In the beginning, there were only two; since the time of his death, no more than seven individuals ever learned the total truth about Arnold's plot to assure that the patriot cause would succeed. Known only to seven individuals for more than two centuries, this secret has been kept from the world over time – until now.

Benedict Arnold: Legacy Lost (A Ghost's Story)

With the belief that *all things are possible and that all truth is not known,* this conviction regarding Benedict Arnold's true motives is based upon an understanding of a soldier's psyche and the following well-documented facts:

1. *Fact* – Benedict Arnold's second wife, Peggy Shippen, was a "very close friend" of British Officer John André.
2. *Fact* – George Washington was a strong and loyal supporter of Benedict Arnold before his "act of betrayal."
3. *Fact* – George Washington and Benedict Arnold met on several occasions shortly before the infamous month of September 1780.
4. *Fact* – George Washington personally arrived "just in time" to thwart the British's attempt to capture West Point. Some say it was "divine providence" or an act of God that placed Washington at a critical location at a critical time.
5. *Fact* – After "the betrayal," George Washington ordered his men to find and capture Benedict Arnold "alive."
6. *Fact* – Due to the circumstances surrounding his meeting with Benedict Arnold and at Arnold's suggestion, young John André disguised his uniform, hid secret papers on his person and, against the direct orders of his superior officers, behaved as a spy.
7. *Fact* – After trial, and upon the order of George Washington, John André, the former lover of Peggy Shippen before she met and married Benedict Arnold, was hanged.
8. *Fact* – George Washington permitted Benedict Arnold's wife, Peggy, a suspected loyalist, to join her husband after the "betrayal."
9. *Fact* – The British were defeated and the Americans were able to win their quest for independence from Britain, while limiting the future involvement of the French in the affairs of colonial America.
10. *Fact* – Benedict Arnold was discretely unfaithful to his wife.
11. *Fact* – Near the end of his life, Peggy Shippen-Arnold learned of the unfaithfulness of her husband and the existence of a son born to Arnold by another woman while married to Peggy.
12. *Fact* – As the Revolutionary War neared an end and throughout the remainder of his life, some would say that George Washington

became overly concerned about his "legacy" and how history would remember him.

13. *Fact* – After George Washington's death on December 14, 1799, Martha Washington burned some of his private papers.

14. *Fact* – After Benedict Arnold's death on June 14, 1801, Peggy Shippen burned some of his private papers.

15. *Fact* – When Peggy Shippen-Arnold died on August 24, 1804, she still possessed a locket containing a snippet of hair given to her by British Officer John André, twenty-six years before…

Love runs dark. Love runs deep. Love complicates life. And love explains all.

CHAPTER 1

ROAD LEADING TO SARATOGA – DECEMBER, 1785

The noon-time sun was as high as it was ever going be on this gray, overcast day as a lone rider and his horse ambled down the frost-encrusted road leading to the northeastern New York colonial Township of Saratoga. It was his first journey back to America since the end of the Revolution; unlike the last time he had ridden this road, it was now empty, the landscape barren, desolate…and peaceful.

To protect himself from the harsh elements of winter, the traveler wore a long winter coat, tricorn hat, and a dark blue hooded cape. And, remembering a lesson of an Indian elder from his youth, he also wrapped a long, oversized deerskin blanket over his shoulders and the exposed flanks of his horse. Nonetheless, the frigid temperature caused each to expel gentle puffs of vapor from their nostrils as they continued their lonely journey over this rutted path leading to their next destination. Slumped low in his saddle, the shivering rider reached out with his brown leather glove to slowly brush snow from his horse's dark brown mane. "Hang in there my boy. It's not much farther now. Not much longer until we'll be warm again."

The solitude of travel experienced on this day was in stark contrast to the time he was last at this location, in the fall of '77. At that time, men by the score crowded this very road; all carrying long-barreled muskets, powder horns, leather pouches stuffed with cartridges and spare balls of lead. Clutching onto satchels of food, cooking utensils, dreams of glory, and little else, young and old members of the militia descended upon these rolling hills. They all came to join forces with the Continental Army in its effort to stop the British's advance to Albany – the heartland of colonial America. And that they did.

Deep in thought of days gone by, the rider all but ignored the lightly falling snow as it cast a white shroud over him and his horse.

Passing beneath a towering, leaf-barren oak tree, the only sounds to be heard were the muffled clomps of the horse's hooves as they met the hardened ground beneath. Among the lofty branches of the enormous tree's outstretched arms sat a solitary large, black crow. Turning its head to look, first with one eye and then the other, the crow watched intently as his momentary visitor passed beneath. Once beyond the aged oak, the rider then heard the distinctive call of the crow and the echo-like retorts of invisible crows from more distant perches.

Looking upward at the now cackling observer, the rider informed his horse, "Some would say that this crow is an omen my friend, and is perhaps even trying to tell us something. Problem is, I never did take the time to learn to speak 'crow' and I can't be certain if our encounter is a good omen or a bad one." With a sigh, he turned back to look in the direction of the path ahead, "Time will tell. Time will tell."

Continuing his travel, the rider mumbled to his horse, "Eight years. It has been eight long years since I've ridden this path." The rider's horse appeared to be listening somewhat attentively as he continued his faithful service to his passenger. "Although history will show that the war is long ended, few will likely ever know that battles are yet being waged. The war of independence may be over, but the battlegrounds have not yet settled matters still outstanding."

By late-afternoon, the sun rested low in the sky and white clouds cast vast shadows that danced quickly over the snow-covered, tree-topped landscape blocking the sun's fleeting warm rays from reaching the earth below. Weary from his long day of travel and with a heavy sigh, the traveler looked about him with a melancholy stare. "Although much has changed, it is my expectation that some fragments of my past yet remain."

CHAPTER 2

SARATOGA

When the rider finally reached the small township of Saratoga, a dull grey shroud of thinning clouds masked dusk's sun as it slowly dipped behind forested hills in the west. Passing a smithy and sawmill on the outskirts of town, the horse and rider wandered slowly down its empty main street. He took notice of a general store to his left and a barber shop on his right. A painted sign hung on the barber shop wall announced the services available at this humble establishment: 'Haircuts, Tooth Extractions, and Other Treatments of Medical Necessity.' Turning toward an apothecary beyond the barber shop, the rider also smirked at that proprietor's message, painted on its window: 'Elixirs, Potions, and Concoctions Guaranteed to Help Mend Most Common Ailments of Human Misery.' Leaning forward the rider whispered to his horse: "Looks like we've come to the right place, Governor."

But, to his disappointment, all were closed; the storefront windows dark and the merchants warm in their homes. Yet, in a distance, one building did appear to have life inside. At this hour, the dim glow of candlelight from a storefront window and smoke coming from its chimney were telltale signs of an inn or saloon. Making his way to the establishment's door, he noticed yet another sign slowly swinging above the establishment's entrance door. Reaching up to hold it steady, he squinted to read its message in the waning evening light. Three simple words faintly painted on weather beaten wood confirmed his hope: '*The Bryan Inn.*'

Entering the inn, the distinctive sound of a crackling fire and the hushed mumbles of people talking could be heard. The sweet scent of burning apple and maple wood aroma filled the room. Looking around as he entered, he noticed the silhouettes of three men seated near a large open-hearth fireplace to his right. They were broad-shouldered men; dressed in heavy woolen clothing, with unshaven faces and tufts of unkempt hair sticking out from beneath fur-covered hats. As he looked in their direction, they all turned to carefully study their new visitor in return. To his relief, he recognized none; nor did they appear to recognize him. After their mutual exchange of glances, one raised his mostly empty glass with a partially deformed, scar-covered hand in the direction of their new arrival. "Welcome in from the cold my friend. It is not often we get strangers passing through these parts at this time of year. Where're you from?"

"Thank you. I'm from Quebec, passing through on my way to Albany." Taking off his hat and shaking snow from its crevasses onto the floor, "And I've got to admit, 'tisn't often that I spend much time in the saddle this time of year either."

Studying the faces of his new acquaintances and guessing at their ages, the traveler expected that one or more of them would have likely been involved in the Revolution. And, given the inn's location, he thought it was likely that they would have also been at the battles that occurred on the fields a short distance away eight years before. His suspicions were all but confirmed when his eye caught sight of a solitary crutch sitting on the floor next to a man missing his lower left leg, just below the knee. *But for the grace of God*, thought the traveler who was somehow pleased to see that, despite the pains of life the amputee must have endured, he was still able to laugh, joke and drink.

Glancing away from the men, he strained his eyes to make out more details of the tavern. However, the dim glow coming from several small candles scattered throughout the room filling the inn with faint yellow hues of light and deep shadows, made it difficult to see much more than vague images of the tavern's interior. The glow of the candles gave the tavern a warm, home-like feel. Despite the room's darkness, he was able to see three rusting cannon balls: two 24 pounders and a 12 pounder, sitting on a large wooden mantel above the fireplace. Light from the candles mounted on the mantel gave each a burnt orange appearance – as though they had just been pulled from a forger's furnace.

Drawn by curiosity, he walked toward the mantel to inspect the items more closely. He was then able to also see several balls of musket shot sitting on the mantel as well, some flattened on one side with jagged, odd-shaped edges; others that appeared to be unused. Pointing toward the mantel, the traveler smiled at the three men seated next to the fireplace, "Interesting ornaments you've got here."

One of the men looked in the direction of the mantel and shook his head slowly, "That's Alex. Always wanting to hang onto reminders of the past, when others…" raising his glass in the direction of his companions, "…like us, can't seem to escape it."

While listening to the man's comment, a thin, balding man of middling stature walked toward him from a doorway to his left with an outstretched hand, extended in his direction.

"Welcome to my humble inn sir. I'm the Alex he mentioned; I own the place. As I told these gentlemen several times over, I don't think it hurts to be mindful of our past so that we don't allow the same mistakes to be made by others in the future. And my friend here failed to mention that after I found these cannonballs and musket shot several years back," motioning in the direction of the three men, "…they were the ones to suggest that I place them on the mantel. It wasn't exactly my idea alone to put 'em there."

Shaking Alex's hand and motioning his head in the direction of the mantel, the traveler smiled. "And I take it they were gifts left by the British when they passed through a while back."

Alex nodded with a laugh. "Not sure I would call them gifts as such. But you could say that they didn't seem too interested in hanging onto 'em once they got here…"

One of the men sitting next to the fireplace interrupted, "…and they sure seemed hell-bent on giving them away, free of charge, to those of us who came out to greet them as they were passing through."

Studying the bottom of his now empty glass, the mood of the man with the missing leg was more somber. "Can't help but think how some of these *'ornaments,'* as you call them, may have helped to shape the destiny of some number of men's lives or more likely, their deaths."

Glancing up at the mantel and nodding his head with a smirk, the man with the scarred, partially deformed hand then joined the discussion. "I can remember a time when these spent shards of metal would have been quickly melted down to be used once more – all without giving any second thoughts about their past usage or the men they may have encountered along the way..."

While listening to the comments made by the men at the table, the traveler slowly rubbed his forehead. "That is true, and perhaps I was wrong to refer to them as mere *'ornaments.'* But I, for one, can't help but feel comforted by the thought that these balls of lead will be used no more." Then, pointing toward the man with one leg and looking in the direction of the innkeeper, "Nevertheless, I also can't help wonder if we really need such reminders of our pasts. I doubt that this gentleman here needs any. And, by the emptiness of his glass, I'm guessing he would rather forget more than remember."

Slowly looking up from his glass, the man smiled and grabbed his crutch to raise it into the air. "You got that right my friend. I am reminded of my past with every other step I take." Raising his glass with the other hand, "And this is pretty much all I need to help blur the memories of the past." Then, turning to look back into his glass with a more distant stare, "I, for one, don't need any damn cannonball reminders."

Gently patting the one-legged man on the shoulder, Alex refilled his glass; then turned toward their new arrival with a smile. "I expect you and Jacob here may be quite right. Some are reminded of the past with every waking moment. And I also expect that you didn't just stop in at this time of day just to talk to a bunch of drunkards about rusted old cannonballs. Lookin' for a room?"

Smiling and nodding his head. "Yes, I'm looking for a place to stay for a few days and a stable for my horse. We've been on the road all day and are both in need of a good meal and a warm place to rest before heading on to Albany." Droplets of melted snow fell to the floor when he unbuttoned his long overcoat. Opening his coat, the shiny wooden handle of his pistol stuck out from his waist belt.

After seeing to it that his horse was well fed and groomed for the night, the traveler returned to the tavern for his meal. The three men he met earlier were still seated by the fireplace; still drinking and still talking, although somewhat louder than before. Again, the innkeeper and others watched attentively as he walked stiff-leggedly across the room toward the innkeeper's table to register. Although trying as best he could to disguise his natural gate and to walk normally, one of his boots thumped a bit louder than the other when it met the inn's wooden plank floor. The effect was not unlike the different sounds a horse's hooves would make if it lost one of its shoes.

Noticing their stares as he walked, he reached around to his back with his right hand and, squinching his face as one would who was in pain, "It is tough getting old. My back just can't take the ride like it once could and it even affects me when I try to walk. I can't imagine what I am going to be like by the time I get to Albany."

Raising his crutch once again, the man with one leg added: "Try using one leg and see if it is any easier for you."

"Again, you've got a good point there my friend. I shouldn't complain about my sore back, sore ass or legs."

The man used his crutch to push himself up; nodding his head he limped toward the visitor. "Sure, we can. We can complain all we want, but I discovered a long time ago that most people don't care and it don't do no good." Leaning on one crutch, he held out his right hand. "Name's Jacob. What's your name?"

Reaching his right hand out to shake that of Jacob's, "The name's McGurk, Otis McGurk."

As he introduced himself, he noticed Jacob's two companions turning their heads slowly in Alex's direction. One raised an eyebrow, and the other lifted his glass ever-so-slightly from the table and gave the innkeeper a slight smile. And it even seemed that Jacob's grasp of his hand tightened a bit upon hearing his name.

Listening carefully to the faint comments made by the men at the table under their breaths; some of which he could faintly hear: "...*Otis, Otis McGurk*, an odd-sounding name...," he noticed a distinctive thinning of their lips and a narrowing of eyes when they turned to again look in his direction. It was obvious by the occasional slurring of words that they had been drinking rather heavily before he arrived. And he couldn't be certain if they were simply amused by the sound of his name, suffering the confusion of thought that normally accompanied an evening of heavy drinking, or if there was something more.

Yet, one thing he could be certain of: there was a definite change in the room. Whatever just occurred, it was very subtle and he couldn't quite put his finger on it. Again hearing the crackling fireplace, he discovered the sudden quietness in the room. And he noticed as well, the glances the men at the table made toward each other and Alex when they mumbled his name.

Slowly, the man with the deformed right hand, stood; staggering slightly, he reached out to shake the visitor's hand. "The name is Roeloff. So you're headed for Albany are you, Otis?"

Reaching out and shaking the scar covered hand, he was surprised at the strength of the man's grasp. "It's a pleasure to meet you,

Roeloff." Roeloff's hand was noticeably warmer than Jacob's; even moist to the touch. Otis felt a twinge of danger as he shook Roeloff's hand.

Resisting his instinct to back away, Otis stood firm. "Yeah, I hope to ride the rest of the way to Albany within the next few days. Do you suppose the road is open enough for me to get through?"

First glancing in Alex's direction, Roeloff scratched his unshaven stubble before looking back at Otis. "Yeah, I suppose the road is passable. We got some snow today, but there hasn't been all that much in the last week or two. I expect that it will be well traveled, in spite of the time of year."

Alex spoke up. "Albany is about another day's travel. I'd say about ten to twelve hours. So you may need to rest over in a place a bit further south of here called Halfmoon. You can find somewhere to stay there if the weather is not all that good, or if your back, or your horse need a rest at that point along the way."

As Jacob and Roeloff slowly eased themselves back into their chairs, Alex motioned in the direction of the man who hadn't moved since Otis' arrival. "This here is Albert. He's probably too drunk to stand up or be polite, but he's a nice enough guy. Care to join us and visit a spell? You can tell us all about Quebec. I think it's safe to say, it's been years since any of us have been in that part of the country."

"Thanks for the hospitality, but not tonight. Tonight I need to get something to eat, if it isn't too late, and to get some badly needed rest. It has been a long day for me, my back and my ass; I would much rather be lying down than doing much more sitting."

Alex smiled. "Suit yourself, Otis McGurk. You look tired anyway, and although it might help with your back, I expect that one or two of these would likely do you under!"

Alex and the others then held up their glasses high as they offered a toast to the new guest. "Welcome to our humble quarters…" hesitating before adding, "…Mr. Otis McGurk. May your stay with us be an interesting one."

"And, I believe if you look to the other side of the room you will see that while we've all been out here gabbin', my son, Peter, has cooked you up some dinner."

Otis turned to discover a steaming bowl of beef stew and potatoes placed on a table at the opposite side of the room from the fireplace. When he sat to eat his meal, he first leaned over the pewter bowl to feel the steam on his face, smell the pleasant aroma of onions and admire the simmering chunks of beef, potatoes and carrots he was about to consume. Pleased with his findings, he bowed his head to offer a private prayer of gratitude: "Thank you Lord for this meal that has been prepared for me, and for the safe journey granted to me and my horse. I ask that you equally bless and provide for my wife, sister and children, whom I miss dearly." Finishing his prayer and reaching out to pick up his spoon, he noticed the glances of Alex and the three men by the fireplace. And he saw the less subtle stare of the innkeeper's son who walked slowly by his table.

While eating his meal, the visitor turned to the innkeeper, "Alex, do you know of anyone in these parts by the name of Van Derwerker?" Walking by with an armload of firewood he just brought in from outside, the innkeeper's son stopped, "There are several Van Derwerkers in the area."

"How about Martin Van Derwerker? I knew that he once lived in this area, but it has been several years, and I am not even sure if he is still alive or still in the Saratoga area."

Alex interrupted. "Hurry with the wood boy! The fire needs more wood; we don't want our friends here to catch a chill." Then turning to Otis, "I'm not familiar with the name Martin Van Derwerker. Yes, like the boy here says, there are several Van Derwerkers around. But, it is a common name in these parts and at the moment, I can't seem to recall a Van Derwerker by the name 'Martin'."

As Alex spoke, Otis noticed that Peter hesitated at first and stared back at his father with a slight scowl, leading Otis to conclude that he was either surprised or confused by his father's interruption. Nevertheless, the boy said nothing more and delivered his armful of wood to the fireplace hearth.

Turning to continue with his meal, Otis shook his head, "Too bad. I hoped to locate him and his wife, Martha, while I was passing through the area. But like I said, it has been a long time. Perhaps they have moved on."

After finishing his supper, the traveler thanked the innkeeper and his son. "That was an absolutely delicious meal. Just what I needed at the end of a cold and blustery day of travel, thank you."

With a smile and a wink of an eye in the direction of the innkeeper's son, he paid for his meal. "And I've added a little extra for another bottle of rum for your three friends over there."

He then stood, stretched and slowly walked toward the stairs to turn in for the night. Before Otis reached the bottom of the stairs, Alex stopped him. "So how is it that you knew this Van Derwerker fellow? Mind if I ask what the nature of your business is with him? We get people passing by all the time. Perhaps I can ask around to see if some of the others who come by may know of this Martin fellow."

"It is not business, more of a social call. I met Martin and his wife, Martha, when they were at a hospital in Albany for a spell during the war."

"Oh, so you were a doctor in Albany during the war?"

Thinking it best to let Alex develop his own thoughts about who he may, or may not be, Otis did not directly answer the question. "I traveled to many places during those days and stayed in Albany for only a short period of time. I met the two of them while they were there at that time. Never mind asking anyone else about them; it is not all that important. I just hoped to see them again if they were still in the area."

Alex nodded his head, "Of course. Speaking of Albany: inasmuch as you've been there before, do you know of a place to stay while you are there? I've got a friend who also owns an inn in Albany. It's called the Yardarm Inn; you might want to stay with him while you are there."

Otis was taken aback by Alex's comment. Not knowing how many inns there were in Albany, he wondered what the chances would be that, in this isolated corner of the world, this over-friendly innkeeper would just happen to mention the name of the very inn he had been instructed by others to go to upon his arrival in Albany. He learned long ago not to place much trust in coincidences. And he concluded that the odds were not all that high.

Trying not to disclose his growing concern, he nodded his head and smiled in Alex's direction. "Thank you. I don't believe I've heard of that inn. But I will certainly look for it. What's the name of your friend I should ask for once I get there?"

"His name is Timothy. Be sure to tell him that Alex sent you his way. I am certain that he would be happy to put both you and your horse up for a long as you may need to stay."

"I certainly will." Then, turning in the direction of the men at the fireplace, he raised his hand in a salute like wave, "Good night gentlemen, hope to see you again soon. It's time for me to rest these weary, old bones."

However, to a man, they were now slumped over the table, sleeping. Seeing their condition, Otis probed the psychic innkeeper a bit more. "It's a good that these soldiers of fortune aren't facing any battles tonight."

Looking at Roeloff, Jacob and Albert passed out at the table, Alex nodded. "Yep, whatever skill for battle they may yet have would do them little good tonight." Then, turning his head back in Otis' direction, and with a thin-lipped smile, he added: "But there is always tomorrow, or the tomorrow after that to better prepare for whatever battles may come their way."

Staring back at Alex with steely gray eyes, Otis shrugged his shoulders. "Not so sure 'bout that. There comes a time when everyone's tomorrows will end." Then with a slight smile and a bow of his head in Alex's direction, Otis turned to walk up the stairs. While ascending the stairs, one step at a time; without looking back, Otis added: "And that, my friend, is why we should always be ready for whatever comes our way today. We just can't be too certain about how many tomorrows we have left."

After watching his new guest limp his way up the stairs, Alex turned in the direction of his three companions sleeping next to the smoldering fire. Heads resting on folded arms, legs sticking out at all angles; hats on the floor next to an empty bottle, and hands still grasping now empty glasses.

Then with a quick jerk of his eyebrows, Alex nodded his balding head and whispered to his sleeping companions: "Well, he's right about one thing. The three of you would not have been of much help in battle tonight. It looks like we will need to wait for another day to share in a celebratory drink from the bottle so generously paid for by our new guest: *General Benedict Arnold.*"

CHAPTER 3

VAN DERWERKER FARM

Early the next morning about a mile from The Bryan Inn, the innkeeper's son knocked on a farmhouse door. Dogs barked wildly and jumped upon the other side of the door. But he could tell from the high-pitched sound of their barks, they were more eager to greet him than eat him.

When the door opened, three dogs leapt upon him, their tails wagging swiftly. Two taller, short-fur dogs with splotches of black, brown and white, jumped high enough to lick his face. A shorter, white, belly-to-the-ground kind of dog with big floppy ears licked his boots, as though they were covered with meat sauce. Peter chuckled as he watched the shorter, floppy eared dog try, rather unsuccessfully, to rise up off its front legs and lick his hands.

To fend off the overzealous affections of the dogs, he handed each a small treat he brought with him to gain their favor. Looking up from the blur of fur, he noticed a woman's hand reaching out to help him into her home.

"Shoo, shoo, let the poor boy in. Come in Peter, please come in, this is certainly a nice surprise on such a cold, blustery day."

"Thank you Mrs. Van Derwerker. I'm glad to see that *Logan, Lacey, and Lance* here still remember me. It even looks like they missed me, but, I'm guess'n what they really remember is that I usually bring along a little snack to take their attention off me." With a wink and a smile, he leaned down to pat each of their bobbing heads one more time, and gave each another treat from his pocket. "Yep, they likely remember the food and smell of my boots more than me."

"Oh Peter, how could they possibly forget one of their favorite visitors?" Adding with a wink of an eye in return, "Especially one who brings treats with every visit.

"Here, let me take your coat; come in sit down a spell. It has been some time since we've seen either you or your father."

"Sorry ma'am, but I really can't stay." Noticing the dogs now sitting quietly at his feet, he smiled, "See, it works every time." Then turning his attention back to Mrs. Van Derwerker, "Pop has a lot of chores for me to do around the inn, but he wanted me to come and tell you about someone who stayed with us last night."

From across the room, he heard another voice. "Is that so? Can't imagine who would be so important for us to know about that your father was willin' to let you get away without doin' all your chores first."

Peter looked behind Mrs. Van Derwerker to the other side of the room. "Mr. Van Derwerker, I didn't see you sitting there. Good to see you again, sir.

"Yep, I expect Pop thought it important enough to let me escape my chores for a little while..." adding with a shrug of his shoulders, "...and besides, I think we all know, whatever don't get done this morning, will get done by nightfall anyways."

"And I expect you are right about that, Peter. So what it is that is it your Pop wanted us to know that is so important, son?"

"Well, he thought you would want to know that a stranger stayed over last night who was askin' if we knew anyone named Martin Van Derwerker. He said that he was from Quebec traveling to Albany on business."

"From Quebec you say? And he was asking for me, by name?"

"Yep, actually he said that he was hoping to find both you and the missus." Looking in the direction of Mrs. Van Derwerker, "If you will pardon me ma'am, but he said that he was looking for both 'Martin' and 'Martha' Van Derwerker. That's what he said. He called you both by your first and last names.

Peter heard a mumble from across the room: "I'll be damned. Asked for us by name, did he?"

"Yep, and we've never seen this man in these parts before. And he had a pistol on him when he came in; so when he asked if we knew you, my Pop said we didn't"

Again, from across the room, "I'll be damned…"

"Pop didn't know what he wanted, so he didn't say anything 'bout knowing you or where you lived. But he must've thought about it durin' the night. First thing he said to me this morin' was to come here and tell you 'bout the stranger. I guess he thought that you would want to know someone was in town askin' 'bout you.

"And another strange thing happened that probably got pop thinkn' more this mornin'. When the stranger got here last night, he told Pops that he would be staying for a couple days. But this morning, he paid us and left."

"I'll be dammed."

"Martin, please. Watch your tongue. We don't want the Lord thinking you're asking Him to make things worse for you."

"Well, he asked for us by name Martha. Who the um, dickens do you think might just be passing through here in the middle of winter, from Quebec of all places, and asking for us by name? If that don't beat all…"

"And when he left he told pop that he might stop back on his way to Quebec after he finished his business in Albany. But, he said that he wasn't sure if he would make it back our way. Said it sort of depended upon Providence and the weather and stuff."

"Did he say what his name was or what he wanted?"

"Well, he didn't exactly say what he wanted; only that he was interested in finding the two of you for a social visit while he was passing through. He told pop that his name was Otis McGurk, and he knew both of you while you and he were in Albany during the war.

"Who the h….who the dickens you say? *Otis McGurk* did you say?"

"Yep, that's who he said he was, Otis McGurk. And he said something about seeing you or meeting you at a hospital in Albany, but that is about it." Peter looked down at the dogs who were once again trying to get his attention by licking his hands and wagging their tails. Lancelot, the portly, white dog with floppy ears, spun around in a circle every time Peter glanced in his direction – hoping to get another treat for his effort.

Martin and Martha looked at each other with raised eyebrows and widened eyes. Martin scratched and then slowly shook his head. "Thanks son. And thank your father for us too. I can't say that I rightly recall anybody by the name, Otis McGurk."

Looking in Martin's direction, Martha added: "And, unless we know more about him or what exactly he may want, I would rather not let him know where we are. You can never be too careful with strangers."

"I'm guess'n that's why Pops asked me to come over."

Turning back in the boy's direction, Mrs. Van Derwerker smiled. "Please thank your father for us. We'll keep our eyes open, and please be sure to let us know if he does stop back or if you hear that he may have asked any of our other neighbors about us. I suspect that if he asks enough people in our little village, someone will point him in our direction. Unless we know more about who he is or what he wants, I am not so sure we want to meet up with this Mr. Otis McGurk."

"I sure will Mrs. Van Derwerker. If he comes back, we'll let you know right away." Rubbing the heads of each of the dogs and giving each one last morsel of food, "Well, I guess I better get back. You know Pops. I'm sure he'll be comin' after me if I don't get back soon."

After closing the door, Martin turned to his wife, "It can't be. I've only heard the name 'Otis McGurk' once before and you know that he wasn't really a person, or at least it wasn't a real name when we last talked of it."

Martha looked out a frost-covered window to watch the innkeeper's son walk down the road. "I agree, Martin, it can't be! It can't be him! He wouldn't dare come to these parts now! It has been over eight years since we last heard the name 'Otis McGurk.' It might just be a real Otis McGurk, and we simply didn't know at the time that anyone existed by that name."

"That's certainly true, Martha; someone by that name could really exist. But then why would he be looking for us by name?" Shaking his head in disbelief, "It has to be him, Martha. Who else could it be? Why else would someone ask for us, using that name? It must be him, but why now? If anyone recognizes him, they would surely hang him without even giving him a chance to explain anything to anyone."

"At least he's left town for now. Let's just hope he doesn't come back. I can't believe it, Martin. It doesn't make any sense. Why would he come here in the dead of winter and stop here to see us? How would he even remember our names after all these years? It just doesn't make sense, it can't be…"

Martin sat in one of the rockers by the fireplace while Martha cleaned up after their morning meal. Staring into the fire and rubbing his forehead, he couldn't help but think of the man they both once knew. A man so different from themselves and a man who led quite a different life. A man they became so close to during a relatively short period of time so many years ago. And the man they later learned to detest as a self-serving traitor.

A short while later, Martha joined Martin in front of the fireplace. The two of them sat quietly, rocking and staring into the odd and peculiar shapes of the flames and the images formed by the glowing embers. With distant stares, they both rocked and thought about the man who once called himself *Otis McGurk,* as a lark.

The sudden barking of their dogs and the distinctive sound of footsteps on the front porch startled them both out of their trances. Martin leapt from his chair and Martha clutched her sweater to her chest. Step, thump; step, thump; step, thump. The sounds of the footsteps were odd and distinctive.

While the dogs barked, Martin grabbed a musket from a corner of the room and slowly approached the door. The dogs barked incessantly and were in a frenzy by the time their visitor knocked at the door. The dogs then leaped and clawed at the door to get at the intruder, Martin pointed the musket toward the door; motioned Martha to open the door.

Martha slowly stood and moved to the backside of the door. Then, with one fluid motion, she reached for the door's latch, opened the door quickly and swung it wide to let the dogs at their prey.

The splotchy brown, black and white dogs leapt at the intruder and began licking his face and hands; their tails wagging feverishly. The man at the door looked down to see the white, floppy eared dog spinning in circles at a dizzying rate of speed. He awkwardly bent down to pet the dogs and, gave each a treat he, too, had taken from his pocket.

Smiling, he looked up at a wide eyed Martin and his trembling wife. "Really, is this any way to greet an old friend?"

With furrowed brows and squinting eyes, Martha and Martin stood in silence staring at their visitor.

"Your home is getting cold with its door wide open. May I come in for a short visit, or would you prefer that I simply turn and walk away?

Looking at Martin's now quivering musket, the visitor smiled. "That won't be needed, my friend. The war is long over and I certainly mean no harm to anyone."

Shaking his head slowly, the visitor once again looked briefly toward the dogs who were all now seated quietly behind Martin. Then looking into Martin's eyes, his smile faded and his face became sullen.

"Martin, Martha, I am here to simply say, 'thank you.' Thank you to the both of you for saving my life. Having said that, I can now leave if you wish. The choice is yours. I can leave, or I can come in and help you stoke the fire to warm the room up a bit and perhaps...," offering a small cloth bag to Martha, "...share in some of this tea I brought with me from London for just this occasion."

Martin and Martha stood motionless. The only movement was in their eyes, looking back and forth between each other and the man at the door.

With a faint, ever-so-slight nervous smile, Martin slowly lowered his musket and Martha motioned their visitor into their home.

Taking off his hat, cloak and coat, "I knew I could count on the innkeeper or his son to lead me to your home. When I mentioned your name last night, the boy's expression, and that of his father's, clearly told me that they knew exactly who I was asking about. Their concern for you was written all over their faces."

Martin whispered softly, "How did you ever know where to find us? It's been so damn long, and yet...here you are..."

"You may recall Martin, I once made a living out of listening, not only to the words people used as they spoke, but also reading the expression on their faces as they were telling me what it was they wanted me to hear or believe. You see, people, by nature, don't make good liars. They may make good friends and neighbors, and perhaps even good innkeepers. But, by and large, they all make terrible liars."

Again with a barely audible whisper, "I guess you got that right…but it has been so long. How could you possibly know where to find us?"

"Well, after talking to the innkeeper and his son last night, and after seeing their reaction when I asked them if they knew of you, it was clear that they knew exactly who it was I was asking about. They said that they didn't know you, but I knew better. So this morning, I decided to leave, or at least let them think I was leaving. But rather than actually leave, I went over the hill and circled around to the tree line at the top of the hill to watch the inn for a while. I wanted to see if anyone would try to follow me or leave the inn in any hurry."

Looking in Martha's direction, "And as I expected, it didn't take long before the boy left the inn, and he seemed to be in a hurry. So, I just followed the lad to your front porch."

Then, motioning in the direction of the now silent dogs, he smiled. "And when I used my scope to see the way your greeting party here met the boy after you opened the door, I knew that if I were to have any hope at all of being allowed to walk through your door, I would need to share some of my rations."

Looking down at the dogs at his feet, Martin rubbed the back of his neck. "Always prepared…just like before."

Their visitor smiled, "It is probably best that it worked out this way. After talking to your innkeeper last night, it is just as well he doesn't know of my visit with you. Not sure what there is about that man, but I don't trust him. And the more I thought about the conversation I had with him last night, the more I regretted ever mentioning your names to him."

Martha looked up at their visitor. "I wouldn't be concerned about Alex. He is such a nice neighbor. As a matter of fact, and as you said you expected, he sent his son to tell us about your, or at least of Otis McGurk's showing up at the inn."

"That's true, but considering the circumstances, one can never be too careful, and I don't know what his reaction would be toward you or your family if he were to discover exactly who I am. Thus far, I believe he may think I am a doctor. As long as he doesn't ask me to heal any illnesses or set any broken bones, I saw no harm in letting him think whatever it is that he wanted to think about me."

Martin pensively bit his lower lip. "I agree with Martha. I wouldn't worry too much about Alex. He's a nice enough fellow."

"Nonetheless, it is just as well that he doesn't know of my coming here. I was careful to cover my tracks in the snow after I left the inn and headed for Albany. Nobody followed me and he won't have any way of knowing that I actually found you."

Watching Martin and Martha stare back with their persistently furrowed brows, he nodded his head. "I know that this must be awkward and unsettling for both of you. I've been planning this visit for years, and so I've had time to get accustomed to the idea of possibly seeing you both again."

Martin looked at his wife, "To be honest, I don't think either of us ever expected to see you again."

"I know, and I honestly wasn't sure you wanted to ever see me again. But I just needed to see you, and to let you both know that you meant so much to me during a most difficult time in my life. After I left Albany and after the war ended, I could not help but wonder and worry about the two of you. I hoped and I prayed that you and your family all survived and were doing well. And I hoped that one day I would have the opportunity to say thank you."

Shifting his feet, "You know, Martin, we could all stand here for a very long time, but I am afraid that your dogs will tire of their licking and tail wagging. Can we sit?"

Martha was the first to speak. "Yes, of course. How rude of us. Please have a seat and let me get you, no, I'll get all of us some tea."

Without taking his eyes off their uninvited guest, Martin added: "You might want to bring some rum with that tea, Martha."

Looking deep into the visitor's soft grey eyes, Martin whispered, "I can't believe it. I simply can't believe it. It is true. You are here, standing in our house, as big as life. General, please forgive my confused state. I just can't get over it. General Benedict Arnold, here in our home."

"Yes, I am here in your home to thank you and Martha. I would not have survived without you. Thank you my friend."

Martin rubbed his eyes with his left hand, "It has been years; a lifetime, really. I've often thought about you after you left Albany and wondered about you and your life."

Motioning with his musket Martin shook his head adding: "I've got to admit though, General, there was a time when I would not have thought twice about using this thing had we met at a different time, under different circumstances."

Benedict smiled, nodded his head in return and, with a jerk of his eyebrows, looked back into Martin's eyes. "Yes, I understand. I would have expected you to use your musket had our meeting come at a different time and place. That's, in part, why I waited so long."

Pointing toward Martin's musket, "And I remember what a good marksman you were with that thing. I wouldn't have stood a chance with you at the other end of the muzzle."

Turning in Martha's direction, "But these are different times, and the war is over. And I am here, in your home to offer my thanks to you and your dear wife Martha for all you did for me while we were recovering in Albany."

Looking toward the floor and with a softer voice he added: "I would have died there in that hell-hole had it not been for the two of you. And for the care you gave me, I am grateful. I know that circumstances make it difficult for you to welcome me into your home without reservation or concern, but please know that I've come to offer my hand in peace and friendship. Our war is over and victory has come to America. Congratulations, my former comrade-in-arms."

While Benedict stood with his hand extended, Martin just stood and stared back into the face of his former General, turned enemy. "I'm sorry General. I am simply having difficulty expressing what I am thinking."

Pointing to his head, "Words are racing through my head, but…but the right ones are having trouble finding their way out…don't quite know what to say…"

Recognizing her husband's dilemma, Martha shooed the dogs away, wiped her hands on her ruffled apron, stepped forward to give Benedict Arnold a welcoming hug, a big smile and kiss on his cheek. "Welcome to our home, General. We are confused, yes, but nonetheless glad to see you. You, too, have been in our thoughts and in our prayers. Both before you left Albany and afterward when, I must confess, praying for you was made somewhat more difficult by your deeds."

Tears swelled up in Martin's hazel green eyes as he watched his wife hug Benedict Arnold. His musket hung limp at his side in his trembling hand.

Benedict walked to Martin, each staring at one another. Martha joined the two men as they all hugged and sobbed, allowing eight years of emotion to run its natural course. Rubbing his eyes, Benedict stepped back to look at Martin and Martha. "Yes, much has changed, but by God's grace, much remains the same and for that I am grateful. Thank you, from the bottom of my heart, thank you."

CHAPTER 4

VAN DERWERKER FARM

During the first few hours of his stay, Benedict, Martin and Martha were all uncomfortable and awkward during their conversation about inconsequential matters like the weather and general health and well-being. But nonetheless Benedict was gratified with the opportunity to rekindle the bond of friendship, comfort and, to the extent possible, trust that once existed between him, Martin and Martha.

By mid-day it started to snow more heavily; Martin and Benedict took his horse to the barn for shelter and food.

"This is a beautiful animal. How long have you had him General?"

"Only a month now. I got him shortly after I moved to St. John's from London and I needed a good steed to get me around. When I saw him, there was something about this horse that reminded me of a few others I rode during the war. I think it was his eyes. It seemed as though he was watching me as I was looking him over. It was as though he was as interested in appraising me as I was in studying him. Most horses I've owned over the years did not have as expressive eyes as this one. So I guess he was as much responsible for picking me as I was for picking him."

"That is a good quality in a horse; a sure sign of intelligence," Martin offered as they closed the barn door and slid the heavy plank latch into place to keep it from blowing open.

On their return to the house, Martin pointed upward to the tops of the large pine trees in the distance starting to sway back and forth from the effects of the increasing winds. The snow was falling heavier now and blowing sideways as the wind picked up beneath the trees as well. "Looks like you may want to stay on a bit until we see what the weather is going to do. No point in you starting out in weather like this. Got to admit, General, I would have thought you would have a bit more sense than to set out on a cross-country journey in the dead of winter."

Looking first at the tree-lined landscape, which was becoming more difficult to see in the distance, Benedict appeared a bit more pensive. "The timing of my travel was not of my choosing, Martin. I too would have picked better weather in which to journey."

Then turning to Martin with a smile, "By the way, if you have not yet noticed or been informed, I am no longer a General. That time of my life is over. I am a simple man of business trying to provide a living for my family just like you. It is probably best that you and Martha not refer to me by that title any more. You just never know who might be around to overhear and start asking questions. Don't need to increase anyone's normal curiosities."

Martin laughed, "Guess you're right about the name thing. The war is over, and I imagine our friends in the Continental Congress stopped paying your General's salary long ago."

They both smiled at the thought. "But I don't think that you need to worry about anyone overhearing anything we might call each other. Aside from my niece and her boy, who live in the cabin in the back over there, the next farmhouse is more than a quarter mile away. It is quiet in these parts, which is one of the reasons Martha and I love it so much here."

Benedict studied the rolling wooded hills that surrounded Martin's farm. "Yes, it certainly is peaceful and quiet."

"Other than our friendly innkeeper, Alex, and his son, nobody pays much attention to our comings and goings. In any event, how about if I simply call you 'Ben.' Any name with more than two syllables in it trips over my tongue every time. 'Ben' is a strong, friendly-sounding name…sort of like that good ol' Franklin guy I've heard talk about." Martin smiled as he added, "And you can just call me 'Mr. Van Derwerker,' or 'Martin' for short."

Looking at Benedict with a sheepish smile, Martin raised his right eyebrow a bit leaving Benedict to wonder if his friend was looking for a reaction from him regarding his newly christened name: "*Ben.*"

Benedict was taken aback by his friend's use of the word, "*syllable,*" wondering wherever in his education, which was minimal, or his life experience as a farmer in this isolated part of the world, he learned what a syllable was. His use of the word was so natural in his conversation. And he was relatively certain that Martin knew that Franklin's first name was Benjamin and not Benedict. "I see that you still have that sense of humor that I've missed so much. I guess it would be all right for you to call me Ben. The only people ever to call me 'Ben' were my mother and my first wife. So you are in good company, and I would be pleased if you and Martha would just call me plain ol' Ben."

Benedict looked down at the snow-covered ground, noticing that the footprints they made on the way to the barn were being quickly covered by the freshly falling snow. "You just might need to put me and Governor up for a bit if there is room. If not, I am sure that I can get my room back at the inn up the road."

Martin looked at Benedict with a quizzical look. "No need to go back to the inn, and who the hell names a horse Governor? I'm assuming you are talking about your horse and not someone or something else?"

Benedict laughed and then whispered, "I named him after my great-great grandfather."

"You can bet that no one in his right mind would leap to any conclusions about who you are by the name given to your horse, that's for sure! Someone might think that the name may be a reference to some other horse's ass!" They both laughed as they continued their blustery walk back to the house.

"You mentioned your niece and her son who live in the cabin over there. I don't see any smoke coming from the chimney. Are they not here?"

"Not now, but they are expected back from my brother's place tomorrow if the weather doesn't keep them away. My niece's name is Theresa, Theresa Van Arenum. Her son, John, was born in the spring of '78 and will be eight his next birthday. He is the love of her life and ours, I might say.

"She and her son moved in after the boy was born." Then, looking downward and shaking his head, "Her husband, whose name was also John, died during the first battle at Saratoga. When he was killed, they were expecting their first," glancing skyward, "...and as fate would have it, their only child. The poor soul never got to see the birth of his namesake."

"What a shame Martin, I'm sorry to hear of your family's loss. I didn't realize..."

"You had a lot of problems of your own, so Martha and I never said anything about it at the time. My brother and his wife were not doing well at that time either; so after the baby was born, Martha and I built the cabin over there so Theresa could be close to family and have some help raising the boy."

Listening to Martin describing his niece's circumstance, Benedict sighed. "Too many children growing up without fathers. And too many women trying to raise families without husbands."

Shaking his head and looking downward Benedict continued his lament, "What may seem to be a lonely sacrifice a solitary man pays on the battlefield is seldom felt by the soldier alone. The pains of battle are not simply the physical and emotional pains the individual soldier may feel, but also the mental and emotional pains long felt by the families thereafter. Yes, it is also a sacrifice that affects the family left behind, and unborn generations for years to come. What a sad state of affairs, I must say."

Martin nodded, "Ah, the invisible victims of war, sad and tragic in so many ways. You are undoubtedly right. The after-effects of battle are also long felt by not only those of us who survive on the battlefield, but the families of those who do not." Turning away from each other, they each lowered their heads, continuing their conversation as they slowly lumbered back to the warmth and comfort of Martin's home.

When they neared the house, a single horse-drawn wagon turned onto the road leading to Martin and Martha's home. Raising a hand to shield his eyes from the driving snow, Martin lifted his head, squinting his eyes, "Can't imagine who that might be."

Holding onto the brim of his hat, Benedict squinted into the blowing snow as well to see two shadowy figures humped over in the wagon as it drew near. He leaned in Martin's direction, "Remember, as far as anyone else is concerned, my name is '*Otis McGurk*.'"

Martin then nodded, "No need to worry; I recognize the wagon now. It's my niece and her son. I expect they're trying to get home before this weather really settles in."

"Nevertheless, it would be best if you and Martha stick with Otis McGurk..."

From the wagon, Benedict heard a woman's voice as it strained to penetrate the snow and wind. "Uncle Martin, we are certainly glad to see you. John and I came home early thinking we would be able to return before the storm; it seems to have come on a bit quicker than we thought it might."

Martin called out to Theresa, "Glad you made it in time. Looks like it's going to be a bad one..."

Martin then looked in Benedict's direction, "Here Otis, hold on to this." He then handed Benedict the horse's bridle and ran into the house.

Theresa and her son stepped down from the wagon and, with their heads lowered in the direction of the blowing snow, hurried into the house, each nodding their heads in Benedict's direction as they quickly passed him by.

Martin soon returned. "I told Martha that we were going to call you '*Otis McGurk*' while Theresa and John were around."

After unhitching the wagon and putting the horse and wagon into the barn, Martin and Benedict returned to the house where the pleasant aroma of food cooking permeated the air. They each looked toward the fireplace to see Martha holding a long-handled spoon, stirring a pot hung over glowing red coals.

Martin smiled, "Smells like chicken soup to me."

Martha continued to stir as she turned to look over her shoulder. "Actually, it is chicken stock soup with vegetables and dumplings."

Brushing snow from his shoulders as he entered the house, Benedict removed his hat and coat; then turned to meet the new arrivals. He was stunned to see a beautiful woman dressed in a long, emerald green, velvet dress with sleeves gathered by lace at the wrists. Her soft, cream colored cheeks, still rosy-red from the cold journey, were caressed by the high collar of a white ruffled blouse. Her hair, tucked neatly into a bun at the back of her head was covered with small, diamond size droplets of melted snow. Sitting softly upon curly ringlets of light brown hair, the small beads of water glistened in the candle light, giving her a sophisticated, duchess-like appearance. It was not the appearance he expected to see of someone who just maneuvered a horse driven wagon through a blowing snowstorm.

Noticing Benedict's expression and apparent loss for words, Martin smiled as he introduced each to the other. "Theresa, John, this is Mr. McGurk, Otis McGurk. Martha and I knew Mr. McGurk several years ago during the war. He's going to be our guest until the weather improves. Otis, this is our niece, Theresa Van Arenum, and her son, John."

Benedict bowed slightly and reached out to kiss Theresa's hand. "My pleasure ma'am. Handsome and strong-looking young man you have there, Mrs. Van Arenum."

"Why thank you Mr. McGurk."

Benedict looked in the boy's direction, "And, someone once told me that a boy's strength comes from his father and manners and appearance from his mother. I can clearly see that he does get his appearance from his lovely mother."

Bending down on one knee to look the little boy squarely in the eyes and to shake John's hand, "And I can see that your father was undoubtedly a very strong man, my boy. It is my pleasure and honor to meet you both."

The lad smiled, stood tall, puffed out his chest a bit and looked into Benedict's eyes in return. "Thank you, Sir. My dad was indeed strong and I am told that I do look a lot like him, too!"

Standing upright, Benedict noticed Theresa's furrowed brow as she turned toward Martin, "'Mr. McGurk', did you say, Uncle Martin?"

Before Martin could say anything, Benedict interrupted, "Yes, my name is McGurk, Otis McGurk." While knowing full well what the answer would be, he asked: "Have we met before?"

"Your name does sound familiar, but I am positive we have not met before. I certainly would remember such a meeting."

Benedict smiled and bowed his head slightly in Theresa's direction.

Theresa blushed and quickly covered her mouth with a silk-soft hand at the apparent forwardness of her comment. "I'm sorry Mr. McGurk. What I mean is that I don't believe I've ever met anyone named Otis before. I think I would remember if I did. Welcome to our home Mr. McGurk. How long will you be staying?"

"Please, call me Otis. Depending upon the weather, I may be here a day, perhaps two. However, I do have business in Albany that I must attend to; therefore, my stay will only be for a few days at most, if that would convenient. I told Martha and Martin that I can undoubtedly get a room at the inn up the road…"

"No, no, Mr. McGurk, um, er, Otis. That will not be at all necessary. You are certainly welcome to sleep in John's and my house out back, while we stay with my aunt and uncle here. This way you will have the room entirely to yourself, and John and I can stay here in the loft."

Benedict smiled, bowing his head slightly in Theresa's direction, "Thank you for such hospitality, but I couldn't possibly put you and your son out."

"Nonsense Mr. McGurk. We wouldn't be put out whatsoever. And although our home is not all that large, once we get a good fire going, it will heat up nicely for you. You can make yourself comfortable and stay in our home for as long as you need. Please, I won't take no for an answer!"

"Please call me Otis."

Theresa smiled, "Of course, I'm sorry, Otis."

When Theresa smiled, Benedict noticed just a hint of her age by the slim, ever-so-slight wrinkles in the outer corner of each of her beautiful hazel-green eyes. He couldn't help but contrast her natural beauty against the stressful life she must have endured over the years, raising her son on a farm in this isolated community.

Benedict concluded that Theresa was certainly a strong-willed and outspoken woman, reminding him somewhat of his wife. "Thank you, it is very kind of you and your son. I appreciate the hospitality that you all have shown me since my rather unexpected arrival."

After finishing their evening meal, they all sat by the fireplace to talk and catch up on the last eight years of life, and lost years of friendship, as best they could with Theresa and John in the room. From their conversation, Benedict could tell that Martin and Martha knew enough not to ask him about his past, but it appeared that they didn't see any harm in asking about what he was doing at the present. Theresa and John mostly sat quietly and listened as others talked.

The hours passed quickly. Just before sunset, Martin excused himself. "Well, I best feed and check on the horses, and I'll get a fire goin' in Theresa's cabin so our guest here will be comfortable for the night."

Benedict put on his hat and heavy coat to join Martin. "I'll get the fire started Martin; then I'll join you in the barn to help with the horses."

In this northern part of the New York colony, darkness comes early in the month of December. Martin and Benedict each carried lanterns to help them see their way through the still blowing snow. Martin headed for the barn, and Benedict headed in the direction of the cabin.

As he approached the door to the cabin, Theresa caught up with Benedict. "Otis, please let me help to get you settled into our home."

Stepping into the small one-room cabin, Theresa lit a lantern on a table near the middle of the room, as well as one near a fireplace on the far end of the room and another next to the bed in one corner of the room. Yellow hues from the lanterns flickered and cast a warm yellow glow throughout the room.

Simple, even stark in appearance, the room was nevertheless clean, neatly organized and welcoming. "Very nice home, Mrs. Van Arenum" Benedict said, nodding his head in a pleasing and accepting manner as if to let his hostess know of his satisfaction with the accommodations she was offering.

"Otis, please. Call me Theresa. I am not sure of your age, but I expect that our years are not that far apart and if, in keeping with your wishes, I am going to call you Otis…" At this point in her conversation she hesitated and looked directly into Benedict's eyes. "You did say that I was to call you Otis didn't you? That is the name you want me to call you isn't it?"

Benedict was a bit confused by her question. "Yes, Otis. And although you are undoubtedly much more youthful in spirit than am I, I suspect you may be right about our ages." Feeling uncharacteristically flustered, he hesitated slightly before remembering the name she was to call him. "I will call you Theresa as long as you remember to call me, um Otis."

"Then it's agreed. Um Otis, it is."

He then felt his cheeks flush, but was certain that Theresa would not have noticed in the dim light of the room's candles.

Looking around the cabin, it was as he envisioned. Small, with comfortable furnishings, which he surmised Martin probably made himself with all the skill and attention to detail one would expect from an artisan craftsman.

It was a single room with a loft at one end where Theresa's son, John, likely slept. At the other end of the room stood a large, stone fireplace with cooking pot hooks and utensils. A short distance from the fireplace sat Theresa's bed, with its four large, solid oak posts and heavy duck or goose down-stuffed covering. On the table in the middle of the room lay a few books, a few items of sewing and partially completed quilt work.

As Theresa moved candles about the room and straightened the bed, Benedict lit a kindling fire. As the growing flames in the fireplace brightened the room, Benedict could better see that, although Theresa and John were not wealthy with many material objects, they did nonetheless have a very comfortable, warm and inviting home.

Curious about the type of literature Theresa might be interested in, Benedict casually picked up a book from the table – *Meditations and Contemplations* by James Hervey. He had in fact heard of its author; thought he even read one or more of his books while in London.

Lost in thought over the book as he strained to glance at its contents, he was startled back into the present by Theresa's voice. "These will keep you warm, no matter how cold it gets outside and if you need more, there are additional coverings in John's loft."

"Thank you. You are very kind and considerate." Placing the book back on the table, Benedict looked directly at Theresa, "I feel badly about putting you and your son out of your home and having to inconvenience Martin and Martha with my visit."

Theresa approached Benedict. "Please, Otis…" as she spoke, he noticed that she appeared to glance up at him each time she mentioned his name, "…think nothing of it. John and I are glad to do it, and staying with Uncle Martin will give him a chance to tell my son more stories. John just loves to sit and listen to stories Uncle Marty has to tell about the war and his father." Looking back into Benedict's eyes, "And Uncle Marty is certainly a man with many tales to tell."

"I bet he is."

"And they do enjoy each other's company so much. Tell me, Otis, how is it that you and Uncle Martin met?" Theresa continued to look into Benedict's eyes as she asked the question; leading him to wonder if she were looking for a reaction.

Benedict Arnold: Legacy Lost (A Ghost's Story)

The question did, in fact, catch Benedict off guard, making him a bit uncomfortable with its directness. Looking back at the self-assured woman before him, he could not help but feel that it was as though she were looking into him and not at him. It was a look that was familiar to him. He recognized it as the attentive look he often gave to others while judging the truthfulness of the answers being given. He knew that it would be best to stay as close to the truth as possible when answering her questions.

"I met Martin and Martha during the war while I was in Albany several years ago. They are wonderful people, and I have often wondered about them since I last saw them. So, while I was in the area on business, I just wanted to see if they were still living in Saratoga, hoping that they were still both alive. I am happy to see that they are both indeed very much alive and doing well."

Theresa smiled, "Yes, quite alive and doing quite well for themselves."

With a more somber look, Benedict added, "Martin told me about your husband. I am truly sorry for you and your son's loss. Many good men died at Saratoga, and I have always thought that the men who fought to stop the British here truly saved the country from what surely would have been its eventual defeat had they not done so. I hope that you and your son both understand the significance of what your husband and others like him did for this country on the battlefields of Saratoga."

Theresa looked downward as he continued. "Your husband and the others like him helped to save not only Albany, but the country. In my opinion, the war was won at Saratoga. It may have taken another four or five years for it to be understood by others, but this was indeed the beginning of victory for the country. You and your son should be very, very proud of your husband. I am grateful for his contribution to the ultimate victory…"

Benedict simply stopped in the middle of his thoughts and looked away from Theresa and then back in her direction. "I am sorry, Theresa. It was so long ago in time but only yesterday in my mind. It was a very difficult time for a lot of people, especially for those who died then and their families…"

When Theresa looked up to speak, Benedict noticed tears forming in the corners of each eye. "Thank you, Mr. McGurk. Thank you for your appreciation for my husband, your understanding," and, gesturing toward his left leg, "thank you also for the sacrifices that you undoubtedly gave of yourself during that very difficult time. It was a difficult time for everyone involved."

The two of them stood in front of the now blazing fire, looking into each other's moistened eyes – neither knowing what to say next.

Martin entered the cabin brushing snow from his clothes. "Everything is all set at the barn. The animals all fed, watered and cared for." Glancing in Benedict's direction with a smile, "I guess it took quite some time to start that fire and I am glad to see that you got it going so well. The room will heat up in no time now."

Theresa turned away from Benedict, "Sorry Uncle Marty, I delayed him by my gabbing." Then, patting Benedict on the lapel of his jacket, she walked toward the door. "I'll leave the two of you and go get John into bed. I am sure the two of you still have a lot of catching up to do. Good night Otis, Uncle Marty."

CHAPTER 5

VAN DERWERKER FARM

"Sorry I didn't get out to the barn to help with the horses, Martin. Theresa and I got to talking and she seemed somewhat more inquisitive than I would have expected. I didn't want to be rude or insensitive to her interests in getting me settled into her home for the evening."

"Believe me Ben, I understand. We don't get many visitors here and when we do, we take full advantage of hearing the voice of the newcomer in our midst and to try to learn what is going on in other parts of the country." Taking off his overcoat, "Besides, one extra horse does not make any more work. The Governor is all set for the night."

Martin then motioned toward the fireplace, "However, like Theresa, I too would like to hear more from you before we all turn in. If you don't mind, I'd like to sit a bit and talk. This is really the first time we've been alone since you arrived; like Theresa said, we've got some catching up to do."

Before sitting and lighting his pipe, Martin poured each a cup of rum. The two men then sat in rocking chairs near the warmth of the fireplace, and stared at the flames and rising smoke from the burning wood. Listening to the hiss and crackle of the fire, Benedict turned to watch as Martin stared into the fireplace and slowly puffed on his pipe. "What are you thinking, Martin?"

"Martha and I are glad you came, Ben. Ever since you left Albany in '78, we often wondered how you were and what you were up to. We certainly heard about the little matter of your moving to the other side."

With a jerk of both eyebrows Benedict smiled, "Well, I am glad you brought that up. I was a bit worried about what the two of you might have thought about that."

"Yeah, Martha and I wondered about you often. It seemed to us that much must have changed in your life shortly after you left us. What we were hearing at that time didn't exactly match our expectations, and, frankly, Martha and I had a tough time believing anything about what was being said. At first, we simply thought that they were talking about some other Arnold fellow…"

Martin hesitated before continuing, "…At least that is what we wanted to believe. However, as time passed, it became clearer that they were talking about our Benedict Arnold and not some other fellow, and you were branded a traitor!"

Turning his head in Benedict's direction, "Martha and I have often wondered if you would ever come back to this place – to the place that seemed to be the beginning of your end." Martin stopped suddenly and turned his head again to study the flames.

Benedict rocked slowly as he took his turn at staring into the dancing flames. "Well, this place was the end for many of my enemies; I am certain that some would also say that it was the beginning of the end for me as well."

Looking toward the ceiling, "Ah, had my body been buried here with those who gave their life's blood on either side of the battle-line. Those poor souls had no way of knowing the importance of what they did at that monumental moment in time. The young and not-so-young lads of the militia who fought so bravely, so fiercely, and so selflessly… They just knew what needed to be done; they did it. And that made all the difference in the world."

Martin mumbled, "That they did."

Benedict continued to study the flames. "Martin, I don't know about you, but my memory is seared with the images of many of their nameless faces. Some oddly smiling with crazed looks of excitement; some frightened; some crying; and too many suffering not only the physical pains of battle, but the mental insults as well.

"To this day, I am haunted in my sleep by the gut-wrenching smells of blood and torn flesh as well as visions of the knowing stares of acceptance on the faces of many of my companion soldiers and their bloodied, maimed bodies as they each awaited their last moments of life."

Martin rocked, "I've let that demon go quite some time ago…however, I've often wondered about John…right after he was wounded and looked at me. He didn't even have time to say anything, but that look had many messages. I'm sure he knew it was over for him, and I've often wondered what it was he was thinking when he turned to me. What was he thinking? He didn't say, but I'm sure it had something to do with Theresa."

Benedict nodded his head, "I, too, have often wondered what they thought as their time on earth was about to end and they breathed their last breaths. Some were luckier than others. Some died suddenly and had little or no time to think. I've long ago concluded that it is better to have it end quickly; not to have any time at all to know, to feel, to understand or to think…"

Benedict hesitated and rocked in silence for a moment before continuing… "I can't help but wonder what it was like for those who knew it was their time to die, and to look around at what was to be their last vision on earth and see others who were going to live on for at least another day. What would I feel knowing that I was about to die and that others around me were not?"

As Benedict continued, Martin turned his head to listen, and to watch.

"Would I be angry or upset in some way with those who would live on? Or would I simply be relieved to know that I was about to learn what men from the beginning of time have sought and yearned for in so many ways: the knowledge of death and what it means to die."

They both sat in silence, rocking slowly and staring intently into nothingness…

Then Martin spoke up, "After John's death, Theresa has devoted herself entirely to her son since his birth." Shaking his head, "It isn't right for either her or the boy that there's no man around to care for them."

Martin turned his head to glance around the room. "A husband and father are needed in this house. Sometimes I feel so bad for the woman. She is just a year younger than me and hasn't had a man in her life since '77. That just isn't right. Not right for her or the boy. But, like I keep telling Martha, everything happens for a reason. We often don't understand or know why…sometimes we just need to accept things for the way they are."

Then turning his head in Benedict's direction, "But there is no law against hoping for better."

As Martin spoke, Benedict couldn't help but wonder why Theresa hadn't been able to find a man in her life to help care for her and her son. *"There must be a reason…everything happens for a reason…"*

Martin surprised him by changing the subject altogether. Turning toward him with a quizzical look he asked: "So, General, speaking of *reasons*, tell me. Did you really think that the British were going to win?"

Martin's questioning caught Benedict off guard on several levels. It was not so much the straightforwardness of the question, and not so much the question itself. But it was now being asked by perhaps the only person in the world he could call *"friend,"* and he did not want to lie to the man who once again just now called him General…why did he use that title again? Yes, Benedict was truly conflicted and uncharacteristically speechless. Turning to Martin, he simply said: "Give me a moment to compose my thoughts, my inquisitive friend."

After hesitating for a brief moment of silence, Martin continued with his inquisition. "So, Ben, if you are unable to tell me what went on with you, perhaps you can tell me what are you up to, traveling to Albany at this God awful time of year?"

Benedict knew that he could not confide everything to his friend. Perhaps one day, but not now; he was uncertain about what to say. "Although history will show that the war is long ended Martin, few will likely ever know that battles are yet being waged. The war of independence may be over, but the battlegrounds have not yet settled matters still outstanding."

Martin scratched his head and squinted his eyes, "What the hell is that supposed to mean? What battles?"

With a smile, Benedict turned toward Martin, "It's complicated. All I'm able to say at this point my friend, is that *my* final battle of the war is not yet over. And there's certainly no point or benefit in bringing any others into the struggles being fought at this point. It may get dangerous before it is all over and God certainly knows that your family has given quite enough."

Martin scratched his head again as he wondered about what Benedict had just shared with him.

Seeing Martin's obvious bewilderment, Benedict attempted to ease his confusion. "Martin, of all our talks while in Albany, do you recall one of our discussions about the importance of honesty in a man's character, and our agreement that honesty was perhaps the single trait that ultimately accounts for one's honor on earth and ultimately his salvation? We agreed that if one weren't honest with himself or others while alive, he probably wasn't going to be honest with God either."

Turning toward Martin he asked: "Do you recall our discussions about ethics and honesty?"

His forehead was now deeply wrinkled; without looking up, Martin continued to focus upon the embers within the fireplace, slowly nodding his head as he listened.

"Martin, although I haven't always been honest with everyone in my past, I am going to be honest with you – to the extent that is prudent to do so. And I am going to let you know now that I can't yet tell you everything that you may be interested in knowing. Nonetheless, I can tell you that I have given others my word of confidence about certain matters of importance, which are of interest to me."

Rubbing his chin, Martin turned his head in Benedict's direction. "But maybe Martha and I can help out in some way Ben…"

Benedict cut him off, "…Martin, although I truly wish it were within my power to discuss all matters with you, I cannot." With a deep sigh and looking upward at the ceiling as he spoke, "You can't imagine how much I truly wished that I had someone I could confide in, to talk to, and to have someone to help me to think things through. Life can be so complicated at times, and I wish I had a confidant, but that was not then, and is not now to be."

Martin once again turned away, "So, what's stoppin' you, Ben?"

Before responding, Benedict hesitated and stared into the fireplace as well. He then offered his explanation. "Some things take on a life of their own and, as I said a moment ago, things can get risky. Let's look at it this way. Knowledge and understanding are like the flames of this fire. From a great distance, there is no particular benefit or interest. It appears to be nothing more than a flicker or a spark of curiosity. However, as one draws closer, knowledge becomes attractive and somehow comforting, like the warmth we now feel from these flames. Then again, if one gets too close…"

"...One could be burned..." Martin offered with a grimace on his face as if to let his friend know that he was following the analogy.

"Or worse," Benedict added. "Many good men have been killed for no other reason than for what they knew... and because they were thought not to be trustworthy." Turning to Martin with a smile, Benedict added, "So you see, as long as I remain trustworthy, I have nothing to worry about."

Martin then slid his rocking chair a bit further away from the fireplace and smiled back at Benedict, as if to assure him that he wasn't seeking anything that Benedict was not able to share. "I would never ask a man to violate his confidences. You know that! God knows, there are too few people who can, in reality, be trusted and one never knows..."

Martin stopped in mid-sentence and then smiled. "Enough said." And then, turning his attention to another subject altogether, "You said earlier that you were headed to Albany on business. Might I ask what form of business you have in Albany?"

"My business is in shipping. And Albany might provide me with a means to ship some goods down the Hudson to the West Indies a month or so sooner than I could from Canada where spring thaws come late. That is my story...should others ask. However, for you I can only say that it is my hope that my business in Albany will permit me to clear up some past misunderstandings, which may enable me to move my family back to America where my children and I belong."

"Misunderstandings! That is a bit of an understatement, wouldn't you say?"

"Well, I think of them as misunderstandings. People do not understand all that was done or the reasoning behind some of the events that occurred. Consequently, people are missing something, and that something is understanding..." With a smile, he concluded,

"...therefore, it seems only reasonable for me to refer to them as *misunderstandings*."

Both men laughed and Martin poured a second glass of rum to toast their reunion. "To our past and to our futures! Wherever Providence shall lead us, let the road be clear and trouble free. And to our families, may we all live in peace and in good health!"

After drinking to the toast, Martin turned to face Benedict directly. "Can I ask how you hope to clear up your little misunderstandings?"

"Of course you can ask, but I am afraid that the less said about this matter the better. I've been invited to Albany to meet with someone who may be able and willing to help me straighten out this whole mess."

"Can I ask who invited you?"

"You can ask, but again...As you recall, as the war unfolded, we were all living in such uncertain times; not knowing from one day to the next what tomorrow would bring. Not all that different from now, as I think about it. After Saratoga, I wasn't much good for the battlefields any longer; yet I wasn't quite ready to give it all up either, or to be turned out to pasture so to speak."

As Martin continued to rock, Benedict continued with his explanation, as best he could under the circumstance. "One thing led to another. Not that we knew what the outcome was going to be; we were all doing what we thought was best. Things got a bit out of hand and, before I knew it, I became the single most hated man in this country. It wasn't supposed to happen that way, but it did, and it seemed to serve its purpose."

"Sorry Ben, I can't help myself...what purpose?"

Benedict shook his head. "Nope, I can't say... Then the war ended, and lo and behold, I was still the most hated man in this country. All I am seeking now is that the truth be told. However, being the most hated man in the country, I can appreciate the irony of my wish. I am not in such a good position to be demanding the truth from anyone, or so it would seem."

Martin looked again at Benedict and offered a comment. "And some men wouldn't know what to do with any truth, should they ever encounter such a thing."

Benedict nodded, "And who would listen to me? I am certain that there are men who would hang me at the first opportunity. Some of those who now wish me ill were obviously my enemies. But not all of my enemies then, or now, were British. I am now certain, that among those who would wish that I simply disappear, are men who were once considered to be my comrades and even close companions."

With a sigh, Benedict leaned back into his rocker. "But it has all become so confused. I don't exactly know who my enemies are anymore. One cannot always tell by the uniform or clothes one wears or even what one says. As we both agreed many years ago, not every man is trustworthy or believable for that matter."

After rocking in silence for a moment longer, Benedict then continued: "I just need to sort out who among them can be trusted and who would now rather see me dead than allow the truth to be told. I am not so sure that I, or my family for that matter, are safe at this point in time – even in England. I cannot go on living in such uncertainty; I need to be assured that my children and family will be safe, even if I am not. Therefore, I am here on this journey to see what, if anything can be done to make this world a better place for my family and, if at all possible, for me as well, God willing."

Martin listened carefully and then offered an observation: "Yep, it seems that one thing we are good at is misunderstanding others and holding a grudge."

With a sigh equal to Benedict's, Martin added: "You may or may not recall, but the one human trait that I have the most trouble with is arrogance – as if we are all perfect beings and in a position to judge others. There was so much suffering, so much pain and so many personal losses during the War. However, it also seems natural or understandable that people need to hold someone responsible, to be able to blame someone else for their misery and sufferings."

Benedict looked to the heavens, "Isn't that the truth."

With a shrug of his shoulders, Martin continued. "As luck would have it Ben, it appears that circumstances have put you in a position to be blamed. Like it or not, General, you've been selected. Like Christ in His day, you are to be held accountable for all the sufferings that have occurred. And I mean everything. From the death of the soldiers on the battlefields, to the failure of the crops in the fields…"

Looking directly at Benedict, Martin added: "Yep; you're the guy to blame. It worked out okay for Jesus. However, I don't hold out quite as much hope for you;" with a quick jerk of his eyebrows, "if you know what I mean. I wish I understood better. I wish I could help make things better for you and your family."

Martin hesitated for a second and then continued his discussion with his friend on a much less troublesome topic. "Speaking of family, you haven't told me about your family. I know that your first wife died a few years before we met at Saratoga and you had three children then, and a sister. And I also heard that you married again after you left Albany. Mind telling me a bit about your family? Where are they now?"

Benedict smiled, and lit up the room with his grin as he told Martin of his second wife, twenty years his junior, who coincidently also shared the same name as his first wife, Peggy. He also told Martin about his eldest son, Benedict, who was about to turn 19 and now enlisted in the British military. He told him as well about Richard, who turned 16 last August, and Henry who just turned 13 a few months ago. These were the children that Benedict had with his first wife, Peggy, that he told Martin and Martha so much about during his convalescence in Albany. They were definitely his pride and joy and told Martin that they were all being cared for by his sister, Hannah, and his new wife in London.

Benedict then told Martin about the children that he had not heard about before: Edward, 5; James, 4; and finally Sophia who was now just about six months old. Benedict told Martin that his wife also gave birth to two other children, one who lived for just 7 months and another who died during infancy a few years back.

"With all the death and suffering I've witnessed over the years, I initially thought that experiencing the death of one's own would not be quite so hard." Shaking his head and looking to the floor, "I was wrong on so many levels. The death of a child leaves scars on the mother and the father, some of which never heal. To witness this little, helpless child do all it can to survive. And then to survive one day more, only to die the next…it was so hard and so very difficult to understand…"

After a moment, Benedict looked up and smiled, seemingly adjusted to the reality of the loss of his two infant children. "All my surviving children are with my wife, Peggy, and sister in London. Once I get my business matters settled here, I hope that they will all come to live with me on this side the ocean."

After listening to Benedict as he listed his children and their ages, Martin smiled. "I doubt that the name, 'Peggy,' shared by your first and second wives, was such a coincidence. What are the chances of that happening? And I can see that you've been one active man off as well as on the battlefield! Tough to keep a good man down I suppose! And I don't suppose that you purposely waited until now to finally have that daughter, Sophia."

Benedict shook his head slowly. "No, it was neither purposeful, nor anticipated. As a matter of fact, the child who lived for 7 months was a girl; we named her Margaret, after my wife. Thinking back now, I suspect that giving her the same name as my wife's may have made our daughter's death somewhat more difficult for my wife to bear – if that was even possible to do after carrying the baby to full term and caring for her day in and day out until she could breathe no more..."

Turning his head in Martin's direction, "You just take what the good Lord provides. Although I must admit, if Sophia had come along sooner, perhaps James may have been in jeopardy somewhat."

Martin stoked and added a few more logs to the fire; bade his long-lost friend good night and returned to his home. After extinguishing the room candles, Benedict crawled into the bed Theresa had made for him. Staring at the various shapes and images formed by the glowing embers at the base of the fireplace, Benedict drifted off to sleep to end his busy and eventful day.

During the evening the wind continued to blow and the snow continued to fall lightly. At one point in the middle of the night, Theresa was awakened by what sounded like the shouting of a man coming from the direction of her cabin. Sitting up, she looked at the three dogs. Each sitting side-by-side near the center of the room; their heads cocked in different angles as they stared into the darkness toward Theresa's cabin.

Theresa slowly got out of bed to look out a window. The snow had stopped falling. Moving to the door, she held it slightly ajar and listened carefully. The shouting was indeed coming from her cabin.

Theresa quickly went to Martin and quietly shook her uncle's arm. "Uncle Marty, wake up. There is shouting coming from my cabin. I think something might be wrong with Otis."

Martin sprung from his bed, arms flailing about and in an obviously confused state. After standing next to his bed for a few seconds to clear his head and regain a normal level of consciousness, he then heard the noise Theresa was talking about. Grabbing his musket, he quickly slipped on boots and went outside toward Theresa's cabin to investigate.

In a few moments, Martin returned. "It's okay, Theresa. Everything is fine. Otis appears to be dreaming and shouting out in his sleep. It is probably best not to disrupt or surprise him at this point of unrest."

Theresa disagreed. "No. He should be awakened, comforted, and assured that he is safe and among friends."

Nevertheless, Martin sternly told Theresa that they should leave Otis to himself. "He is undoubtedly accustomed to this condition and would be very embarrassed or troubled even more if he thought that his disturbance awoke us. Chances are, he isn't even aware of it; we should leave him alone."

While gently patting Theresa on the shoulder, Martin added: "Otis is a very, very proud and private man Theresa. I am certain that he would rather keep his unconscious, unguarded, personal nightmares private. Trust me, it is best to leave him alone."

Theresa reluctantly returned to her bed. Listening to the sounds of periodic shouting, a multitude of thoughts ran through her head: "I can clearly hear his voice, but I am unable to discern any of his words…the more I listen the more the sounds seem more like screams than shouts."

Eventually the sounds coming from her home and her bed subsided; Theresa then also fell back to sleep, apparently glad that their troubled visitor was finally at peace and at rest.

The next morning the sun shined low in the sky. By all appearances, the day promised to be storm free. The clouds had cleared, and the sky was brilliant blue. Benedict was up and about, seemingly refreshed in spite of his restless evening. Seeing that the weather had changed for the better, he gathered his belongings and prepared to leave Martin and his family to continue his journey to Albany.

After sharing a morning meal, Theresa, John, Martha and Martin all bade their guest goodbye. Walking Benedict to his horse, Martin wished Benedict well and said that he hoped that his *"business meeting"* would go as well as he might want and asked Benedict to stop back for another visit on his way home again.

"Ben, I know that we live different lives and have very little material objects in common. I am honored that you thought enough of Martha and me to remember us at all…and to take the time from your travels to pay us a visit. One day, I hope that our paths will cross again in a world that will permit us the freedom to be totally open and frank with each other."

Shuffling his boots in the snow with the appearance of a shy school boy trying to talk to the first girl he ever met and not knowing exactly what to say, Martin looked up at Benedict. "I would be honored to be your confidant should you ever need someone to talk to. We may not always agree or understand the other's motives, but in spite of whatever differences may exist between us, you can be certain that I will never judge you."

Benedict looked down from his horse. "Martin, it is never the material objects that form meaningful bonds among men. What bonds our lasting friendship comes from within each of us. It was our relatively brief encounter at Albany during which our bond of friendship was forged by the forces of compassion, understanding, gratitude and care."

Gesturing in Martha's direction, he added: "It is my undying gratitude that forever formed my bond of friendship with you and your dear wife. I suspect that it is your and Martha's understanding and endless compassion for others that bonds your friendship for me.

"I certainly will return on my way back to Quebec if I am able to do so. Thank you for your friendship and understanding." Leaning down from his saddle, Benedict smiled, patted Martin on his shoulders and then whispered, "It is time for me to finally face my demons my friend."

Waiving to Martha, Theresa and her son, John, Benedict then turned his horse up the road to face his uncertain destiny.

CHAPTER 6

ALBANY

Arriving at his destination, Benedict could not help but reflect upon the time he was last at this location. For him, and many others at that time, it was a place of hell and unbearable pain. While everyone else referred to it as Albany, Benedict aptly called it *"Agony."* When Benedict last left this place eight years before, he expected that his life would never be the same again because of the changes that occurred within him during his stay here; his expectations proved to be well founded.

Riding slowly into the heart of the city, he once again saw its omnipresent river, its narrow roads sloping up hillsides away from docks along the riverbanks. While taking in some of the changes that have occurred among the city's all too familiar buildings, he was surprised by the ringing in his ears and a quickening of his heartbeat. Benedict was taken aback at how emotional this part of his journey had become.

Before seeking out the location of his long-awaited meeting, Benedict first visited a long wooden, two-story, building with long wings added perpendicular to each end of its length. Nestled on a hillside next to the city's Masonic Lodge near the crossroads of Steuben and Lodge Streets, the now-vacant building overlooked the banks of the North River a short distance to its east. Once a bustling hospital during the Revolution – particularly after the Saratoga campaign – it was at this location that Benedict suffered most during the longest four months of his life.

Benedict stopped in front of this all-too-familiar building; from his horse, he peered up at the windows located on the second floor. It was from these windows that Benedict spent countless hours watching boats, merchants and fishermen at a distance moving up and down the majestic waters of the North River with serenity and a freedom that Benedict could only envy. Confined within the walls of this lifeless structure, he spent much of his time strapped to a large wooden brace to immobilize the bones, muscles, and blood vessels in his left leg while they mended. Trapped within this building for more than four months, any movement he made often resulted in pain. For days, weeks and months on end, all he could do was to look out these windows and witness the ability of others to come and go as they pleased. It angered him. He had no such freedom. The body and the mind can only handle so much; when its threshold is reached, the mind shuts down. On many occasions the pain was more than he could bear, and he would lose consciousness. There were times during his stay here where his only escape was that which was provided during periods of unconsciousness. For Benedict, these periods of unconsciousness meant relief.

Doctors who treated him wanted to amputate his left leg, just above its knee. Benedict refused, and told them that he would rather die than become an invalid for the rest of his life. Nevertheless, doctors insisted that amputation was the only way to ensure that his leg would not become gangrenous due to the severed arteries and the diminished circulation of blood to the lower part of his leg. For doctors, removing his leg was the only treatment; for Benedict, it was not an option. He remembered the doctors telling him that unless he allowed them to amputate his leg, poisons from his infected leg would spread throughout his body and he would more than likely die. He remembered as well telling the doctors that he was prepared to die. Their comment to him in return was to simply suggest that he make good use of the time remaining to him by making peace with the world.

At an impasse with Benedict on how to best treat his injuries, doctors at this hospital stopped treating him for much of anything. Some told him that if he refused to let them treat him and wanted to die, so be it. There were others who needed and wanted their care.

They did not invest much time with Benedict; they simply did not expect him to survive. As far as they were concerned, his fate was in the hands of God. Yes, on several occasions during his stay here, he wished that he were dead and often prayed for the physical and mental peace that death would provide. Although these prayers went unanswered, it did not occur to Benedict at the time that Providence had other plans for him.

Staring into the building's darkened windows, he was reminded that this was also the place to which Martha Van Derwerker traveled from Saratoga to care for her husband. While here, she also provided care for him as well. She cleaned his wound, fed and encouraged him to eat when he had neither the strength nor the will to feed himself. Martha would change not only his bandages, but also his bed clothes when he was unable to move and soiled himself. Indeed, caring for Benedict was no easy task for anyone. Nonetheless, Benedict remembered Martha later telling him that Martin instructed her to care for him because he was too important to be allowed to wither away unattended and needed more care than Martin.

Benedict smirked when he also recalled that at that time even his aide, David Franks, had given up on him. His actions lead Benedict to understand that his aide's loyalty and devotion would only go so far; it was certainly apparent to Benedict that his aide resented having to care for him while he was at the hospital. He remembered hearing Franks whispering hurtful words to another when Franks thought he was sleeping: "I did not enlist in the Continental Army to become a nursemaid for the dying…my time and talents are being wasted with this man who is too stubborn to die…" Benedict believed that Franks was of the opinion that everyone would be better off if he simply died. Benedict even later found out that at one point, Franks was so hopeful that Benedict was going to die that Franks even began to plan his funeral.

Benedict Arnold: Legacy Lost (A Ghost's Story)

Fortunately for both David Franks and Benedict, Martin and Martha witnessed Benedict's plight as well, and they cared for Benedict as they would have for any other human being in need. Benedict never forgot the time when they both spent days-on-end caring for him at a time when others had given up on him and were more than willing to allow him his death wish. It was this kind and selfless care provided by Martha and Martin that renewed Benedict's interest in life, and brought him back from the brink of death on more than one occasion.

Contemplating this part of his past, Benedict realized that although the passage of time had eased the physical pain, the scars on his memory nevertheless remained and would likely never completely heal. And, although he did retain the use of his leg, he was now willing to admit that perhaps he and everyone else around him at that time would have been better off had he listened to the doctors and allowed them to use the saw.

While sitting on his horse, Benedict was finally able to acknowledge that the memories of this place lived on and would likely accompany him to his grave. Not being able to escape them, day or night, he now understood that his greatest demons after leaving this place were his memories.

Nevertheless, over the years since his last stay at this location, Benedict learned that he could cope with his memories and live a normal life as long as he simply accepted them for what they were – a mirror of his past, but not his present or his future. He long ago discovered that he needed to keep the memories of this as well as other parts of his past in their rightful place.

The thought also occurred to him that, although this lifeless building was the place where he suffered most, it was also the place where he, Martin and Martha developed their lifelong bond of friendship, mutual respect and trust. And, in addition to this benefit of loyalty and friendship, this was also the place where he was given "*the gift.*" The gift of untold hours with which he could do nothing –

nothing but think. Benedict had time to think about his family, those living as well as those dead. He had time to reflect about his past life; his future, and the future of this fledgling country.

During times of delusion, passing into and out of consciousness, Benedict used his capacity to think to assure himself that he was still alive. *"Cogito, ergo sum...I think, therefore I am."*

Glancing to the heavens and then bowing his head, Benedict was now willing to acknowledge that this was also the place where he finally came to terms with God and his own mortality. Once believing that he was impervious to injury and perhaps even invincible, it was at this spot, during that time, that he came to accept death as an inevitable event – for all men. It is only a matter of time. Sooner for some, and later for others. It was here that Benedict began thinking in terms of *"the greater good"* and not simply in terms of self-interest.

As his wounds began to heal, and to keep his sanity during his long, brain-numbing, monotonous convalescence, Benedict spent days, weeks and months devoted to the development of battle strategies. The only unknown variable for Benedict and his plans was when. In war, as in life, timing was everything. Carefully weighing the options and possible outcomes of untold tactics, he was determined to make good use of this *gift* of time.

Soon after his arrival at this location eight years ago, it became clear to him that his wound would limit his mobility and he would likely be of little value on the battlefield ever again. It didn't take long for Benedict to realize that perhaps he could be of greater service off than on the battlefield. It was at that moment of realization that his concentrations turned from battlefield formations and troop movements to that of strategic information analysis. Considering known information and postulating variables of unknown information to develop probability equations.

Benedict Arnold: Legacy Lost (A Ghost's Story)

As the days droned on, Benedict spent more and more of his time in consideration of the unknown to develop strategies that may be of some use to those on the battlefield. What is known? What is not known? How does one bridge the gap between the two elements of fact to ultimately determine what actions might have the best odds for success when not all facts can be known?

During the early days of the Revolution, Benedict realized that all soldiers, American or British, are first and foremost, human beings. And humans have strengths and weaknesses. Although many believed that fighting an enemy was more physical than mental, Benedict disagreed. Benedict believed that in battle, as in the more cerebral game of chess, it often comes down to knowing how one's opponent is likely to react under stress, and knowing which actions would provide the greatest likelihood of success. This early lesson weighed heavy in Benedict's strategies. It was during this time that Benedict also developed a particular strategy that he subsequently called a "*victory plan.*" A plan that changed his life forever and laid the foundation upon which the remaining years of the Revolution were to become rooted.

During his recovery in this *H-shaped* building he often thought of as an asphyxiating sarcophagus, Benedict honed his sense of observation. Watching and listening to others from all walks of life became an obsession. He once believed that he could tell what a person was thinking, simply by carefully watching their eyes while listening to the intonation in their voices as they spoke. Becoming almost intuitive for Benedict, he was amazed at how often his assessment of others' thoughts turned out to be accurate – in spite of their words.

In conjunction with honing his observation skills, Benedict learned the skill of listening. Lying in bed for hours on end with eyes closed, he often listened to the conversations of others – some nearby and some more distant and far away. He became skilled at focusing upon a specific individual's voice, while blocking those of others, as well as noises, sounds and other distractions from his mind. He discovered that as he listened, he could discern anxiety, worry or hesitation in the voices of the speakers – characteristics of those who were not telling the truth or attempting to deceive the listener. Benedict learned not to listen so much to the actual words used, but the tone and pitch of the speaker's voice as well as changes in speech patterns. They are different for those who are telling the truth and those who are not.

These lessons of watching and listening acquired while confined within this building were indeed gifts that would prove invaluable to Benedict in the years to come. As he sat looking at this now empty building, Benedict was amused by the thought that this building and the time he spent here may have been responsible for changing the history of the Revolution and the country, if not the world.

He never gave it much thought before, but with the advantage of now being able to look back over time, it seemed like an obvious conclusion for Benedict to make. Nodding his head slowly, he softly mumbled: *"Yes. This building was indeed a place of consequence."*

Wondering how history may one day view this structure, Benedict couldn't help but also notice that, like the effects of time upon the body, the passage of time appeared to have taken its toll on this building as well. It was now empty and lifeless.

Before continuing on his way, Benedict slowly raised his right hand to his forehead and gave a respectful salute. He then lowered his head and offered a silent prayer for all the men who did not survive their stay at this now-empty tomb. *"May our spirits be one day reunited, and may we all one day be resurrected to walk at the right hand of our God and Savior, Jesus Christ…Amen."*

Staring at the empty structure once again, Benedict realized that he had now come full circle to this time and place. Although haunted by its memories, Benedict was resolute in his conviction that although a painful place indeed, some good did come from this building. And he was determined that he was not going to allow this part of his past to interfere with his efforts to chart a new course for his and his family's future. That part of his life was over, and he was now ready to face those who would help shape the years to come.

His horse seemed to instinctively know when Benedict was ready to move on. As Benedict turned his head away from the building as if to block its vision and its memories, Governor once again continued his faithful journey up the hillside road leading to his passenger's next destination – Benedict did not look back.

CHAPTER 7

ALBANY

Benedict reached into his chest pocket and unfolded a document containing the name of the inn at which he was told to register. Although expecting that he would remember the name of his meeting's location, Benedict wrote it down to keep with him during this journey in the event that his memory failed him along the way. Being a man of the sea, Benedict liked the chosen location in this northern, in-land port city. It was an inn with a nautical name. Riding up one of Albany's hilly roads near the center of the city, he noticed a large wooden sign on the side of a three story building that looked promising. It was a large sign with a weather-beaten image of a square-rigger sailing ship under full sail, listing to port in emerald green, frothy waves. Under the ship, was the inn's name, *The Yardarm Inn*. Benedict tied his horse to a hitching post and hobbled up the wooden stairs leading to the inn's wide porch that led to its entrance.

Entering the inn's lobby, Benedict stopped just inside the door for a moment to allow his eyes to adjust to its darkened interior. The room was large, cold, dark, quiet and musty. Heavy velveteen curtains hung over each of the lobby's large, floor to ceiling windows and two shiny-banistered staircases ascended from both sides of the room in a semi-circular fashion to the floor above. As his eyes adjusted, he could more clearly see the registrar's desk along the back wall of the lobby and situated just below a second floor balcony that overlooked the lobby's main entrance. Two candles flickered at each side of the registrar's desk, offering guidance to new arrivals. A door behind the desk creaked as it slowly opened just wide enough for someone to peer out into the lobby. The opening spilled light and warmth into the lobby; a head silhouetted from behind with a yellowish hue could be seen peeping into the room silently studying the new arrival.

The door then closed abruptly, darkening the room once again. Just as abruptly, a door beneath the staircase to the left opened and a man quickly scurried into the lobby. "Sorry for my delay, we don't get many visitors at this time of year. I am the innkeeper, may I be of some assistance to you?"

"Yes, my name is McGurk, Otis McGurk and I would like a room and I will also need to stable my horse for a few days as well."

"Mr. McGurk. Yes, yes, I've been told to expect you. My name is Brother Timothy." As he introduced himself, the innkeeper reached into his desk and handed an unaddressed envelope to Benedict. "I've been instructed to give this letter to a Mr. Otis McGurk upon your arrival."

Inspecting the envelope carefully, he saw that it was sealed with red wax into which a small, rectangular shaped paper containing a multi-colored symbol had been pressed. It was an odd symbol, resembling a red heart in the center surrounded by several arms reaching inward grasping a circle as if to stretch it. Benedict could not clearly discern the meaning which he assumed was intended by a seal so ornate and detailed.

"This was left here for me? Are you sure you have the right person?"

"Yes, of course, as long as your name is Mr. McGurk. Not that many Otis McGurks passing through these parts at this time of year; I am quite sure it is intended for you."

Exchanging glances with the innkeeper, Benedict broke the wax seal and, being careful not to damage the paper symbol, opened the envelope. The note was simple and direct:

Dear Mr. Arnold:

It is with regret that my colleagues and I are not able to join you at this time. Please accept our most sincere apologies. In our effort to make amends for past sins, please contact Brother Sparks who is also staying at the inn to discuss the schedule of our next meeting. Time and place to be mutually determined.

Your most humble servant,

L. Q. C.

Benedict did not know nor ever heard of anyone with the initials "L.Q.C." And he was alarmed that someone would be so careless as to use his real name in a written document. He became even more concerned when the thought occurred to him that, although he used his assumed name, *Otis McGurk*, the innkeeper handed the unmarked envelope to him containing a letter addressed to his given name, *"Arnold."* Glancing up from the letter, Benedict asked: "Why did you give this to me?"

Benedict carefully watched and listened to the innkeeper as he spoke. "I was told to give the envelope to a Mr. Otis McGurk should you register at the inn. Why, is there a problem, Mr. McGurk?"

As he listened to the innkeeper, Benedict thought that it was possible that the innkeeper did not know of its contents, and he did appear to be straightforward in his response. Either he was sincere or a very good liar. Although the innkeeper did appear relaxed and at ease, Benedict could sense himself becoming tense, agitated and increasingly concerned about the events that were quickly unfolding around him.

Benedict shook his head as he carefully folded the letter and put it in his coat pocket. While doing so, he casually unbuttoned his overcoat in the event that he needed to retrieve his pistol quickly. "Is a Mr. Sparks staying at the inn?"

Glancing in the direction of the staircase to his right, the innkeeper said, "Brother Sparks arrived two days ago and is staying in a room at the end of the hallway at the top of the stairs."

Benedict continued to ignore the innkeeper's use of surname preface, *Brother*. "Good, please give me a room as near Mr. Sparks as possible."

While bowing his head slightly the innkeeper smiled. "You can have any room you want. At this point, there are no other guests in the inn other than Brother Sparks, and now yourself."

It was the sly smile on "Brother Timothy's" face that tipped the balance for Arnold. He now knew that the innkeeper, whoever he was, was lying about something. However, not wanting to give any indications of his increasing concern about the situation facing him, Benedict asked to be given the room next to Mr. Sparks. Nonetheless, Benedict was not at all comfortable and now became uneasy to the point of being fearful. Too many unanswered questions. *Why was the meeting he was invited to canceled? Who was the person with the initials, L.Q.C.? Who was this "Brother" Sparks? Why were there no other guests at the inn? Why did the innkeeper, who appeared relaxed on one hand, keep looking around the room more than looking directly at him?* Benedict's instincts for survival told him that something was not right with this situation and that he was in danger.

CHAPTER 8

REFLECTIONS

This was Benedict's first trip back to America since the war; he had hoped that this meeting would establish the terms, conditions and timeframe for his repatriation. For him, the time had come and he was ready. But were others ready for his return, and just how would it be orchestrated? The Treaty of Paris officially ended the war two years before, and he was hopeful that the passage of time would make his return at least within the realm of possibility. Nonetheless, believing that once the full truth about his past actions became known, Benedict half expected that it would make his return to his country of birth a natural and understandable event. That said, he was also keenly aware of the continuing uncertainties that existed among those of power and influence in this country. He was also certain that, several among them would not, under any circumstance, welcome or even permit his return – if they had anything to do with it.

Benedict understood that his return would be dangerous on several counts. Certainly, his past has not been forgotten among the former soldiers and the populace at large. In virtually every corner of every colony, word had quickly spread of his traitorous actions. Joining the British and attempting to turn over the key fortress of West Point to the British in September 1780, his actions galvanized the country. At that time and as the war with Britain dragged on over the years, Benedict understood the need for a unifying force for the country that was sorrowfully lacking. He was hopeful that his actions would provide the unifying thread so desperately needed to sew the colonies together in their opposition to the British and the loyalist supporters of the crown. His fellow patriots needed a focus, and he was willing to become the catalyst to unite their energies. Indeed, in the fall of 1780, Benedict Arnold provided a name and focus, for the hatred that grew exponentially in the hearts of patriot soldiers and their families. He was just not prepared for how vitriolic the feelings of his countrymen would become, or the depth of their beliefs about the wrongness of his actions. As beneficial as this component part of his strategy was at the time, he was now concerned that its success would prove to be the single, insurmountable element that could possibly prevent his return.

Benedict nevertheless did take solace in the fact that this aspect of his victory plan strategy, conceived in that nondescript hospital a year and a half before its execution, did have the expected side-benefit for the country at a crucial time in its struggles for freedom. Yes, he became the most singularly hated person in the United States, and that fact provided a common cause to unite the nation. At that time he took pride in thinking that he was perhaps the single reason the colonies could again, truly call themselves united.

The fact still remained that, given what is now commonly known about his past among the general populace, Benedict understood that any number of them would kill him outright if they recognized him for who he was. He was not at all certain that his return would be welcomed by anyone, even by the one person who had a better understanding of his past actions, and the motives behind them, than anyone else in the world.

Before moving to Canada in November of 1785 to be closer to his ultimate objective, Benedict had been informed that although the war for independence had ended, the struggle for freedom, power and influence in this country had not. Consequently, those who were now attempting to establish a functioning government and chart the future of the nation would certainly feel threatened by the presence of Benedict Arnold in their midst. The balance of power between the separatist state and the more centralized, federalized government factions in this newly-conceived nation was simply too fragile and too uncertain. He was asked to further delay any efforts to return until a functional government could be solidly put into place and not be threatened by the scandal and confusion that would likely result from his return. Benedict had firsthand experience in dealing with the unscrupulous actions of some members of the Second Continental Congress who crossed him during the early days of the Revolution.

Therefore, Benedict often feared that if his countrymen were not careful, they would be simply tossing off the yoke of one form of tyranny for that of another. Consequently, Benedict was apprehensive about waiting too long before returning to his country of birth. He wanted to become a part of this country's struggles for even greater freedoms for men and women like Martin and Martha Van Derwerker and the countless thousands like them. He wanted to join the ongoing struggle of shaping the government of this newborn nation to ensure that its leaders were responsive to the needs of all the people on whose bodies the country's struggle with Britain was won. In spite of the circumstances and the sudden turn of events surrounding this planned meeting, he had come too far. Benedict could not turn back now.

CHAPTER 9

THE YARDARM INN – ALBANY

Many years before, Benedict learned to respect his senses and feelings regarding danger. This was one of those times. While looking at the innkeeper who calls himself, 'Brother Timothy,' the hair on the back of his neck literally stood on end!

Benedict determined that it was best to respect his intuition rather than now face the man on the second floor, at the end of the hall. He was also certain that his every move was being watched by someone other than Brother Timothy. Not wanting to alert the innkeeper to his suspicions, or any others who might be watching or waiting for him to make any unexpected moves, Benedict finished registering as Otis McGurk and paid in advance for his room.

However, rather than go directly to his room, he looked for an excuse to leave the inn.

"Before I go to my room, I am going to first care for my horse." And he turned to walk toward the door.

As he turned, the innkeeper smiled and raised his right hand in a quick gesture. "That won't be necessary, Sir. I will have one of our stable boys groom, feed and water your horse."

Benedict noticed a slight quiver in the innkeeper's voice, confirming that Arnold's instincts were correct. Benedict turned toward Brother Timothy and spoke with directness and determination so the innkeeper could make no mistake about his intentions to personally care for his horse. "I am sure that your stable boys are quite able, Sir. However, many months ago, I made an agreement with my horse. If he would take care of me and deliver me safely to my destinations, I would take care of him in return and personally see to it that he is properly groomed, fed and watered."

Benedict then smiled, "It is sort of a gentleman's and gentlehorse's agreement that we have. He has maintained his part of the bargain and I am damn well going to do the same."

With that, Benedict slowly walked out of the inn while carefully watching and listening for the sounds of movement of any others around him. As he walked Governor to the stable located behind the inn, he casually glanced up at one of the windows in the back of the inn on the second floor. The movement of shadows of more than one person in the window suggested that 'Brother Sparks' was not the only person in the room at the end of the hall. Benedict smiled and thought to himself: *Curiosity is a common weakness among the dim-witted. It will give them away every time.*

Entering the stable, Benedict also noticed four other horses in the stalls within the stable, each of whom appeared to have been settled for some time. For having only one guest at the inn, it struck Benedict odd that there would be so many horses at the stable.

Talking gently to his horse as he normally did while settling him down for the night, he first offered his horse water and then a bit of grain from a food bucket. He intended to prepare Governor for any exertion that may be needed before this day was finished. While caring for Governor, Benedict continued to listen and to watch for movement of any others in the dimly lit stable. As his horse ate, Benedict retrieved a short saber from his saddle. He removed his pistol from his belt and, standing next to his horse to shield his actions from anyone that may be watching, Benedict loaded powder, wad and shot into its muzzle and prepared a small amount of powder to be placed upon the flash-pan quickly if needed. He then carefully placed the pistol under his left arm beneath his cloak and draped his saber within its scabbard under Governor's saddle blanket.

However, rather than remove his saddle to stable his horse, Benedict now got back onto Governor's saddle and with his right hand tucked inside of his cloak holding his revolver, he rode slowly out of the barn; down a road leading away from the inn toward the Hudson River. Benedict took an indirect and convoluted route toward the river; all the while subtly looking for others who may be watching him or would attempt to follow him. It wasn't long before Benedict noticed two horsemen who appeared to be following him, taking the same oddly construed path as he.

At one point, Benedict circled around and back onto his path ending up at a crossroad intersection a few blocks away from the docks on the Hudson. Crossing his path to the other side of the road, he quickly moved off the frozen street to a wooded area where he could conceal his horse and himself among the evergreen underbrush, and yet be able to get a good look at the men who were following him. Benedict dismounted and used a small tree limb to quickly brush the snow to obscure his horse's tracks leading off the road. It would now appear that he circled back and took the same path that he and the others had previously taken.

Although his actions would soon send a clear message to those who were following him that he was aware of their presence, Benedict believed that it was a risk worth taking. It wasn't long before the two riders approached and passed his vantage point as they followed their old path once again. Concentrating their attention on the tracks they were following on the road, they slowly ambled by without noticing Benedict as he carefully watched and studied his pursuers.

They appeared to be in their mid-to-late forties, but he recognized neither rider. *Dim- witted indeed*, Benedict thought as they passed him by. After these riders rode out of sight and as he prepared to mount Governor and leave his vantage point, Benedict noticed a third horseman approaching from the same direction and who appeared to be following the previous two riders. From the distance between them,

Benedict concluded that the first two riders were unaware of the third horseman's presence.

The third man was larger than the other two. His face and features were well covered by his tricorn hat and dark blue cloak. Although there was a familiar air about the rider and his appearance; Benedict could not get a good look at the third rider. Unlike the first two horsemen, this rider hesitated at the crossroad intersection and looked around before he, too, continued in the same direction as the two previous riders. Once he slowly ambled by and was out of sight, Benedict got back onto his horse and continued his exit in the direction of the crossroad leading away from the river. Not having any other place to go, Benedict had no other alternative but to begin his return trip to Saratoga where he thought he might be safe.

Before long, however, Benedict noticed a single rider following his path; he concluded that this rider was determined and perhaps not as dim-witted as he once thought. Benedict then decided that it was time to confront this nemesis on his own terms. Benedict turned into a narrow alley and dismounted his horse behind one of the buildings located on the riverbank. With his pistol at the ready and saber in his left hand, Benedict prepared to greet his follower. It wasn't long before he heard the hooves of a horse approaching the rear of the building. Benedict slowly cocked the hammer on his revolver and placed powder in its flash-pan. It was time to determine exactly why he was being followed and by whom.

Awaiting the horseman, Benedict felt the pounding of his heart and noticed a bitter taste and dryness in his mouth. Recognizing the long-forgotten feelings of battle, Benedict smiled. It was not an altogether uncomfortable feeling for him; one that he was well able to control in years past once he recognized it for what it was. Benedict credited many personal victories on the battlefield to his ability to control his emotions and its effects upon the mind and body at a time when full control of both was needed. For some, the effects of emotion in battle manifested itself as fear; for others, near paralysis.

It was often the fear felt by his enemies that doomed them in battle as they struggled with not only their enemy, but also with themselves. Although Benedict, too, felt fear, he was able to control his emotions and its effects. This ability made him appear fearless to others. Some would say foolhardy if not insane. He also knew that people feared the insane, primarily due to their unpredictability. Knowing this, Benedict often faced his close-combat enemies with an unexpected and exaggerated grin, along with laughter and a piercing stare that provided an even greater distraction to the poor souls who had the misfortune of confronting Benedict face-to-face on the battlefield. In battle, seconds matter; the momentary confusion implanted within his enemy was all that Benedict needed to ensure that he would be the one to survive.

Benedict heard the horse stop before rounding the turn to the back of the building. *This rider was no fool.* Hearing the rider beginning his dismount, Benedict thought it best to confront him while he was in the awkward position of dismount rather than after he had both feet on the ground. Benedict leapt into the alley from behind the building and hobbled quickly to confront his follower who slowly, but purposefully, completed his dismount. He was a large man, and someone with physical features familiar to Arnold. Benedict wasn't certain, but thought that the shadowed outline of the rider's features were familiar, perhaps of someone he knew. The rider then slowly turned to face his prey. Benedict and the horseman that followed him for the last half hour stood face-to-face; Benedict was bewildered.

Facing Benedict in an alley behind a building in Albany near a riverbank on the Hudson stood an old friend. Someone Benedict believed that he had truly known and trusted. It was also someone Benedict expected that he would meet on his return visit, but hardly under these unusual circumstances. Benedict's expression quickly changed from that of a crazed man, to one of a man filled with uncertainty and confusion.

As the lone horseman stepped from the shadows, he greeted Arnold: "General, it is an honor to once again see you and to know that your survival instincts are still intact and have not dulled with age. It has been much too long." He removed the glove from his right hand and reached out to shake that of Arnold's.

Staring back, Benedict lowered his pistol, allowing the powder to spill from its flash-pan, and grasped the hand of his long-ago friend. "General, it is indeed my honor to see you as well, and to see that you still know how to make an entrance. Yes, it has been much too long. I trust that you and Martha are doing well."

"We are. However, I am not so sure that either you or I will be doing quite so well if we do not immediately leave this area. You are in danger. It appears that there are men here who have enticed you to join them in hopes of significantly abbreviating your stay on this earth, if you know what I mean. I learned of your planned visit to Albany twelve days ago; I came to see if it was true. I see that you are somewhat surprised to see me as well as I am to see you, and I know that we both have much to discuss. However, we must now leave here for somewhere safer. No one knows of my being here, and I fear that if we are seen together, it may very well be the end of both of us. Get your horse; we must leave."

Benedict was more than surprised. He was stunned. He was ready for almost anything in that alley. But meeting his former General, George Washington, here and under these circumstances was not one of them.

He couldn't quite think clearly. "Where will we go? It is getting dark soon, and it will be difficult to travel at night," as though darkness was his greatest concern after what Washington just told him.

Benedict Arnold: Legacy Lost (A Ghost's Story)

Remembering his friends in the more isolated community of Saratoga, Benedict then offered: "I know a place north of here. I believe that it will be safe there, but I am not sure how we will get across the river at night. I expect that the tender will not be willing to take us across by the time we reach the ferry."

Washington looked down upon Benedict from his horse, "I am not sure who these men are. Although they are not able to track and follow other riders too well, I doubt that they are totally ignorant of your journey here and the path you would likely take to get here. They will expect you to leave by the same course. They will likely be at the most commonly used ferry to await your return. I don't think it would be safe for us to use that same ferry any time soon

"I know of another route you can take that will not be so obvious to them. We can rest at a location west of here where I stayed the last two evenings in a small village on the Mohawk. Traveling at night will not be the most pleasant. Nevertheless, we both must leave this city now. Providence has provided a near full moon, which should help light our way. And I expect that those looking for you would be searching for a lone rider, and we should therefore travel together. Two men traveling together would likely draw less attention than either of us traveling alone."

They traveled quickly, and quietly, not speaking at all along their journey to a location near a ferry on the Mohawk River, west of Albany that was operated by Nicholas Fort and his family.

Taking over two hours to reach their destination, a small cabin in an isolated area near the banks of the Mohawk River, it was dark when the two men dismounted and walked their horses into a barn for food, water and a quick grooming. It was clear by their silence that both men felt awkward by their circumstance – each glancing at the other as if trying to absorb the thoughts of the other.

Although these men did have much to discuss, neither spoke as they cared for their horses. Brushing Governor, Benedict did consider the thought that Washington's ability to get him to this isolated location was much too easy. Despite their past friendship, Benedict was fully aware that it was Washington who possibly stood to lose the most if his return was not well planned and orchestrated. In spite of their past friendship and bonds of trust, much time has passed; *one can never be too certain about the effects of time upon the minds of men.*

As he groomed Governor, Benedict was cautiously aware of his surroundings – looking and listening for anything unusual. After the men settled their horses for the evening, they went into the cabin, started a fire and made themselves comfortable.

Benedict was the first to break the silence with a torrent of questions. "Perhaps you can now tell me what is going on. Why was our meeting canceled? Who are the other two men that were following me? Who are the men at the Yardarm Inn who go by the names Brother Timothy and 'Brother Sparks'. And just who the hell might someone with the initials, L.Q.C. be?"

Leaning back into his chair, Washington looked tired and confused. "You question me as though I should know something. You want to know what happened to a meeting you apparently planned, and the primary question I have is what the hell are you doing here?"

Rubbing his forehead with his right hand, Washington continued. "With all honesty, I cannot tell you why your meeting was canceled . I don't know who arranged the meeting with you or who was to attend. I was not even aware that the meeting was planned until Philip Schuyler sent me a letter less than two weeks ago to let me know that you were traveling to Albany to meet with a group of men who were also coming to Albany from out of the area."

"General Schuyler, Philip Schuyler? What does he have to do with this?"

"He was the one who told me of your possible arrival back in this country and the meeting that had been planned for you to attend in Albany. I don't know how Philip learned of your meeting, or where he got his information; however, based upon the fact that you are now standing here before me, it is reasonable to conclude that his information was accurate."

Washington shook his head slowly. "And, based upon the content of his letters to me on this matter, I do not believe that he had anything to do with it either. He obviously knows nothing of our previous agreements. And he was quite concerned about your return, as well as the intentions of the unknown men who would also be traveling to Albany to meet with you."

Benedict looked confused as he sunk further into the back of his chair. "What do you mean that you didn't know that I was coming?"

Washington shrugged his massive shoulders. "I was not made aware of any of the specific arrangements for your meeting until Philip sent me another note six days ago telling me that your meeting was then being canceled. His note indicated that apparently only a limited number of people were aware of the planned meeting; neither he nor I were among them."

Extending his hands toward Benedict with his extended fingers separated, "Fortunately for you, in spite of his lack of knowledge about our past understandings, he is a compassionate man. His note said that he was concerned for your safety here. Although he was primarily concerned about the motives behind your return now, Philip was also of the opinion that you were not apprised of the meeting's cancellation, and was concerned that you were apparently being baited into coming to Albany as some form of elaborate plan to hold you accountable for your, shall we say, unpopular acts during the war."

Looking directly at Benedict, Washington concluded, "Philip was not positive about their exact plans; however, he believed that some individuals wanted you to come to Albany so they could dispatch you and, by doing so, make a name for themselves in history."

While attempting to make sense of it all, Benedict continued with his questions. "What about those who were at the inn, do you know who they were?"

"I do not know anyone by the names of Timothy, Sparks or anyone with the initials 'L.Q.C.' that you specifically ask about. These men are strangers to me.

"However, based upon what has thus far occurred, our friend, Mr. Schuyler, does appear to have a very reliable source of information. I simply cannot be certain what he knows or what his source of information is. Virtually everything he said about the meeting appears to be accurate. At an appropriate time, I will talk to Philip to see what more I can learn from him and see if he knows who these men are."

Nodding his head of graying hair, Washington added, "Nevertheless, he may very well be correct regarding their motives. As you can well imagine, not everybody in this not-so-united country is willing or able to greet your return with open arms. Some would rather meet you with a rope, and others would think them to be heroes in doing so."

Looking directly into the eyes of Washington, "And, as long as we are on the topic of my potential demise, I would be interested in knowing on which side of that line you stand regarding this point as well."

With the wave of his hand, Washington dismissed Benedict's comment. "Don't be ridiculous, Benedict. As you may recall when I wrote you last August, I told you then that I wasn't at all certain that the country is quite ready for your return at this point in time. There is simply too much uncertainty and political confusion right now. Our battle for control in shaping this country's government is at its zenith. If we were to attempt your return now, all that we struggled for may come to an end; tyranny would once again reign over this blood-soaked land."

Benedict now looked more puzzled than ever. "What do you mean that you didn't know anything about my planned trip to America, or that you still believe that the time is not right for the country? I received other letters, more recent than August from you suggesting that the time has indeed come for us to meet to plan for my return and our country's future."

"What do you mean other letters?

"I received the last letter from you in October, a mere two months ago. Within that letter, you agreed upon a meeting date, location, and even the names that we would use to register at the Yardarm Inn where our meeting was to take place in Albany. Are you trying to tell me now that you had no knowledge of my coming to America, or our planned meeting?"

Washington looked downward and shook his head. "I had no idea whatsoever!"

Benedict was exasperated. "If that is true, who the hell wrote those letters? And, at the risk of sounding terribly self-serving, have you given any consideration whatsoever to me and my family? As one result of *our* actions, mind you, you are the hero of the revolution. This nation's savior! And that is fine by me. Without your steady hand on the helm during the revolution, our nation's ship would have been rudderless. God only knows that you deserve all the accolades that this nation can bestow upon you.

"On the other hand, as another result of *our* actions, mind you, I've acquired the brand that is leading me directly to the gates of hell. You have no way of knowing the personal price my family and I have paid for our victory."

Throwing both arms upward in exasperation, "Do you know what it is like being thought of as a traitor all these years by my former friends; my comrades, Generals Knox and Schuyler; and even my children, for God's sake? I have uprooted my family from our rightful homeland. I have abandoned claims to any friendships I might have had, save yours, and maintained the ruse of being a loyal subject to the Crown and the aristocratic British bastards until I've literally become sickened by it all.

"Five years ago I was naive. I couldn't possibly have known where the paths we chose to take then would ultimately lead me or, more importantly, those I love. You and I had a war to win, and we did so."

Hearing this, Washington slowly nodded his head. "Yes we did. But as I said before, although the war may be over, the battles for power and control of this country's future continue."

Looking downcast, and with a higher pitched voice than before, Benedict responded with a slap on the table between them. "*Now* is time for me to claim my rightful place here on this stage and live as a true American in this country for which my family and I have sacrificed more than any man will ever know. It isn't right for anyone to ask my family to suffer more. How much more can we suffer? How much more must we endure? What more can you possibly expect of me? I am here! This is where I and my family belong! Looking back upon my actions, both on and off the battlefield, and knowing the intended outcome of our plans for West Point, I frankly do not understand your personal objections to my return now."

Sitting back into his chair once again and with a softer, even faint voice, Benedict continued. "What right do you or anyone else have to insist that I not return to my heritage and become part of this nation's victory celebration and its plans for the years ahead? Why in God's name are you still so afraid of the truth now? It has been five years for God's sake!"

Benedict Arnold: Legacy Lost (A Ghost's Story)

With his typical, steely lack of emotion, Washington looked in Benedict's direction. "It is not the truth that concerns me. It is what others may do with it to undermine our final victory that I am concerned about..."

Leaning back into his chair, Benedict continued with his tone of resignation. "The war is over for Christ's sake! I beg, indeed, my soul begs for the truth to be told. Nobody would believe me now. Why would they? It needs to be you. You need to be the one. You need to tell my family, my friends and the world what happened and why. They need to know that I am guilty of nothing more than being a part of a successful attempt to bring victory to this country."

"Regardless of who it comes from, the secret we share could be equally dangerous to you and your family if it should become known now."

Shaking his head, Benedict responded, "I am now willing to risk the perils of the British lot again when they learn of my being an intelligence agent for you over the last five years. They are no more dangerous to me now than these men here who are apparently trying to kill me for what they now believe I did over five years ago. I am 43 years of age and not in great health, all things considered. I am truly not afraid of any man now, British or American, or what they may attempt to do to me now."

Washington sat in silence, staring into the dancing flames within the fireplace, apparently not knowing what to say.

While continuing to look in Washington's direction, Benedict persisted. "What I fear most is dying with a flaming letter "$\underline{T}$" seared upon my soul. It is not that I am afraid of death itself, or to face my God now for what I have done to my enemies or to myself for that matter. However, what I fear most is to face my God for what I've done to my family and to my progeny for the years to come. I ask God every day for His forgiveness. And then, each day I look into the faces of my children. If I cannot forgive myself for what I have done to them, how can I possibly expect God to forgive me?"

Looking away from Washington and joining his stare into the fireplace, "George, my family needs to know. You and I need to come forward with the truth. I need to have this brand removed. My soul needs to be cleansed and my spirit resurrected. I cannot do so alone, and I cannot do so while living a lie."

Slowly shaking his head, "I have been living a lie and, by association with me, my family, too, have become unwitting victims of our victory and are also living a lie with me and for me. I can't even stand to look at myself in a looking glass any longer, knowing that I took them away from this glorious country to live in a snobbish, uncaring land where the aristocratic life is a birthright and not something one can aspire to achieve with dedication and hard work."

Benedict leaned back into his chair and rubbed his face with his burly hands as though attempting to rub the exasperation from his face. "Now at this moment when, at what I believed to be your invitation, I finally thought that my time had come…Here I thought I was going to meet with you to bring this nightmare to an end. And you now tell me that you knew nothing about my coming to the America or our planned meeting. How could you possibly not know?"

Washington glanced at Benedict and hesitated for a moment before standing up. Leaning over with his fisted right hand on the table separating the two of them, he looked Benedict squarely in the eyes. The lantern on the table below cast yellow hues and deep shadows upon Washington's stern face; he spoke with a deep, soft; yet firm tone.

"Benedict, I want you to watch me very carefully as I speak…I knew nothing. Nothing until Philip Schuyler first told me less than two weeks ago of your coming to Albany. I know that we need to settle this matter, but I want you to know now that I had absolutely nothing to do with your planned meeting in Albany.

"This is all catching me rather off guard, and we both need time to think and to plan. We cannot allow our actions to be dictated by the actions of others. I am asking that you believe me on this score, and to know that I do understand you and your family's sufferings, and I am willing to work with you to prepare your rightful place at our country's table. I just don't want the table to be that of *The Last Supper!*"

Shaking his head, Washington continued, "Our war is not over. Our victory is at hand but not yet in our grasp. Now is not the time. We have come too damn far to allow our personal wants and needs to outweigh the needs of this country and the collective futures of all our nation's children."

Benedict looked up from his chair and then stood up slowly. Leaning toward Washington with his right hand on the table between them and supporting himself with his left hand on his cane, Benedict looked directly into Washington's eyes in return. His face was equally as stern as Washington's and totally void of emotion.

After a few seconds of silent contemplation, Benedict's expression slowly morphed from that of anger to sad resignation and then, with a slight smile and in a low whisper, Benedict responded. "Well, I've got a few things to say about that my friend. First, George, you look older than I remember. It must either be the passage of time or the close vantage point from which I stare. Second, it looks like we have a mystery on our hands. Who are they? Who the hell was I communicating with in my letters if it wasn't you? And, why did you come to Albany?" Sliding back into his chair and folding his hands behind his head, Benedict sighed, "And...of not the least importance at this moment in time, do you have any brandy or rum to commemorate our long-overdue reunion?"

Sitting back into his chair as well, Washington stretched his legs outward and rubbed his wrinkled forehead as he thought about what Benedict said and the questions asked. "Right now, I only have answers to two of your perplexing questions. First of all, I came to Albany to see if what Philip said about your return was true. As you might very well expect, your coming back to America would be of reasonable concern and of particular interest to me. And secondly, yes, I just happen to have a choice of brandy, rum or one of my personal whiskey blends to help commemorate this moment."

After standing to stoke the fire, which then brightened the room, Washington turned to look at Arnold, stretched his arms toward the ceiling and yawned. "Perhaps it would be best if we rested for the evening and see if we can sort all of this out in the morning when we both have clearer heads."

Walking toward a cabinet in the corner of the room, Washington continued. "I imagine that you've had a difficult day, and being here must be unsettling for you on many levels as well. As pleased as I am to at last have the opportunity to see you again after five long years, wrinkled-face-to-wrinkled-face, I must, nonetheless, admit that my mind is conflicted, confused and that I, too, am not able to think clearly at this hour."

Reaching into the cabinet to retrieve a bottle and two snifters; Washington then returned to the table where Benedict was sitting. Before he reached the table, he hesitated. "Ben, I knew that we would need to meet one day. I simply could not imagine how we could do so, or what the outcome of our meeting would be. Yet, here we are. And, it would appear that, whether I like it or not, the time has now come for each of us to consider our options."

Washington placed the two glasses on the table, uncorked the bottle and, while carefully pouring brandy into each glass, he raised his eyebrows in a quick jerk and glanced in Benedict's direction. "Right now I am mentally tired and need a good night's rest. I well imagine that the same can be said for you. After pouring two glasses of brandy, Washington gave one to Benedict and then raised his glass: "To the United States of America. May Providence provide each of us with the strength and wisdom to understand where we go from here."

Benedict stood to join Washington in his toast, raising his glass to meet that of Washington's. "To the souls of those who died for Liberty, Independence and Freedom. And to all the families of our nation who suffered and sacrificed in the long…" raising his glass a bit higher; winking his right eye, "…and apparently never-ending struggle for freedom."

CHAPTER 10

DEWEES MANSION, VALLEY FORGE PENNSYLVANIA THRUSDAY, MAY 21, 1778

As the morning fog lifted from the surrounding hillsides, General Washington sat at his desk reviewing field reports and correspondence while awaiting his first visit with Benedict Arnold since the victory at Saratoga and Arnold's recovery at a military hospital in Albany.

This past winter had been a long and arduous one for many. While Benedict suffered in Albany, the British occupied Philadelphia and men at this Valley Forge winter encampment died by the thousands from exposure, hunger and disease. It was the opinion of a growing number of colonists, both those within the military and their family members at home, that the war with Britain was dragging on much too long with no end in sight.

As a consequence, Washington's popularity among the men within the Army, as well as an increasing number of individuals within the Continental Congress, was waning with each passing day. In spite of the American success at Saratoga the previous fall, neither Benedict Arnold, who was instrumental in orchestrating the battlefield movements leading to success there, nor Commanding General Washington, whose troop movements to the south near Philadelphia kept British Generals Howe and Clinton's attention diverted from Saratoga, received any recognition for the American success at Saratoga.

Sole credit was claimed by Major General Horatio Gates, Field Commander of the Continental forces at Saratoga. Gates used the victory at Saratoga to enhance his own standing among the members of the Continental Congress and a means to discredit Arnold's and to undermine Washington's leadership as Commanding General. Having political aspirations of his own, General Gates wanted nothing more than to have Washington step down as Commanding General of the American forces. And, based upon his claim for the northern victory at Saratoga in the fall of '77, politically naïve Gates was certain that members of the Continental Congress would now turn to him as a natural successor to George Washington as Commander in Chief.

After the Saratoga campaign and before Arnold's responsibility for the Army's success there became fully known, Washington was simply annoyed with General Gates for not respecting the chain-of-command protocols by providing his battlefield reports directly to members of the Continental Congress. As Arnold's leadership and responsibilities for success at Saratoga became more widely known, Washington was further troubled to learn that, in spite of what he was told by others who were at Saratoga, General Gates' report did not recognize any of his subordinate commanders who were instrumental in leading the American forces to victory.

Washington was a hands-on leader and, like Arnold, instinctively understood that it is better to lead men into battle from the front rather than push men into battle from behind. Leadership means getting dirty and taking calculated risks. From what Washington had been told, Gates barely broke a sweat at Saratoga. He was particularly annoyed at the petty slight given to Benedict Arnold by General Gates who did not say a word about Arnold's fearless and dedicated leadership on the fields of battle; only mentioning that Benedict had been wounded. However, others who were at Saratoga spread the word about Arnold's courageous, selfless actions and informed Washington that the credit for victory was rightfully Arnold's and not Gates'.

Before the battles, General Gates' general orders were to meet the enemy once they attacked the American's established fortifications; Benedict wanted to meet the enemy in the woods and the rugged terrain that was both advantageous to the Americans and would prevent the British from being able to mobilize into their customary battle formations. Benedict knew that it was best to engage the enemy on American terms and not wait until the British had enough time to reconnoiter, position their field artillery and plan their attacks.

As more and more field reports about the victory at Saratoga were received, Washington also learned that even British General John Burgoyne, commander of the doomed British forces at Saratoga, acknowledged Benedict Arnold as the individual responsible for his loss. Although Burgoyne had been told that Major General Horatio Gates commanded the American forces at Saratoga, his battlefield commanders only confirmed that General Benedict Arnold had been active at the first and second battle engagements and was seen by several of Burgoyne's officers who were directing their forces. It was not until the smoke and dust of battle had settled, and the blood began to be washed away by torrential rains into the soil of this now-hallowed ground, that General Gates communicated directly with General Burgoyne to negotiate the terms for the British surrender. Only then was Burgoyne certain that Gates was even present during this campaign.

Gates' self-serving reports, and lack of respect for the men deserving of acknowledgment for their contribution to success, troubled Washington and gave him reason to question the character and motives of this gutless and now untrustworthy general. It wouldn't be until later in the Revolution, during the Battle of Camden, South Carolina, in August of 1780 where General Gates' predilection for caution and retreat would become apparent to even the most casual observer. Both Washington and Arnold would one day smile and shake their heads at stories of General Gates' hasty retreat where he reportedly not only left the battle field, and all 3,000 members of his command behind, but drove his horse into the ground during his lone 60-mile dash north into North Carolina and relative safety.

Benedict Arnold: Legacy Lost (A Ghost's Story)

Washington looked out a window as the sun's light strained to shine through the heavy morning fog. The dew hung heavy on the blades of grass and the newly formed, emerald green leaves on the trees. The clomping of hooves and the squeaking of an approaching horse-drawn carriage could be heard long before it could be seen through the dense fog. Finally, the shadowy shape of black horses followed by a cloaked driver, then carriage parted the wisps of fog. Major General Arnold had arrived at General Washington's Valley Forge headquarters.

As General Arnold was being helped out of his carriage to enter Dewees Mansion, Washington came out of his home and, akin to the arrival of a ghostly apparition, emerged through the morning mist. Washington simply appeared out of the fog and mist to greet his valued commander. It was as though, Washington wanted those present to see that Generals themselves were not immune to the sufferings of war and must also endure the hardships of battle – just like the enlisted men of the Continental Army and members of the militia.

"My Northern Admiral of Valcour, and hero of Saratoga, welcome! I am so pleased to finally be able to see you once again in the flesh." Benedict was supported by crutches; assisted by his aides and two other soldiers who greeted his carriage.

Standing as erect as possible under his circumstance, Benedict saluted his Commanding General. "I hope you pardon my feeble frame sir, I am not as tall as I once was, but my heart is larger and I too am proud to be with my esteemed Commanding General. We have much to catch up on and discuss."

Rather than offering a customary return salute, Washington showed uncustomary feeling, approached Benedict and embraced both his shoulders with his large, firm hands. Smiling and looking directly into Arnold's eyes, his words were warm and welcoming, "Yes, we do have much to talk about General, but first let's get you inside and comfortable. God knows how much you've suffered as well as these men here who also join me in welcoming you to our humble headquarters."

Benedict looked around as he was being helped onto the porch. Men in rags and tattered clothing could be seen through the fog, some smiling with toothless grins and others saluting Benedict as he passed them by. A few simply removed their shredded hats and placed them over their chests in honor of their beloved battlefield leader.

One of those present shouted, "I was with you at Quebec." Another: "I was with you at Ticonderoga and Valcour Island, that is until my ship was splintered and I ended up damn near swimming all the way back to Ticonderoga." Benedict smiled and waved.

Yet another shouted, "I was with you at Quebec, Valcour Island and Saratoga! I used to love fall; it was always my favorite time of year. But it was never before as exciting as spending that time of year with you! It was never so rewarding either! What shall we do this next fall?"

With that Benedict stopped, turned and saluted his admirers. "We will see, my sons, we will see." Motioning in the direction of General Washington, "We'll need to see what our commander here has in store for us. But whatever it is, and as Providence will allow, I assure you, it will very likely be as exciting and rewarding to each of us as were our past campaigns."

Removing his tricorn hat from his head, General Arnold concluded: "I am grateful for all your efforts in our continuing struggles for freedom and independence. And I look forward to serving with you all in future engagements, God willing."

With waves to their tattered group of greeters, Generals Washington and Arnold then entered headquarters where they visited for the remainder of the day as well as throughout the evening and well into the next morning. The two Generals did have much to discuss.

The after-dinner drinks flowed freely as the two men sat alone in Washington's study. Well after the midnight hour, Benedict turned to Washington and said with a slight slur to his speech, "George, I cannot describe clear enough the changes that have occurred to me during the last six months."

After struggling to stand, he looked about the room, felt somewhat dizzy and then, thinking better of it, Benedict slouched downward into his chair.

"As certain as I am now here with you, I am equally certain that you and I have each survived for a reason. I want you to know that I am not the same man you once knew. I was once a self-centered, egocentric bastard. Greed and personal advantage played a major role in my past life's decisions, and I must now admit that I am ashamed of my past."

Shaking his head slowly, Benedict continued his statement. "I do not yet know what Providence has in store for me. But I can tell you this: both you and I will be part of Power's plan for our country's survival and its success into the future."

Pouring Benedict yet another drink, Washington also stumbled slightly as he stood to toast his newfound friend, "To Benedict, the new man! May he lead a healthy, happy life and may he continue to demonstrate the vision and courage needed to help lead this country to victory." Washington laughed as he, too, fell into his seat. "You know Ben, I cannot honestly tell you when I was last this drunk. I cannot honestly tell you, because I am too drunk to remember…"

The two men laughed. And so it was at their first meeting after Albany. With that, Washington and Benedict raised their glasses and continued to drink themselves into oblivion.

During the wee hours of the morning, the two men talked of family, of fanciful tales of women and their personal losses in the battles with the sexes; the likes of Sally Fairfax, a married woman, for

Washington in his early years; a more recent skirmish with the untouchable Miss Betsy DeBlois for Arnold. Both men agreed that the wounds of the heart inflicted by the fairer sex can be as debilitating and long-lasting as wounds of the flesh received from men during the more obvious battles for life and death. In addition, they both confirmed their opinion that it was often difficult to know whom to trust in a world filled with self-centric women and self-serving egomaniac men. They agreed that, although most women were honorable by nature, men of true honor and trust are far and few between.

On a more familiar subject that each had greater knowledge of, and were more comfortable with, they also shared stories of personal experiences on the battlefield offering testimony to the apparent interventions and protections of Providence in their lives. As the night wound down and the effects of liquor subsided, the two leaders discussed the more intrinsic political struggles of power and influence with Washington recounting his recent power struggle with General Gates' and others' recent, unsuccessful attempts to unseat him as Commanding General.

As the evening ended with arrival of the morning sun, both men had sobered up enough to become more serious in their parting remarks to one another. Benedict stood and hobbled to look out a window as the sun crested the distant hillside to cast its reddish-orange hue over the brown, brush-covered landscape.

Staring out the window, Benedict sighed and his expression was solemn. "I want you to know, Sir, I will give my life to you and to our country and I will be with you until the end. I do not yet know where my path will take me or what contributions I will be able to make in consideration of my current physical limitations. But you can believe me when I say that I will keep my eyes open and listen to the wind to learn where my journey in this war shall lead me next."

Turning toward Washington who was listening with his head resting on his arms at his desk, Benedict added, "You can count on me to do whatever you ask of me. For the moment however, I must care for my family."

Once again looking out the window, "As you know, my dear Peggy died a few years back, just as this whole mess started. My sons, now 10, 8 and 5, are being cared for by my loving sister, Hannah. It has been so hard on them all." Looking downward, "They don't understand the importance of what we do, nor should they at their innocent ages. All they know is that their mother died, and their father is away. I need to spend some time with them.

"Nonetheless, I do understand that our work is not yet completed; although they can't possibly understand, what I do here with you, I do for them and their futures. So please keep me informed of how I may best serve you and our country. Great challenges simply mean great opportunities!"

Looking up at Arnold, Washington offered his condolences, "Benedict, I am sorry for the loss of your dear wife. I sincerely hope your young children have been well cared for by your sister in your absence."

"Thank you sir, we were all blessed by Peggy's presence and her care for us all while she was with us. Fortunately for my sons and to my peace of mind, my sister, Hannah, has dedicated herself to their care ever since my dear Peggy first became ill."

Washington stood, stretched and, while yawning, joined Benedict at the window to also witness the morning's birth. "This is the beginning of a new day for all of us. I am always marveled and intrigued by life's mysteries. As wise as we all like to believe we are, we just never know what will become of us, from day-to-day. We both need to place our trust in Providence and pray for the best for all of us and our nation."

Reaching up to place one of his large hands on the top of the door casing, Washington glanced in Benedict's direction. "I wish I knew where our paths are both headed. This Power you speak of, as you might know, I am not a particularly religious man, in the strict interpretation of the phrase. However, I do believe in God and the powers given to others by God. And, as evidenced in my past skirmishes with death, I too have been blessed by His protection and divine guidance when difficult times presented themselves. I, too, will keep my ears into the wind, as you say, to see where we go from here."

Turning to face Arnold, Washington smiled. "Right now and for the next few weeks, you need to rest, get well, be with your sons and heal your leg. I will find a rightful post for you as soon as you are able to return to active duty. At the moment, I am looking for someone to help manage the liberation of Philadelphia once the British occupiers depart, which they appear to be planning to do. I am afraid that unless we control the transition once the British abandon the city, there will be lawless retribution inflicted upon the hapless inhabitants who remained while the British occupied their city. There are men of influence in Pennsylvania who will use any excuse to punish those who are thought to be loyalist supporters of the crown.

"We are striving to become a better nation of laws, of civility and of compassion. I need someone of strong will and character who can control men of influence and the unknown situations that will confront us there. I need someone who can face up to those who would be king and cut them down – with words and not by sword or tomahawk. I need someone like you in Philadelphia."

Putting his hand on Benedict's left shoulder, Washington looked out the window once again. "The battlefield there will not be as dirt filled or bloody as those you have become accustomed to, but it will be a dirty struggle nonetheless. I need someone who can set an example and can let the populace of Philadelphia know that our strength is in our laws and that we mean to enforce the laws for the protection of all its citizens, regardless of their personal positions on matters of state."

Locking his eyes upon Benedict's, Washington concluded, "Simply stated, we will need a man like you to manage this delicate situation. You let me know when you are able and ready. We will then see what Providence has in store for us at that time."

Less sturdy on their feet than before, and still staggering somewhat from the combined effects of drink and the lack of sleep, the two men then departed the study, startling three young, exhausted sentries in the foyer.

Benedict overheard one whisper to another, "I would not have believed that these two *old-timers* could sustain themselves throughout the night and into the next day." With visions blurred by drink and sleep deprivation, Washington and Benedict simply smiled.

As he was being helped into his carriage for his trip home to get some badly needed rest, Benedict turned to salute General Washington. "Until we meet again, Sir."

This time, Washington returned Arnold's salute. "Indeed, until we meet again my fighting general; my comrade. Until we meet again. Godspeed!"

CHAPTER 11

FORT'S FERRY – DECEMBER 19, 1785

B enedict was awakened by the sound of crackling and the smell of food cooking over a wood-burning fire. While yet in a semi-conscious state of awareness, his mind drifted back to the days of his early youth when he would be awakened by the smell of the morning meal being prepared by his mother over an open hearth.

The memory of his loving mother's care for him and his younger brothers and sisters brought a smile to his lips, and moisture to his eyes. Benedict sat up slightly, leaned on one elbow, rubbed his eyes, and looked across the room to see not his mother, but his former General, George Washington.

There he stood, as big as life, with spoon in hand, stirring a pot over the fireplace hearth. Benedict was amused by the image before him. *Behold! A leader of thousands! There stands a man whose decisions tipped the balance of life and death for soldiers on both sides of the battlefield. Wearing calf-high socks sticking out over his oversize boots, a long, white nightshirt gathered at the waist with a rope belt; graying hair pulled into a ponytail-like knot in the back of his head; stooped over an open hearth, and stirring a pot.*

Benedict smiled and slowly shook his head as though in disbelief. He never expected to witness such a personal image of his former General. It was indeed humanizing and affirmed Arnold's opinion that underneath all the exterior, superficial trappings of every man, exists a human being. Nothing more, and nothing less.

This image reinforced Arnold's belief that the only difference between men of power, wealth and influence and men thought of as *salt of the earth*, is simply circumstance. It is typically circumstance of birth, of educational opportunities and of family and personal connections that, in large measure, determines one's destiny.

That said, Benedict also understood that God also provides each of us with free will, and how one adjusts to his or her particular circumstance can indeed make a difference in one's life. Benedict often considered himself an example of someone who overcame the stranglehold of limited circumstance.

He also often thought of the limitations placed upon his friend, Martin Van Derwerker and his family, and how they, too, adjusted to make the most of what they had in order to build a satisfying life for themselves. At this stage of his life, Benedict realized that money, power and influence did not necessarily translate into happiness. Washington seemed to have it all, but one would never look at him and say that he was particularly happy.

On the other hand, Martin and his family had few material goods; yet they all seemed quite content and in high spirits. Staring at this image before him, Benedict wondered if Washington ever needed to prepare a meal for himself or another in his life before now. Nevertheless, here he was, preparing their morning meal – in his sleepwear for God's sake! It appeared to Benedict that time and circumstance have indeed changed for Washington as well.

Still leaning on one elbow, Benedict called out to Washington. "Well, either I am still dreaming, or the day I have longed for during the last five years has finally arrived. If you are indeed real and not an apparition in my mind's eye or a dream, I am ready to correct the historical record and join our countrymen once again. That is, of course, if you are willing to grant me my dream."

Washington stood upright from his stooped position, turned toward his guest, and bowed his gray head in Arnold's direction. "And a good morning to you too, Mr. Arnold. You don't waste much time with the pleasantries of small talk, do you, Benedict?"

Turning his attention back to his morning chores; he stooped to inspect the progress of the meal being prepared in his pot, "The word is not so much my 'willingness' but more accurately my 'ability.' It is not my willingness to grant you your dream that is up for discussion; it would be more precise to say that it is my ability to do so that needs to be considered."

Smiling, Washington turned his head again toward Arnold. "However, I think better with nourishment to warm my stomach. Let us enjoy a celebratory meal before we try to rectify the historical record and tax our creativity so early in the day."

Benedict smiled and stretched his arms as he yawned. "There is probably a better word to use other than '*tax*.' As I seem to recall, that is what started this whole mess and got the British into so much trouble in the first place. Perhaps a better word would be *challenge*. To challenge our creativity so early in the day. Of course, you are quite right. Understand that I've wasted over five years waiting for this moment in time. Please accept my humble apology for my impatience. I'm simply anxious to begin my final journey home. Yes, the day is young and we have nothing but time."

Getting himself out of bed, Benedict added, "For you it may be a nourished stomach that comforts you and clears the mind, however, for me it is the relief gained by the use of the necessary that allows me to concentrate better."

As Benedict quickly dressed and left the house to relieve himself. Washington simply smiled with his pursed lips and spooned them each a hot bowl of oatmeal with a molasses covering and poured each a cup of hot herbal tea. The two men then sat quietly to savor their morning meal and to prepare, each in his own way, for the day ahead.

CHAPTER 12

ALBANY

While Washington and Benedict enjoyed their breakfast, four men gathered in the lobby of the Yardarm Inn in Albany to try to determine what became of their prey and to understand what went wrong with their plan to capture the elusive Benedict Arnold.

"Damn it! What do you mean he disappeared? No one simply disappears without a trace, especially if he is on a goddamn horse in the middle of winter!"

"I knew we should have shot him when we had our chance. But the Colonel gave clear and direct orders. '…Bring him to me alive!…' His orders were unmistakable. Had we killed him when we had the chance a few days ago or again yesterday, the Colonel may have missed out on his glory, but Arnold would no longer be a worry to anyone! It's not clear to me what the Colonel's motives are. Is he interested in the betterment of all members of the Society or a select few? Is he interested in the betterment of the country or something more personal?"

"Regardless of his motives, it is necessary that the job simply gets done. None of us, including you or the Colonel, should worry so much about which one of us gets the credit for ridding the earth of this scourge. Brother Roeloff could have done it when he found him in Saratoga three days ago; or Brother Timothy could have done it when he had him right here in this very lobby just yesterday!"

Another joined in the discussion. "We should have anticipated Arnold's cunning gift of survival. He has not lived this long for no reason! We should simply kill him when we find him and be done with it. It is not about glory any longer. Mission above glory for God's sake! The glory days are over; we must, above all else, first get the job done.

Then you, the Colonel and others can worry about any glory or credit that may fall upon the shoulders of the Society."

"This isn't a discussion we should be having here. Let's go to the Colonel's room to see what we need to do next." The four men ascended the stairs and knocked on the door of the room at the end of the hall.

"Colonel, we've searched the city and asked everyone we know. Nobody knows where our invited guest is. We think it is likely that he met up with someone else yesterday after he left the inn, and it is possible that he may still be in the area, hiding at someone's home."

The door quickly opened. "Who the hell would he know here? Who in the world would ever put Arnold up now? That is, without using a rope to do it?" Motioning the men into his room, "I can tell you one thing for certain. As sure as I am standing here, everyone is somewhere. The question we need to answer is where Arnold's somewhere might be. I am not so interested in trying to figure out what happened yesterday or why his natural instinct for survival overcame his equally relentless curiosity. Perhaps he has become somewhat wiser with age."

Walking to look out a window toward the river, "What was done is done. What we need to do now is to determine how we can find the bastard. He is too close to permit him to escape yet again. The Hudson is frozen; neither the Vulture nor any other British ship is here to serve as a safe harbor for him this time."

One of the men who had remained silent up to now mumbled: "Arnold must have believed that he had someone here he could trust, or he would not have come in the first place. Who did he really think that he was going to be meeting with yesterday? If we knew that, we might possibly know where he might be now."

The other men in the room all glanced at one another and then looked to the Colonel, each with puzzled looks of exasperation.

The Colonel all but ignored the question and looked directly at one of the men standing to his left. "Brother Roeloff, I want you to return to Saratoga. Stop at Halfmoon along the way and ask everyone you encounter if they've seen any strangers on horseback within the last day or two. He is probably still using his alias, so ask everyone if they've seen a traveler who goes by the name Otis McGurk. There is no point in raising any suspicions about our interest in Arnold now, so don't use his real name when questioning others."

"Why not let others know that Arnold is in the area? If we can't get him, perhaps someone else can."

Turning quickly, the Colonel shook his fist. "No! We all agree that Arnold needs to be killed; however, it is important that the Society be responsible for dealing with Arnold. We have no idea what stories he may tell others to save his life. We just need to deal with him swiftly and not let the country get bogged down now in any lengthy, controversial and undoubtedly distracting trial for treason. Could you imagine what would happen if Arnold was captured by someone else and put on trial now?"

Sitting back down, he continued his rant. "We need to ensure that he does not get that far. It is critical that we find him and put an end to the risk of his distraction to the efforts now being made to put this country back on its feet again. There has been too much physical and emotional suffering; we do not need any additional emotional turmoil in our countrymen's lives at this time. Enough is enough!"

Brother Roeloff lowered his head. "We know that he was in Saratoga three days ago and also here yesterday. That much we know. He must have stayed someplace between those two days. I'll go back to see if he has returned there on his way back to Canada and try to see if I can get any indication as to where he might have been for the last few days. Sir, if I come across Arnold, what should I do?"

"I am afraid that 'Brother Sparks' is undoubtedly right…we need to get the job done. But be careful, I would not attempt to confront him alone. He is like a cat that has expended each and every one of his nine lives and yet lives on. I wouldn't be surprised if Arnold has made a pact with Satan himself to grant him extended life in exchange for an eternal damnation! If that is the case, he will have the devil on his side. Should you come across him again, get other members of the Society to help with Arnold if you possibly can. That said, if you have the opportunity, take it. We may not get another. Kill the son of a bitch!"

Shaking his head, "No court in this country will convict you or anyone else for eradicating this land of its greatest traitor. Our band of brothers, indeed all good citizens of this land, will stand by you or anyone else who brings this dark chapter of our country's history to an end."

CHAPTER 13

FORT'S FERRY

After their morning meal, Washington looked at Benedict and smiled. "It seems that the time has come for us to discuss your dream as you call it. Ah, what is a dream but a fanciful illusion of reality? I don't know what kind of dreams you are accustomed to, but perhaps those you were having last evening are more like nightmares than something to be wished for."

"I am sorry if my restless evening disturbed you. It is one of the curses acquired during the war. On occasion, I am more active in my sleep than I am during the daylight hours. My poor wife or others in nearby rooms are often awakened by my restlessness; it embarrasses me, but there is little I can do about it. Please accept my apologies."

Washington offered Benedict another drink of hot tea. "I understand and was not troubled at all by your restlessness. I, too, had active and restless nights on occasion during the first year following the war. I expect that we are not alone in this regard. It is the baggage that many of us carry forward as we attempt to forget, or at least reconcile, our pasts. I suspect that the conscious part of our being is better able to cope with our lives after the war than the unconscious part. At least, that is how I understood my nightmares."

Staring at the ceiling, Washington added: "However, for me, it was sweaty fits where I awakened drenched. On cold nights like these, it was quite uncomfortable. But at least my discomfort was a more private and personal reaction and not necessarily one I was required to share with others sleeping in adjacent rooms. Let's hope that we are both not living a real nightmare by the time this day is ended."

"Unlike you, my restless nights continue. It is my sincere wish that they would all come to an end soon."

Benedict rubbed the frost from a window to peer out. "It is certainly a dark and overcast December day. It is a good day to stay indoors and remain out of the elements. So here we are. Just you and me, and the whole day to ourselves. Where to begin? That is the question on the floor under consideration of this assembled body of two. Where do we even begin this discussion?"

To which Washington responded. "I believe that it is safe to say that for each question you may have about the future, I have as many about exactly how events unfolded five years ago at the very beginning of our current situation."

Putting two fingers from his right hand to his lips, Washington added. "In my opinion, clarifying the past for each of us will help shine a light upon the path we should take into the future. At least we will have the same understanding of the facts of our collective pasts. I expect that we will then be able to establish a sound foundation upon which we can plan for our respective futures."

Benedict laughed. "I wouldn't doubt that you may need to have some answers settled before we focus upon tomorrow and the tomorrows after that. It is true that we must begin somewhere; so what would you like to discuss first?"

Washington placed a few logs on the glowing embers in the fireplace and fanned the coals beneath with a bellows to ignite the freshly placed fuel. He then sat in one of the rocking chairs next to the fireplace and Benedict joined him. Both men appeared rested as they settled back into their oversized rockers to begin their long overdue journey toward their respective futures, and that of the fledgling nation they each helped forge with their swords of sharpened steel.

Washington was the first to begin the journey down the uncertain path of discourse they were to explore on this eventful day. "This is our first real opportunity to talk to one another directly in five years and without cipher, which only confuses the hell out of me. There are some events that occurred in the beginning that have perplexed me even to this day and, frankly, left me wondering about your true motives over the years. Yes, things did eventually work out as we had earlier hoped, but believe me, there were plenty of times that I frankly did not think they would."

While looking at Benedict, Washington explained. "I must confess, in the beginning when I first saw the documents that Colonel Jameson delivered to me that you had provided to Major André, I was frankly startled by their content – a map of West Point fortifications with artillery placements, and troop strengths and weaknesses. Even a copy of the minutes from a recent Council of War meeting that I held at that time…That, in and of itself, was treasonous and a personal affront to me, for God's sake. When I saw that, I wondered if I, too, had been taken in by your scheme, and if I were even to become a casualty of your plot with the British."

Turning to stare back in the direction of the dancing flames, "As events were beginning to quickly unfold, I was at a loss, concerned and honestly did not know what the hell you were up to! There were times when I truly believed that you had actually gone over to the British, and that I was a foolish victim of your plot.

"I might add that your Mrs. Arnold was quite beside herself when I first saw her shortly after you departed your West Point Headquarters at the Robinson house. Her ordeal was quite convincing. Too convincing. I even thought that you had also thrown her and your child into the heap of victims in your plot. She was either living a day in hell or quite the actress."

Benedict glanced in Washington's direction. "She wasn't acting. When she found out that our young Major André was captured, she went into one her hysterical fits that she is quite capable of turning on and off. The possibility of my leaving her behind was never discussed with her ahead of time. I saw no point, and I could not be certain how she would behave if she knew that she would one day be allowed to join me."

Folding his hands in his lap, Benedict continued. "Therefore, dear Peggy had no way of knowing that you were going to permit her to join me once I made my way to the British camp. When she and I had talked about my eventual movement to the other side of our lines, she always believed that we would both go to New York together. There was only so much preparation I could do for her without giving her too much information.

"As upset as I was to leave her in that condition, it did seem fitting at the time. After she learned of André's capture, frankly it was not clear to me if she was more upset with his capture or my leaving without her. Her whole world was crumbling around her; she needed a valuable lesson that life often is not what she would wish it to be."

Turning his head toward Washington, Benedict concluded. "She was spoiled by her parents, and I expect that this one experience alone undoubtedly added several years of maturity to her young soul and made her character even stronger in the end."

Washington looked back at Benedict with one of his characteristic stern, steely looks. "I was never as angry with anyone as I was with myself on that first day. I thought I was duped; everyone believed that I was angry with you, which certainly would have been natural and understandable under the circumstances. However, the truth was that I was mostly angry with myself for being taken in by what I then believed to be your self-serving plot to truly go over to the British and leaving your dear wife and child behind! Had I the opportunity then, I would have killed you on the spot myself!"

Noticing Washington's flushed face at recounting his concerns, even after so many years have passed, Benedict raised his eyebrows. "Lucky for me, my horse and boat were ready. I certainly can understand the momentary confusion as events unfolded for the world to see. I was accustomed to Peggy's histrionics and tantrums; I knew that she would soon recover."

Laughing as he shook his head, Benedict mused. "Poor you, never having witnessed such behavior, it must have been distressing. Hopefully, it added to your mood so that you were even more convincing to others with you at the time. However, the truth be told, I, too, was very uncertain about everything that was happening around us at the time. It was all so tenuous."

Benedict thought for a moment before continuing. "With regard to the documents that I gave to our Major André, you may recall that we had previously discussed and agreed to what type of information I would need to use. It had to be of such complexity and detail that it could not be committed to memory by Major André, the British's rather *intelligent* Intelligence Officer."

Then folding his arms across his chest, "Evidence was vital for our plan to work; the transfer of documents from me to André was, therefore, crucial. The documents needed to be carried on his person and he had to be caught transporting the information that I had provided. And the documents needed to be convincing, not only to young André, but to any others that would see them as well."

Leaning forward in his rocker as he contemplated, Benedict continued. "As you may recall, we did not have the smartest of militia guarding the trails leading to and from New York at that time. Consequently, it needed to be obvious that the documents were important, confidential and secret by their very nature. I could not leave this judgment on the part of our freelancing militia to chance."

Benedict held out his left hand, "On the other hand…if André had been able to escape my little snare and was somehow able to make his way back to Sir Henry, the General must also be convinced of the value of the information I provided if I were to be welcomed into their camp with little suspicion."

And then once again leaning back into his seat, "Yes, the documents were telling and confidential and perhaps secret to most mortals. However, if they were to be considered individually for their true value to our enemy, one could determine that the information provided was that which could be easily learned by any run-of-the-mill, rogue spy or Loyalist at the time; thereby confirmable by the British and their network of goons. The detailed documents I gave to young André were a necessary condition if the British were to accept me for what I was purporting to be."

While nodding, Washington turned to another topic. "I knew that it was your goal to have André caught transporting secret documents, but I've often wondered how were you able to get him to then travel back to his New York headquarters on horseback and not return to the Vulture under the protection of a flag as he had come to you."

"Sir, you know that I'm a firm believer in Providence and the hand of God in most of what I do. Sometimes I need to just plant the seeds and let human nature take its course. I had earlier ordered the cannon be moved to the lower river below West Point from the highlands. Knowing that the Vulture was to travel upriver, I was simply hoping that those transporting and setting up the cannon would see the British ship and take it upon themselves to fire at the target so generously provided by the British themselves."

Scratching the stubble of his unshaven face, Benedict winked. "If they didn't sink it, the Vulture would certainly need to pull anchor and move down river to be out of cannon range. Once that was done, André had no choice but to stay a bit longer and ultimately return to New York by other means."

Folding his hands behind his head, Benedict added. "I'll tell you what, when I heard the cannon fire, I was never as proud of our enterprising cannonries as I was then, and never so thankful to the Almighty!"

Benedict grinned and shrugged his shoulders. "I try not to argue with success, nor do I question the hand of Providence."

Washington smiled. "It was my understanding that the band of men that roamed the trails and roads north of New York at that time were primarily mercenaries, working for the greatest profit more so than working for the benefit of any one camp. How, then, was it that you arranged to deliver Major André directly into the hands of your three militia guards, and how did you know that they would turn André over to their superior officers and not simply rob him or kill him on the spot?"

Washington rubbed his eyes as he spoke. "As you apparently realized, the militia in that no-man's land between our forces in that area were, shall we say 'creatively challenged,' to be polite. Nor were they the most loyal of our camp. Counting on them to deliver André was certainly a gamble."

Benedict shrugged his shoulders and smiled broadly once more. "Again, Providence. All of life is a gamble. In this instance, all I had to do was to plant a few seeds of misinformation among the local militia in that theater shortly before André was to make his fateful journey."

While adding another log to the fire, Benedict continued with his explanation. "About a week or so before André and I were to meet, I let it be known that important British agents often traveled on horses that had some form of distinctive marking below the forelock on the bridge of its muzzle and forehead. I told them that it was a 'secret' marking that British agents used so that they could be recognized by their own kind and not confused with any of our agents…At least that is what I had told to others whom I knew would talk to their mercenary friends to the south."

Smiling proudly, Benedict added, "I also let it be known that if any agent were caught on a horse with a star marking on its forehead, a handsome reward would be paid to those who would capture such an agent."

Now chuckling, "This was only one of many rumors that quickly spread throughout that group of not-so-loyal members of the militia in those days. It is amazing how gullible some people can be and damn near willing to believe anything if they think that it will bring them glory or money. Mr. Paulding and his two companions were simply the lucky ones. However, you can rest assured that there were many more than three members of the militia looking out for British *star* agents during that period."

Washington looked at Benedict with a thin lipped smile. "Annuit Coeptis. I can't help but wonder how many innocent riders suffered the consequence of this bit of misinformation."

"What the hell is *Annuit Coeptis?*" Smiling and shrugging his shoulders with his hands outstretched, Benedict continued with his accounting. "Hopefully, any such souls were able to prove their innocence if confronted by confused militia trail guards. All the same, when my meeting with André was over and the damning documents were delivered to my young nemesis, I simply arranged to have him placed upon a horse that just happened to have a distinguishing characteristic of a white star on its forehead and sent him on his way homeward."

Looking toward the ceiling, "Again, it was all in the hands of Providence. As I said a few moments ago, by that time I was convinced that Providence was on our side and, therefore, I was hopeful. The rest, as others can truthfully say, is history. Young André was intercepted by Paulding and his friends. The documents were discovered and delivered ultimately to your hands."

Benedict rubbed his forehead with his burly right hand. "Thanks, in part, to your forethought in sending Colonel Hamilton to my headquarters at the Robinson house to subtly inform me of your pending arrival, I was able to make my way to the Vulture. I was then accepted by the British bastards as a traitor to the American cause. Keeping your part of the agreement, André was tried as a spy and ultimately hanged. Paulding, Mr. Wert and Mr. Williams were handsomely rewarded – just like I said that they would be, by the way. And I became the scourge of the earth among my friends, former comrades and our friends in the Continental Congress!"

Leaning forward in his chair, Benedict's stare was more distant. "A perfect plan! Perhaps a little too perfect. All we need to do now is to figure out the best way to let the world know that it was all part of our victory plan for the nation."

Benedict was now more somber as he stared at the ash and glowing embers that remained of the logs. "Unlike these embers, but like the ashes of the Phoenix, it is my hope that my past can be reconstituted to its original form before that infamous day at West Point."

Washington turned away from Benedict to look at the embers within the fireplace as well. "*Annuit Coeptis* is a phrase that appears on the Great Seal we adopted a few years back as an emblem for the United States. It is Latin; when translated in the context of its placement over the all-seeing eye as it is on the seal, it means something like, *Providence has favored our undertakings* or something very close. I made the comment earlier because it seems to be a saying that pretty much characterizes your beliefs as well. *Annuit Coeptis.*"

After a moment, Washington continued, "My next inquiry has a little to do with both our past as well as our futures. And, now that you've broached the topic, I can't help but wonder: what will be thought of our dealing with Major John André? Who, by the way, was not only popular within his own camp, but also admired by many in our camp at that time as well."

Turning his head in Benedict's direction, "Once it becomes known that young André was a pawn and the first casualty of our efforts to get you into the British camp, how are we going to explain his ultimate demise? I can't help but also be curious as to how your dear Mrs. Arnold will likely take to learning that she, too, was an instrument used to get to and, ultimately, bait young, impressionable and naïve André into meeting with you – a meeting that the entire world now knows, ultimately lead to his death by my hand."

Washington appeared to unconsciously rub his neck as he spoke of André. "Once all the facts surrounding your, shall we say, 'negotiations' with the British and Major André become known, reasonable men, and women I might add, may conclude that young André's death could be construed as a premeditated act of murder, with you being the conspirator, and me the executioner. One of the questions that will need to be answered, as we look into our futures, is how we are going to explain away this young man's life, given in service to his country?"

Now looking toward the ceiling with his massive hands gently folded behind his head of graying hair, Washington's voice grew more somber. "I am afraid my friend that his death places a shroud over both our shoulders that together we must wear into our respective futures."

Again looking in Benedict's direction, hands still folded, he added. "On a more personal level for your consideration, I particularly wonder about Mrs. Arnold, and what she will think or say about this and other matters once the truth be told about this rather delicate subject."

Benedict slowly turned to look at Washington who then looked away to stare into the burning embers. "Why must we begin by climbing the highest damn mountain first?"

Without making eye contact, Washington shrugged his shoulders. "It may not be your highest mountain, Benedict, but it is an obstacle that must be overcome at some point. Why delay the inevitable? If we can conquer this potential impediment, others may seem less formidable."

Unable to restrain himself, Benedict stood up and paced back and forth between Washington and the hearth, looking at Washington as he talked. "Major André got what he deserved! He was my enemy in more ways than the world will ever know. Regardless of what you and I planned as a means to get me to the other side, he was a spy. I was willing to take the risk for my country, for Christ's sake, and so was he for his!"

Bending backward at the knees and putting both hands to his chest, Benedict added: "However, unlike me, that young fool was captured in the act of espionage and he paid the price. Nobody needs to know of *my intent* that he be captured in the process. As far as the rest of the world will ever need to know, it was my hope that he would indeed be able to take the documents to General Clinton so that they both could be convinced of my value and usefulness. As far as anyone else is concerned, the fact that he did get caught only provided me with the reason to leave our camp sooner than later, but neither the British nor anyone else needs to know that André's capture was part of my objective from the beginning."

Standing in front of Washington, Benedict concluded: "He was a victim of espionage. As the head of the British intelligence service at the time, in my humble opinion, the punishment was deserved on any number of different levels."

Washington looked up at Benedict, "Some may say that he was entrapped."

"Just like the time he entrapped and took advantage of my dear Peggy when she was only eighteen years of age and equally naïve and impressionable. He knew what he was doing when he plotted his attack on her innocence and her virginity! My dear Peggy mistook the temptation of passion of youth for an opportunity for escape from her controlling parents. She, too, was young, impressionable, naïve and too damned trusting."

Flailing his right arm in an arch like motion, Benedict was fuming with anger. "Just as he took advantage of my dear Peggy's youthful ignorance, I took advantage of his egocentric greed for glory. That bastard took advantage of my sweet flower and dishonored her, her family and, ultimately, me. He believed he could simply have his way with my young Peggy and that would be the end of it."

Sitting once again, this time at the edge of his chair, Benedict's expression became less emotional. "When he and I met that fateful night on the banks of the Hudson, I doubted that he even considered the possibility that I knew of his and my beloved Peggy's fleeting imprudence."

Now looking in Washington's direction, "Even at the moment he closed his eyes for the last time and gasped his last breath, I am certain that he believed he was dying a nobleman's death. What more can a military officer aspire to than to sacrifice his life for his nation in such a public fashion! He had no clue that what he was doing was paying the price for depriving me of a husband's honor. Little did he know or suspect that his life was sacrificed not for his military misadventure, but a lustful indiscretion."

Leaning back and shaking his head, Benedict continued to explain. "I have no regrets on this matter. As far as the public or anyone else will know, he was a Major in the British Army; he was appointed by Sir Henry as Chief of the British Secret Service, he behaved as a spy, real or imagined and, like the sacrifice of young Mr. Hale, he paid the price and died with honor. It was more than he deserved."

Now looking into his fisted hands, "It was all I could do to keep from killing the bastard myself when we first met that dark September night."

Benedict Arnold: Legacy Lost (A Ghost's Story)

With a wave of his hand, Benedict dismissed concerns over John André's death. "His death is of little concern to me now, and I am sure that I can persuade Peggy to believe me on what I have to say on this matter. Much time has passed since then. Children have been born into this world, and I am certain that her love for me and our children will ease whatever feelings she may have once had for that son-of-a-bitch."

With raised eyebrows, Washington added, "Nevertheless, Benedict, others who are less passionate, and more objective, will look at the facts and certainly will have an opportunity to build a case against you and me regarding the death of Major André."

Washington looked at his pocket watch. "And, I am certain that you and I could very well spend the next several days talking about nothing other than this one factor alone. However, all of this is overshadowed by an even greater circumstance. We are now in the midst of creating a government to rule these not-so-united States. The Confederation is struggling to hold the states together; some members of this body are resisting others' efforts to bring us together as a singular nation."

Now looking in Benedict's direction, "As you may recall, under the Articles of Confederation, the Congress has little power to compel the states to comply with any of its decisions. Other than an interest in mutual defense which has even now waned, nothing else seems important to the states. They all appear willing to go their own way with little semblance of any meaningful overarching government. Individuals who once seemed inclined to join a more federalized system of governance are now less willing to serve in the Confederation."

Now standing, Washington stretched his arms toward the ceiling. "Even some of our leaders during the time of the Revolution, who you would have normally expected to come together to form a strong government, appear to have a preference to serve in state government. That is where their real personal power exists. You can't believe the intrigue, the divisions that have occurred among those you would expect to be of the same mind, and the brawls that have occurred since the end of the war regarding the formation of our government."

"Perhaps not. I have little tolerance and no stomach for politics. Therefore, I avoid the subject altogether and leave these matters to the likes of others for whom I have little patience," bowing his head in Washington's direction, "present company excluded with all due respect."

As he sat back down in his chair, Washington returned Benedict's bow. Benedict smiled and continued his comment. "However, I can tell you that all I've been hearing in Europe is that everyone is expecting the States to implode by their own devices in their futile attempts to form any semblance of a meaningful government. Many in Britain and, I hear, France and Spain as well, are of the belief that, although the Colonies were able to come together and exhort themselves on the battlefield against a common foe, they do not have the vision necessary to look beyond their immediate states' borders in order to be able to truly unite in any meaningful way."

Looking back into the embers of the fire, Benedict reflected. "Other nations appear to be sitting back, waiting and positioning themselves to come forward to our assistance – as long as they are the ultimate benefactors in any alliance that may be needed at that time. Regardless of the nature of the conflict, be it regional between the north and the south, or the east and the frontier states, between the states and Indian tribes, or even more global, as long as there are opposing forces, there is money to be made."

Looking again in Washington's direction, "As you may expect, Britain, France or Spain could not care less about what form of government you and others may fashion."

"I realize that, Benedict. Accordingly, we cannot allow regional differences to divide us, and it is for this very reason that I am concerned that all you, I and others fought for is at risk of being lost. As soon as any one of the States becomes more dependent upon a foreign power than upon other members of the Confederation, our collective independence is at risk."

Shaking his white head, "It appears that very few of us understand this basic fact. After traveling the entire length and breadth of this great nation before, during and after the war, I've seen so many common threads that can bind us as a single nation in a manner keeping with our Templar Freemasonic philosophy. Yes, there are differing interests among the states, but there are also many common needs and expectations shared among the citizens of every state, indeed in every other country as well, that must be addressed."

Benedict looked befuddled. "And…?"

To which Washington responded, "I and a few others have been attempting to mend our differences among ourselves as well as between the lodges on each side of the ocean, and to shape a government structure that will work to the benefit of all States and peoples of the world as we set the example for others to emulate. Not just the south or the north, or not just those on the east coast. We are envisioning a government that will bring all the people of each of the states together as a singular nation. If we are successful in doing so, together we can resist the warmongering interests of the European countries."

Washington sighed, "They have their own problems; the less we have to depend upon any one of them on that side of the ocean, the better off we will all be. But I am afraid that, individually, each of the states will be not able to resist the temptation to become aligned, one way or another, with any one of the foreign countries."

While seated, Benedict leaned forward in his chair with his elbows on his knees and his hands folded under his chin, "That is all well and fine, but what does all of this have to do with me? As I said before, I too want to be a part of the building of this nation's next government!"

"Well as I see it, Benedict, it is not so much that it has anything to do with you directly, but more to do with me at this particular moment in time. During the last year, I've been trying to subtly position myself as someone that others can again turn to in this country's time of need."

Slowly rocking, Washington looked pensive. "Like I did as a Virginia representative during the First and Second Congresses, I sit and listen and let others do the talking, the debating and the testing of waters. Over the years, I've discovered that listening is my greatest skill, more so than my lack of eloquence at speaking at a debate or other public forum."

With a shrug of his shoulders, he added, "I am a miserable orator. Therefore, while others are half-listening while trying to think of things to say at the same time, I have the luxury of concentrating upon what is actually being said by others. By listening, I can pretty well determine how a man will vote or what a man will decide when presented with a scenario of differing facts."

He paused and then continued with his story. "When I attended the meetings of the Second Congresses for endless months in my military dress, I did so for a reason. By listening to what was being said by the other delegates, I knew that, ultimately, most of the 55 other men in the room, with the likes of Samuel and John Adams, Patrick Henry, and even John Jay and my fellow Virginian, Richard Henry Lee, who, by the way, was not particularly keen on the idea, were all, sooner or later, going to come to a position of independence."

Washington smiled, "I watched Franklin's masterful maneuvering with each of the egos in the room, mold the group into a single mind regarding the need for independence. He was a magician with words and men's minds. He was truly a visionary like no other. Few of us realized it at the time but what we were setting out to do in 1776 was essentially rooted in Franklin's Albany Plan which he first penned in 1754. He is a very patient man..."

Benedict commented, "...And I am less so."

"Time will tell, Benedict. However, by watching and listening carefully to what was being said, I knew that, one way or another, that body of men was going to, ultimately, declare war against the British. I also knew that, if they were to move in that direction, they would need to appoint someone to lead the army that would need to be established."

Brushing the lapels of his woolen dress coat for apparent emphasis, Washington added, "Inasmuch as I was the only one in the room that looked the part, I made it easy for many of the weary delegates to look in my direction as a natural selection."

Then shaking his head, "However, as you would expect, not all the Colonies at the time were ready for a *Southerner* to lead any army of any sort – particularly Samuel and John Adams. It was really my fellow Virginian, Richard Lee, who convinced others of my worthiness at the time. All I needed to do was look the part, be humble and be ready."

Jerking both eyebrows quickly, "I think you will appreciate this. As everything was unfolding at that time, I could never see myself as a long-term member of Congress, sitting around talking each other to death. I would much prefer death by bullet than to be bludgeoned to death by the pompous words of my fellow representatives. I knew that, to be of greatest service, I needed to be a part of the army. Of all the men in the room or elsewhere at the time, I, frankly, was not aware of anyone else who I believed could do the job that needed to be done to lead this country's ragtag, ill-equipped and ill-trained army."

Before continuing with his description, Washington paused and pensively pinched his lower lip with his manicured thumb and forefinger. "We had little equipment, but at least I had experience and the training – thanks to the British during my early military career. Nevertheless, I must admit that, to call it an army at that time was a bit of an exaggeration. Then again, to call the Continental Congress a form of government was a bit of an exaggeration as well. But that was all we had."

Benedict interjected, "And don't forget, we had Annuit Coeptis."

Washington was not amused. "The way I see it Ben, this country is now in much the same kind of predicament that we were in back in '75 and '76. Now that the war has ended and we have gained our independence, none of us knows exactly where this nation is headed. As you might very well expect, there are many men of influence who believe that the States should each retain the ultimate power of government and are rather pointedly resisting the formation of any truly centralized form of government with any substance or power."

Now leaning back into his rocker, Washington quipped. "Although retired from public life since the end of the war, I've nonetheless been working with others who agree that this nation will be best served with the formation of a government with a strong, centralized base of power. We are working behind the scenes, as it were, to get others to agree that the future of this country, even with all its differences among the states, will be far better off with a federalized government."

Benedict looked toward Washington with a confused expression, "…And?…"

Washington's lips turned up at each corner, "…And, like it was in '75, I am not directly involved in any of the discussions, but I am certainly listening and aware of what is being discussed and the direction that the States appear to be going at the moment. It is my expectation that, if everything goes well and according to plans now being made, the Congress will again be looking for someone, someday, to lead the new government to be formed."

Benedict Arnold: Legacy Lost (A Ghost's Story)

Again, Benedict baited his host, "...And?..."

Washington's smile became more apparent, "...And, Ben, can you imagine what could happen if some of our former 'friends' in Congress were to become the leader of a newly formed nation? Who knows what they will do with uncharted and untested power, or if they will serve the needs and interests of all the people of this land?"

After finishing his comment, Washington added a few more logs to the embers and sat back into his rocker and looked at Benedict. Benedict looked into the embers and the flames now engulfing the newly added logs. He sat in silence for some time.

Washington watched Benedict as they both contemplated their exchange. Some number of moments passed before Benedict turned to Washington and rubbed his face with his burly hands. "Well, for one who is more skilled at listening than speaking, you have been doing quite a bit of the talking...and I've been doing quite a bit of listening. Although I, too, fashion myself as a good listener; again, I must ask, what does all this have to do with me and my coming back to America?"

Washington laughed and tossed both arms up into the air as he slid back into his rocker, "This, my friend, is what happens when two egocentric personalities try talking to each other!" Then, standing straight up with outstretched arms and turning slowly in a circle to add emphasis, "As I said before, it is all about me and not about you!"

Then, sitting back down and, in a less animated way, Washington continued. "For the sake of this argument, Ben, let's assume for a moment that what I just said is true. Think about what it would be like should the day come when others in this nation may turn to me in their consideration as some form of leader of some form of government."

Benedict added, "Perhaps I should have added another...*And*..."

"Perhaps so. But now, think about my earlier question about the late Major André. What do you believe the chances would be of my being selected to lead this nation if my detractors…" pointing his finger in Benedict's direction, "…and there are many…what if they were to now learn of our *victory plan*? No matter how noble the cause or how successful our efforts to win victory, our plot also resulted in the hanging death of a popular member of the British military."

Pausing a moment and giving Benedict time to process his words, Washington then continued. "Ben, try to remain objective and try to imagine what might happen if a man like John Adams or Thomas Jefferson were to hear of our victory plan and end up being selected to lead our nation. What direction do you believe they may set? What direction might they take this nation with foreign matters? What precedence might they establish? What kind of government might we expect if someone other than I takes the helm in this country's formative years?"

Shaking his head, Washington concluded, "We do not need an elected monarchy, for God's sake! As you and others know, I have spent my entire public service building others' confidence and trust in me. That is the one quality that I seem to have that other talented and otherwise-gifted men appear to lack."

Benedict looked up, "You certainly have a point about that."

"Yes, and I am certain that if we were to now come forward and tell the world about our victory plan, regardless of its success, no one would be able to place his trust in my word ever again. Regarding your interest in becoming involved in our nation's deliberations, you can rest assured that if we were to come forward now, neither of us would be in a position to lead a prayer meeting, let alone a nation's government."

Both men rocked and stared more at the fire than at each other during much of the remaining conversation. As the day wore on, each would take his turn at replenishing the wood in the fireplace and stoking the embers to ignite the newly added fuel.

Later in the day, Benedict eventually turned to Washington and asked about the other mountain that he had alluded to earlier in the day. "You indicated that the subject of Major André may not be our most difficult peak to climb. We might as well get a look at all the obstacles that must be overcome. What is it that you were referring to earlier?"

Washington did not answer immediately and simply rocked as he appeared to focus all his attention on the dancing flames and glowing embers of the fire. Without glancing up, he finally uttered in a low, hardly discernable voice: "This is not so much 'our' mountain, as it is yours and yours alone...New London, Connecticut, Fort Griswold, September 6, 1781..." He needed not say more.

Benedict lowered his head and nodded in understanding, "Sir, what happened there was not of my doing. I sincerely hope that you believe me on that score. As you and most every soldier that has been in battle knows, the consequence of battle among soldiers is a fact of life; some die, some live on. Every man on the field understands and accepts this fact of battle. However, the killing of the helpless once defeated is repugnant to any civilized man to say the very least. Regrettably, in the heat of battle, when friends and comrades are lost, not every man on the field remembers that there is civility, even on the battlefield."

As he continued his explanation, Benedict sunk down in his rocker and looked to the ceiling. "The world will never know how I felt on that day." Turning his head in Washington's direction, "You and I both knew and expected that I would be tested by the British bastards before they could fully accept and trust me in their camp. For over a year, they did their best to put me in limited engagements in the south and elsewhere to test my loyalty to the British effort. I believe that it was their final test to send me to my former home front to see if I had truly come over to their side, or if I would show any signs of faltering in my trustworthiness."

Washington nodded his head; Benedict continued. "The battle at Griswold was so quick, I had no idea what happened until after it was over. The poor souls at Fort Griswold put up a valiant effort, but they were simply overwhelmed by the number of forces we used to advance upon them. It was my expectation that, once they recognized the futility of their situation, they would surrender and save themselves in doing so. I even offered a flag before the beginning of the hostility in hopes that they would surrender before any of the poor souls suffered any injury at all. Those brave boys stood their ground."

Benedict stopped and motioned in Washington's direction, "Sir, you would have been proud of them. They were perhaps too good and, despite the odds, they fought ferociously and effectively. Early on in the engagement, your brave soldiers inflicted very heavy casualties on my troops, in spite of being so greatly outnumbered. I suspect that the early casualties suffered by my regiment are what led the men under my command to lose their honor and commit their crimes against humanity."

Benedict wiped a tear that slowly rolled down his right cheek. "It was wrong. It was horrible and it was dishonorable…"

Then, extending his hands outward from his sides, with his palms upward as he turned toward Washington, "But being in the predicament that I found myself at the time, there wasn't much I could say or do about it. Not without compromising our effort."

Looking directly into Washington's eyes, Benedict added, "Like our dear General Montgomery who gave his life while we attempted to take Quebec in '75, the British, too, had a Montgomery, a Major Montgomery, who was popular with his forces as well. What was ironic is that Major Montgomery was my second at Griswold whereas I was second in command to our General Montgomery at Quebec."

Benedict Arnold: Legacy Lost (A Ghost's Story)

Benedict rubbed the back of his neck. "Against my nature but in keeping with British rules of engagement, I stayed back at a headquarters position near the fort to direct the theater as the battle began. Early in the engagement, British Major Montgomery suffered the same fate as our General Montgomery. Communications between the field of action and my headquarters then broke down and I did not know of his death or the American defenders' attempt to surrender until it was over."

Washington shook his head as Benedict continued his tortured story. "The British troops were distraught over the loss of their Major Montgomery and their comrades during the initial thrust at the fort. They apparently took their grief out on the poor American soldiers who ultimately surrendered once the tide had turned against them. Later in the day I was informed that your commander at Griswold, Colonel Ledyard, was the first to be killed after he surrendered his sword to one of my officers."

Benedict then stood to slowly pace about the room with both of his hands clasped behind his back. "You would have no way of knowing, indeed, nobody will ever know, but during a subsequent action in another theater, I personally saw to it that the British bastard, who killed your American Colonel at Griswold, suffered the same fate."

Nodding his head as he slowly paced about the room, Benedict told Washington, "The officer who killed Colonel Ledyard with Ledyard's own sword met his maker in a similar manner within a month after the battle at Griswold. During a subsequent nighttime skirmish, I was near him when he received a flesh wound on his right arm, which caused him to drop his sword. Captain Beckwith was his name. It was dark, the air was filled with musket smoke, and there was much confusion as there usually is during battle. I saw his sword, picked it up and gave it back to him."

With a frown on his forehead and a distant look in his eyes, Benedict continued, "I can still see his face as he watched the blade of his own sword enter his chest. He was quite surprised, to say the least. I believe that it can be safely said that he was undoubtedly the only member of the British military who ever knew for certain that my treason was perhaps not sincere."

Now sitting back down next to his former Commanding General, Benedict concluded his story. "As he gasped for breath with his left lung perforated, I leaned in close and whispered that he was dying for Colonel Ledyard and the innocent lives of my countrymen he, and others under his command, took at Fort Griswold on that day. He could not speak and I did pity the poor bastard. While on his knees looking at me in shock as the blood drained from his body, I suggested that he spend his remaining time praying to our God for the forgiveness of all his sins."

Once again slumping down into his chair, Benedict looked pensive. "It is my sincere hope the poor son-of-a-bitch took my advice. He was dead within a minute." With a sigh, Benedict added in a low, deep voice, "*An eye for an eye and a sword for a sword.*"

Benedict then turned away from his General. "As satisfying as this act of revenge was to me at the time, the face of that British officer often haunts me on many of my restless nights. He looked so helpless and was clearly scared of his pending death. He looked so alone. Probably not much different than what your Colonel Ledyard must have looked like when he was mercilessly killed." Looking downward, Benedict softly mumbled. "I, too, pray for forgiveness, each and every day."

Washington's and Arnold's reddened eyes locked in anguish. "Nonetheless, Mr. Arnold, should you ever have any hope of returning to this land, you will need to convince not only me of your innocence at Griswold, but the rest of this country as well. It may be that while I, and some others, may believe you and even understand the circumstance that may have occurred at Fort Griswold, it is likely that your former homeland of Rhode Island and Connecticut, if not the whole of the Northeast, save New York perhaps, may find it difficult to forgive you in their hearts."

Benedict nodded. "I am afraid you may be right. I have trouble forgiving myself for that day. I can well imagine that it would be nearly impossible for others to do so."

The two men then stood, stretched and walked outdoors when they heard the distinctive honking of a flock of migratory geese making their late journey southward for the winter.

The clouds had cleared and the late day sun brightened the sky. As they both watched the formation of geese fly overhead, Benedict glanced at Washington. "I expect that it is not likely that I will be in this country to watch the return of these geese next spring. How long do you expect that it is going to take you and others to complete the work that will need to be done to bring this country together? When do you think that the country might possibly be ready for my return?"

Washington placed his large right hand on Benedict's left shoulder. "I only wish I knew. I only wish I knew. All I know is that the time is not right for you to come. Not now at least. I truly appreciate your understanding and the continuing sacrifice that I must continue to ask of you and your family. We need to continue our fight until our goal is attained."

Washington looked toward the heavens once again to observe another approaching flock of geese. "In the meantime, we need to give some serious thought as to how we should address the André matter, and you need to determine how best to present your defense regarding the Griswold affair. And I will also try to determine who the men were that invited you here in the first place. We need to see if we can determine what their specific intentions might have been."

"George, I think we both know what their intentions were. Whoever they are, they never want me to return."

"I am certain that you are right, but we need to decide how best to ensure that your life and those of your family are not in danger. If they went to the trouble of inviting you to come here, they would probably not hesitate to track you down on whatever continent you may be. May I see the letter they gave you at the inn?"

Benedict reached into his pocket and pulled out the envelope and letter, as well as the wax seal with its picture still intact, and handed it to Washington.

"Interesting seal. *'Brother Sparks'...Your most humble servant,* '*L.Q.C.'.* Odd initials, if they are initials. I don't believe I ever heard of a middle name beginning with the letter, 'Q,' other than Adams' eldest son, John Quincy, but the 'L' and 'C' would then make little sense. I would like to make a copy of this letter's contents? I can't imagine who these men might be, but I will find out what I can. We can't have a group of men going around plotting to kill you now, can we?"

"If they were to succeed, your worries about my return would be over, wouldn't they? I hesitate to ask, but inasmuch as you mentioned the 'all-seeing eye' that appears on the Great Seal and the reference in the note and their speaking of *Brotherhood*, might it be possible that our Templar friends are involved in this matter. Is there any chance that you may have confided in any of our fellow Masons about our efforts, either during or after the war?"

"To be honest, I don't know if any of the Mason brotherhood are involved or not. It is certainly possible, I suppose. However, you can rest assured that I spoke to no one, Mason or non-Mason, about our plans, either during or after the war. As you know, many of our Mason friends and brothers are closely tied to members in British lodges. The war presented our brotherhood with a vexing and confusing dynamic.

It was, and still is difficult to know exactly what each of our member lodges' true allegiance is."

They smiled at one another as they both looked to the heavens to watch the remaining geese pass them by on their journey to their winter home in the south.

In a soft voice, Benedict commented, "It is ironic. These lowly geese and their eventual effort to return to their summer home next spring will be undoubtedly more successful than mine. Again, nature humbles me."

Washington looked at Arnold, and once again placed his hand upon his shoulder. "Humility is a good quality for both man and beast, Ben. We all need to keep our eyes open for the lessons nature has to offer."

Then, from an invisible perch from a distant tree, a solitary crow cawed.

Upon hearing this, Benedict nodded his head and smiled. He understood that the omen he encountered earlier in his journey was neither a good omen nor a bad one. It was simply an omen that something was indeed going to happen, just not in the timeframe he had hoped.

With that bit of understanding, and knowing that his life was in the hands of Providence, Benedict was satisfied.

CHAPTER 14

VAN DERWERKER FARM
FRIDAY, DECEMBER 23, 1785

A s was their custom during the winter months to help ease the long, dreary nights away, Martin and his family gathered after their evening meal. To pass the time, they talked, they read and they shared stories. From the middle of their round table, a lantern brightened the room and cast a golden hue upon the faces of those gathered for their evening ritual.

After learning that there would be only conversation and no reading or storytelling this evening, young John frowned. "I think my ears hurt. And I am sleepy tonight. I am tired from our sliding on the pond today, Mommy. It was fun, but all the running and sliding also made my bottom sore too. Can I go to our cabin so I can take care of the fire and go to bed?"

Martin and Martha smiled as Theresa kissed John on each of his tired little ears and patted his sore bottom with a mother's loving touch, effectively excusing him from tonight's *"gathering"* as they referred to it.

John was obviously content at being freed from the discussions that can sometimes be confusing to a young boy. To the amusement of others, he would on occasion need to remind them: "I'm just a boy. Is it okay if I don't understand what you are talking about?"

Martha poured each a cup of hot tea from the gift that Benedict had given during his visit, and John made his escape to the door. As he moved away from the glow of the table's lantern, John's shadow danced on the cabin walls mimicking his movements, and revealing just a hint of his delight.

Martin relished these quieter, less hectic moments shared with his family over the years. He missed this luxury of conversation during the spring, summer, and early fall months when the days were longer and there were simply too many chores that needed to be finished during the evening's twilight hours.

After Martha rejoined Martin and Theresa at the table, she noticed that Martin appeared distracted. "What are you thinking about, Martin?"

Glancing first at Theresa sitting to his right and then Martha, he winked his left eye so that only Martha could see. "I saw our inquisitive innkeeper, Alex, this afternoon. He told me that someone from Albany spent the night at the inn last night who was asking if anyone had seen another traveler within the last few days named Otis McGurk, who would be passing through our area on his way to Canada. Alex said that this guy, named Roeloff, told him that he was supposed to meet Otis a few days ago in Albany, but he wasn't able to get there before Otis left for Canada."

Scratching his chin, Martin added, "Alex told me that he thought it was odd because this fellow, Roeloff, stayed at the inn with two other men just last week at the same time that Otis spent the night there. He said that he even saw him and Otis talking to one another. He also said that all of them, Roeloff, Otis, and the other two men, who were with this Roeloff fellow, all left the inn within a day or two of each other."

Martha commented, "You don't say."

"Yep, and Alex thought that when he saw the two of them talking to each other, it didn't appear that Otis and this Roeloff fellow knew one another. Thinking that they first acted like strangers and now being told that they were to meet with one another in Albany, Alex thought that it simply didn't make sense."

Now shaking his head, "While he was telling me all of this, I had to admit that it didn't make much sense to me either. Then it got even more interesting when our confused innkeeper told me he also remembered that Otis had asked about us while he was here. But our instinctively protective proprietor said that Roeloff looked like he was up to no good; so he didn't tell the stranger that Otis had asked about us."

Martin ended by saying, "Alex may have been confused, but he at least had enough common sense not to tell this stranger about us. And the confusing thing for me is that Otis didn't say anything when he was here about knowing anyone in the area named Roeloff. Frankly, I don't know what to make of any of this."

Theresa looked at Martin, "Did you tell Alex that we haven't seen Otis since last week while he was on his way to Albany?"

"No, I didn't think that it was important to mention it."

"Not important, or not advisable?"

Looking downward as she continued, "I know who Otis McGurk is. I know that it troubles the two of you to be deceitful, and I want you to know that you don't have to be deceitful around me any longer about who Otis McGurk really is. I certainly will not tell anyone and reveal your, or more accurately, his secret. I know how the two of you feel about honesty. I think that you both would be much more comfortable with yourselves, and me, if we were all honest with each other about your General Arnold."

Neither Martin nor Martha said anything as Theresa added, "There's no reason for John to know however. Not that he would even know who Benedict Arnold is or anything about him, but there's no need for him to become involved in our little family secret. I really don't want him to think that it is okay to deceive others at such a young age, but we can never know whom he may talk to, or what others may make of what he might say, if he were to mention his real name to anyone else."

Martha looked embarrassed, fumbling for the right words: "What are you talking about, dear?"

Theresa raised her eyebrows, tilted her head upward while looking at Martha with a sheepish smile. "Aunt Martha, you shouldn't allow yourself any further stress with your and Uncle Martin's act of deception among our little family. I know that *Otis McGurk* is really Benedict Arnold, and I know that it was he that visited here last week."

While shuffling her feet under the table, Theresa informed the Van Derwerkers, "When you first introduced the two of us, I knew that the name, Otis McGurk, sounded awfully familiar to me. It is an unusual name, and it took me a little while to figure it out. But then I remembered when the two of you talked to each other after Uncle Martin returned from the hospital in Albany, and the stories that the two of you shared with me over this very table several years ago."

Theresa smiled, "You probably thought nothing of it at the time, but I remembered the stories you once shared about taking care of Benedict Arnold while the three of you were at the hospital. As I recall, you said that one day when you entered his room, he told you that General Arnold had left the building and that his name was Otis McGurk. He said something about the General writing out some form of orders instructing the two of you to take as good care of Mr. Otis McGurk as you had taken care of him. Your comment to each other at that time was the General had a smile for the first time since he was wounded, and that it was the first indication to the two of you he was likely to recover."

Martha's eyes blinked nervously as she listened to Theresa. "And I remember you and Uncle Martin telling stories about how you both toyed with the General by telling '*Otis McGurk*' that it was time for him to take care of the two of you inasmuch as he wasn't a General. He then behaved as a manservant for you as the three of you continued to entertain yourselves during his and your recovery."

Looking in Martin's direction, "Besides his name, I remember your comments to Aunt Martha about discovering how relief from pain and misery could apparently be gained by good humor, and you were convinced that the distraction given to the General while acting out his little skits as master Otis McGurk actually had true healing benefits. I simply thought that was odd; so I guess that is why I remembered the stories that you once shared with me about General Arnold and *Mr. Otis McGurk.*

"I also couldn't help but notice his limp. And when I saw that the sole and heel of his left boot was somewhat thicker than his right, it all came together for me. This man was Benedict Arnold. I have to be honest with you, once I figured it out, I was confused about why he was here and didn't know what to think or say. So I said nothing."

Scratching her head, Theresa added, "Then I thought more about the stories you told me about him. And what I recalled most was the smiles each of you had while talking to each other about the General. As I sat quietly years ago listening to your stories, I remembered thinking it was odd that although it was undoubtedly an excruciatingly painful time for you and the General, it was also likely among your happiest times."

Glancing back in Martin's direction, "At least that was the impression I had when you shared your stories with me about General Arnold. So I assumed that the reason he was here was just to see you both again. Your time together in Albany was likely as memorable for him as it was for the two of you."

Martin looked at Theresa. "Well, I can say that they were certainly memorable, but I wouldn't say that they were among our happiest moments. Nonetheless, as strange as it may sound, Theresa, they were among the most carefree times Martha and I ever had. However, I can't say that they were so carefree for the General because he was so ill and was always thinking about something. But the General undoubtedly appreciated our being with him during that time, and he stopped here last week on his way to Albany to thank us for helping him through his recovery."

Looking more sheepish than Theresa had ever seen him, she could tell that he was uncomfortable. "Theresa, we are sorry that we were not honest with you when the General surprised us for his visit last week. We simply did not know what to make of it, and, given the circumstances surrounding his becoming a traitor after he left us in Albany, we were uncertain about telling you, or anyone else, about who he was."

Now, looking directly into Theresa's eyes, "You can well imagine that others may be very concerned and upset with us if they knew that Benedict Arnold had visited us. Others still likely despise him for what he did; some may even try to kill him if they knew who he really was. When you and John arrived home last week from your visit with your father, the General asked that we simply tell everyone that his name was 'Otis McGurk,' and he did not want anyone else to know of his real identity."

Looking in Martha's direction, "We simply went along with it, thinking that it was best to limit the number of people who knew. Frankly, I believed he was right then, and I now regret that your memory of our stories was so good. In spite of what others may now think about him, or what he did during the war, we know that he is a good, God-fearing man."

Martha added, "Dear, the war is over, and we would now like to treat him as a friend and not an enemy any longer. However, we know and appreciate that others will not be so quick to overlook or forgive what he did."

Theresa smiled, "Now that I've had a chance to meet the General myself, he does seem like a kind and gentle man. It is difficult for me to imagine that he was once a General and some of the…"

Before Theresa could complete her thought, the dogs started to bark and darted toward the door. At first, everyone assumed that the dogs were barking at John, returning from his cabin. However, the sound of the footsteps on the porch was much heavier than those John would make.

And then, the knock at the door. An evening visitor, especially during the winter months, was seldom good and usually meant that one of their neighbors needed help. Martin quickly opened the door only to find not a neighbor, but their reacquainted friend, Benedict Arnold, at the threshold of their home once again.

Martha and Theresa looked carefully at each other as Benedict entered the room, neither exactly sure what to say. Theresa was the first to greet their nighttime visitor: "Good evening, Mr. McGurk, I mean Otis." Theresa appeared somewhat coy, but had a smile that let the others know she was pleased to see their uninvited guest once again.

Believing that Martin looked distracted before, Martha now thought that he looked downright bewildered. She couldn't help but notice his unnatural look of confusion as he took their guest's cloak, coat, and his tricorn hat. It was also obvious to Martha that Martin wasn't quite certain what to say to Benedict after the discussion they just had with Theresa.

After greeting his hosts, Benedict walked directly to the fireplace to warm himself. As Benedict faced the fireplace, rubbing his hands together for warmth, Martha immediately busied herself by making another pot of tea and preparing a meal for their new arrival.

While Benedict ate, Martin took Governor to the barn for grooming, food and water. Once Martin returned, he appeared a bit more collected. "Well Otis, it is certainly good to see you again so soon. How was your trip to Albany?"

Benedict looked first at Martin, then Martha and finally Theresa. "Is there something that I should know? Ever since I arrived here this evening, the three of you look like I stood too close to the fireplace and my hair is on fire. Either that or there is something else troubling you and that you want to tell me."

Looking around the room, Benedict noticed that John was not there. "Is it John? Is he all right? Has something happened to John?"

Martin was the first to answer. "No, it has nothing to do with John." Hesitating for a few seconds, he added, "It has more to do with Theresa."

With that, Theresa reached out and grasped Benedict's left hand as if to comfort him. Studying him carefully with her forest-green eyes, "The problem is that, in spite of your wishes and in spite of Uncle Martin and Aunt Martha's best efforts...before I tell you, I want you to know that it is all right and there is no reason for concern..."

Theresa hesitated, looking at Benedict for some type of reaction, but received none.

Benedict returned Theresa's intense look. "If I may ask, does it have anything to do with me?"

Theresa, Martin and Martha all glanced at each other to see who would be the one to answer the question. Theresa finally broke the awkward silence, "Yes Mr. Arnold, I mean Benedict, it does have something to do with you."

With that, she did get a reaction. To which Theresa smiled broadly at Benedict's initial expression of surprise, immediately followed by one of embarrassment. "Mr. Arnold, although I may not be a sophisticated city lady that you may be more accustomed to, nonetheless, I do have a pretty good memory and reasonably good powers of observation."

Theresa patted the back of Benedict's hand, "Please know Mr. Arnold, my aunt and uncle did not betray the trust you had placed in them. They didn't tell me who you were. They just didn't remember that I was with them many years ago when they once shared delightful stories with each other about their meeting General Benedict Arnold while the three of you were at the hospital in Albany."

Glancing at Martha and Martin, "They simply didn't remember telling stories years ago about the name, *Otis McGurk*, that you had adopted for yourself while recovering and the pleasant times the three of you had with each other while you passed the time as Otis McGurk, manservant."

Benedict sat looking at the three of them, not knowing quite what to say; thinking that it would have been better if his hair had burst into flames.

Theresa smiled, "It is okay. I can be trusted to keep your secret, Mr. Arnold. To the best of my knowledge, no one else was around when Uncle Martin and Aunt Martha once proudly shared their stories years ago about their friend, General Arnold and Otis McGurk."

Martin looked at Benedict and shrugged his shoulders. "Would you like a little rum with that tea, Otis?"

Benedict offered a quick smile and, nodding his head, held his cup up in Martin's direction. "Frankly, when I was here last, it did appear that there was something Theresa was keeping to herself."

Looking directly into Theresa's eyes, "When we talked before, I had an uneasy feeling and wondered if you had somehow learned of my identity then. I hoped that my trust in Martin and Martha was well placed, and I am glad that my confidence and trust has indeed been upheld. As I adjust to the idea that you know who I am, Theresa, I am honestly relieved. Asking Martin and Martha to be less than honest with a member of their family was not appropriate of me; I am frankly pleased to now be honest and open with you as well."

After taking a long sip from his cup, he added: "Although it was enjoyable to portray Otis McGurk while we were passing time in Albany, it is not enjoyable at all to deceive family members, friends or others that are close to us. Believe me; I know the personal price paid by the soul for the deceptions we inflict among family and friends."

Benedict then frowned, "Does John know? Where is the lad? Is he okay?"

Theresa laughed, "He is fine. However, our conversations tend to bore a seven-year-old, so he went to our cabin to keep the fire going while the three of us were visiting after dinner. And no, he doesn't know your real name. As a matter of fact, I only told Uncle Martin and Aunt Martha that I knew who you were just a few moments before you arrived here this evening. They didn't know anything about my knowing until now."

Theresa folded her hands before her and appeared a bit more reflective. "Although I too am troubled by keeping secrets from family or those close to me, I do think that it would be in everyone's best interest if my son does not know anything about Benedict Arnold. If you all would agree, I suggest that we address our guest as Mr. Otis McGurk. I truly do not want to try to explain to John why it might be okay for grownups to keep secrets or to deceive others."

Shaking her head slowly, "John has plenty of time to learn of life's unfortunate lessons when he gets older. I see no point in starting him down the path of deception just yet."

Nodding his head in agreement, Benedict stood up, bowed gently with his left arm tucked in front of him at the waist and his right hand extended to his rear. "So, *Otis McGurk*, it is; once again at your service."

A short time later, Martin told Benedict about his conversation with the innkeeper earlier in the day. "He told me that a fellow named Roeloff from Albany was here asking if anyone had seen you, that is, Otis McGurk. Apparently this Roeloff fellow told the innkeeper, Alex, that he missed your meeting in Albany and was trying to catch up with you on your way back to Canada."

Martin scratched his head slowly, "The odd thing is…Alex also said that this same fellow was one of three men who stayed at the inn when you spent the night there last week. He said that it seemed to him that, if this *Roeloff* guy had a meeting with you in Albany, he might have said something about it to you when you were apparently talking to each other at the inn."

Looking directly at Benedict, "When telling me all of this, Alex seemed confused, more so than usual. It apparently didn't make any sense to our inquisitive innkeeper. And to be honest, Ben, inasmuch as you didn't mention anyone named Roeloff to us when you were here last week, it didn't make much sense to me either. Then again, whom you were to meet with in Albany was none of my business."

Martin leaned back in his chair, "Although I couldn't help but to be just a little curious, I was not curious enough to risk getting burned, if you know what I mean."

Benedict thought for a moment. "I do know what you mean. You know, the more I hear about your Alex, the more it seems to me that, for such a small community, your little inn and its innkeeper certainly are at the hub of activity and intrigue."

Shaking his head, Benedict added: "I don't know anyone named Roeloff. However, I do remember briefly meeting three men at the inn when I was here last. One had his leg amputated, and another did call himself Roeloff. You can trust that I did not have any meeting scheduled with him in Albany or anywhere else. However, I suspect that he and others did have plans to meet with me."

Looking at Martha, "I told Martin before I left that I had a meeting in Albany with someone who might be able to help me and my family return to the United States."

Then turning back to Martin, "But it was not with anyone named Roeloff."

Martin asked: "So how did your meeting go? Did everything work out as you had hoped?"

"Well…not exactly. Apparently I was invited to Albany under false pretenses by individuals unknown to me. It would appear that it may have been with this Roeloff fellow and, perhaps, the others who were at the inn last week as well. Nevertheless, it was not with the person I had expected. It would appear that they had plans to ensure that I would never return to this country alive."

Now sitting back into his chair; stretching his legs outward and clasping his hands behind his head of thick brown hair, Benedict mused. "I must admit that I agree with you, all of this does sound strange indeed. If they had intentions of doing me harm as I suspect, it would seem that they would have made an attempt when I was at the inn last week. However, it was obvious that they had been drinking quite heavily before I arrived; so I doubt that anyone of them would have been in any condition."

Leaning forward once again, "Or perhaps there was a reason to wait until I arrived at Albany. Who knows? It doesn't make any sense at all." After thinking about the question he'd just asked, Benedict turned to Martin. "Do you know if this 'Roeloff' fellow is still here? I think that I would like to have a little discussion with him to see exactly what he is up to and why he is looking for me now."

"I don't think so. Alex told me that he left earlier today. At least that is what Alex believed, but I can check with him again in the morning."

Glancing in Martha's direction, Martin told Benedict, "He also told me that he remembered you asking about us when you were here. But he made a point of telling me that he didn't say anything to Roeloff about that."

Martin rubbed his chin, "However, now that I think of it, it was easy enough for you to find us after talking to Alex and his son. I don't know who this Roeloff fellow is, but I don't want him poking around and showing up on our doorstep unexpectedly either."

"I am sorry, Martin. I truly didn't expect my visit to create any problems for you or your dear family. If this Roeloff is one of the men who attempted to follow me in Albany, I wouldn't worry too much about him being able to track you down. One main difference between him and me is that I knew about you; he, obviously, doesn't. Nonetheless, I will leave first thing in the morning so that you and your family are not caught up in matters that do not have anything to do with you."

Martin's reaction was immediate, direct, and cautious. "No, no, no. That won't be necessary, Ben. We don't know where this Roeloff fellow might be. If he is expecting you to be on the road to Canada, he will likely be waiting for you somewhere along the way up north. Let me see what I can find out from our unofficial town crier in the morning. We may be simple folk, but this is a pretty close-knit community and we know how to deal with inquisitive strangers. You can stay here as long as it takes to ensure your safe journey."

Theresa looked directly at Benedict. "I am confused. Considering things that you did during the war, why would you expect that people are now going to simply forget and pretend that nothing happened? How is it that you would expect people to treat you differently knowing what you did? Isn't it reasonable to expect that there would be people who would prefer that you never returned?"

Martin was taken aback at Theresa's attack. "Theresa, please! He is a guest in our home and…"

"Uncle Marty, Mr. Arnold, I don't really mean any disrespect. I am just saying that it may be dangerous for Mr. Arnold to return now, even after all these years."

Benedict Arnold: Legacy Lost (A Ghost's Story)

Benedict stood; shadows once again danced along the cabin's walls as he moved about the room. "Please, Martin, Theresa, do not argue on my account. All I can say at this time is that my trip did not go as planned and the time for me to return to the United States has not yet arrived. However, I am not going to give up on my efforts to do so. This is the country in which I was born. This is the country for which I, as well as you my friend and thousands of others, shed blood. And this is the country in which I wish to be when I die…although not just yet."

Looking at Theresa, "I understand your sentiments. Nonetheless, all I can really say now is that none of you know everything there is to know about me and my actions during the war. What you don't know, Theresa, is that I did share a bit more information with Martin last week about my plans for return."

Looking toward Martha, "I don't believe you were aware that I told Martin either. I apologize for keeping this from you as well. However, I am unable to say anything more to anyone at this point. But, just so you all know, what I did tell Martin before I left is that one day more information will be known about my actions, particularly about West Point, and my activities thereafter. Once more is known concerning all the facts surrounding my actions during and after the war, perhaps then I can be judged in a clear light."

Sitting back down with his head bowed. "Perhaps then I can have some hope and expectation that my family and I can safely come home again. I am just not able to share anymore information with you, or anyone else now, for everyone's safety. But, hopefully, this day will soon come."

CHAPTER 15

VAN DERWERKER FARM

The snow continued to fall and the wind howled through the needles of the trees surrounding the Van Derwerker home. Once again, Theresa and John spent the night in Martin and Martha's home allowing Benedict the privacy of their cabin during his stay.

After they all turned in for the evening, the snow changed to a bitterly cold rain. The rain froze immediately when it landed on the snow, houses, barn and trees. At first a thin, and then a thickening layer of ice formed on everything the raindrops touched.

Late in the night, Theresa was awakened by the sound of tree limbs cracking, breaking and falling under the weight of the ice. Once awakened, she also heard the faint, now familiar sound of shouting coming from the direction of her cabin. Looking about the room, it was apparent that John, Martin, Martha or the three dogs were not disturbed by the howling winds, the breaking branches or the sounds coming from the cabin next door.

Expecting that Benedict was again having nightmares, and knowing that Martin would prefer to do nothing; Theresa chose not to awaken her uncle. Slipping on boots and putting on a hooded cloak over her nightgown, Theresa decided to investigate the shouting herself. She silently left the house while being careful to not disturb any of the others, to include the soundly sleeping, not-so-on-guard, dogs.

The wind whipped her cloak against her body and the pelting sleet slashed at her face as she walked the short distance to her cabin. Slipping on the sheets of ice and tripping over broken tree branches, Theresa fell on her knees several times before reaching the safety of her cabin's porch. After taking a moment to catch her breath, she quietly opened the door to investigate the sounds coming from within.

Benedict Arnold: Legacy Lost (A Ghost's Story)

Entering the room, Theresa could then clearly hear what Benedict was yelling, and she could see him thrashing about in her bed.

"The wolves! Kill the wolves! They're killing the men. Some are yet alive and the wolves are eating 'em! Kill the wolves…shoot the wolves! It has my leg! For God's sake, kill the wolves! They are eating the wounded! My leg! My leg! Shoot the damn wolves!" Thrashing about in his sleep, Benedict kicked the coverings to the floor as he continued to yell. "The wolves! Shoot them! Kill the wolves!…"

Theresa rushed to him, trying to awaken him by shaking his shoulders. Benedict struck out in his sleep, pushing her to the floor. As she fell, Theresa's cloak flew over her head and one of her boots came off, sliding to the other side of the room. Picking herself up, Theresa threw off her cloak and kicked off the remaining boot as she drew near Arnold. This time she leaned in, grabbing him, and held him as close to her as she could with a firm hug.

Holding Benedict with a tight hug, she continued her struggle to awaken him. "Ben, Ben, wake up. There are no wolves. It is me, Theresa. You are having a nightmare. Wake up, Benedict, wake up!"

She firmly held him as close to her as possible to keep him from pushing her away. "Wake up, Ben, it is okay. There are no wolves. It is just me, Theresa. Wake up, Ben." She continued to hold him close until his thrashing eased as he awakened, startled to find Theresa leaning over his bed, hugging him, with her arms around him and her hands holding the back of his head next to hers as she continued to comfort him. "There are no wolves, Ben. It is just me, Theresa, wake up. You are having a nightmare. Please wake up. You are okay! You are with me, there are no wolves…"

Her shouts softened to a whisper as his thrashing eased and he appeared to regain consciousness. "Shhhh, it is okay, Ben, you are with me. There are no wolves. It is just me. Shhhh, you are going to be okay…" She continued to cradle him in her arms, rocking back and forth to gently awaken him. Shhhh, Ben, you are okay, it is only me, Theresa, there are no wolves…"

When Benedict became fully aware of Theresa's presence and what had happened, he reached out to hug Theresa in return. "I'm sorry. I'm so sorry, Theresa. I didn't mean to awaken you. I am sorry. Thank you. Thank you for your concern. I am sorry." His voice turned to a whimper as he seemed to slip back into his subconscious, "I am so sorry, Theresa. I am sorry about the men. I couldn't help them…they were so helpless, please help me, I am so sorry….they didn't deserve to die like this…the wolves. I am sorry, I am sorry, I can't help them. Help the men, for God's sake, shoot the wolves."

Still hugging Benedict close, Theresa crawled into bed to lie next to him. "There are no more wolves, Ben. I am here with you. You and the men are safe now. That time of your life is over, Ben. You did what you could for your men. You couldn't protect them from everything. That time has passed us all. It is over for all of us. We are here in my home and there are no wolves. Shhhh, it is okay, Ben. It is just you and me, here and now…there are no wolves."

The two continued their embrace as she rocked him in her arms. It became clear to both that each was comforted by the warmth of the other's embrace. Looking into his eyes, Theresa grasped his face in her hands and kissed his eyes, his face and then his lips. "I am sorry, Ben, it is going to be okay…There are no more wolves. It has been so long. I've not been this close to any man in over eight years…I am sorry, Ben. I am so alone and I don't understand, but I just need to be close to you now…There are no wolves, just you and me…here and now, there are no wolves. Just you and me…"

While they comforted each other, the unrelenting sleet continued to fall and the ice continued to build on the trees, breaking more limbs under its weight. Theresa remained with Benedict for the remainder of the night. Neither slept, and there was no more talk of wolves or loneliness.

CHAPTER 16

VAN DERWERKER FARM

The next morning, Theresa cooked breakfast for Benedict and the two of them were sitting at the table when Martin knocked at the door. "Come in, Uncle Marty; there is no need to knock."

Obviously feeling awkward about their circumstance, neither Benedict nor Theresa looked directly at Martin when he first entered the room.

"I was worried about you, Theresa. When I woke up and didn't see you at home, and then seeing all the tree limbs that had fallen during the night, I thought something may have happened to you. If you haven't looked outside yet, everything is covered with so much ice that with the morning sun, it looks like everything is covered with glass crystals. It is absolutely beautiful out there, but walking on glass is dangerous as hell. I fell twice, damn near breaking my ass, if that is even possible!"

Theresa and Ben looked up toward Martin; smiling, Theresa tried to explain. "I am fine, Uncle. I woke up very, very early and came to talk to Benedict and make him breakfast…I, I couldn't sleep with all the noise of the trees and…"

Looking at the two of them, Martin offered each a gentle reminder. "Do you remember each of your comments to Martha and me just last night on the subject of deception? You need not say anything more. It is not necessary for either of you to explain anything to either Martha or me. Neither of us needs any explanation and John is still fast asleep. I am just glad that you are both okay."

Turning back toward the door, "I am going to check the barn and the horses to make sure that there's no damage or problems there.

Finish your breakfasts. I will tell Martha that only John and I will need breakfast this morning."

Benedict got up to put on his coat and help Martin with the animals.

Martin looked over his shoulder, "No, please, Ben, I can easily take care of the horses. If I need your help with any of the tree limbs, I will let you know. Please sit and enjoy the remainder of your breakfast. You are our guest. And if I have my days straight, I believe that tomorrow is Christmas. Martha and I hope that you can stay with us a few more days."

When he reached the door, Martin stopped and turned toward Benedict once again. "After the ice melts and I am less likely to kill myself walking on the roads, I will go talk to Alex to see if I can get any more information about that 'Roeloff' fellow. Until we know more about him or where he might be, I think that it would be better that you stayed indoors and not wander the roads alone."

Benedict said nothing, but sat back down at the table and nodded. It was apparent from his demeanor that he was the most uncomfortable person in the room. Nonetheless, as Martin requested, nothing more was said.

Later in the day the ice melted and Martin was able to pay Alex a visit. During his conversation, Alex told Martin: "This Roeloff fellow left the inn yesterday. He was traveling alone and based on the direction of his route, he was undoubtedly headed south, back toward Albany."

CHAPTER 17

VAN DERWERKER FARM
SUNDAY, DECEMBER 25, 1785

After their evening meal, Benedict joined Martin, Martha, Theresa and John at the fireplace for the evening's after-dinner gathering. John looked at Benedict: "Mr. McGurk, do you have any stories that you can share with us? I've heard most of the stories that we have to tell; yours might be somewhat better than ours."

Glancing at John and noticing for the first time John's light brown hair sticking out in one spot near the back of his head in an odd cowlick angle, Benedict smiled. "I don't know that my stories will be any better than those that you, your mom or your aunt and uncle can tell, but let me see. I think that I have one that might be of interest to you all and worth telling on this day. I can tell you a true story about the most moving and wonderful musical concert that I attended in London about this time last year."

Benedict picked John up and placed him on his lap. "But first I want to give you a little gift, John." Reaching into a large, brown leather pouch he brought with him, Benedict uncovered a small wooden ship that he had carved from a piece of driftwood found during one of his earlier ocean voyages. "This is what one of my ships used to look like, only it was quite a bit bigger than this one I made for you."

Handing John the small ship's replica, Benedict reached back into the pouch and pulled out 3 separate quarter-inch round sticks, each about 8 inches long with cross beams at half and three-quarters to the top of each small pole. "Here are three masts that you can place and secure in the holes I made on the ship's deck so that it looks more like a sailing ship. Perhaps your mom or Aunt Martha can sew some cloth sails that your Uncle Martin can then add to the masts here so you can sail the boat like a real ship in a pond or river this next summer."

Adding as he smiled in Martin's direction: "With your uncle's help of course."

John's face beamed with an ear-to-ear smile; even his cowlick seemed to stick out a bit further from his head than it did just a few moments before. "Thank you, Mr. McGurk. I've never had a toy ship before! I will take good care of it and keep it forever!"

Looking up into Benedict's friendly gray eyes, "Will it really float like a real ship?"

Benedict laughed, "Well it should. The piece of wood from which it was carved likely floated in the ocean for several months, if not several years. You will need a little breeze to push it around like a real ship, but I think that it will float and sail quite well if you are careful with it. Just make sure your uncle doesn't put too much sail on her. The wind may take it away too quickly if there is too much sail, or it may tip over. If it tips, you may need to add a bit of ballast in the hull. I think your uncle can help you figure out if any lead will need to be added to the bottom of the ship to keep her from tipping over when under full sail."

Turning to the others, Benedict smiled as he bowed his head in their direction to acknowledge their expressions of appreciation for his attentiveness to the imagination of their "little John" as they occasionally referred to him.

With tears in her eyes and without making a sound, Theresa mouthed the words, "THANK YOU" to Benedict; then added: "How about telling us of your story now, Mr. McGurk?"

Settling John comfortably on his lap, Benedict began. "About this same time last year, I attend a concert at one of the most beautiful music halls of London. It was called the Theatre Royal. They tell me that it was originally built as a cathedral over 500 years before. It was very old, very big, very beautiful and a very, very appropriate location in which to witness the particular concert about which I'm going to tell you."

John looked up into Benedict's face: "What's a concert? What's a music hall? And, if you don't mind my asking, where's London?" Although he looked confused, he seemed truly interested in learning more from the storyteller as he asked his questions.

Benedict laughed. "Okay then, I am sorry, John. London is a very large city with many, many people living in it. It is a city in another country thousands of miles away, on the other side of the Atlantic Ocean. A concert is when a group of people, called musicians, come together and play several different musical instruments, or sing on a stage to others who are sitting in chairs in front of them as they perform their musical selections."

Looking out of the corner of his eyes toward John, "A musician is someone who plays a musical instrument like a violin, or harpsichord, trumpet, oboe, cello, or sings songs." Noticing John's expression, he added: "A trumpet is like a horn."

"Oh, I know what a horn is. And I know what a violin is, too."

"Good. And a music hall is like a very large room that has a ceiling that is thirty or forty feet above the floor. Many of the music halls in London are beautifully decorated with carved woodworking, large statues, heavy wooden paneling with carved, golden inlaid images, oil paintings and other works of art. This particular music hall also had what they call a balcony located 10 or 12 feet above the first floor where people also sat to watch the performance. It was so big that more than 200 – 300 people could all sit and watch the musical performance at the same time. It was a very majestic place."

Benedict glanced down at John again to see if he had any other questions...John let the word "majestic" go. It seemed that he was now beginning to visualize the story being described by his new-found friend, *Mr. McGurk*.

"Anyway, last year I was told about a concert that included music that was written in 1741 by a composer named Handel. His full name was George Frederic Handel. I had never heard of him before then, but I was told he had written this sacred musical composition that they called an oratorio."

Looking again at John, "Don't worry, John, I didn't know what an oratorio was either until last year. It is like an opera or a play that is mostly sung with an orchestra…just try to stay with the story, John. It might help to close your eyes and try to imagine the most beautiful room ever built by man with 200 – 300 people in it listening to other people telling a story with music.

"This concert caught my attention because, as I said before, it was written in 1741, which just happens to be the same year that I was born. Inasmuch as the music and I were both created in the same year, so to speak, I was naturally curious. However, what is most remarkable about this particular composition is that, as the story goes, the composer, Handel, wrote the whole thing in a matter of three or four weeks! The musical composition had at least 3 main parts, each with between 4 and 7 individual scenes in them and more than 50 musical scores."

Glancing in Theresa's direction, "It took this gifted genius less than a month to create what is undoubtedly the world's most beautiful composition – certainly the most beautiful one I have ever heard. Although I did not know of this composer before then, now that I've listened to his musical creation, I shall remember the name, George Frederic Handel, and his music for the rest of my life."

Benedict raised his right arm high into the air. "The reason I am sharing this story about this particular concert with you tonight, this being Christmas night, is that the composition, called Messiah, was essentially a story about the birth, life and death of Jesus."

Looking into John's eyes, "Do you know who Jesus is, son?" John smiled and nodded that he did.

Benedict smiled broadly in return and continued with his story. "It is the most moving music the world will ever hear. The story tells of the Old Testament Biblical prophecy of Christ's coming, and a New Testament telling about His life, His suffering and finally Jesus' death. The music also tells the story of Christ's victory over death. Anyone sitting in that music hall, who wasn't a believer when they walked in the door, could not have possibly left the music hall without a firm belief in the power of God as conveyed to them by Handel's music. With this one work, which I think must have been partly written by God Himself, Handel undoubtedly saved hundreds, if not thousands of souls of former nonbelievers."

Putting his hand over his heart, "I must now admit that before that point in time, I didn't know what to think. My mother was a very firm believer in Jesus, and as a young man like you, John, I learned about Jesus and His life. But as I got older and as I experienced life, I began to have doubts. I wondered how Jesus, if indeed he was the Son of God, would permit such bad things to happen to good people. Like the deaths of my young brothers and sisters; my God-loving mother; or the death of my first wife and mother to my young children."

Giving John a soft hug, "Or the death of your father who was your mother's life's companion. Most of my adult friends did not believe in any single religion, but believed in a Power, or something like a supreme architect, but not necessarily in Christ. So, as much as I hate to admit it to all of you, at that point, I guess I needed some convincing myself. However, when I walked out of that music hall that fateful evening, I no longer needed such convincing. The musical experience so affirmed my beliefs in Jesus as the Son of God that when

I left, there were tears streaming down my face. I was so moved. It was simply overwhelming."

John looked up, "You cried because of the music you were listening to? Isn't that a bad thing? Why would you cry when hearing a story about Jesus?"

"No, my son, a man can also cry when he is happy. It moved my soul to the point where I cried to express my happiness about being reminded of the story about Jesus and God's gifts to those of us, like my mother, who believe. I was reminded of the same stories that my dear mother used to share with me and my brothers and sisters when we were little. We all suffer at one time or another, and it was comforting to be reminded that we are not alone in our personal and private sufferings. It made me happy, not sad."

Continuing his story, "There were two specific selections that I heard during that night that I remember most. One was about His birth and comes from the Old Testament, Isaiah, I think. Handel named it, *'For Unto Us a Child is Born.'* And the chorus from this movement was repeated again and again, *'For unto us a Child is born and His name…we shall call him Wonderful, Counselor, the Mighty God, the Everlasting Father, and Prince of Peace…'*

"This chorus was sung to us, time and time again, so that it would always be remembered, … *'and His name…we shall call him Wonderful, Counselor, the Mighty God, the Everlasting Father, and Prince of Peace.'* This movement was engraved in my brain in a way that I can never forget. *'For unto us a Child is born and His name…we shall call him Wonderful, Counselor, the Mighty God, the Everlasting Father, and Prince of Peace.'*

"This movement also reminded us that the government shall be upon His shoulder and of His government and of His peace there will be no end. When they sang the word 'government,' I took it to mean the world…the world will be upon His shoulder and the world and the peace that Jesus gives to us will never end.

"It was absolutely an astounding telling of Christ's birth. So you can see why it seemed appropriate for me to share this specific musical score of Handel's with you today."

Benedict noted that John's eyes had grown as wide as his mouth was open, "We must always remember His birth, His life, and His gift of peace to us each and every day, my son. When you grow older, you will have a better understanding about what I am telling you now." John simply nodded his head in agreement.

Benedict turned his attention to the others. "There was also another movement that simply left me and the others in the hall spellbound. Handel called it his '*Hallelujah Chorus Hymn,*' and it was so appropriately named. He was indeed a genius who must have been touched by God Himself as he wrote this score."

"Are you ready, John? Listen carefully to the words, close your eyes and imagine them being sung by angels. '*... Hallelujah! Hallelujah! Hallelujah! Hallelujah! Hallelujah! King of kings, and Lord of lords, King of kings, and Lord of lords, And He shall reign, and He shall reign forever and ever, King of kings, forever and ever, and Lord of lords, Hallelujah! Hallelujah!*'

"Again and again, the chorus sang this verse, or something very much like it. It was just so majestic; you could feel the breath of God upon your face as it was sung. People stood, as was their habit during the performance of this particular movement. Imagine 200 to 300 people all standing; listening to all the musicians singing and playing their instruments as beautifully as they possibly could."

Shaking his head, "It was the most emotionally moving music I've ever heard. So moving that I and others in the music hall could not contain ourselves, and again we cried." Looking quickly at John, "And we were unashamed. It was like we could feel the hand of God upon us as His music entered our souls through our ears. It was like an awakening of the spirit!"

With a beaming smile, Benedict concluded his story. "Every Christmas, I will think back to the day I sat in that cathedral with 200 or 300 total strangers and know that, at that moment and at that place, I was personally touched by God. It was like I experienced Christ's birth, life and death, not with my eyes, but with my ears and my soul. It was amazing how the music so moved everyone in the same way."

Glancing at John, "I was surprised at myself, and somewhat pleased as well, if you don't mind my sounding like a bit of a braggart. Before that day, I didn't know how easily I could be brought to tears in a public place without feeling badly or ashamed. I learned a bit more about myself on that day and I was even somewhat proud of this realization. I didn't know that I had it in me to allow my emotion to show in such a public way and not be ashamed or embarrassed in doing so."

Tears swelled up in Benedict's eyes as he shared this aspect of his life with them.

Once he was done, he looked down at John, who then seemed to understand each and every word of his story. Theresa, Martha and Martin, all just sat in silence; Theresa dabbed a handkerchief to her eyes.

They were all moved by listening to the story given to them by this seemingly rough and rugged man, Benedict Arnold, on this Christmas day. It will be a tale remembered for many Christmases to come.

John eventually broke the silence. "Thank you, Mr. McGurk. I am glad you visited us and told us this story. I will remember it forever. Someday I am going to go to London myself and listen to the music you told us about with my own ears."

Benedict gave John a long hug and handed him over to his mother, ending this evening's gathering.

CHAPTER 18

VAN DERWERKER FARM

While preparing for bed that evening, Benedict realized that his spirit had indeed been lifted by the act of recounting his experience of listening to the Messiah. And he realized that many positive changes have occurred in his life since he attended this concert. Being here at the home of his friend, Martin and his family, as well as meeting with his former Commanding General were only two examples of such changes. For these changes and more, he was thankful.

Before turning in for the night, Benedict took a moment to look out a frost-covered window of Theresa and John's home at the glistening snow and ice, blanketed by the full moon's bluish light. Having shared his story about being touched by God with Martin and his family, he was reminded of other instances in his life where God had made His presence known to him.

Looking out the window, and thinking once again about the music of the Messiah, Benedict recalled other days in his past where God most touched his life. He thought about the days spent as a child, with his mother and father, sisters and brothers in their modest home in Norwich, Connecticut. *'For unto us a Child is born and His name...we shall call him Wonderful, Counselor, the Mighty God, the Everlasting Father, and Prince of Peace.'*

Thinking about his youth, he was reminded of the suffering of his younger brothers and sisters, all but one of whom died of yellow fever. He considered the emotional scars their deaths left on him when he was only 12.

He thought as well about the anguish felt by his mother and father at the loss of their young children. While his father sought solace with alcohol, he was thankful that his mother had God to fall back on during her times of grief and need.

He remembered the death of his mother when he was just eighteen and the death of his father when Benedict was twenty. At twenty years of age, he was on his own. He wondered why he and his sister, Hannah, were the only two members of his family permitted to survive those years of disease and poverty. Benedict had an inkling that God might have spared the two of them for reasons unknown to each at the time. While remembering this part of his past, another verse of Handel's Messiah came to mind: *'The trumpet shall sound, and the dead shall be raised incorruptible, and we shall be changed, for this corruptible must put on incorruption, and this mortal must put on immortality.'*

Benedict also thought about the life he'd had with his first wife, Peggy, who gave him the gift of three sons… *'For unto us a Child is born and His name…we shall call him Wonderful, Counselor, the Mighty God, the Everlasting Father, and Prince of Peace'.* . . He thought about her death while he was away at Ticonderoga during the early days of the war. Not being with his wife and young sons at that time, when they undoubtedly needed him most, would always be one of his greatest regrets. *'The trumpet shall sound, and the dead shall be raised incorruptible, and we shall be changed, for this corruptible must put on incorruption, and this mortal must put on immortality'.*

Although saddened by the loss of his life's companion, he was also comforted by the knowledge that her spirit was with God and at peace. *'Hallelujah! Hallelujah! Hallelujah! Hallelujah! Hallelujah! King of kings, and Lord of lords, King of kings, and Lord of lords, And He shall reign, and He shall reign forever and ever, King of kings, forever and ever, and Lord of lords, Hallelujah! Hallelujah!'*

Continuing to stare at the moon's blue light, the music of the Hallelujah Chorus Hymn continued to echo in his head… *'Hallelujah! Hallelujah! Hallelujah! Hallelujah! Hallelujah! King of kings, and Lord of lords, King of kings, and Lord of lords, And He shall reign, and He shall reign forever*

and ever, King of kings, forever and ever, and Lord of lords, Hallelujah!
Hallelujah!'

The snow-covered fields outside his window reminded Benedict of the sufferings of those brave souls who traveled with him through Maine to Quebec City in the most intolerable conditions he ever experienced. Traveling the Kennebec River in the Maine wilderness to the Chaudière River in bateaus and canoes just over ten years ago, in the late fall of 1775, many drowned as their poorly constructed and overburdened bateau capsized. Others froze walking chest high in the ice-encrusted water of the Chaudière.

Men also froze while sleeping unprotected from the elements. Lacking blankets, coats or any other protections, many of his men covered themselves with dead leaves and pine needles at night to provide a modicum of insulation from Maine's harsh weather while they slept. He remembered the visions of snow-covered mounds that quivered and moved when the men awakened to discover it had snowed as they slept. He was saddened by the memory that some mounds didn't move with the next day's light, or ever again.

Lacking provisions lost from their capsized bateaus, men starved. In desperation, many ate candles to give their stomachs some form of sustenance. In their attempts to seek strength enough to face yet another day, others boiled and ate leather cut from their boots to gain whatever nourishment they might leach from the former animal hide.

Of the 1,100 or so men who began this journey through hell with him, some 370 turned back in shame; more than 50 died along the way from exposure, fatigue and starvation. Nonetheless, with God's grace, just over 675 weary souls were able to withstand their 8 week journey of depravation to reach their destination of Quebec City. *'Hallelujah! Hallelujah! Hallelujah! Hallelujah! Hallelujah! King of kings, and Lord of lords, King of kings, and Lord of lords, And He shall reign, and He shall reign forever and ever, King of kings, forever and ever, and Lord of lords, Hallelujah! Hallelujah!'*

Benedict recalled the anguish he experienced the first time he was wounded by a bullet fragment to his left leg while storming the British Fortress at Quebec during an early morning blizzard on New Year's Day of that momentous year, 1776. His wound made it impossible for him to walk or move, let alone run forward any longer. Having come so far, and having to wait so long for this moment of opportunity, Benedict was devastated to realize that he would be unable to lead his men any further into the citadel of Quebec City.

It was this life experience which taught him that intervention of fate did not necessarily result in the success one desired. His Field Commander, General Richard Montgomery, was killed, and he was incapacitated by a wound to his leg. Indeed, Providence did not shine upon Benedict and his men in their effort to capture Quebec in the early days of the Revolution. '*The trumpet shall sound, and the dead shall be raised incorruptible, and we shall be changed, for this corruptible must put on incorruption, and this mortal must put on immortality.*'

The blue haze of the moon's evening glow also brought forth images of the waters of Lake Champlain. He thought of the men who joined him on this lake at Valcour Island nine years before, in the month of October 1776. It was at this location he commanded America's very first navy flotilla in this country's very first naval battle. Benedict and his paltry fleet of ragtag ships built from freshly cut trees challenged the British fleet on Lake Champlain as they made their way toward Albany in their strategy to defeat the Americans by cutting the nation in half.

At the forefront; standing in their way, was Benedict and his green fleet of 4 row galleys, a schooner, 2 sloops, and 8 gondolas. All poorly rigged, modestly armed and sailed by an army of landsmen, all trying their damnedest to develop sea legs. Facing the British naval armada consisting of a flagship, 3 schooners, a 2-masted ketch and 20 gunboats, Benedict understood from the very beginning that his fleet was outgunned and outmanned. He knew in his heart that this battle on the lake was not to be won in the traditional sense of victory.

Arnold's fate, and that of his ships' novice crews' again rested in the hands of Providence. However, unlike Quebec City, this time Providence did shine upon Benedict and his ships and crew in a not-so-obvious way. To the amazement of sailors on both sides of the battle line, Benedict as well as most of his ships and crew survived the daylong onslaught of British cannon fire, grapeshot and the devastation of being hulled above the waterline and ships' decks raked with burning metal.

Against all odds, some damage was inflicted upon several British ships, and Arnold's badly damaged flotilla remained mostly afloat as darkness settled upon the Bay of Valcour. Nonetheless, with three quarters of its powder and cannon shot exhausted, Benedict knew that his fleet would face overwhelming odds, death and certain destruction with the dawn's new light.

To further humiliate the Americans and, as a demonstration of their day's victory after the sun had set, the British set fire to the American ship, Royal Savage, which had run aground at the southern tip of Valcour Island and was abandoned by the Americans early in the battle on the lake. Knowing human nature, and expecting that most, if not all sailors in the British fleet would be paying more attention to the illumination given by the burning ship than his badly damaged fleet, Benedict took full advantage of their folly as well as Providence's twofold gifts of a moonless night and a ghostly thick fog that mysteriously blanketed the lake just after the sun dipped below the horizon of distant mountains.

Upon orders from Benedict and with oars muffled to lessen their sound on the water's surface, the remnants of Arnold's badly damaged fleet hugged the shoreline, and, one by one, rowed passed the inattentive British armada in single file. While staring at the eerie-looking, flickering orange glow that unevenly penetrated the cold mystic fog, the British sailors, to a man, believed that they had Benedict and his ships trapped in the Narrows of Valcour Island's shallow waters after the day's long battle.

However, when the mist and fog lifted from the lake at mid-morning the next day, the overconfident British were astonished to discover that Benedict and the remnants of his damaged flotilla had vanished. Some thought that the whole of the American flotilla must have sunk to the bottom of the bay during the night. Others who knew of Arnold's cunning reputation, thought better. They understood that Benedict and his fleet had somehow escaped their grasp to live on to fight yet another day.

Looking back at this battle on the lake, Benedict understood that the outcome of his actions was always in the hands of Providence. Although all but three of his ships were ultimately destroyed in the ensuing day's battles, his previously untested sailors and their paltry fleet nevertheless did slow the advance of the British movement southward in 1776. He and his crew did give the British pause to reconsider their circumstances.

After the battle on the lake was over, the British ultimately decided to return to Canada to take up their winter quarters in a safer haven. Arnold's delaying tactic was successful, and although soundly defeated on the waters of Lake Champlain, he and his landlubber sailors did provide his Commanding General and the country another year in which to prepare for the next British campaign. *'Hallelujah! Hallelujah! Hallelujah! Hallelujah! Hallelujah! King of kings, and Lord of lords, King of kings, and Lord of lords, And He shall reign, and He shall reign forever and ever, King of kings, forever and ever, and Lord of lords, Hallelujah! Hallelujah!'*

The haze-covered landscape outside his window also took Benedict back to the last time he was at this location eight years ago in the fall of 1777. The blue light cast by the moon upon the snow-covered field reminded him of the blue grey, smoke-filled haze that engulfed the battlefields at Saratoga where he fought what he truly expected to be his final contest. He remembered the fearless militia, to include his friend, Martin, and Theresa's husband, who faced the British Army as they advanced toward Albany in their renewed efforts to divide the nation in half.

At a location not far from this very window, Benedict and the good soldiers who accompanied him into battle stood their ground and, again with God's grace, stopped the advance of the world's greatest military force. Thinking about Theresa's and her son's loss of a husband and father, as well as his own personal anguish when he was again wounded with a bullet to the same leg previously damaged at Quebec two years before, Benedict came to understand from life's lessons that triumph can often be accompanied by a balance of tragedy and disappointment. *The trumpet shall sound, and the dead shall be raised incorruptible, and we shall be changed, for this corruptible must put on incorruption, and this mortal must put on immortality.'*

Finally, Arnold's thoughts turned to meetings he had with his leader and friend, George Washington, just over five years ago, during the summer and early fall of 1780, as they planned for their country's final victory. *'For unto us a child is born, unto us a son is given and the government shall be upon his shoulder: and his name shall be called Wonderful, Counselor, the mighty God, the everlasting Father, the Prince of Peace…the government shall be upon his shoulders Hallelujah! Hallelujah! Hallelujah! Hallelujah! Hallelujah! King of kings, and Lord of lords, King of kings, and Lord of lords, And He shall reign, and He shall reign forever and ever, King of kings, forever and ever, and Lord of lords, Hallelujah! Hallelujah!'*

Benedict smiled. "And the government shall be upon his shoulders, all right."

Crawling into bed for the evening, Benedict mused that the similarities between Jesus as a leader of *man* and George Washington, as a leader of *men* were unavoidable and continued to resonate in his brain as he allowed sleep to overtake his weary body. *Indeed, the government shall be upon Washington's shoulders. And perhaps, he shall reign forever. And some may call him wonderful, counselor, the everlasting father; the prince of peace…the government may indeed rest upon his shoulders. I can't help but wonder what Providence has in store for each of us in the years to come. May God guide him and have mercy on him, our families as well as our nation.*

CHAPTER 19

TIME IN A BOTTLE

March 13, 1786
Mount Vernon

Dear General Schuyler:

I am traveling to New York City next month for purposes of State and would appreciate an opportunity to meet with you at that location if you are in good enough health and well-being to make the trip to New York from Albany at that time.

I am interested in learning more about the matter you previously brought to my attention regarding a possible meeting between parties both known and unknown to us, that was to be held last December.

It is my understanding that such meeting did not, in fact, occur. Nevertheless, regardless of the meeting's last minute cancellation, it is also my understanding that <u>all</u> parties were present at that location. As you can well imagine, and will be no surprise to you, I am deeply interested in, and concerned about, the intended nature of the meeting, as well as learning more about the meeting's organizers. At this fragile stage of nation building, I believe it is critical that those involved in the planned meeting understand the latent ramifications of the actions they may take - no matter how well intended or how pious the motives of their ill-conceived actions may have been.

Please let me know at your earliest convenience if you will be able to join me for a discussion on this matter while I am in New York.

Please extend my best wishes to your dear wife, Cornelia.

I remain your most humble and obedient servant,

George Washington

August 14, 1786
St. John's, Canada

Dear Martin:

It has been several months since my visit with you and your lovely family. It is my sincere hope that this dispatch finds you and your family well and in good spirits.

I set sail Sunday next for Campobello Island off Nova Scotia, and then to Jamaica, on a lengthy voyage of commerce to gather goods of interest to my associates on the European continent. Once I complete my purchases in the Caribbean, I will then cross the Atlantic to sell and exchange the goods purchased there for others of interest to the residents on this continent. It is *also my plan to bring my dear wife and children back to St. John's to take up (hopefully temporarily) residence with me here until we reach our final destination. My sister and oldest sons have already joined me and will be looking after my business interests at this location in my absence.*

As I prepare for this voyage, I am reminded of my younger days when such a trip was more about adventure than business – although business was the primary purpose of my travels at that time. Seeing other parts of the world and dealing with other peoples as a younger man gave me a better understanding and appreciation of not only our differences, but the similarities that are common to all men of this earth. With this life experience in mind, I would like to offer Theresa's son, John, an opportunity to join me on one of my future voyages when he comes of age. Perhaps one day John can work with my sons and me for a year or so to see if he has an interest in shipping or commerce that he could, perhaps one day, carry out from the Albany docks on the Hudson. Depending upon the timing of such a trip for John, and should his mother permit it to be, of course, I may also be able to arrange for a trip to London so he can personally witness the Messiah that I described at your last Christmas gathering. I believe that he would remember such a trip for the rest of his life, and it may shape a lifetime interest in the shipping trades should he take a liking to the seas and the benefits that such travel has to offer a young man of business. This is a discussion Theresa and I can have at an appropriate time should, God willing, the opportunities present themselves favorably when he grows older.

To my knowledge, there has been no further progress in the efforts that I mentioned last December. As might be expected, communications toward that business adventure have been difficult from afar at best. I expect that my voyage will last well into next year, and I hope to participate once again in direct discussions with my associate in the United States on this point once I return from England. Should you find it within your powers to do so, I would appreciate hearing from you with news regarding your activities and the well-being of your dear Martha, Theresa and John. Inasmuch as my travels will be varied and my stay at any single location unknown in advance, please send any communications of your interest to the attention of "Lord Sheffield" at the St. John's Business location. I am leaving instructions with my sons and business associates here to forward any and all such letters that I may receive to my temporary locations of which I will inform them as they become known to me.

Until then, I remain your most affectionate and obedient servant,

Lord Sheffield

August 19, 1786
St. John's, Canada
No. 9

Dear Sir:

It is with considerable gratification this date that I received your communication of 23 June. I am pleased that progress has been made regarding the formation of the business enterprise of concern to you that we briefly discussed at our last reunion. It is my sincere hope and expectation that the management of the business to be newly established is bestowed upon the shoulders of my trusted friend and former comrade in arms, as it will be well-deserved, and the venture shall, therefore, succeed as envisioned, bonum commune hominis.

The timing of my receipt of your letter could not have been better. For I write to inform you that tomorrow my business will take me from this location to the Caribbean for the winter months and Europe in early spring. I expect to return to this establishment early next summer to complete my venture. On a happy note, I anticipate relocating the business associates, personally close to me, from their current London location to St. John's. Based upon the news contained in your letter, it is my hope and expectation that, within the very near future, circumstances may permit the expansion of my business to the location where we last encountered one another in December of the previous annum. That is, if future transactions unfold favorably and it is believed profits can be gained at that location. Indeed, consideration may be given to relocating all my personal business associates to that location as a permanent business headquarters, where I may live out the remainder of my days.

I regret to hear that little information has been learned about the failure of my investment meeting at that same location last year. I, too, have had no further communication from those who hoped to profit from my last visit. Perhaps their interests in my business have diminished, and they are no longer pursuing the implementation of their ill-conceived plan to take over my personal business interest. Upon my return to this continent next summer, it is my hope that we may then meet again to assess the business climate at that time and give further consideration to our mutual business interests. However, should your plans advance at a quicker pace than anticipated and should you wish to meet sooner to consider the relocation of my personal business to a more favorable location, please send such communications as you may deem necessary to the attention of "Lord Sheffield" at my St. John's location. I am leaving instructions with my business associates here to forward any and all such letters I may receive to my temporary locations about which I will inform them as my business voyage unfolds before me.

P.S. I hope it is not indelicate of me that I have not acknowledged, before this point in my communication, your mention of General Greene's untimely death on June 19, and your mention of your former aide-de-camp's, Tench

Tilghman, passing earlier in the year. I know how important these men were to you and your efforts during the campaign; such events can only serve as a reminder to us all that our time grows shorter with each passing day.

Until then, I remain your most grateful, obedient and humble servant,

Lord Sheffield

November 3, 1786
St. Vincent, West Indies

Dear Martin:

It has been approximately one year since I had the pleasure of your company and consult. To date, I have not received any communications from your area since my last letter, sent to you from St. John's, before I departed for the Caribbean.

I hope that you did receive my earlier communication, sent to your attention in August, and that it has not caused any community or personal concerns or problems. Please send a message to the St. John's location directed to the attention of Lord Sheffield; any *such communications will be forwarded to my current location.*

I trust that you, Martha, Theresa and John are all doing well as the harvest comes to an end and you prepare for the long winter ahead. I find myself becoming somewhat melancholy and in want of seeing my family and friends. Therefore, I am preparing to depart soon for London to be with my family in time for Christmas, should Providence bestow favorable winds as is customary for this time of year in the Atlantic. I fondly remember the time of my last Christmas spent in the company of my good friend and his family... in particular, young John sitting in my lap as I recounted my story regarding my London music hall experiences. He is quite the inquisitive lad; an eager listener and learner like his uncle and mother, I might observe. He will do well in life. Please let them all know of my interest in their well-being. I wish each of you a happy Christmastide again this year.

Until then, I remain your most affectionate and obedient servant,

Lord Sheffield

January 7, 1787
London
No. 7

Dear Sir:

I have not received any further communication from your location since your correspondence of 23 June of the previous annum, to which I responded in August of the same year.

My personal business is growing, and I am ever anxious to expand its base of operation to a more central location referenced in my last communication to you on this subject.

I have plans to return to my northern port mid-year to pursue the expansion of my trade ventures further. I am, therefore, apprehensive, as a result of not hearing further from you since your letter of last June. I await more information on the subjects of our mutual interests. I trust that our respective company interests would likely prosper should we be able to conclude our business negotiations by the end of this year. I, therefore, seek an opportunity to meet with you at a location of your choosing upon my return. At which time, I hope to be of greater service to you and your interests.

Until I am certain that our communications are received without intervention, I shall limit my additional thoughts on this matter.

I trust that both you and Martha are in good health, as am I. It appears that my wife and I will be adding to our family by year's end; it is my sincere hope that the birth of my next, and likely last, child will be in the same nation state as was the birth of his (or her) father some 47 years before....

Until then, I am, Sir, &c.,

LS

<hr/>

May 30, 1787
Mount Vernon
No. 8

Dear Sir:

I am in receipt of your communications of August last year, and January of the present annum. I have been extremely busy with the development of the business enterprise briefly discussed at our last meeting.

Nonetheless, the fruits of my interest enable me to now report that the business of interest to you is progressing on its natural course of development, with the possibility of maturing to its fullest potential in the very near future. By all accounts, however, I doubt that you will be able to relocate your business from its current safe harbor to a more southern port by the end of this year. However, I offer the hope that such a prospect is not out of the realm of possibility in the not-too-distant future.

I have yet to personally invest myself in the day-to-day planning of my business venture; however, all reports indicate that I will soon need to engage directly in the planning as a demonstration of my personal commitment to the business structure and to foster the business values in which others may seek to invest. The projected profits to be gained appear reasonable.

I am also pleased to inform you that I have a somewhat better understanding of the meeting in which you participated briefly during your last visit. Such detail will need to be discussed when we meet again. However, rest assured that I am relatively certain the risk to you or your personal business associates appears to be minimal at this time. This is not to suggest that the concerns of your business venture I previously expressed at our last meeting have been addressed; it is only to extend assurance that any personal risks to you have been minimized to the extent possible at this time. This good tiding does not imply that your plan to relocate your business can be advanced at this time. Only time and further considerations of our unique circumstances at our next meeting will provide insights into the investment strategies that should be implemented at that juncture.

Investors appear to be extremely cautious; the conditions remain delicate. Nonetheless, I remain optimistic that each of our business objectives, although in potential conflict, can yet be attained if we are vigilant.

It is my sincere wish that this communication finds your former and newly added personal business associates in good spirits, good health and well-being. Notify me upon your return. I believe that it would be advisable to meet to assess our mutual business interests in the early fall while the weather is yet favorable and before the crops are in need of harvesting.

I remain, &c.

———

August 3, 1787
St. John's
No. 5

Dear Sir:

I am pleased with the information and direction described in your letter of May 30 and will be honored to meet with you. I returned to St. John's in June but didn't receive your letter until now, inasmuch as it was initially forwarded first from St. John's to my location in London. However, I had already departed for my return trip to this continent, and it needed to be forwarded to me from that location.

Please be advised that I can arrange to obtain passage on a business associate's ship to New York harbor whereupon I can then forward a message to you once docked, to inform you of my arrival at that time.

It is anticipated that I will be adding another personal business associate within the next month or so; however, it is likely that my presence will not be required upon his or her arrival should your meeting date coincide with such occasion. Please inform me of the time period in which such a meeting would be convenient to you.

I understand the delicacy of the times and the need for confidentiality in our business investments. You can trust that I would never do anything that might, in any way, detract from your capital investments or anticipated rates of return.

Until then I am, Sir, &c.,

LS

September 3, 1787
New York
No. 6

Dear Sir:

In response to your letter of August 3, please ask your business associate to arrange delivery of previously discussed cargo during the third week of October when I, again, expect to be at this location.

I remain, &c.

CHAPTER 20

CHERRY STREET, NEW YORK
APRIL, 1786

While in the library of his temporary New York residence awaiting his guest, Washington studied the copy he had made of a letter given to Benedict by an innkeeper while in Albany four months earlier.

Looking at the letter's referral to 'Brother Sparks,' he remembered Arnold's comment that the innkeeper persistently used the preface, "Brother," while referring to others. He knew that many former members of the Continental Army often referred to each other as a "band of brothers." It never ceased to amaze him that, when used in a context that many could relate to, a simple phrase could become so popular among others in such a short period of time. He had noticed its growing use, time and time again, since he incorporated the Shakespearian phrase within his last set of orders delivered to the Continental Army in his final act as its Commander-in-Chief, three years before.

It was one of those phrases that seemed to stick in the listener's mind. Indeed, many used the word, "Brother" with pride in recognition of their participation in the greatest war ever fought. Nonetheless, it was also the case that the term, "Brother," was commonly used among his fellow Masons in their reference to other members of the Freemasons. Based upon these facts, Washington was able to conclude that the source of the letter and the men referred to by the innkeeper were either former members of the Continental Army or members of the Freemasons – or both. Consequently, these observations alone did not help Washington narrow the field in his endeavor to identify specific individuals involved in an attempt to ensnare Arnold.

Washington's thoughts then turned to the location of the planned meeting. Why Albany, and why now? What was there about Albany that made someone believe Benedict would feel comfortable traveling to a meeting at that location? And finally, he thought about the letters Benedict said he received from someone posing as Washington himself. To deceive a man like Arnold, it was reasonable to conclude that the letters were written with delicate care and detail. Sufficient care to convince Benedict that the letters were from him...

Who would know that Benedict would be willing to risk a meeting in this country with him at this point in time and be able to craft such believable letters? These thoughts did, in fact, help Washington narrow the list of probable conspirators significantly. Yet, he needed to be certain before confronting those responsible.

Standing next to the fireplace in his library and staring at the glimmering hues of yellow, blue and orange flames flickering over the surface of the crackling wood, Washington mumbled to himself, as he occasionally did when in deep concentration. *"There is too much going on at this point to risk any controversy, or to arouse suspicions among those working with me to form a more perfect union. I need to determine if others are attempting to use Benedict to discredit me and our efforts."*

Shaking his head slowly, his eyes focused upon the mesmerizing flames. *"I need to be certain. I do care about Benedict and his family on a personal level. And I know that I would not likely be here, in this city or possibly anywhere else on this earth at this moment, if it were not for the risks and sacrifices he's made. Yet, I must keep the focus of our energies upon our final victory, as he often referred to it. We must make sure that the nation does not suffer from either his desires or the planned actions of others. I even expect that Benedict would agree with me on this point. Although he has suffered much, it would appear that he may yet need to endure more."*

Walking to his desk to study the Arnold letter, Washington mentally summarized the facts presently known to him. Philip Schuyler lives in Albany. . . he was the only one to inform him that Benedict was traveling to Albany to meet with individuals unknown to him...he was correct about the meeting being planned, if not canceled...he is a long-time resident of that area and a highly influential participant in the Albany political arena. At the very least, he must have a source that could point to the parties involved in the Albany meeting.

Consequently, it is reasonable to conclude Schuyler would know the individual, or individuals, responsible for inviting Benedict to the Albany meeting – even if he were unaware of the individual's direct involvement. Washington also knew that General Schuyler was also one of Arnold's few supporters after Benedict was assigned to the Northern Theater to assist the Army's efforts to thwart the British's southern march to attack the country's heartland from the north. While preparing himself mentally for his meeting with Philip Schuyler, Washington was comforted by his knowledge that Schuyler's character included traits of honesty, trustworthiness and compassion – as evidenced by his concern regarding Arnold's safety expressed in his December letter.

Washington's contemplations were interrupted by a quiet knock on the door leading to his library.

Placing his copy of the letter in his desk's top drawer, Washington looked toward the door. "Yes?"

The door opened slightly and his faithful servant, Billy Lee, looked in without entering the room. "Mr. Washington, Master Schuyler is here to see you."

Standing up from behind the desk and walking toward the entrance to his library: "Please show the General in directly, Billy. Don't keep him waiting a moment longer."

Philip Schuyler and Washington greeted each other as they would long-lost brothers; each grabbing the shoulders of the other with broad smiles and glistening eyes. "It is so good to see you, Philip. Thank you for taking the time from your dear wife, Cornelia, children and grandchildren to join me."

Benedict Arnold: Legacy Lost (A Ghost's Story)

"Sir, when one's former Commanding General requests an audience, one gives the Commanding General an audience. When one's friend asks for help, one jumps on his horse without hesitation. And besides, this trip gives me an opportunity to visit my dear daughter, Eliza, and my two grandchildren as well. I, too, am glad to see my friend once again and to see that you are in good health and, hopefully, good spirits."

After the formal pleasantries, common courtesies, and the sharing of information about their families, health and the relative monotony of their day-to-day lives since the war's end, Washington wasted no time in getting to the point of his invitation and his desire to learn more about the meeting that Philip had brought to his attention the previous December.

"As I suggested in my letter, Philip, I need to learn more about the meeting that was planned last December in Albany between our former General, Benedict Arnold, and others. I can't imagine why anyone would invite Benedict to return or want to meet with him now. What would the motives be? As you know, many are not at all satisfied with the Confederation, and discussions are currently taking place to address these dissatisfactions. It is not clear what path this nation may take of the options under consideration. As a statesman and politician, you can very well imagine that this is all-too-delicate a time for this country to now face the prospect of Benedict Arnold returning to this land for unknown purposes. Might it be possible that such a meeting could be part of a foil to upset plans under consideration to chart the course of this country's government?"

Washington's tapping of an index finger on the top of his desk as he spoke provided Schuyler with a hint of his host's anxiety as he continued to speak. "Being a politician engaged in the public arena in this state, you are undoubtedly aware that I and others are occupied in discussions concerning the Confederation. I suspect that your knowledge of my interests in this regard was primary among the reasons that you knew I would be interested in learning about any meeting involving Benedict taking place anywhere this country, let alone your home city."

Looking at Philip Schuyler with a scowl, "If my suspicions are proper, I confide in you now that my curiosities were then, as they are now, focused squarely upon the impact this matter may have upon the forward movement being made to establish a new order within these United States. It should be of little surprise to you that the intentions of Benedict and those he planned to meet do concern me. So please, what more can you tell me about this matter? How did you come to learn of the meeting?"

Washington then leaned back in his chair behind his desk and folded his hands together behind his head, pushing a bulge of gray hair out on each side of his face.

Schuyler slowly paced about the room, seemingly interested in studying the covers of the books within the library. "Well, Sir, it is complicated. And I am not quite certain where to begin or exactly how to say what needs to be said."

Turning his head in Washington's direction, "First, let me begin by assuring you I will tell you all that I know and will keep nothing from you relating to this matter that may be of interest to you. For reasons that will become clear in a moment, I also need to let you know I have interminable confidence in what you may do with the information I am about to share with you. I trust your judgment and the wisdom you've demonstrated over the years about the confidences that I and others place in you."

He paused before continuing, "For you, the interest is political. However, for me it is personal. As you may suspect, the matter involves a member of my family and personal trusts members of my family expect of me. It is my sincere hope not to lose the trust of those I care dearly about. It would likely be devastating for my family and, I daresay, for me as well. Having said that, I need to add that like you, I, too, am concerned about the path this nation may take into its uncertain future. I, too, am concerned about the divisions that have emerged within our camp and their unknown consequences for my grandchildren and generations yet unborn."

Shaking his head and looking downward at the floor boards once again. "As I grow older with each passing year, I yearn for a rocking chair, a garden to tend and the feel of a cool summer breeze upon my face as I watch the sunsets of each passing day while savoring the cool waters of High Rock."

Washington glanced with a smile in Schuyler's direction, "Ah yes, High Rock Springs. What a lovely place, not to mention the medicinal benefits of its waters. I fondly recall my trip to your summer estate in '83 while visiting the battlefields at Saratoga. And I recall as well, the time you took Alexander and me to the springs to experience the magic of the waters there. After our visit, I felt so refreshed."

Looking away from Schuyler, Washington smiled sheepishly. "I am pretty sure I never before shared this with you, but after our visit to High Rock, I did attempt to purchase some of the land near the springs, thinking that I may wish to one day grow old, or perhaps stay young there. But the damn Livingstons…between them, the Waltons;" looking back in Philips's direction, "and the Schuylers I must add. Thanks to all of you, the land around the entire area had already been deeded. There wasn't enough land to purchase in that area on which to place a necessary, let alone a home in which to live."

Schuyler laughed, "Sorry about that my friend. Had I known of your interest there, I may have made some inquiries. Nevertheless, that was then and this is now. There is obviously work yet unfinished and, consequently, such pleasantries of watching sunsets and sipping the waters of High Rock will need to wait for another time. I am afraid you are correct, if left to the devices of others, who knows what will happen to this country, or the legacy we are about to relinquish to this nation's next generation?"

Looking up from his desk, Washington smiled at Schuyler and nodded his head in agreement, "I understand, Philip. Believe me, I understand…" Moving from behind the desk, Washington placed two straight-backed chairs next to the fireplace whose flames were now reduced to glowing embers. "These are not rockers, but if you will indulge my curiosities, I would like to learn more. It is my sincere hope and expectation that the confidences you and others have entrusted with me over the years will not be dishonored at this time either."

Sitting with his arms folded across his chest and his right leg crossed over the top of his left, Schuyler looked somewhat perplexed. "Well, Sir, I am not sure where to begin. Yet, before I do, there is something else I would like to confide in you that has occupied my mind for more than five years now. It is not clear to me what others know about this matter and I have not discussed it with anyone, to include Eliza or even my son-in-law, Alexander."

Placing a finger to his chin, "As you may recall, Colonel Hamilton married Eliza, while he was your Aide-de-Camp in December of '80. Less than two months after the nuptials, I received a rather disconcerting letter from Alexander telling me that the two of you had a falling out of sorts and he was no longer a member of your family. Being his new father-in-law, it seemed that poor Alexander felt compelled to convince me that the reason for his leaving your service should not reflect badly upon him and intimated that the reason for the split was more of your doing than his."

Tapping a pocket on the left his chest, "I brought the letter with me in the event that I had the opportunity to talk to you on this matter to see if I can resolve my puzzlement before the end of my days. I will certainly address your curiosities about the Arnold meeting in Albany to the extent that I can, if you would be so kind as to indulge my curiosities about why Alexander left your service for more than two years." Looking at Washington, Schuyler winked his right eye, "Consider it a *quid pro quo*."

Reaching into the left chest pocket of his dark blue, double-breasted jacket to retrieve the document, Schuyler offered a nervous smile. "The letter is dated February 18, 1781, and was written by Alexander while at your Windsor headquarters. It is quite lengthy, but if you would allow, I would like to simply extract some of its contents that have puzzled me over these many years. In his letter, he attempted to offer what he purported to be a reasonable explanation for his separation from your service. He wrote that as you were walking up a staircase to your office, he passed you in the opposite direction as he descended the staircase."

Glancing in Washington's direction, he smiled, "So far, simple enough."

Looking back to the letter, "Then the letter goes on to state that while passing each other on the stairs, you informed him of your interest in speaking with him. He indicated that he was courteous and respectful of your request, but first completed a few tasks, which took only a few moments, before returning to you as requested."

Looking in Washington's direction, "Again, simple enough. However, Alexander then stated that upon his return, you were waiting for him at the top of the stairs and scolded him for keeping you waiting for more than ten minutes. He further wrote, and I would like to read this portion of his letter so that I make no mistake in recounting it, you told him that for the delay in his return, '...*I must tell you, Sir, you treat me with disrespect.*'

"Alexander's letter then goes on to explain that he informed you that he didn't think he kept you waiting for quite as long as you seemed to believe. However, if you thought strongly enough about his lack of respect to tell him so in such a direct manner, he saw no alternative but to leave your service."

Slowly looking up from the letter, "Sir, I know you both all too well to accept that something so simple and insignificant as the passage of a few moments…even if it were all of ten minutes as you may have then believed…could possibly have led to your anger with Alexander or his decision to leave.

"After a fashion, he later stated, and again I need to read, for this is the most puzzling of all, '…*With this key you will easily unlock the present mystery. At the end of the war I may say many things to you concerning which I shall impose upon myself 'till then an inviolable silence.*' That is what he wrote…'With this key'…" Schuyler stopped reading and looked up at his puzzled companion.

Looking back with both eyebrows raised, Washington could not contain himself, "What the hell does that mean?"

Shrugging his shoulders, Schuyler sighed, "I do not know, Sir. Alexander never did say anything more about the letter after the war ended as he suggested that he might. He never again raised the subject of his split with you or anything about the 'mystery' referred to in his letter."

Then standing to pace about the library again Philip Schuyler continued recounting his concern. "He never raised the subject again and, inasmuch as the two of you did reconcile whatever differences you had as the war came to an end, I never addressed the matter with him. At least not directly, and the mystery therefore remains a mystery to me…to this day. Not to say that my curiosity ever ended. I just didn't feel it appropriate of me to present the question to him as directly as I am presenting it to you. Frankly, I awaited opportunities to subtly raise the subject of his letter, and did so on more than one occasion."

Shaking his head, "However, Alexander never took my inducement to explain anything about what exactly happened between the two of you. After a few feeble attempts on my part to seek clarification, it became obvious that he did not want to discuss the subject any further."

Looking over his shoulder at Washington, "I believe you can understand why my curiosities continue to this day. Inasmuch as Alexander has been unwilling, or unable, to put his father-in-law's mind to rest on this matter, I am hopeful that you might help ease an old friend's curiosities."

Taking a seat beside Washington before the fading, and now smoldering, embers, Schuyler patted Washington on the knee in a friendly gesture. "And there are a few more things Alexander said in his letter that I believe important for you to be aware of. He stated in no uncertain terms that it was his firm belief that your popularity was essential to the war effort and the future of America.

"If you will again allow, I quote: '*The General is a very honest man. His competitors have slender abilities and less integrity. His popularity has often been essential to the safety of America, and is still of great importance to it. These considerations have influenced my past conduct respecting him, and will influence my future. I think it is necessary he should be supported.*' He also requested my silence in the matter, stating: '*It is also said in confidence, for as a public knowledge of the breach would in many ways have an ill effect. It will probably be the policy of both sides to conceal it and to cover the separation with some plausible pretext.*' Looking up at Washington and raising his eyebrows, "I am not so sure that the *raison d'être* offered in this letter was quite as plausible to me as he hoped it would be. So, General, I trust that you can understand why my curiosity regarding this matter was piqued at that time, and why it troubles me to this day."

Washington slowly shook his head as he stood to take his turn at pacing about the room. "I can certainly understand your curiosities and confusion, Philip. And it will not comfort you to know that the letter you share with me today only perplexes me more about what was going on around me then, as well as now. Life is just so full of uncertainties and confusion. How the hell can one ever possibly think that he has any of the answers when one can't even be certain that he knows what the questions are?"

Walking in slow pace, as though searching for thoughts that might be hidden in the cracks of the floorboards, "This is not going to make sense to you now as it didn't make sense to me at the time it occurred, but let me explain my recollections about Colonel Hamilton's departure from my service in '81. When Colonel Hamilton left my family, he was angry with me for some unknown reason. Like you, I, too, was confused by his actions and therefore remember the events leading up to his departure as clearly as though they were yesterday."

Washington stopped and turned toward his guest. "As he said in his letter, I was climbing the staircase leading to my headquarters office as he was coming down at an unusually rapid pace. It was as though he were being chased by a ghost. When the two of us met midway on the staircase, he accosted me in a hushed but angry tone, accusing me of being a traitor to the cause and telling me that I was a greater risk to the nation than any enemy General ever was. As you can well imagine, I was unaccustomed to being addressed in such a manner; what he was saying was, quite frankly, incomprehensible. His words were that of a mad man, and his look was that of a desperate and frightened man. I believed him to be suffering from a lapse in mental capabilities."

Looking up from the floor toward Schuyler, who was sitting with his arms and legs crossed, "To be honest with you, Philip, it concerned me enough to cause me to reach for the scabbard I carried with me at the time. As I think back to that moment, I am embarrassed to have concluded that Alexander and I could possibly have any form of physical confrontation. And even now, I have trouble looking back at that moment and imagining it as well."

Again shaking his white head of hair, "Nevertheless, he appeared desperate, and I had no idea what action he might take. Therefore, I ordered him to leave and to return only when he could explain his absurd and injudicious behavior. Before that moment in time, I was quite fond of your son-in-law, totally confident in his abilities, and I relied heavily on his counsel. As you undoubtedly know, the man is brilliant. Up until that moment on the staircase, he was one of my most trusted advisors. However, after his inexplicable outburst of vitriol toward me, the likes of which I never before or since experienced from any man, I was, quite frankly, uncertain that I could ever entrust him with any work in my camp ever again."

Washington again joined Schuyler sitting next to the fireplace. "He soon thereafter departed, and never did attempt to explain his outburst. As you are aware, our direct association was estranged for nearly two years. It wasn't until the war neared its end that he took the initiative to reach out as a gentleman to offer me unsolicited counsel. Although he never did come forth with any explanation of what occurred two years before, his opinion and advice were so refreshing and focused, I was, frankly, glad to receive it. Our renewed relationship remained fragile for a considerable period, and we both addressed each other in cautious, more formal ways than we did before his departure. However, since then, our confidence in each other has been renewed, and I again count heavily upon your son-in-law for his sound advice. He is such an innovative and earnest young man."

Reaching out with his right hand toward Schuyler, "May I see the letter?"

After studying its content carefully, and handing it back to Schuyler, "I am sorry, Philip. But I cannot offer any further information concerning Colonel Hamilton's departure from my service or the mysteries imbedded within his letter. He seems to have since recovered from his inexplicable anger with me; I believe it best if you set the matter aside, unless he comes forward to offer additional commentary on his own about the '*key*' he refers to in his letter or the '*mystery*' the key was to '*unlock*.' I suspect that nothing positive would likely result if you should pursue this matter, which occurred over five years ago now. I've gotten over it; he apparently has as well." Smiling at

Schuyler to comfort him with an easing of tension, "I can certainly understand your confusion and interest in your gifted son-in-law. Nonetheless, I suggest that you release the demon of this mystery from your mind and not give it another thought."

Washington's invited guest then turned his attention to what he knew of the Albany meeting of interest to his host. "Let me see if I can do any better at addressing your curiosities concerning Arnold's planned meeting in Albany than you were at resolving my mystery. As you know, Colonel Hamilton is very active in the New York Chapter of the Society of the Cincinnati in Albany since its inception in '83, and meetings are often held at our home."

Lowering his head, Schuyler peered up at Washington through his bushy eyebrows. "Being the national President of the Society, I hope you do not take any offense, but for political reasons, and some concerns about the Society of a few of my more vocal constituents, I have limited my activities in the Society and do not attend many of its meetings. Nonetheless, it is not uncommon for meetings of the Albany chapter membership to be conducted in my home without my participation or involvement whatsoever."

"No offense taken. Believe me I understand."

"Thank you, Sir. Nonetheless, it was at one of these meetings last August I first heard the name '*Arnold*' mentioned as I passed by the door leading to the study where the meetings are often held. Understandably, the name caught my attention and I hesitated for a few moments outside the door to see if I could determine what was being discussed. I could not hear all of the banter, yet the name '*Arnold*' came up, time and time again, during that evening as well as at subsequent meetings.

"And, it was during one such meeting in early September that I overheard one of the members tell another that Benedict had been sent a letter inviting him to Albany in December. I also overheard them refer to something or someone as *'Brothers Pheme'* in connection with this planned meeting. Yet I had no idea who they were talking about, as I could not clearly hear everything being said.

"My anxieties concerning Alexander's involvement with the Society of the Cincinnati and Mr. Arnold increased as a result of the portions of the conversation I could hear. I subtly tried to get him to tell me about the group's activities; however, when I did so, he would only smile and offer me assurances that those at the meeting were spending more time reminiscing about their activities during the war than accomplishing anything to further the cause of either the Society's objectives or in support of the new republic.

"I thought it best not to mention the Brothers Pheme and give him cause to believe that I was paying too much attention to what was being discussed at any of their meetings. Nevertheless, by his responses, and his demeanor, I knew that he was not telling me everything. At the time, I assumed he was shielding me from knowing too much about something that could get a politician into trouble."

Washington looked directly at Schuyler. "That may very well have been the reason he didn't share more with you, Philip. He may have been protecting you from becoming involved in controversy. I have never heard of the *Brothers Pheme,* or any such person. Do you know if it was it Colonel Hamilton who arranged to have Benedict Arnold invited to Albany?"

Looking up at Washington in return, "Sir, I honestly do not know. I trust not. However, I did learn indirectly from Eliza that a meeting at the Yardarm Inn was planned for the third week of December. In November, Eliza told me that Alexander had earlier informed her that he expected to be busily occupied in a series of lengthy meetings during the third week in December that would likely require some number of overnight stays at the Yardarm's lodging.

"The inn is not all that far from our home. Just up the hill from the Masonic lodge, and not far from where Benedict was hospitalized after the Saratoga campaign. Therefore, it was somewhat unusual, to say the least, that Alexander would feel the need to stay away from our home for a number of days while yet so nearby. Subsequently, just a few weeks before the meeting was to take place, Eliza also told me that Alexander informed her that the meeting had been canceled. But in all likelihood, the guest speaker," glancing in Washington's direction, "that is how he referred to him to Eliza and not by name, he said that the guest speaker was traveling from a great distance and would likely already be on his way to the meeting and therefore wouldn't be informed of the meeting's cancellation until after he arrived."

With a shrug of his shoulders, Schuyler added: "It didn't take me long to figure out who the 'guest speaker' was. Nevertheless, I have no idea exactly who planned the meeting, or canceled it for that matter. Eliza later told me that the odd thing was that, even though the meeting was canceled, Alexander may nonetheless need to be away for a few days in the event that some of the invitees did not hear of the meeting's cancellation and showed up unexpectedly."

Looking in the direction of the floor, Schuyler sighed. "It was all very befuddled and not clear at all if the meeting had been planned, if Benedict was invited, or if the meeting was or was not going to be held. While all of this was going on, I also overheard two other state senators, whom I knew to also be members of the Society, talking about a meeting at the Yardarm Inn. At first I believed that they were discussing a meeting of a subcommittee of the senate, until it became clear that they were talking about a meeting among a select group of the Society of the Cincinnati members. It was at that time I sent you a letter informing you about the possible meeting and to let you know that Benedict may be returning to the country. I thought you would want to know, and I, frankly, had no one else in whom to confide."

"I appreciate the fact that you did, Philip. The importance of such a planned meeting, and the likely consequences of Arnold's return to this country, is the reason I invited you here today. I need to know who planned the meeting and what the motives are for his return now. When you were listening to others talk about the meeting, did anyone mention the name 'Brother Sparks'?"

"No, I don't recall anyone named Sparks being mentioned. Should I?"

"No, I was just curious if you knew of anyone by that name. I've heard it mentioned by others who have recently traveled through Albany, and I assumed that he was a member of the Society in Albany. How about the name Otis McGurk? Did you ever hear Colonel Hamilton, or any of the other Society members speak of someone named Otis McGurk?"

With this name, Schuyler did noticeably raise his eyebrows. "I do recall someone mentioning the name McGurk, Otis McGurk. I remember, because it is an odd name. But I was never able to learn anything about him or if he were a member of the Society. Does he have any involvement with my son-in-law?"

Looking to the ceiling of the room, Washington sighed. "I am not certain about him either. It is a name that I've heard others mention when they've spoken of Mr. Arnold in the past. I do not know what association he may have with Colonel Hamilton at this point. But it would appear that our Colonel, and others in the Albany Society membership, may know of this Otis McGurk and his association with Benedict Arnold as well."

Inching closer to his guest, "Philip, I need to ask for your confidence about what we discuss here today. It is imperative that our Colonel Hamilton, or any others, not become associated with our former comrade, Benedict Arnold, at this time. And I intend to address this issue with Alexander directly. I need to put this matter to rest so that he, I and others can all focus upon our nation-building efforts and achieve what has been years in the making. Your son-in-law is an important figure in helping to shape our nation's future. He and I have worked together diligently to attempt to shape a meaningful form of government that will, hopefully, serve this nation's needs."

Sliding back into his chair once again, "We've come so far and we are so close, we cannot now allow ourselves to be distracted by any involvement with Mr. Arnold. I can't imagine what Colonel Hamilton's interest in Mr. Arnold might be at this point in time, but I need to find out. I need to be assured that Benedict is not plotting a return with others, or planning some other form of disruption to our nation's efforts to right itself. If Alexander knows something about this matter, and it appears that he does, I should be apprised. If rogue members of the Society are simply attempting to exact a price for what Benedict did during the war, they need to be stopped. This is a nation of laws and vigilantism has no place in our society, no matter how justified the aims may be."

Shaking his head, "The war is over; Benedict is undoubtedly paying the price for his actions with every waking moment."

Placing one of his large hands on Schuyler's shoulder, "I know this is about your family, your daughter, your grandchildren and their father. For you and your family, this matter is indeed personal. Believe me; it is personal for me as well."

Turing away from Schuyler to once again pace about the room Washington added, "I've become very close to your Colonel over the years. Like you, I look upon him as a son as well. I believe that he may look upon each of us as fathers for the man he seldom saw. For me, he is like the son I never had. And, much like what I expect normal father-son relationships to be, Alexander and I do have our differences. Yet, the renewed bond of respect and care for each other, forged by the billows of war and political stress, remains strong."

Benedict Arnold: Legacy Lost (A Ghost's Story)

Pausing as though to collect his thoughts, "The truth of the matter is that, other than my dear Martha, your son-in-law is the one person I feel that I can confide in and trust. Every man needs to have at least one person he can place his trust in; for me, that person is Alexander. He and I have spoken to this point and he understands my feelings toward him as well. I believe he and I have settled our past differences. So if you are willing to allow me, I would like to tell Alexander of our conversation this morning and to ask him, directly, about his and the Society's involvement in any matters relating to Benedict Arnold."

Joining Schuyler once again in a chair next to the smoldering embers, Washington leaned forward with his elbows on each knee and his hands folded under his chin as if in deep contemplation. "When General Knox first conceived of the idea to form the Society of the Cincinnati at the conclusion of the war effort, I initially saw no harm. I was, frankly, of the opinion that it would be a worthwhile endeavor for any number of reasons. However, not everyone was in agreement at the time."

With a smile he added: "Certainly, Thomas Jefferson and John Adams were vocal opponents to the formation of any such fraternal organization that had a restricted membership. Ostensibly, and with intent, the membership in the Society was to be limited only to Generals, Colonels and officers of the army. Mr. Jefferson publicly argued against the Society's establishment, based upon the grounds of its resemblance to an aristocratic, closed society. It was my supposition at the time that Mr. Jefferson and Mr. Adams were insulted by the fact that, in spite of their obvious social standing, they were not eligible for membership within the Society of the Cincinnati. And I could, frankly, understand their umbrage."

"As could I."

Washington nodded in agreement. "Yes, however, in private, Mr. Jefferson also expressed concerns to me about the formation of any such organization external to the government – particularly an organization that was to have its members limited only to former officers of the former Continental Army. He confided that his true concern was that this group of military minds could prove to be a threat to any newly formed government – particularly when that government lacked any such army of its own. And frankly, I did not altogether disagree with Mr. Jefferson's expressed concerns."

With a wink of an eye, "As you may suspect, this concern was the primary reason that I agreed to serve as President of the Society of the Cincinnati. As its President, I expected to be kept informed about this group's activities. But, as you know, the span of control over any group spread out over distant parts of the country can be limited. And it would now appear that some members of the Society may be acting in the name of the Society on their own accord. If any of the Society's members are operating independently of the national charter, Jefferson's and my worst fears about this organization may then be realized. Such action would be a risk to both the Society and, in this example, the nation."

Looking away from Washington, Schuyler's words were hardly audible. "I know not about the Society's risk to the nation." After a considerable pause, "With all due respect, Sir, it would appear that I have limited option in what you do with the information I willingly shared with you today. Please know that I have unbridled trust in your judgment, and my son-in-law, regarding national interests."

Then, turning back in Washington's direction, "I have difficulties dealing with the more narrowly focused and insular matters relating to New York State issues; I cannot imagine the stress that must be upon your and Alexander's shoulders during this time of national transition. The war has ended, yet the fog of uncertainty sits heavy upon this nation. I know as well, Sir, the strain of brokering this nation's future rests heavy on your shoulders. And I know that Alexander is indeed a gifted individual who is invaluable to you in your efforts."

Benedict Arnold: Legacy Lost (A Ghost's Story)

Moving to the study's window, Schuyler peered beyond its velvet curtains looking at a more distant place. "Regarding any concerns I may have about Alex's reaction to my discussion with you on this matter...I have none. I personally believe that, within each of us, there exists two driving forces that ultimately influence our actions and reactions. One such force is guided primarily by the emotion and the other by the intellect. Although I expect that, on an emotional level, Alexander will initially think that I betrayed some amount of family trust placed in me. Yet, I am equally confident that his undeniable intellect will reign in this instance as it does in most facets of his life."

Joining Washington once again at the fireside, Philip Schuyler continued his assessment. "Based upon past more private comments and discussions we've shared with one another about the sacrifices one must be willing to make for one's country, I know he understands there are matters that transcend us all. Matters that, from time to time, require us all to put our personal opinions and lives aside. This would appear to be one of them."

CHAPTER 21

CHERRY STREET, NEW YORK
MAY, 1786

It was a typical, rainy spring day in New York as dusk arrived. The sound of gently rolling thunder could be heard in the distance when Washington's dinner meeting with Alexander Hamilton, James Madison and John Jay, ended. As the others quickly prepared to leave his home to enter their carriages before the storm and heavy rains arrived, Washington asked Alexander to stay behind. "Mr. Hamilton, can you please stay with me for a while longer? I have another matter I need to discuss with you."

Once the others left to return to their homes for the evening, Washington poured two snifters of brandy and handed one to Hamilton. "Please sit with me, Alexander. I have a few things that we need to settle."

After a few sips from his snifter, Washington began: "Alex, I know that over the years you and I have had many differences. And I know that over these same years, you may not have particularly cared for me as a person..."

With that beginning, Hamilton sat upright in his chair and started to respond to Washington's comment, "But, Sir, whatever..."

Washington was not willing to allow Alexander to continue his objection and held up his large right hand toward Hamilton's face. "Be silent for just a few moments and do not interrupt! You will have an opportunity to say whatever it is you wish to say, but before you do, I must first finish what I have to say. And I want to tell you what I know of you...just so you do not state things now that will leave me no option but to conclude that you lack true integrity and are no longer trustworthy."

Benedict Arnold: Legacy Lost (A Ghost's Story)

With a determined expression, Washington cautioned Alexander. "This is a time when you and I need to be totally, even brutally, honest with one another. This is not so much about you or me as it is about the country and our respective plans for the new Confederation. During these next few moments, you and I both need to set our pride, our personal interests and even our emotions aside. Indeed, for the remainder of this day and into our future, you and I need to be as objective and open with one another as we humanly can. If we cannot do so now, we may as well go our separate ways from this day forward and let others have their way in the formation of the next government. Do I make myself clear?"

Hamilton sat for a moment to absorb Washington's unexpected candor. Then, raising his eyebrows in a quick jerk and leaning back in his dark brown English wing chair, Hamilton raised his snifter toward his host as one would in making a toast. "To honesty and openness. And to wherever it will take us and our country."

With a slight swirling motion of his snifter, he then tested its bouquet and took a delicate sip of brandy. Crossing his right leg over his left and holding his snifter gently with his right hand, Hamilton attempted to give the impression of being relaxed and confident. "Please, Sir, let us begin."

As he settled into his chair, a clap of thunder from the approaching storm shook the room. Washington glanced upward and, raising his snifter in Hamilton's direction, adding to Hamilton's toast: "And to Providence, wherever it may take us this fateful night."

Washington then began in earnest. "You may have wondered why I asked Billy Lee to take the other household servants from the house for the evening after preparing our evening meal. Mr. Madison and Mr. Jay may have concluded that it was because I didn't want to risk anyone overhearing the conversation the four of us were having over dinner. The fact is, it was because I didn't want any other man alive to overhear this conversation. This is a conversation that will only be heard by you and me. And, this is a conversation that, if we are to be successful in our efforts, should never be repeated to another.

"I now know why you left my service during the height of the war in '81. When you accosted me on the staircase at the Windsor headquarters, I had no idea that you had then discovered that I was in communication with Benedict Arnold."

In spite of Hamilton's effort to appear relaxed, his snifter smashed to the floor when he lifted his right leg to stand bolt-upright out of his chair.

"Mr. Hamilton, as I said at the beginning of this discussion, we are to set our emotion aside – and I meant what I said. Now sit down, take a deep breath, keep your mouth shut and open your mind as well as your ears. Listen very carefully to what I say and take time to consider my words before offering a reaction." Hamilton sat back in his chair, not nearly as relaxed as he was when he first joined his host in the library.

"I want you to know that Mr. Arnold is not the Catiline you and others believe him to be. He was not a traitor to our cause. He was one of my most beneficial spies who, by his efforts, ingenuity and personal sacrifice, was able to provide information to me from the highest levels of the British military."

Washington's caution to Hamilton had not yet taken hold; again, he was on his feet. Standing agape above Washington, his eyes darted about the room, giving the appearance that he was looking for a place to run or hide. He also gave Washington the impression that he was about to faint. "I...I...You...You...You...But!"

Washington slowly stood up; placing both hands on Hamilton's small framed shoulders, gently pushed him back down into his seat. "Please, Mr. Hamilton. Again, breathe deep and clear your emotion. I'll give you a moment to compose yourself while I pour another brandy to help you through the rest of the evening."

Benedict Arnold: Legacy Lost (A Ghost's Story)

Hamilton simply did not know what to say. He just sat there, staring at Washington as he moved about the room. Flashes of nearby lightning strikes cast Washington in an eerie light as he poured each another brandy and returned to sit opposite his guest. "Here you go. Please try not to spill this one; it is one of my finest blends.

"Perhaps it would be better if I try to give structure to our situation and give you a foundation upon which you can build your thoughts and form the words you will undoubtedly choose more carefully than your blithering utterances of a moment ago." Smiling, Washington raised his glass in Hamilton's direction, "To you, Sir, I sincerely hope that you neither faint nor swallow your tongue before the night is over."

Washington took another sip of brandy; then with a more serious expression and a firmer tone of voice, he continued. "Mr. Hamilton, what we have to discuss is no laughing matter. The outcome of this evening will, in all likelihood, determine in large measure what you and I do for the rest of our God-given days. So, let me begin from the beginning.

"As you recall, not long after the Saratoga campaign, General Gates and others were actively attempting to have me replaced. My battlefield strategies were being challenged at all levels of my command, as well as by those in the Congress. When we lost Philadelphia, and after the harsh winter of '77 at Valley Forge, even I wondered if the nation would be better served with another as its Commanding General. The British spies were not my only worries. I also needed to be concerned about Generals Lee, Gates and others who were conspiring, each in their own way, to have me replaced. Turncoats were aplenty, and the intelligence that was being received from our supporters in the British ranks was becoming less reliable and more suspect.

"As you also know, once the British abandoned Philadelphia and it was again under our control, I assigned General Arnold as

Philadelphia's Military Governor to maintain control over the militia and civilian populations. At that time, he was still recovering and was unable to assume an active command. Without going into too much unnecessary detail with you about how he proposed to accomplish it, in early '79, General Arnold informed me that he believed he would be able to establish a direct line of private communication with Major John André, who, as you know, was in British General Clinton's family, and he proposed that we attempt to recruit Major André into becoming a spy on our behalf."

Washington rubbed his index finger against his nose. "At the time, I thought it preposterous to think that André would be willing to turn against his country. Needless to say, I was correct in my opinion regarding Major André's allegiances and General Arnold's efforts to recruit him were futile. Nevertheless, while attempting to do so, General Arnold came up with another plan. One that he often referred to as a 'victory plan' whereby he would defect to the British and, in time, become a spy himself."

Glancing in Hamilton's direction, "As you can attest, his efforts were somewhat successful. Although the world over believes him to be a traitor to this nation and a spy on behalf of the British, the exact opposite was indeed the case. The record will show that at the time of his apparent defection, the war had raged for more than 5 years."

Sitting back in his chair Washington added: "And a closer inspection of the record will also show that within one year of his movement to the British camp, we were able to successfully bring the war all but to an end with our collaborative victory at Yorktown."

Another bolt of nearby lightning lit up the room and framed Hamilton's expression of disbelief as the ensuing thunder shook the room.

Continuing his tale, Washington became a bit more reflective. "Once his defection was realized, one of his first objectives was an endeavor to cleanse our ranks of true loyalist sympathizers by recruiting and attempting to attract others from our camp who would be tempted to join in his apparent defection. Before that point, we had many sympathizers in our camp, and we both believed that it would be better to draw them out of our ranks if we could. However, this part of his victory plan was not so successful."

Now nodding his head, "I believe that those who may have been tempted to defect changed their minds upon hearing others talk about Arnold and witnessed the loathing everyone quickly developed for their former hero after his defection. This universal reaction toward General Arnold may have opened their eyes, and I suspect that many British sympathizers did not want to be thought of by their friends and family as a turncoat or branded a traitor as was General Arnold. His apparent defection may have, in fact, rejuvenated their interest in our cause."

Glancing in Alexander's direction, "Seeing that you are still vertical and ventilating, I will continue. General Arnold and I did have a rather elaborate means to communicate with one another, which is not important for you to know, with the exception of the following fact: the couriers used to transmit letters between our lines did not know who the letters were from or to whom the letters were ultimately to be delivered. Over time, it was a rather ingenious means of communications that no one suspected…until you stumbled upon a partially decoded letter I carelessly left hidden in my desk while at our Windsor headquarters."

While watching Alexander carefully, Washington continued with his version of events. "After our confrontation on the staircase, I returned to my office to try to figure out what was raging through your mind that caused such anger toward me. It was a phrase you used that gave me pause. You said I was a 'traitor to the cause.' This phrase led me to think about General Arnold and then I remembered the letter that I had hidden in my desk drawer in my office. As was my habit, once I decoded and read any letter from General Arnold, I always destroyed them so that no other would ever be able to uncover them. However, on that day, I was called away from my desk before I was able to complete the decoding of his cipher. When I checked the drawer upon return, I saw that it was partially opened."

Looking at Hamilton, "You see, I remember being careful to close the drawer when I was called away, and then I discovered that it was not fully closed when I returned to my office. I then wondered if I had been careless about fully closing the drawer in my haste to leave my desk. Perhaps I did not close the drawer, as I thought. I couldn't be certain. I then concluded that you could not possibly have accidentally come across the letter and I, therefore, dismissed this as a possible explanation of your otherwise mysterious actions of that day."

Raising his eyebrows, "Even when Mr. James McHenry showed me a copy of the letter you had written him at that time concerning our split, the reason for your action was not clear to me. It wasn't until more recent events involving Mr. Arnold, and a conversation I had with your father-in-law last month, that it all became clear to me."

Hamilton could no longer remain seated, "Sir, I will continue to respect your wish to keep my mouth shut for the time being, but at least allow me to move about. My body is about to jump out of its skin, and I can no longer remain seated." With that, Hamilton finished his brandy with a large gulp, placed his glass down on an end table and began to pace rapidly about the library.

Keeping his eyes on Hamilton as he paced, Washington continued. "I also know that you and others within the Albany chapter of the Society of the Cincinnati attempted to meet with Mr. Arnold last December…"

Hamilton immediately stopped his pacing, and slowly turned toward Washington. "It was you! It was you, wasn't it? You were the one. You were the one who snatched Arnold from our grasp."

"In keeping with my request for total honesty...yes, it was I. I was in Albany last December and prevented you and others from making a grave mistake and possibly exposing this nation to an untimely scandal at worst or an unnecessary distraction at best. Now may I continue to lay the rest of the foundation for your consideration?"

Without giving Hamilton any opportunity to respond, "As I was saying, after finding Benedict in Albany, he and I did meet for the first time since his departure from West Point five years earlier. During our meeting, Mr. Arnold told me that he received letters, supposedly from me, inviting him to a meeting in Albany. Knowing that I obviously wrote no such letters, I immediately thought of you as a natural suspect and likely author of such letters. You know me and my writing style better than any man alive. It was reasonable to believe that you could prepare a letter to another who would easily believe that it was from me."

Looking into the embers of the fire once again, "Then when Philip shared information about meetings of the Society being held in Albany at that same time, it was clear that you were certainly involved in this matter and, I concluded, the likely mastermind of the attempt made to capture Mr. Arnold."

With a quick pat on Alexander's right knee, Washington smiled. "The initials 'L.Q.C' used to sign the note given to Benedict when he arrived confused me for quite some time. However, once I was able to conclude that you were the author of the note given to Arnold, I knew that the initials had to have meaning of some significance, but for the life of me, I couldn't figure it out. After learning of your activities with the Society and Arnold, I then remembered. . . 'L.Q.C.': the initials of the Roman farmer, Lucius Quintus Cincinnatus, after whom General Knox named the Society of the Cincinnati. It was so subtle, yet so obvious."

Hesitating for a moment, Washington took his turn at raising his eyebrows and looked in Hamilton's direction. "It was also careless of you and presented a risk to all of our brothers within the Society. Your actions make it clear, Mr. Hamilton, you are no Cincinnatus! Your actions betrayed the cause of the Society of the Cincinnati."

"Although I was then certain that you were involved in the Arnold affair, I nevertheless still did not have any idea as to your motive, or why you would risk such an undertaking at this critical point in time. It wasn't until I met with your father-in-law and he told me of the letter you had written to him concerning our separation in '81. This was the last piece of evidence I needed to understand not only who, but why."

Resting back into his chair once again, "Mr. Hamilton, these are the facts as I know them to be. Now I want to tell you of my interpretations of these facts and give you an opportunity to comment and correct my interpretations should I be incorrect in any way."

A distant roll of thunder suggested that the storm outside Washington's home had passed them by, leaving Washington to wonder if the storm within his home was about to do the same or to brew even stronger yet.

"I believe that you did come across the partially decoded letter I received from General Arnold while at our Windsor headquarters. I believe that you may have noted that the communication was numbered – a system he and I used to track our communications so we could determine if any were missing or the delivery interrupted before another was received. I know that you did not know of Benedict's and my plans and you had no idea what the communication was about; therefore, I believe that you may have thought me to be a possible traitor as well.

"Consequently, I believe that you wrote your letters to your father-in-law and Mr. McHenry in order to distance yourself from me and to provide evidence that you could use, if necessary, to convince others that you were not involved with me as others once thought General Arnold's Aide-De-Camp, Mr. Franks, was with him.

"I also believe that you have not shared your fears with anyone else...that is, up until now. I believe that, after you recovered my trust, thereby gaining total access to my private study, day and night, you also came upon recent communications Mr. Arnold sent me concerning his interest in returning to this country to claim his rightful place among us. I believe that you intercepted our communications and, knowing our numbering system, continued to write to Arnold, as though you were me, to invite him to a meeting with you and others in Albany."

Folding his arms and stretching his legs outward, Washington concluded. "And, finally, Mr. Hamilton, and this is important for you to understand: I believe that your attempts to capture Benedict were not to put him on trial for treason, but to kill him in order to protect me or, more accurately, to protect your plans for the federalized government that we are attempting to establish."

With those final remarks, Washington stood up to pour another brandy and turned to Hamilton who was still frantically pacing about as a trapped fox would once ensnared and placed within a cage. "So, Mr. Hamilton, how am I doing in my understanding and interpretations given to your actions over these many years?"

Periodically looking at Washington, who now seated himself again to enjoy his drink, Hamilton continued to pace about the library for several minutes before saying anything.

Washington raised his glass in Hamilton's direction and smiled when catching Hamilton's glances in his direction. "Whenever you are ready, Mr. Hamilton...but I caution you. Choose your words carefully. Set aside your emotion. And be honest. If you are not honest at this time, our time together will come to an abrupt end this night. Just as it did in '81... however, at least this time, we will both know why."

Raising his glass to his lips, Washington leaned back into his chair. "Take your time, Sir, we have all evening."

Hamilton eventually stopped pacing and refilled his snifter. Sitting next to Washington, and swirling his snifter, "Well, Sir, it appears that this night will be more eventful than I ever imagined it could be. Yes, while at Windsor, I did inadvertently uncover a partially decoded letter General Arnold had apparently written to you. His penmanship is quite distinctive; although the letter was written in cipher, I recognized that it was written by his hand. I didn't take the time to study your decoded letter, but what little of it I did see led me to conclude that the two of you were conspiring against our war effort.

"I was looking for another document sent to headquarters from General Greene concerning a need for supplies that I placed in your desk drawer earlier in the day. Apparently, you placed Arnold's letter over the top of General Greene's in your haste. In keeping with our pledge of honesty and openness, I want you to know that I was not prying into your personal papers. I was only looking for the letter from General Greene that I knew to be in the drawer.

"When I saw the letter from Arnold and your partially decoded copy, I believe that my heart stopped beating; I didn't know what to think. With so much uncertainty swirling about at that time, and with General Arnold's defection just a short five months before, it was not an altogether impossible conclusion to think that you, too, were tempted to defect. I was simply flabbergasted, and when we encountered each other on the stairs, I couldn't restrain myself. I honestly do not remember my exact words, but I remember that they were not kind."

"I remember your exact words, Mr. Hamilton, and it is true, they were not kind. But under the circumstance and, in retrospect, if you truly believed that it was even remotely possible that I was considering such an act, your words were not altogether unreasonable. I was careless to leave the partially decoded letter anywhere, other than on my person."

Benedict Arnold: Legacy Lost (A Ghost's Story)

Hamilton raised his glass in the direction of his host, "Again in keeping with our pledge of brutal honesty, I must tell you, Sir, I have difficulty believing that all of what happened at West Point on the day of the General's defection was all part of a plot to get Mr. Arnold into the hands of the British…as a spy for us. With Mrs. Arnold and all that she was going through? The actual risk to the fort made by the General's intentional weakening of its fortifications? All this was all part of a plot? Shakespeare himself could not have crafted such an orchestration. What about Mr. Varick and Mr. Franks? They were suspects and, themselves, could have been hanged for God's sake."

"Although we had a plan, I admit that we did not have all the details worked out fully. General Arnold and I both understood that each of us would need to address unplanned events as they unfolded before us. Mrs. Arnold was not informed of our plan for her own sake. The General was not willing to risk involving Mrs. Arnold in the details of our collaboration; frankly, I insisted that she not be made aware of any of our plans. In fact, Mrs. Arnold was of the mind that Benedict's true motives were to defect to the British.

"And, as you may have guessed by now, Mrs. Arnold was the means by which General Arnold established communications with Major André. To the best of my knowledge, Mrs. Arnold's beliefs regarding this matter remain unaltered to this day. Yes, she did go through hell on that day, but there was no avoiding it. As for Richard Varick and David Franks: I, of course, knew of their innocence and would not have allowed anything untoward to happen to them should they not be able to mount a plausible defense."

"What about me? Was I part of your plan? I could have been brought under suspicion as well. I recall that as we were approaching General Arnold's headquarters at West Point that morning, you sent me ahead to let General Arnold know of your pending arrival. At the time I thought it highly unusual to do so, but I did as you ordered. As a consequence of my advance warning, General Arnold was allowed to escape before you and the others arrived…"

"Yes, you were part of my ploy to let General Arnold know that the time had come for him to depart. However, you were with me before, during and after his apparent defection, and there was little likelihood of your becoming caught up by any form of suspicion. As you undoubtedly recall, you were never asked to explain yourself or any of your actions concerning Mr. Arnold's defection. Your reputation remained intact and unscathed."

"Who else knows about this? You earlier stated that you had recent discussions with my father-in-law. Does Mr. Schuyler know?"

"No. Neither Mr. Schuyler nor any other man alive knows anything about Benedict Arnold's true motives or my involvement with his defection. Just Mr. Arnold, me and now you.

"However, I did need to draw out of Mr. Schuyler some additional information regarding your actions last December and those of your fellow members of the Society of the Cincinnati. He informed me about some group or individuals referred to as 'Brothers Pheme' and the planned meeting with Mr. Arnold that was to take place at the Yardarm Inn sometime during the third week in December.

"During our discussion, I informed him of my belief that you and other rogue members of the Society were apparently attempting to ensnare Arnold. But he knows nothing more. That said, I do know that he is concerned about having violated family trusts you may have placed in him by talking to me. You should know that it was his sincerely expressed wish that none of this would interfere with your relationship with him."

With the look of a compassionate father, Washington added: "Alexander, like you, and me, Philip Schuyler loves this country. And he believes well enough in each of us to be open with me during our discussion on the subject of Benedict Arnold and your actions of last

December. He also told me of the letter you wrote to him to offer an explanation for our separation. As it was with me at that time, it didn't make much sense to him, and to this day he remains concerned about your wellbeing as a result of our past separation. I suggested to him that he let the subject drop from his mind, and I make the same suggestion to you now. Neither he, nor any other individual should ever learn of the real reason for your leaving me at that time."

Washington lowered his voice and spoke with a very determined expression on his face. "Alexander, I want you to also know that if you, or any other member of the Albany Chapter of the Society of the Cincinnati, ever again act outside the Society's Charter, I will have your chapter disbanded. You, of all people should know that we are a nation of laws. If you would have been successful in your efforts to kill Mr. Arnold, you would have killed an innocent man, guilty of nothing other than sacrificing his reputation and his life for this nation."

Hamilton stared at his host for a full moment's time before responding: "Mr. Washington, Benedict Arnold cannot now return. No one would believe him or you for that matter, about what you are telling me here this evening. Even now as I listen to your words, they do not register with anything I believed to be true. Even now as I listen to your explanation, I must tell you, Sir, it does not sit well on my mind. There are too many unanswered questions; too many misplaced facts. He cannot now come into our midst."

Again pacing quickly about the room, "If he were to do so, can you imagine what Mr. Adams, Mr. Jefferson or even Misters Madison or Jay would say or think? There is not another man in this world so hated as Benedict Arnold by virtually every citizen of this nation, rightly or wrongly. It wouldn't matter what you or Mr. Arnold now say about this so-called victory plan. Others will think him guilty, regardless of what you or any other soul on this earth has to say about his or your true motives."

Pausing to think a moment, "What about the families of soldiers who were at Fort Griswold, for God's sake? They will never, ever forgive him. And, should you be linked with Benedict in any plot, regardless of its ultimate outcome, they will hang you right alongside the swaying body of Benedict Arnold. He can't return to this country now or ever again. If he were to do so, someone will certainly kill him sooner or later. And it would be the end of your public career, if not the end of your life on this earth as well."

"I agree to this point, Mr. Hamilton. Mr. Arnold must not return at this time. However, he was instrumental in our nation's victory, and the time should one day come when others learn of his actions and his sacrifice. He cannot, and I will see to it that he does not, return during this delicate time. However, the day will come when the truth will need to be told and Benedict permitted to return to his homeland."

Hamilton stopped and stared at his host. "Not now and not ever, Mr. Washington! Mr. Arnold can never return and the truth, as you know it, can never be told to any other person alive! If that were to ever happen, at that very moment of disclosure, you would be driven into political oblivion. Neither of us can allow that to happen. This nation needs you! You need to be this nation's leader. You cannot now allow yourself to be aligned in any way with Benedict Arnold. It would not only be political suicide for you, but the death of this nation as well."

Turning to face his host with a mesmeric, steely look, "Do I make myself clear, Mr. Washington? Not now and not ever."

"The truth? The truth, Mr. Hamilton? What is the truth? Is it that this nation needs me? Or is it that *you* need me?"

Standing to face his guest in return with a look that would have made Medusa proud, "From where I stand, Mr. Hamilton, the nation needs me more than it needs you. And you and your associates need me more than I need you. The harsh truth, Mr. Hamilton, is that without me, you and your federalized ideals, which I happen to share, would evaporate into eternal oblivion.

"Listen to my words very carefully. If you, or this 'brother' Sparks fellow, or if anyone else brings harm to Benedict in any way, or so much as scuffs one of Mr. Arnold's boots, I will let the truth be known. Neither you, nor your conspirators, nor the nation for that matter will then be able to use me as a buttress ever again.

"We do this together and we do it my way, or we will both suffer the certain consequence of humiliation. With our defeat, the fate of this nation will then be left for others to sculpt."

With his glistening, steel-blue eyes focused into those of Hamilton, he slowly swiped his top lip with the tip of his tongue. "Do I make myself clear, Mr. Hamilton?"

CHAPTER 22

NEW YORK HARBOR – OCTOBER, 1787
(Seventeen Months Later)

B enedict Arnold remained below deck while the ship docked at an isolated berth in the New York harbor shortly after six bells. The ship's five-man crew, including Benedict's two sons, Richard and Henry; his business partner, Munson Hayt, immediately set about furrowing and stowing sails, as well as securing the ship's shrouds, stays, and halyard rigging.

As soon as the ship was appropriately secured, Munson immediately departed to explore the docks, warehouses and city merchants to determine what goods he could purchase for the last leg of their voyage to St. John's. Knowing that it would take his partner the better part of the day to complete the tasks before him, Benedict instructed his sons and the remaining crew to seize the opportunity to discover for themselves what they could of this bustling city's treasures.

As they quickly prepared to depart the ship, Benedict gave them one final instruction. "Men, you will not have many occasions to visit this city while in my employ. Therefore, I order you to spend the entirety of this day to look the city over from the starboard to larboard. From the banks of the river to its east, to the North River on this city's western shore; I want you to gather as much information about its merchants, their goods and supplies as you can. Pay attention to not only what they have in their stock, but make note of what they don't have to offer that might be provided by an enterprising shipping merchant from another shore."

Shaking his finger in their direction, "Should any of you return to this dock before nightfall, I will presume that you did not take this task seriously and may not be cut from the cloth of a successful merchant –

and likely not worthy of remaining on this ship's muster. Now all of you, be off! Richard, before you begin your reconnoitering of this fine place, I want you to deliver this letter to a home at One Cherry Street.

"It is my understanding that it is located not far from these docks; no more than one or two kilometers to the north east, near the river's shore. Knock on the door of the house at this address and hand this envelope to the gentleman that answers. Tell him that the letter is from the Lord Sheffield and ask that it be delivered to the Master of the house. He will know what to do with it. If anyone there asks for your name, be prepared to give them a name of another. I don't want either you or your brother to use your surname while in this city. Now be off with you all. Don't forget, if I see any of you here before eight bells, you will have me to answer to for your lack of effort."

With a big smile he added, "Enjoy this city while you can my boys, but, remember, we set sail at sunrise. So don't be too tardy in your return, unless, that is, you plan on taking up residence in this fine city for the winter."

With that, Benedict cleared the ship of all its crew, save himself and three cats who prowled the ship's deck for mice or rats that may tempt to board ship from its spring or stern line rigging.

Before descending into the relative darkness of the ship's hold, Benedict hesitated on deck for a few moments to watch the sun rising higher in the eastern sky. For just a moment, he used this time alone to think back to the long-ago mornings when he frequented the docks along the Connecticut shores not far to the east of this location. With a sigh, he then retreated to the Captain's cabin to prepare for this long-anticipated day ahead, and the arrival of his guest.

Within the hour, Benedict heard footsteps on the deck above. Remaining in the Captain's cabin, Benedict listened to the sound of the visitor's steps as he slowly descended into the ships hold leading to his quarters. "Lord Sheffield, are you here?"

Benedict opened his cabin door to greet his invited guest, George Washington, and to welcome him to his floating home away from home. "It isn't much, Sir, but welcome into my most humble quarters. When one is at sea, other than a solid hull that does not leak, a calm sea, and canvas full of wind, there is not much else a sailor needs. A stark way of life aboard ship makes seafarers more appreciative of the creature comforts of a landlubber's life."

"I am not so much taken by the ship's stark furnishings as I am by its continuing movement and sounds that seem to emanate within the ship's bowels. It is as if it were alive."

Watching a cat scurry across the room in pursuit of its prey, Washington added: "I can see that the ship is indeed alive, and…" reaching up to touch the cabin's low ceiling, "…I can now better understand why most men of the sea are not tall. My only real experience on a sailing ship was when I accompanied my brother, Lawrence, to Barbados in an effort to cure his consumption. I was 19 years of age and somewhat shorter. Although my brother did benefit somewhat from the change in climate, the only thing I had to show for the experience was several days of seasickness immediately followed by a case of smallpox, followed by several more days of seasickness upon our return voyage. I expect that this early sailing experience somewhat tainted my love of the sea."

Benedict looked up at his ship's companion and laughed, "I've often wondered what I would have ever done had I been any taller or the possessor of a more delicate stomach."

Both men laughed as they sat at the Captain's table to get down to the business at hand. "Sir, there is no other aboard ship. I sent the crew ashore for the remainder of the day, but one can never know if something may cause any to return unexpectedly. Therefore, we should make our visit brief, and as productive as we can during the time that we have to ourselves."

"Agreed, Mr. Arnold. I shall get right to the point, and begin by telling you that it is not possible for you to return to your beloved homeland just yet. You will need to delay your return for at least one more year. Perhaps as long as two, or possibly even three years into the future. I know that this does not sit well with you. Nevertheless, as I've said before, you must understand that this nation is at a monumental crossroad that Providence will not likely present ever again."

With a sweep of his long arm across the table, "The path that we must now take will lead to a new order of governance, the likes of which the world has never before seen. The other path, which must be avoided at all costs, would quickly lead us back to the roots of our history – roots that are now severed as the result of our successes during the Revolution. The first path will lead to freedoms of the mind, body and soul; the second would only lead the citizens of this nation back to the yokes of subservience and control. If this was to happen, the soul of this nation would once again suffer the pains of hell."

Placing both hands on the table, Washington continued his argument. "Never! Never again damn it! By our collective efforts in the '70s, we harnessed the people's energy needed to sever ties to our country's master. And now, in the '80s, we are charting our country's course leading to a new assembly of government. By the end of this decade, this nation will arrive at its destiny. And, much like you and this ship, our country's mother ship will then be docked."

Waving his arms, in a wide, outstretched arc-like motion, "This will be the new land once again. This will be the land of the new order, and the citizens of this new nation will undergo a rebirth. This will be the time of this country's arrival at not only its final destination but its new beginning as well. Indeed Mr. Arnold, this is the making of the new world order that you, I, and the bodies of our comrades have all helped to conceive."

Slapping the top of the table with one of his massive hands, "The sails of our nation's ship are now being set and, unless we run aground on some uncharted obstacle, I believe that, within the next one to three years, we will have a new government in place that will provide the foundation upon which a great nation is to be established. Nonetheless, there are political battles yet to be waged that will enable us to bring the ship safely into harbor and to succeed in our enterprise."

Looking directly at Benedict and with a slight smile, Washington continued: "When we last spoke in December, you confided in me that you did not have the stomach for politics. And you were right. In your dealings with people, you speak your mind and tell them exactly what you think. This is not such an endearing quality when negotiating within the political arena. Such honesty is often, if not always, a detriment. No, your strength is not political affairs. Rather, you have always been well suited for more physical clashes and the management of men in a more predictable and controlled theater of operation."

Stomping his left boot on the ship's floor-planks, "The grounds upon which the ongoing political battles are being waged are neither firm, nor controlled in any real sense. But rather, they are fluid, shifting and sometimes sinking, as is the time-limited sand within the hourglass. Your presence is not needed on these battlefields. Although much deserved, and to be one day welcomed, your return to this land at this time, would only serve to undermine our efforts. General, I expect that deep in your gut, you understand why I cannot permit you, or any other man alive, to jeopardize our efforts at this time."

Saying nothing, Benedict stood up, poured each a cup of tea, and sat back down to face his antagonist. While sipping slowly from his cup, Benedict looked into the eyes of George Washington and then uttered three simple words: "So be it."

Shaking his head in disbelief, Benedict added: "Being a politician, you have a convincing way with words and, by your bearing, I know of your conviction. I suspect that you thought long and hard about what you were going to say to me on this occasion and, as I would have

220

expected, you chose your words carefully. I understand that there is nothing that I can now say that will change your mind."

With a long sigh Benedict added, "I was thirty-four years of age when this journey began; although it has all the feeling of a hundred years, I have aged but 10 years since. God willing, I hope to be around when this journey to the door of this nation's new beginning ends. Until the time arrives when my family and I can return, I will lay my head down each night to dream of the freedoms of the spirit and soul you say is to be shared by all citizens of this nation. Truly, my only wish is that these same freedoms be also shared with me and my family when time permits our return to these shores."

"The time will come Benedict, the time will come. But until then, I can tell you that you can rest somewhat more comfortably knowing that your life is no longer in danger from the group of rather spirited patriots who invited you to meet with them last December. I was able to identify the individual responsible for that effort and I convinced him of the error of his ways.

"I don't know if you would have ever heard of a fraternal organization that our good friend, General Knox, was instrumental in founding at war's end. It is called the Society of the Cincinnati. It was the General's desire to create a supportive network to assist former officers and their families as they adjusted from wartime careers to private citizens. We believed that it was important to provide our fellow officers with a meaningful mechanism to channel their energies in a positive way that would be of benefit to themselves, and their families, for generations to come."

Glancing out one of the cabin's portholes, Washington continued to describe this newly formed group. "It is a worthwhile organization, and I was chosen to be its first President. A position I yet hold to this day. The Society has chapters in each State, and among its chapters, the Society has several hundred active members…some apparently more active than others. It would appear that some limited number of

Society members living in the Albany area, took it upon themselves to address, shall we say, some unfinished business. It appears that they were seeking to make a name for themselves and the Society by bringing you to justice for what they believed to be crimes committed during time of war. As I said a moment ago, once I learned of the identity of the leader and organizer of this endeavor, I saw to it that they immediately ended their efforts."

"Who were they; do I know any of them?"

"I see no advantage of your knowing the names of any of those that were involved in this matter. What is important now, however, is that you know that I have taken steps to stop their action. However, I should also tell you that a few of those involved in the failed attempt to capture you were not members of the Society. Apparently the leader of the Albany chapter, who was the organizer of this effort, enlisted the assistance of some residents north of Albany to track your arrival into the city.

"One of those recruited was a former operative who provided intelligence to General Gates when General Burgoyne was advancing to our positions at Saratoga back in '77. This individual was apparently not outwardly aligned with either camp at the time and was, therefore, able to travel among the British encampments to our north. Consequently, he was able to provide General Gates with reasonably accurate information concerning the British's time of arrival at the Saratoga fortifications.

"This operative is the one they referred to as, 'Brother Sparks,' in the note given to you upon your arrival in Albany. As I said, he is neither a member of the Society of the Cincinnati, nor is he a fellow Mason. Nevertheless, he and three of his companions called themselves, 'Brothers Pheme.' And they joined with the Albany Society of the Cincinnati members in collaboration to capture you while in Albany."

Shaking his head, "I do not know much of anything about this Sparks fellow; the only thing that I was able to learn was that his last name is Bryan, he lives somewhere north of Albany and that he apparently has an affable personality, which it has been said that he often uses to his advantage. The leader of the Albany effort did inform me that, to protect the Society from getting its hands bloody in this matter…"

Washington paused, looked at Arnold, and then continued, "…should it have become necessary to kill you in the process of your capture, it was 'Brother Sparks' or one of his Brothers Pheme cohorts that were to be the ones to do it. They were to be your executioner if that was the only way they could accomplish their task at hand."

"It sounds so cavalier of you, to speak of it in this way…"

"I agree, and I apologize for having to be so straightforward and direct about such a subject, but that is what their plan was and I know of no other way to express it to you accurately. Having said all of this, I can nonetheless give you my assurance that the Albany members of the Society of the Cincinnati are no longer actively seeking you. They have ceased their operations altogether. You have my word on this. However, you should also know that I do not know what actions this 'Brother Sparks' person might take should your paths cross again."

Thinking back to his travels to Albany and the stops he made along the way, Benedict asked: "So, this Sparks fellow may be the death of me, you believe that he resides north of Albany, and you do not know exactly where he is from or any name that he may go by other than the last name of Bryan?"

Washington shook his head, "That is correct. There is little known about him or the Brothers Pheme group. My source was not clear in his own understanding about exactly who he was, or where he was from. Apparently, whoever he is, he was careful to remain anonymous and covert in his dealings with General Gates in '77 and his more recent dealings with the Albany Society members.

"And, frankly, they thought that, based upon what they were asking him to possibly do, the less known about him, the better. Although they didn't say specifically, I believe that should a complication have developed in their plan, the Society members would deny knowing who he was or what he was planning. If Sparks ended up killing you, that would have been fine...," glancing at Arnold, "...from their point of view, of course. And, if you ended up killing him, they would deny any knowledge about him, what may have happened, or why."

Benedict snickered, "It sounds like the planner of this contrived scheme may have been a lawyer by trade...concerned more about details of appearances and deniability of his client, and less so about the body of the first or the body of the second part. Just as long as the body is neither that of the lawyer nor his client."

Shrugging his shoulders, Washington commented: "You may be right."

Benedict smirked, "So, this Sparks fellow remains an unsolved mystery, and your Society of the Cincinnati compatriots have ceased their efforts to engage me. I hope that you will pardon my lack of jubilation, but I can't help but think that if the truth about me had been made known to others when the war ended, perhaps your Society friends would not have attempted to abduct me in the first instance. It was the delay in telling the truth about my real objectives that created the circumstance that occurred in Albany."

Standing to pace about his small cabin, "And, it seems to me that any further delay is only going to make matters worse...," bowing his head in Washington's direction, "...in my humble opinion, that is. Nevertheless, there is no changing that now.

"Now we must again weigh the balance and determine how much more time must pass before I can achieve reconciliation with my true history. Sir, I must ask, how will you even know when the time does come that I and my family can return to our home again? What will be the determining factor or factors in your mind? Knowing that there will never likely ever be an ideal time to come forward, exactly what circumstance or conditions are you awaiting?"

"That is a fair question, Mr. Arnold. And the truth is, I don't know the precise answer. You may be correct. Had we come forward immediately after the war to clear this up and had dealt with the aftermath of the revelation then, we may have been better able to endure the controversy that would have confronted us at that time. But I doubt it. We could not then, and we cannot now ignore two facts. The first fact is that in order to get you ensconced into the British camp, your reputation in this country needed to suffer.

"The more hatred your fellow countrymen held for you here, the more successful your efforts would be to convince the British that your defection was genuine. You knew that from the very beginning, and, as I recall now, it was even part of your initial strategy. Like it or not, your strategy on this measure was more than successful, and you did prove to become the most vilified person on these shores. I alone cannot be held accountable for this outcome.

"The second fact has little to do with you and more to do with me. In order for me to be successful as the Commander of the Army and subsequently to keep the reign of power within this country from falling into the hands of despots, I needed to be viewed as trustworthy and ethical. As you know, power brokers, both those in this country and those abroad, were positioning themselves to fill the vacuum of order even before the war had ended.

"Members of the Confederation were looking to the spoils of war before the last shot had been fired. Even our fellow Masons, on both sides of the ocean, had apparently lost focus of the object of our collective efforts. In all of this, I needed to be held above the fray. Both the politicians and the citizens of this land needed someone to trust; someone who could maintain their confidences of honesty and integrity."

Smiling in Benedict's direction, "For better or worse, there was no other; that someone became me. And, now, when the wolves among us are forming their packs and attacking each other for political dominance, I need to be more than human in the eyes of those who are looking for a safe harbor to trust. The time was not right before; the time is not right now for us to come forward with the truth. As paradoxical as it sounds, my coming forward with the truth, either then or now, would cause others to mistrust me more. Our countrymen and the new order are not yet able to survive this truth at this time.

"To answer your question more directly, I can tell you that our primary objective, which I believe will be accomplished within the next year, is to establish a new government structure that will establish stability for this nation. During the last four months, the members of the Philadelphia Convention created a Constitution that is designed to replace the Articles of Confederation.

"To be successful in implementing our strategy, we now need all the leaders within each of the States to come together under a single roof and pool our collective efforts to establish a more civilized society than our imperialist forefathers did. A society that values freedoms of all its citizens; a society that promotes the general welfare of all its citizens; and a just and trusting society that understands and embraces the blessings of personal liberties among its citizens.

"At this juncture, I appear to be at the apex of this effort. Having been the Commander of the Army that was successful in our effort to defeat this nation's former master, others are now approaching me to be the likely leader of this effort to establish our new order, and, if successful, to allow myself to be hoisted up to assume the dubious honor of becoming the first leader of a new nation. I am now convinced that, should I choose not to participate, or should I be found to be unworthy to lead this effort, by my deeds, Mr. Arnold, other power mongers await the opportunity to step into the vacuum and to pitch their less-noble designs for governing the citizens of this nation."

Looking downward with a frown, "Regrettably, not everyone shares values which you, I, and others believe to be of benefit to the citizens of our nation, or the societal structure that will be needed to support our newfound freedoms.

"Therefore, Mr. Arnold, I must continue to ask that you delay your return to this land a bit longer. I need to marshal all the energy I have remaining in this aging body of mine to dedicate to this effort. As much as I may care about you and your family, I cannot allow myself to be distracted by the effort it would take to safely see you home again. Once this nation is settled, its future charted and its sails are set, then, and only then, can we both come forward and see to it that you, and your family, are returned to your rightful place at the table of our feast."

CHAPTER 23

ST. JOHN'S, CANADA – AUGUST, 1791

B enedict's long-suffering patience had run its course. It has now been four years since his former commander last asked him to delay his return; eight years since his first request for the same consideration. Benedict was 34 years of age when the Revolution began; he has now entered his 50th year of life. Benedict was now convinced that he had been more than accommodating of his former commander's wishes and his country's needs.

Although reluctant, he did nevertheless give Washington the time needed to complete the journey they had begun together many years before. It is now Washington's time to grant Benedict his long-delayed journey home. In consideration of the changes that have occurred since their last meeting in New York, Benedict reasoned that there can no longer be any meaningful objection to his return at this time.

Within twelve months of their New York meeting, Washington and his associates did successfully negotiate the establishment of a new order of government within the United States. Within eighteen months of their meeting, and as Washington calculated during their last meeting in '87, he was selected to lead the new governing order of this newly created nation. As the nation's *chosen* President, Washington and his new government had since created both a Department of War and a Treasury Department.

The United States now had an established means to address any threats that might come from a foreign nation or the inhabitants bordering its western frontier. And it now had a banking system to monitor, manage and control the flow of monies within the fledgling country. Benedict had even recently heard that Vermont ratified the Constitution and was now a new member State – there were no longer just 13 colony States.

Benedict Arnold: Legacy Lost (A Ghost's Story)

"How much longer must I wait, for God's sake? I have given him two full years in office and time enough to commence the new nation's journey down its path to its worldly destiny. It is now time for me to begin my final journey down the path that is to lead to my final destiny as well. The time of my waiting is ended."

Benedict did, nevertheless, make good use of the time given to him during these same years spent in waiting, to further develop his shipping interests in the West Indies and Europe as well as Canada. In spite of the difficult economic conditions that British-American loyalist transplant citizens experienced in what was recently renamed *Upper Canada*, Benedict's trading enterprise continued to grow and prosper. It was during this time of disparate prosperity that he learned some life experiences have a way of repeating themselves.

He discovered that neither the passage of time, nor a change in location altered human nature when it came to people viewing the relative successes of others. As with his personal achievements during the time of the Revolution, the successes of his enterprising mind and boundless energy in building his shipping trade during this post-war era left others envious of his accomplishments. Consequently, without even trying, Benedict continued to be a magnet for antagonists resentful of his successes in Upper Canada and the economic station his business savoir-faire afforded him and his family. Having little else to do, a number of less-enterprising businessmen in and around his St. John's community attempted to exact a pound of flesh from their more successful competitor.

As a result, Benedict found himself spending more and more of his precious little time and energy in the courts, trying to recover payments for either loans made to others or for goods delivered, but for which he had not been paid. Benedict's endurance of the petty, small-minded members of the St. John's community was coming to an end. As was his patience with George Washington's apparent lack of effort in getting Benedict and his family back home again. For a multitude of reasons, Benedict knew that a change in his life was needed, and the time for change had now arrived.

> *"The world, my country, indeed my life, are all passing me by. Mr. Washington and his collaborators have now been given more than ample time in which to act. The time has now come for me to claim my station along with those who are to cultivate the new life order from the seeds I helped plant during the time of the Revolution."*

CHAPTER 24

PHILADELPHIA – SEPTEMBER, 1791

"Please come in, Mr. Hamilton, and have a seat. I need to discuss something with you in the strictest confidence." Washington paced about his office while Alexander Hamilton took a seat at one end of a dark brown leather Queen Anne style sofa. Alexander liked sitting in stately furniture, believing that it gave him somewhat of a regal appearance.

"Mr. President, I believe that I have demonstrated my fidelity over the years and can be counted on to keep matters confidential when called upon to do so."

"And I believe, Mr. Hamilton, that once we complete this discussion, you will have a better understanding of what true confidentiality means. It is not simply a matter of keeping this conversation off-the-record and private; it is more a matter of never remembering that it ever happened. What we are about to discuss cannot go beyond these walls." Moving to his liquor cabinet, "Would you like to join me in a glass of brandy?"

"Yes, please. It isn't often that one is offered a brandy by the President of the United States." As he uttered these words and watched the President pour two glasses from the decanter, his mind wandered back to the time he and Mr. Washington last drank brandy together. "As a matter of fact, I believe that it has been over five years since we last shared in a glass of brandy, if my memory serves."

"Here you go, Mr. Hamilton. I do believe that your memory does serve you well – New York City, fall of '86 to be exact. May I join you on the sofa?"

Alexander stood to receive his drink from the President. "Thank you. Please, Sir, of course, I would be honored to share your sofa." Smiling, he looked to the President, expecting a light-hearted moment. However, when the President sat without added comment, he could sense that Mr. Washington was in no mood for frivolity.

"Now, Mr. President, what is it that you wish to discuss?"

While swirling his snifter and initially looking directly at Hamilton, "I offered brandy for a reason, Mr. Hamilton. Do you remember the discussion we had five years ago, while in New York, regarding our former Major General Benedict Arnold?"

Hamilton looked at Washington in return to determine if his question was serious. The President had now slumped back into the sofa, staring into the drink held in his right hand. Alexander then knew that the President was deadly serious. "Yes Sir, I remember perfectly."

Continuing to stare at his drink, "You may want to set your drink down for a moment, Mr. Hamilton. What I have to say to you may cause you to react in a convulsive way, and I do not want you to spill brandy on the floor of the President's office."

"Sir, my emotions have grown steadier over the last five years; I believe I can handle anything you may have to say to me."

Shifting his eyes from his drink to look directly at Hamilton, "Well, Mr. Hamilton, if you are quite certain…I may need to ask you to kill someone…"

As Washington anticipated, Alexander was wrong about his ability to control his emotion; he lost grip of his drink as he launched himself upright from his regal position on the sofa. The glass, once in his hand which, in turn, rested on his lap, bounded upward in an arching motion over Washington's knees. However, the President was not altogether surprised by his reaction and caught Alexander's glass by the stem with his left hand as it passed over him on its downward flight to the floor.

"Pardon me, Sir!" Standing bolt-upright and erect; with a high-pitched voice, and sounding much less regal than ever before, "I know you all too well to believe that you would frivolously say such a thing. But I must ask, are you serious? Pardon me, Sir...I don't know what....who...why...what? What did you just say? Did I hear you right? Did you just tell me that you want me to kill another man? Under what conditions would you ever believe or expect that I, of all people, would agree to such an undertaking?"

Pacing about the room frantically, Alexander Hamilton looked more frightened than confused, grasping for understanding. "What? What did you just say?"

Alexander continued to mumble to himself as he paced around the room. "I know you well enough to understand that you damn well wouldn't ask this of me flippantly." Hamilton then took the drink from the President's hand and gulped it down and quickly sat down briefly next to the President. "Sir, please pardon my confusion, but are you serious?" Standing again and flailing his empty glass around, he mumbled aloud to himself: "What? What did he ask me to do?"

"Mr. Hamilton, you need to listen more carefully, I have not asked you to do anything. I simply said that I may need to ask you to kill someone. And you need to pay better attention to your drink, Mr. Hamilton. You just finished mine," holding up the snifter in his left hand, "this is yours."

Hamilton stood motionless and dumbstruck for a few seconds. He then grabbed the snifter from the President's left hand, and finished the contents of this glass as well.

As Hamilton was acting out in his own fumbling way, he did take time enough to notice that the President looked as distressed as Hamilton had ever before seen him. In Hamilton's eyes, the President appeared even more pathetic and hopeless than he did when inspecting the troops at their Valley Forge winter encampment of '77. The

President gave every appearance of looking distant and dejected – similar to the look of someone who had just lost a beloved family member or lifelong friend. It was a look that British General Charles Lord Cornwallis may have had at Yorktown, or even one that Christ may have cast in the direction of the Roman soldiers as they nailed His feet and hands to the Cross.

It was a tortured look that Hamilton never witnessed on the President's face ever before; the realization then set in. The President was serious and obviously in need of help from a friend, to say the least. Hamilton felt a momentary pang of guilt for not being more understanding of the President's needs. Not as understanding as the President had apparently hoped that he would be.

"Please, Sir, forgive me. Give me a moment to absorb your words. Let me say it myself to see if it sounds differently coming from my lips." Sitting down next to the President and taking a deep breath "You may need to ask me to kill someone…You may need to ask me to assassinate someone…You may need me to take the life of another…Is this it? Is that what you may need to ask of me, Sir?" Knowing full well what the answer would be, he needed to ask it anyway. "I may need to assassinate someone. Is this what you are saying, Mr. President?"

"Mr. Hamilton, I know what the words sound like, coming from either of our lips. It sounds no better coming out of your mouth, than it did coming from mine. And yes, that is what I said. However, I prefer not to use the word *assassinate*. That word somehow softens the effect of the action that I may need to ask of you. It is neither an honest word nor as direct as it needs to be in my communication to you. The hard, cold truth is, Mr. Hamilton, I may need to ask you to kill someone."

"Sir, would it be in poor taste, or indelicate of me at this time, to ask who you may need me to kill? And would I be given an opportunity to learn the reason why you would ask me to do such a thing? I can't even begin to recount the number of times that you have personally reminded me, this is a nation of laws. I am an attorney by training, and I know that, unless done in time of war and at the bequest of one's country, it is a crime to kill someone…and I know it is a crime to ask another to kill on their behalf as well. This is one time that I can neither be expected to function nor answer questions in a hypothetical world. In the world of life and death, I need details."

"Believe me, Mr. Hamilton, I've thought long and hard before inviting you to join me here this evening for this conversation. And, as I said before, I know both the importance of the words I use, as well as the offensiveness my words bring to your sensitivities. And I fully expected that you would need to know more should I need to ask you to perform such an unconscionable task. And I am prepared to give you as much detail as you require."

"Excuse me, Sir…I hope this does not sound insensitive. However, in keeping with your sensitivities regarding the importance of the words we use, I suggest that we continue to choose our words carefully. Asking me to perform a *task* trivializes what you may ask of me. Telling me that you may need to ask me to perform a task is one thing; telling me that you may need to ask me to kill someone is something else again."

"You are quite right, of course, Mr. Hamilton. Let me begin by telling you that, in spite of what the world may believe, including you, the war resulting from the first battles of '75 may be over, but battles for power and control of this nation are yet being waged. The cold fact is, Mr. Hamilton, that although the war among nations may be over, there are battles for power that are yet unfinished. Indeed, the more I consider the prospect of this nation's future, it may be reasonable to conclude that the battles among men who would be kings may never end.

"Although I no longer hold the title of Commanding General of the Continental Army, I do hold the title, President of the United

States. As such, I am also the Commander-In-Chief of this nation. As you very well recall, while we proudly stood on the balcony of Federal Hall in New York, I took the oath of this office. With a noticeable degree of trepidation, I said that I would, to the best of my ability, preserve, protect and defend the Constitution of the United States. Do you recall my oath of office, Mr. Hamilton?"

"Article II, Section 1. 'I do solemnly swear that I will faithfully execute the office of the President of the United States, and will to the best of my ability, preserve, protect and defend the Constitution of the United States.' You may recall, Mr. President, I helped to write it. I do remember it quite well.

"I also remember Section 4 of this same Article. It mentions something to the effect that the President of the United States 'shall be removed from office on impeachment for, and conviction of, treason, bribery, or other high crimes and misdemeanors.' As an attorney, and someone, shall we say, familiar with the Constitution, allow me to hazard an opinion that if the President of the United States asks another to kill someone, it would likely rise to the level of at least a misdemeanor."

Pacing about the President's office and shaking his head, "We appear to be at a very tenuous stage in this nation's very young history, Mr. President."

Standing to stretch his arms, "Now you are perhaps beginning to understand what I meant by our needing to keep this consideration in the strictest of confidence, Mr. Hamilton. I agree. We are at a very tenuous stage in the development of this nation's history, and its future. However, I would argue that the nation is in no more tenuous a position now than it was in the fall of '74, when the First Continental Congress met. Or no more than we were in the summer of '76, when the Declaration of Independence was signed.

"I would also argue that we are in no more of a tenuous position now than we were during the winter of '77, when the heart of this nation damn near froze and starved to death. This moment only appears more so because it faces us directly, in the here and now. It is not yet in our past. However, I can assure you, Mr. Hamilton, this, too, will soon be in our past, and it will then appear to be somewhat less tenuous to you then."

Moving again to his liquor cabinet to refresh both their glasses, Washington spoke as he poured. "Mr. Hamilton, I long ago decided that I am prepared to die so that this nation can live. I ask you, Sir, have you ever been willing to do the same for the sake of this nation?"

Turning to hand Alexander his drink, Washington was startled to discover that Hamilton had quietly joined him at the liquor cabinet. "Mr. President, I have always been, as I am now, prepared to die for this nation. What's more, I am prepared to die so that you and the nation may live on if that ever becomes necessary. Mr. Washington, I am at your service and will do whatever you, Mr. Washington, may ask of me. I may be less willing if the President asks me however. I would argue that the oath of office was intended to protect the Constitution, and not the President. They are not one and the same…if you understand what I am suggesting to you."

Washington offered a cautious smile. "I understand, Mr. Hamilton, and thank you for adding clarity. It is my sincere hope that nobody will need to die, or to kill another at my bidding ever again. Nevertheless, I ask this specific question to make a point. That being, if you and I are willing to sacrifice our lives so that this nation can live on, is there any reason to expect that Mr. Arnold would be any less willing to do likewise – should it became necessary to this nation's survival? I have every reason to believe so. Yet, should he have changed his convictions in the intervening years since the war began, I need assurance that he will not jeopardize our efforts to sail this ship of state on its proper course."

Washington offered a concession to Hamilton. "You may feel a twinge of satisfaction in knowing that I have now come around to your original way of thinking on the matter regarding Benedict Arnold. I may need assurance that Mr. Arnold will not present a threat to me, or this nation. I once thought that this matter was personal; just between him and me. And perhaps it once was. However, I now realize that it is more than that. As President, it would appear that nothing I say or do is personal, and I will do whatever necessary to preserve, protect and defend this government.

"If, by his intended actions, Mr. Arnold presents a threat to me, and in doing so, a threat to this government, it is my obligation to do whatever necessary to eliminate the source of the threat to this nation. I believe it a reasonable interpretation of the powers granted to the Commander-in-Chief, if not the President. What's more, I believe it is also my responsibility to do so."

"Now you are beginning to talk like an attorney, Mr. President, which, I must confess is somewhat disconcerting to me. And you are dead wrong concerning the powers that the Constitution intends to grant to the President as Commander-in-Chief. However, rather than you and I spending time debating the powers given to your office, why don't you just tell me what Mr. Washington is dealing with and allow me to be of assistance to him in bringing this matter to an end. Do I now make my point clear, Mr. President?"

CHAPTER 25

VAN DERWERKER FARM
SATURDAY, OCTOBER 8, 1791

The morning sun crested a distant hillside overlooking Martin Van Derwerker's farm, igniting nature's brilliant fall palette of deep reds, shades of brilliant yellows, and orange among the leaves of the sugar maples, common in the north country. Gentle autumn winds caressed sleepy trees, causing their leaves to quietly flutter to the ground around Martin and his young nephew, John, as they walked from the barn to their home after finishing their early morning chores.

"It is going to be a long winter, John. When the harvest comes early, like it did this year, and the leaves change colors so quickly this early in the season, we know that we are in for a long, cold winter ahead."

While listening to his uncle and the crunching of dried leaves under their feet , young John pointed in the direction of a rider approaching their home, "Who is that, Uncle Marty?"

"I don't know, John. Take your log for the fireplace into Aunt Martha and I'll see who it is."

As always, John did as he was asked, and Martin awaited the arrival of the slowly approaching rider. Martin watched the leaves swirl about the hooves of the horse while trying to get a good look at its rider. From a shorter distance, the rider raised his right arm to wave. Now recognizing the rider, Martin's heart sank. He could tell from the stature of the rider, and his dress, that it was his long-ago friend, Benedict Arnold. Martin did not return Benedict's wave, but simply stood motionless and in silence as Benedict approached.

Although Benedict did write to Martin several times since his last visit, he had not received a single word in return from his former comrade-in-arms. It was not like Martin, or his wife, Martha, to leave a man wondering for these many years. After several unsuccessful attempts to communicate with his long-lost friends, Benedict became increasingly concerned about their well-being. In spite of past events that have occurred in Benedict's life during this time of year, fall in the northeast was always Benedict's favorite season.

Having planned an October 23rd meeting with his former commander in New York, Benedict opted this time to ride from his home in St. John's to New York so that he could enjoy the fall scenery, and take another opportunity to stop along the way, and check in on Martin and his family. "Well, well, you are still here I see. I've tried to write you and Martha several times over the last six years but never received a response from either of you. I was afraid that something may have happened to you, but I'm glad to see that I was wrong. It is good to see you again, my friend."

Martin stood there, appearing thunderstruck. In his usual manner when not knowing quite what to say, he said nothing. Behind him, he could hear the cabin door slowly open and Martha and John's footsteps as they walked to the porch's edge to see who their visitor might be. Martin and Benedict both looked toward the porch as Martha rushed John into their home, quickly closing the door behind them.

Expecting a somewhat more friendly welcome, Benedict was confused by the obviously cold greeting extended by his friends. Hesitating for a few moments and remaining on his horse, Benedict glanced around Martin's farm. It looked the same as he remembered it. Wood piled neatly in rows next to the cabin's entrance where it could be easily retrieved during cold winter days ahead. Cattle, horses, and pigs all in their pens; the open door of the barn's loft showed that it was well-stocked with straw for the livestock's winter feeding. Chickens wandering about the barn yard with their normal carefree cackle, looking through the leaves for whatever it is that chickens look for while roving about.

The only difference Benedict could readily discern was that rather than three barking dogs, there now appeared to be only one. Expressing little interest in the visitor as well, and lacking any apparent energy, the solitary dog remained in his napping position on the porch, near the cabin door. The only sign of life was in his eyes. Both wide open, and trained upon the new visitor.

Benedict's attention was then drawn to the cackle of a large crow sitting on top of the chimney of Theresa and John's cabin. As he turned to look in the direction of the crow, it and another smaller crow flew off into the distant woods, leaving Benedict to stare in the direction of Theresa and John's cabin. It then struck him. It was different.

Leaves and debris had accumulated on its porch and dead, leafless vines could be seen clinging to its exterior walls, and over the cabin's windows. Benedict noticed that one of its windows was broken and another had been boarded up. The logs of the cabin even looked dust-grey in color, and the cabin itself gave every appearance that it had been neglected for years.

It looked dark, empty and lifeless. Unlike Martin and Martha's cabin, there was no smoke coming from the chimney of Theresa's cabin. A more careful look showed that a crow had built a nest, and apparently taken up residence, at one time or another on top of the chimney. Everything about the cabin led Benedict to conclude that Theresa and John had moved away. Yet, John was obviously still here.

Benedict slowly dismounted and approached Martin. It was clear that Martin was uncomfortable by his very presence. Not wanting to create any more of an awkward moment for his friend, and, seeing no point in exacerbating his obvious discomfort, Benedict was perceptive enough not to extend his hand in friendship this time around. "What is

241

the matter, my friend? It is clear that you and Martha are not as pleased to see me as I am to see the two of you. That is quite obvious. Is everything okay? What is it that is troubling you so?" While he questioned his friend, Benedict noticed tears swelling up in Martin's eyes.

"Oh, Ben, I truly don't know what to say. The truth is, no. Everything is not okay. It might be best if you just got back on your horse and left us. Please, Ben, don't ask any more questions. Just turn around and leave."

Benedict was staggered by what he was hearing; now, like Martin, he, too, didn't know what to say in return. Nonetheless, he knew that he could not honor his friend's request and now simply turn and ride away without knowing what was going on, and without knowing how he could be of help to Martin and Martha with whatever it was they were dealing with. "What is it, Martin? What is troubling you so? You can't expect me to simply ride away now without knowing what, if anything, I can do to help you and Martha with whatever it is. What is it I can do to help?"

"I told you, Ben. The best thing you can do is to turn around and go back to wherever it is you came from. Leaving us alone would be the best thing you can do, for all of our sakes. Please Ben, I ask you again to just leave."

Removing his tricorn hat and rubbing his forehead while shaking his head in disbelief, "I can't do that, Martin. Tell me what is going on."

"I know that you are a good man, Ben; even a God-fearing man. But, for reasons that nobody can really understand, sometimes bad things just seem to happen to good people. And it seems that there are some people that simply can't avoid it…it would appear that no matter what you do, or try as you might, bad things are just going to happen to you, and to those around you. I don't understand it. I doubt that anyone can understand it. It just is. Wherever you are, and wherever you go, bad things just seem to happen. You can't be held to blame. It really isn't your fault. Not really, it just happens."

"Martin, you're rambling and not making any sense at all. What the hell are you talking about?"

From inside the cabin, Martha could no longer contain herself, "It's Theresa! Theresa is dead! It's John! He is dead, too! You came here six years ago, all nice as could be, and within a year, my niece and her son were both gone. Both of them were taken from us by your hand. You are not welcome here any longer. Just do as Martin asks, for God's sake, and leave!"

"What do you mean they are *dead*? I just saw the lad a moment ago. He's in the cabin with…" Benedict stopped before completing his words. It then struck him. Although he assumed the boy he saw with Martin, and then Martha on the porch, was John. It now occurred to him that the boy he just now saw looked to be about the same size as John did, *six years before*. How could this be? He would now be nearly twice the age and likely twice the size of the boy he had just seen.

Martin looked up at his confused and frustrated visitor, "Sir, there are some things that are better left unsaid. What happened is not important any longer. It just happened and now they are gone. Please, Ben, just get back on your horse and leave. You, Martha and I would all be better off if you just turned around now and left…"

Before Martin could finish, Benedict quickly hobbled up the steps leading to the cabin, opened the door and stepped inside. "Martha, what is going on? Why are you and Martin asking me to leave without telling me what happened here? What happened to Theresa and John? Why are you telling me that they are now both dead, for Christ's sake?" Looking at the young boy poking his head from behind Martha's dress, "And who is the boy if that isn't John? Can't anybody tell me what the hell happened here?" Pounding his fist on the door of the cabin, "I demand to know what is going on! I will not leave until my questions are answered!"

In a soft, almost mournful voice, Martin looked downward as he walked up the porch steps. "You are not in a position to be demanding anything more from us. We have given quite enough. Like I said, Ben, some things are better off not said. Believe it or not, there are some things in life that we are better off not knowing. I am telling you now, Ben, just leave. I am no longer asking you, I am telling you. Get back on your horse and leave."

Benedict covered his face with both hands; turning first to Martha and then to Martin, he shrugged his shoulders and with a soft, pleading voice, "Just tell me how I can help. That is all I want to know."

Martin moved to his wife's side. "I am sorry, Ben. I truly am. I know you mean well, but if you really want to be of help, you can just leave and never come back."

Looking again at Martha, and then the boy, Benedict dropped his head, turned and started to walk down the steps leading from the porch. When he reached the first step, Martha buried her head in her husband's chest and burst out crying. "John drowned trying to sail the damned ship you gave him! Theresa died giving birth to your son!"

Martin was bewildered by his wife's sudden outburst. "No, Martha!"

Looking up at her husband, "Why shouldn't he know, Martin? Why should he be able to just walk away and never know the heartache he brought to this family? Why should he be sheltered from knowing the truth? The truth is what the truth is. Why shouldn't he know? For God's sake, we've suffered with the truth all these years."

Pointing in Benedict's direction, "Why should he be allowed to just walk away not knowing? And not letting the man even know of his son's existence is a burden I can no longer accept. He has a right to know. No more secrets! No more lies! Tell him the truth, Martin; just tell him the damn truth. Why must it be so difficult to simply tell him the truth?"

Benedict stopped and stood in silence, still looking away from the cabin's door; with his back yet in Martin and Martha's direction. "Martha, what did you just say? John died trying to sail the ship I had given him? And Theresa...Theresa died giving birth...to a son...," slowly turning to face them, "...to my son. Did you say my son, Martha?"

Martin held Martha in his arms as she sobbed. Turning her head toward Benedict, she nodded. "Yes, Benedict, that is what I said, your son."

From behind Martha's dress, the young boy timidly peaked out at the man now standing before them.

Looking at the boy, "This is Theresa's son? This is my son?"

Martin looked up. "Yes Ben, this is your son, John." Looking to the young boy at his wife's side, "John, this is your father, Benedict Arnold."

Slowly stepping from behind Martha; with a soft, angelic voice, the boy introduced himself. "How do you do, Sir? My name is John. Why are you making my Aunt Martha cry?"

Looking first at the boy and then to Martin and Martha, Benedict asked, "Why didn't you tell me? Why didn't you want me to know? I am so sorry Martin...Martha, I don't know what to say...I – I – I just don't know what to say." Raising both arms toward the heavens, "I simply cannot believe that all of this is even possible. It can't be happening and I must be dreaming..."

Holding his wife after she picked the boy up in her arms, Martin looked at Benedict. "It is not a dream, Ben. Our lives are real. Theresa and her son's deaths were real, and John here is real. There is nothing more to say, Ben. That is the reason we never told you anything. There is nothing anybody can say or now do that can change the past. We've adjusted as best we could and are getting along just fine. There is nothing more to say and there is nothing more to do. Other than you now getting back upon your horse and leaving us."

"Is that really what you want me to do? Is that what you want me to do to the boy…to the boy you are just now telling me is my son? Simply leave? Is that what Theresa would want me to do? I can't believe it. There was only one time…not that it matters, but the circumstance that your loving and caring niece found herself in was not all of my doing alone. Is this what you think Theresa would want of me? To now turn my back on her son, and simply walk away? To now turn my back on both you and the boy, and to simply walk away? Is that what you need? What about the boy, is that what he needs? It is true, as you say, there is nothing we can say that will change the past. But perhaps there is something we can, and should say now that will possibly benefit this boy's future…Theresa's son's future."

Benedict's back slowly slid down a rail that supported the porch roof and he sat at the top of the stairs, facing away from Martin, Martha and his son. "I know my words now sound hollow, Martin. But I am truly sorry for the heartache and pain my very existence has brought to your family. I know that I cannot change what's happened, but isn't there something more I can now do to help in some way? What I did, I did from kindness and caring for both John and Theresa. Please take at least a few moments to reflect on what you would ask of me now. In your considerations, I ask that you to open your heart and be a bit more understanding. Show me some compassion."

He placed his hands over his face as he continued with his plea. "For God's sake, put yourself in my place and repeat the conversation we just now had. What would you do? Would you simply turn your back and walk away from a son you just met? A son you were not even aware of for the first five years of his life and never before told of until now? Is that truly what you would do? Is that truly what you expect of me?"

Benedict stood and turned to face them all. "Take some time to just think this through from my eyes for just a second...What would Theresa do if she were here?"

While still holding onto John, Martha looked first into the eyes of her husband, and then into those of the boy. Ever so slowly Martha kissed the young boy's cheek, assuring him that it was all right, and then turned to put John down in front of her. Wiping tears from her face with her apron and taking a second to compose herself, Martha then looked to John. "John, this is your father. Mr. Arnold, this is your son." With a gentle touch on the boy's shoulder, Martha nudged John in his father's direction. Young John's eyes were wide as he tried desperately to understand what was happening around him as best he could.

The young boy stood silent for a few moments exchanging glances with Martha, Martin and this stranger who was now being introduced to him as his father. And, after a fashion, the boy shuffled his brown, dust covered boots and then walked slowly toward the stranger. As he approached, he extended his hand upward, in Benedict's direction. "I am pleased to meet you, Sir."

Benedict slowly reached down to touch the small, soft hand of the child. Touching his son for the first time in his life, Benedict looked into the boy's hazel green eyes; fell to his knees, and hugged the boy. "This is all so bewildering for me. I can't even begin to imagine how puzzling all of this must be for you, little guy. I am so pleased to meet you, too." Looking with tear-swollen eyes toward Martin and Martha over young John's shoulder, Benedict silently mouthed the words, "I'm sorry. I am so sorry."

CHAPTER 26

VAN DERWERKER FARM

Martha and her husband did permit Benedict to stay a while longer, giving him time to get to know his son and for them all to determine what more would need to be said or done concerning their unique and unusual circumstances. It was an awkward day for everyone, not the least of whom, John. Only five years of age and trying his best to understand who this man was, and how this stranger fit into all of their lives. The only thing he ever knew about his parents was what he had been told over the years, and for as long as he could remember: his mother died shortly after his birth and his father was a great man who had fought during the Revolution...whatever that was.

During the day, Benedict learned that Theresa's father had passed away shortly before her second son was born; Theresa's mother had died several years before that. Consequently, after Theresa's passing, the orphan child spent his entire life in Martin and Martha's care. The young boy's mind only knew that the people who loved and cared for him most were neither his mother nor his father, but those he called Aunt Martha and Uncle Marty. It was apparent, by his shyness and his inquisitive glances in Arnold's direction, he didn't really know what to think about this new man who had just now come into his life – a man who somehow made Aunt Martha cry and Uncle Marty very nervous.

After Martha tucked young John into bed in their loft, she then made a pot of tea as was their custom during the brisk fall evenings after John went to bed. Pouring each a cup, Martha joined her husband and Benedict, who were sitting next to their fireplace, speaking with hushed voices so as to not disturb John, or to be overheard. Looking at her husband and Benedict Arnold as they talked, Martha thought back to the first time they all sat together, at this same fireplace, talking about other difficult days in their past. Days which, when compared with those filled with more recent tragedies, now seemed significantly less troublesome by comparison. As she sat, Martha offered the observation, "What a difference a few years can make in our lives. What a difference a few years can do to change what we believe to be of importance."

Looking up at Martha while taking his cup, Benedict sighed in return. "You are so right, Martha. You don't know how right you are." Turning to Martin, "Why didn't you tell me, Martin? Why didn't you tell me what happened? I still can't believe it. Can you tell me now, what did happen? What happened to Theresa's first son, John? When and how did the poor lad die?"

"We simply didn't know what to say Ben. So we said nothing. In the early spring following your visit, it appears that John took the ship you gave to him the previous Christmas and tried to sail it in the pond behind the barn. Theresa had sewn a wonderful set of sails that I mounted on the masts you had made for it. It was indeed a majestic looking ship; Theresa and John displayed it proudly on their fireplace mantel. One early spring day, Martha and Theresa were taking care of a sickly neighbor and I was busy repairing a fence line...," hesitating and thinking back to Benedict's first visit, "... that had been damaged by a tree limb that fell during the ice storm we had during the winter of your visit.

"Apparently, while I was not paying attention to the poor boy, or his comings and goings, John took the ship from the mantel, and took it to the pond. We don't really know what happened, but it would appear that the ship may have gotten away from him and we suspect he tried to retrieve it; while doing so, we believe that is when he fell into the pond. The water was still frozen over in parts and must have been God-awful cold.

"I thought that John was in his cabin all the while I had been working on the fence line. It wasn't until later in the day after Martha and Theresa returned home and asked me where the boy was. He wasn't in his cabin or ours, and John never before wandered far from the farm. John was like a faithful dog, seldom out of sight and never far away. Realizing that I hadn't seen him for quite some time, it was at that point that we feared something was wrong. We looked everywhere and yet we couldn't locate the lad. Then, while searching John's loft to see if he had fallen asleep, Theresa looked down toward the fireplace, and noticed that the ship was not on the mantel where it had always been kept..."

Benedict noticed Martha wiping tears from her eyes as Martin continued his story. "When I reached the pond behind the barn and, as I hoped and prayed, I didn't see anything – at least not at first. Then I noticed the small footprints in the softened mud, near the pond's edge." Looking at Benedict with tear-filled eyes, "I can still see it in my mind's eye, as though it were just yesterday. His little, blue fingers, grasping the edge of the ice from below the water's surface..." Martin looked away for a moment to compose himself before continuing. "When I pulled him from the pond, he still grasped the ship you had made for him in his right arm..."

Martha continued when her husband could no longer. "We were all so devastated. Theresa, God bless her, could no longer stay in her cabin alone, so she moved in with us that night; , after that day, poor Theresa never again entered their empty home. It remains today pretty much the way it was when John last left it. And as fate would now have it, as Theresa last left it as well."

Martin then spoke up, "It wasn't long after when Theresa told us she was expecting a child. Since her husband's death in '77, we knew that she never since had another man in her life. It didn't take us long to figure out what must have happened during your visit the previous December. Frankly, Ben, you should know that, after John's death, the prospect of giving birth to another child was a Godsend for Theresa. She was as excited as a woman could be under the circumstances."

Martha added, "There was no replacing John, of course, but knowing that she would one day have another child to care for, gave Theresa a purpose to live, and something to look forward to as well. So, as you can well imagine, with a strange and confusing mix of sadness, regret, and apprehension along with a tinge of excitement, we all awaited the arrival of Theresa's next child. Shortly before she gave birth in September of '86, Theresa informed us that she was going to name the child John if it was a boy and Johanna, if it was a girl. She had picked the names in memory of both her husband and their first born."

Martin commented, "Yet, as I said before, sometimes bad things just seem to happen to good people. Theresa's and our joy was short-lived. After giving birth, we just couldn't stop the bleeding and, within two days, she too was gone...Then there was just the three of us – Martha, me and baby John. We did the only thing we could; John became ours to care for and raise as our own."

Martha then spoke up again. "The truth is, Ben, we didn't know what else to do. By the time we received your first letter, John had drowned and Theresa had not yet given birth to her next child...to your child. And naturally enough in your first letter, you asked about John's and Theresa's wellbeing. You even suggested plans for the poor boy's future, mentioning that you might one day take John with you on one of your sailing ships, and perhaps even to London..." Looking downward, she fondled her apron as she spoke, "...It was painful for Theresa to read your letter. Writing about him as though he were yet alive and planning for his future, it was like your letter brought John back to life again. We all knew that you had no way of knowing. And Theresa told us in no uncertain terms, as you may well imagine that only she could do, she didn't want you to know about John's death or how it happened. And, at that point, she did not yet want you to know about the baby either."

"So my letters went unanswered."

"Yes. Your letters went unanswered. Given Theresa's wishes before she gave birth and then, when she died, Martin and I simply decided that it would be best if nothing was ever said about John's death or the birth of her second child. We thought that we would just live our lives, doing the best we can for John, and you would live the rest of your life without ever knowing anything about either of the children, or Theresa. There really wasn't any reason to make our lives, or yours, more complicated than they already were."

Benedict sat in silence for several minutes before standing to add another log to the embers of the fire. While standing near the fireplace hearth and watching the newly added log burst into flame, "Life is so damn complicated. More so than I can ever possibly understand or explain. I am often conflicted with myself and my life. I am not even going to try to explain. It doesn't really matter anyway.

"Mine is a life of contrasts between beauty and blessings and one of destruction and damnation. I spent all of yesterday walking the fields, not far from here, where Theresa's husband and hundreds of other good young men, on both sides of the line, lost their lives. It was exactly 14 years ago to the day that I was wounded on these same fields. As I walked through the grassy knolls, I tried to better understand what happened on that stage."

Looking downward, "And, not knowing of their fate at that time, I thought as well of Theresa and John; the hundreds of other wives, mothers, fathers, sons and daughters who lost loved ones on those consecrated grounds. There was a time when I thought that I could never visit these fields of devastation and despair, knowing what happened there. However, as I walked these same fields yesterday, I was astounded by the peacefulness of that place. I couldn't help but contrast the events of '77, and the beauty of nature that has now laid claim to these fields. Herds of deer now graze the grounds by the hundreds. Hawks circle majestically in the blue sky above, looking for mice, squirrels and rabbits; the scavenger crows are more seldom seen.

"I even found the location of the redoubt where I received my wound. Although once a place of death, destruction, and pain, it is now nothing more than a pleasant, grassy field. As I lay on that spot with my spine to the cool earth beneath, I was surrounded by heavy grass. I listened to the melodious call of the cicada that accompany most hot summer days and I watched again the hundreds of geese flying overhead on their way to their winter home, just as they did in '77, and will likely do for centuries to come. I listened as well to their melodic honking, carried by distant winds as they approached, passed overhead and flew on to the distant horizon. It was beautiful.

"Yet, as I walked these fields I was also confronted by the reality of what happened there. Every now and then I came upon the un-interred bones of poor, nameless souls who were hastily laid to rest in shallow graves. Such a sight provided me with a stark contrast between the now peaceful, still and quiet fields and the deafening mayhem that had occurred on these same fields a mere 14 years before.

"Of all the places in this world that I have ever been, either before or since, with the only possible exception being the hospital in Albany, this single location contributed most to my life and all that has happened to me thereafter. These are the fields where the journey leading me to this spot, and to this time, began. Had it not been for what happened there, I would not now be standing here. Had I not been wounded there, I would not have taken the paths that ultimately led me to your doorstep last December, or now for that matter…"

He hesitated and slowly shook his head, "Had I died on those fields, along with Theresa's husband, she and John would yet be alive. I survived then; consequently, Theresa and John are now dead." Then, looking into Martin's eyes, he added, "I don't understand, Martin. It is not right…it's just not right…."

Turning away from Martha and Martin, Benedict continued. "Just yesterday, I truly thought that I was finally at peace with myself. So much so, I spent the night sleeping under the stars, on those same fields, praying to my God for a better understanding of why some men die while others, like me, live on. Asking as well, why some must die so that others can live. And that was before I knew of Theresa and John, for God's sake. I never thought to ask why I yet live so that others *will* die.

"As I gazed at the heavens last evening and listened to the songs of the crickets, I again heard the cry of the wolves… a sound I shall never forget. A sound I last heard on these same fields when the battles were done and the wolves foraged on the bodies of men not yet buried and other poor souls wounded, not yet dead." Turning toward Martin, "I suspect that you, too, remember the sounds to which I refer…"

Martin did not look up, only slowly nodding his head as Benedict continued to tell of his visit to the former battlefields not far from his home. "What neither of you have any way of knowing is that, ever since that time, one of my constant nightmares was hearing wolves howling and of men screaming as they were being eaten alive. What you don't know as well is that it was this same nightmare that I had when Theresa was apparently awakened by my restlessness, causing her to come to me…and to comfort me."

Hanging his head, "She was so kind, so compassionate and so understanding. She never lived long enough for me to tell her that ever since that evening, I have never again been visited by wolves in my slumber.

"The irony of all of this is that while I lay there under the thousands of stars last night, I foolishly believed for a moment that I was finally at peace with myself and all that has occurred with me in my life. For a fleeting moment, I actually believed that I was going to soon have order once again restored in my life. Ever since I was a young boy, I've always wondered why I was here, in this world, at this time and no other. I've always wanted to know what God's plan was for me, or if He even had a plan for me at all."

Standing to pace about the cabin as he spoke, "And, you may find this unexpected of me, however, ever since I was a boy, I've prayed for His guidance as well, undoubtedly not as often as I perhaps should have. But nonetheless, whenever I've been in need of direction, or confused by what action I should take, I typically looked to Power, whoever, or whatever, such Power may be. There were times, like this, when I would've even settled for a clue."

Stopping to rub the back of his neck, "Invariably, when I've done so, I usually received two feelings in return. The best I can do at describing them are the words 'understanding' and 'compassion.' I've always interpreted these feelings to suggest that I should be more understanding and more compassionate toward others. Sometimes it worked, sometimes it didn't; at least as far as I could tell at the time. What I am trying to say is that today I asked for your understanding and I asked for your compassion when I was trying to deal with all that you were telling me. And I thank you for your consideration in return."

As he paced about the room, Benedict's shadow moved across the walls of their cabin from the light given by the fireplace. "Yesterday and last evening was so beautiful, and I thought that I was finally at peace with myself. I thought that, at the center of my being, I was again in balance. And now today! Is this part of His plan for me as well? Was it my destiny to be an angel of death for Theresa's first son, and then Theresa as well? When one least expects it, Power has a way of turning us upside down, and inside out.

"When am I to no longer be the instrument of death for any other? Here I am! Still among the living! And, because of my very existence, both Theresa and her son are no longer here. The lad in the loft has no mother, and he has been cursed with me for a father." Covering his face with both hands and then looking upward with both arms reaching for the ceiling, "This just can't be. Why do I continue to devastate and destroy those that I care about? Why do others die at my hand, while I continue to live on? Why?"

Walking to the front of the fireplace and turning to face Martin and Martha, Benedict lowered his head and stood in silence, his face hidden by a deep shadow. After several moments, and seemingly without moving a muscle, Benedict simply mumbled, "I need to be alone. I just don't understand. Please excuse me."

Raising his head, Benedict walked to the table, picked up a candle and went outside. As he turned to walk away, Martin and Martha could see the glimmer of tears on Benedict's cheeks reflecting the yellow glow of the candle.

Martha and Martin watched out the window as Benedict walked to Theresa and John's cabin. They watched as his hand slowly pushed open the door leading into Theresa and John's cabin. After staring into its darkness for some time, Benedict walked into the cabin, slowly closing the door behind him.

Watching Benedict enter Theresa's cabin, Martha turned to her husband and softly whispered, "The wretched soul. What must it be like to walk down his path? Perhaps the poor man is cursed."

CHAPTER 27

VAN DERWERKER FARM

Benedict slowly looked around the empty cabin as he entered. In the dim light of the solitary candle he carried, it looked ever-so-much the same as it did several years before, when he last stayed as a welcomed guest. Walking to the table, he noticed the cobwebs and thick film of dust that had formed on virtually everything. Blowing the dust and cobwebs from the oil lamp still located near the middle of Theresa and John's dining table, Benedict removed its glass globe, turned up the wick and lit it from the flame of his candle. While studying its flame to see if the wick was going to remain lit, Benedict wondered who had been the last to extinguish its flame. *Was it Theresa, herself?* To his surprise, the lamp remained lit in spite of the time that had undoubtedly passed since its last use.

Slowly pulling back one of the chairs at the table, Benedict sat down and looked about the room, waiting for his eyes to adjust to the relative darkness in the corners of the now empty space before him.

With his head bowed and in a deep, somber voice, Benedict spoke, "I don't know if you can hear me, Theresa. I don't know if you can hear me, John. I don't know if anyone or anything can hear me…but I am here, Theresa, in your home. I am here in the home which you provided for your son John, and offered him your loving mother's care. I am here, in the place in which you planned to make a home for our son, John." Looking upward, "He is beautiful, Theresa. John has your eyes. When I looked into his eyes today for the first time, I swear I could see you, looking back at me." Casting his eyes downward once again, "Regrettably, for the boy, he also has my nose…"

Now standing next to the table, "Theresa, I don't know what to say. The words, *I'm sorry*, can't even begin to approach the depth of my feelings about what happened here. Words alone are not enough, and so I am here. I've come here to listen. I've come here for your help. If ever there is a place where I can learn from you, this is it. This is the space in this living world that you made into your home. Come to me, Theresa, and tell me, tell me what I should do. Please help me, Theresa. Help me to understand what you would want of me now. How can I now be of help to your dear Aunt Martha and devoted Uncle Martin? What can I do for your son, for our beautiful child? I am so sorry about you and your husband's dear child John. He was such a lovely lad. I knew you were so proud of him, as you had every right to be. Please forgive me, Theresa. Forgive me for what I have done to him. And for what I have done to you. My soul asks for your mercy and your forgiveness. What can I do? I know that we do not walk this earth alone. I know you are here. I can feel you. I know you are here and I am not afraid. If there is a God, Theresa, come to me now and help me to know what I should do."

Hesitating and searching for words that could somehow express his feelings, Benedict looked about the room. He noticed a quilt on the table. It was the same quilt Theresa had begun to make before his first visit six years ago. He touched it gently, remembering the first time he had seen it. Although it remained yet unfinished, he could tell that Theresa had completed more of it than when he saw it last.

He then brushed dust off the cover of a book that was sitting on the table, next to the quilt. Benedict picked the book up and held its cover to the light of the lamp and read the title aloud, *"Meditations and Contemplations."* He remembered that it was the same book he had seen on this same table during his first visit as well. Holding the book to his chest and looking around the room, he remembered holding it and glancing through its pages while Theresa was busy making up his bed for his first night's stay…"Oh, Theresa. I am so sorry…This room was once a home by your presence. I know this is a place of power for you. It was so warm and lovely. Everything in it was blessed by your loving touch. It was so welcoming; it was so much a part of you. Everything in this home was more than simple furnishings. Everything in here was a part of you and a part of John. And now, it feels so empty; so void of any feeling."

Looking around the room as he spoke, his eyes caught the glimpse of a shadow on the wall above the fireplace....It was the shadow of a familiar shape that stopped his heart cold and sent a shiver throughout his entire body. Fear stricken, and with an unexpected feeling of terror, unlike that which he had ever experienced in life before, he quickly turned his head away. But it was too late; the vision seen in his fleeting glance was seared into his brain. It was unmistakable. Opening his eyes slowly, he forced himself to look again in its direction. As he did so, his ears rang with the deafening sound of the beating of his heart. Opening his eyes as wide as he could, he stared at the dimly lit outline of the object of his fear. It was still there, sitting quietly on top of Theresa and John's mantel. Not wanting to move any closer, Benedict sat motionless in his chair. The pupils of his eyes dilated in his involuntary effort to see what he did not want to see. He needed to be sure, and yet, he wanted to be wrong – but he wasn't. Once his brain confirmed his fear, he again closed his eyes in a hopeless attempt to shield him from its sight. Now he knew. It was indeed too late.

He then knew that, no more than ten feet from where he now sat, the ship he had once carved and given to young John as a gift, sat quietly on the mantel of Theresa and John's fireplace. The last object John held in his delicate little hands while yet alive, was somehow now staring at him from the darkness. The last object of this world John held in his hands as he struggled to take his last breath. The last, prized possession young John held when his life's spirit left his body...And it was here, in this room, sitting quietly on the mantel where Theresa and John had once proudly displayed it prior to that tragic day. Benedict saw for the first time the sails Theresa had made with her own hand...

Closing his eyes and turning his head away, Benedict felt the pounding in his chest, the dryness of his mouth, and shortness of breath. For a moment, he believed that he could not breathe; when he tried to speak, all he could do was to moan. Although terrified, and feeling the throbbing veins of his temples, he opened his eyes to confront this fiend. When doing so, Benedict felt as though he was looking at the darkness of death itself. Wanting to turn away, he could not. He couldn't take his eyes off the dastardly demon of death.

He couldn't take his eyes off the ship as it sat mounted once again on the fireplace mantel, mocking him. He watched its shadow on the wall flicker, giving life to the ship and the illusion that it was somehow moving across the mantel of this now empty sepulcher. Straining to see it clearly in the dim light, his mind detected movement of the shadow on the wall as the oil lamp flickered without its glass globe. Benedict reached to the table and placed the dusty, glass globe over the lamp's wick. The flame grew even brighter than before; the illusion of the ship's movement stopped. Benedict sat back into his chair and stared in its direction.

"Theresa, John, what can I do? Please help me! If there is such a thing as a spirit of the soul, I ask you now to come to me and to tell me what I should do! I am no longer afraid of this place and the power it may hold. But I need you. I need you to help me. I can't do this without you. Tell me, Theresa. Tell me, John. What should I do? What can I do, for God's sake?"

Benedict sat at the table and waited quietly, listening as best he could for a sound; a whisper; something…anything. After several minutes of waiting and concentration, Benedict slowly stood and walked toward the fireplace. Staring as he walked, he did not take his eyes off the ship as he approached. The ship grew larger and brighter as he drew near. He could now see the detail he had once painstakingly carved in its hull. He could more clearly see the sails, expertly sewn by Theresa's hand and attached by Martin to the ship's masts. He saw again its lifelike rigging, its carved portholes.

He also noticed the broken spokes on the ship's wheel. He studied the hand-carved planks of the ship's deck and its rudder. Like everything else in the room, the ship, too, was dust covered and cobwebs blended with the rigging of its masts and sails. Now standing before the fireplace, Benedict slowly reached up to remove the ship from its perch. He closed his eyes as his hands carefully touched the same object John held in his hands at the very moment of his death. He wasn't sure if the feeling came from his hands or the ship itself. But it was an unmistakable *tingle*. *The ship's hull was vibrating in his hands*. Was it his imagination or did the ship hold some form of feeling of its own?

While closing his eyes and cradling the ship in both hands above his head, Benedict whispered, "John, John, John…is this what you want of me? John? Is this what you want? Grasping the ship with both hands until both arms were fully extended, Benedict held it high over his head. He then took a moment to look upward at its sails, as the masts neared the cabin's ceiling. Closing his eyes and lowering his head, Benedict listened carefully to the empty, lifeless room around him. "John, is this what you want of me? Are you certain?"

With an abrupt, sweeping motion of both arms toward the cabin floor, Benedict smashed the ship into the fireplace hearth. With his left boot, he stomped the remains of the wooden ship until it was no longer recognizable. He tore the sails from the splintered pieces of the ship's mast, grabbed the candle from the table and burned each sail, one by one – turning the linen once used by Theresa into ash. Once the ship was destroyed, Benedict raised his head and smiled. "Thank you, John. Thank you for the wisdom and the courage. Your brother will never be tempted and suffer your same fate." Bowing his head as in prayer, "May your soul now rest in peace."

Picking himself up slowly from the fireplace hearth and sitting at the table in the center of Theresa and John's cabin, Benedict folded his hands and looked toward the heavens. "Now, Theresa, dear woman, what can I do for you?"

CHAPTER 28

NEW YORK HARBOR –
SUNDAY, OCTOBER, 23, 1791

"**D**o you need me to deliver anything while I go ashore to purchase stores for our return voyage, Father?"

"Not this time, Richard, thank you. However, be sure to purchase oats for good ol' Governor. Although we took our time and the weather was favorable for our travels, it is fair to say that the trip may have been too long in the saddle for both of us. I'm afraid our journey here from St. John's may have been too much for the old boy. There was once a day when a journey on this order would have been better tolerated by our old bones; I believe it safe to say that neither of us are as young and spry as we once were."

"Father, before I leave, I need to ask: are you well? Ever since you arrived here, you do not seem to be yourself. If you will allow me to say, you seem quite melancholy. When we each set out on our separate ways to this city earlier this month, you were quite excited and looked forward to the trip. Now you seem very quiet; even morose to be here. If you will pardon me, Father, but I never did understand why you would ever want to visit this place again. Yet when we did so in '87, and again, when we prepared to depart for this place a few short weeks ago, you were, well, if I can be frank, uncharacteristically excited. One might even say gay with anticipation of your trip here. Before each trip you were smiling and joking about more often than normal…not exactly your normal self. It was like you were in expectation of a great adventure. Each time, however, after we arrived at this destination, your demeanor changed to quite the opposite. What is it, Father? Can you tell me what is it about this place that troubles you?"

Benedict Arnold: Legacy Lost (A Ghost's Story)

With a cautious smile, Benedict looked at his concerned son and nodded his head. "Life is indeed complicated, my son. It seems that there are some destinations that one can never truly hope to reach. As I've aged, I've come to realize that one can never arrive at a place that exists only in one's mind. There are days when I awaken and expect by day's end, I will finally arrive at the top of a mountain. However, when the sun sets on these days, I usually discover that I am in some long-lost valley, wondering how I got there, or if I can ever hope to reach the mountain top again.

"But, thank you for your concern, Richard. Let's just say that I am saddened by both the memories of what happened at this place, and the dreams of what might have been. On occasion, I find myself feeling sorry for myself, and much too distracted and worried about the uncertainties of what will be. But, you can believe me now when I say that you need not worry any longer about me. The clouds on the mountaintop are now lifting, and I can once again see a clearer destination.

"Now, be off with you! Join the others to explore the hidden treasures of this city. I will be fine here. Enjoy your night, but remember, we set sail again first thing in the morning." With a broad smile, he added, "So be a good lad and don't overindulge yourself of all the pleasures this city may have to offer."

Smiling in return, Richard assured his father that he would be gentleman-like at all times, and would be back long before any rigging would need to be set in preparation for their voyage home.

Richard and the others departed the ship, leaving Benedict alone, save his faithful companion, Governor. Checking on his horse, Benedict found him resting quite comfortably in a covered stall Benedict had specially designed and constructed on the ship's deck so that Governor could accompany him on his voyages.

Benedict waited in his cabin for the arrival of his guest at the previously agreed upon hour; it wasn't long before he heard the anticipated footsteps on the ship's deck. However, unlike the last time he and Washington met on board this ship, the footsteps sounded different somehow. For a fleeting moment, Benedict thought he heard the steps of not one, but possibly two individuals walking the deck above his head. Or perhaps a single person walking while carrying or dragging something along the deck...Benedict could not be certain of what he was hearing from within his cabin. Listening carefully, he then heard the steps of someone coming down the stairs leading into the ship's hold and his cabin. Slowly opening the door to his cabin and holding an oil lantern in front of him, Benedict cautiously peered out into the ship's hold to see who was approaching. He was relieved to discover his former Commander, George Washington, carefully navigating his way around some of the ship's cargo toward the door leading to Benedict's cabin.

"Ah, Benedict, you are here. I am sorry to have kept you waiting, but as you might imagine, getting away from either my office or my home unnoticed is not as easy for me as it once was. I've only recently been able to convince Martha that, on occasion and for my own sanity, I need to get away from everyone to be alone, to clear my mind, and to keep myself centered. Since becoming President, I have very little time to myself; frankly, the responsibilities I have allowed to be placed upon my shoulders are oppressive."

Washington appeared uncharacteristically nervous as he continued to ramble on. "Benedict, I can't tell you the number of times that I would have simply liked to get upon my horse, go home, walk among the fig trees and allow the world and this nation to go on without me. Although I did once think that Providence had prepared me for a special purpose, little did I know that what it had in store for me was to suffer the lingering weight of this nation's government. It has taken some amount of time for me to now reach this point of frustration. But like you several years before, I, too, have developed a dislike for politics and the egocentric games that small-minded men play on the shifting sands of the political arena."

With eyes dulled by age, Benedict looked at Washington. "Sir, I have waited eight years. And like you, I, too, would like nothing better than to get upon my horse and ride home. Nonetheless, the only homes I've known since war's end can only be reached by ship." Benedict watched his friend nervously pace the short length of his cabin before inviting him to sit, to discuss his future. As Washington sat, Benedict studied his movements carefully, looking directly in his eyes as he spoke. "And how is Martha, Mr. President? Is it okay for me to call you Mr. President?"

Washington hesitated for a second and, seemingly relaxed, looked directly back into Arnold's eyes in return. "Martha is fine, Mr. Arnold. Thank you for asking. And if it is all the same to you, I would appreciate it if you simply called me by my given name. Other than Martha, I seldom hear anyone refer to me as George. I oddly miss hearing my name, and would prefer that my friends call me by my first name – at least when we are not in the public eye."

Nodding his head, Washington continued, "I know that it has been eight years since war's end, and I can't believe how quickly the time has slipped by us, or how much has changed over these same number of years."

As Benedict listened to him attentively, it appeared that Washington knew the purpose of Benedict Arnold's visit full well. He could tell that Washington was trying his utmost to convince Benedict that he would need to indefinitely postpone any plans for his return to the United States; perhaps forever – or at least until Washington completed his public life in government. It became clear to Benedict that Washington clearly hoped to be convincing enough for Benedict to understand and accept his fate. However, Benedict had no way of knowing that Washington was prepared to follow through on an alternative plan if Benedict was not willing to accept his fate.

Benedict carefully listened to Washington as he spoke. When he was finished, Benedict stood, placed both palms on the table before him, and slowly shook his head. "I can see it in your eyes, my friend. And, I can hear it in your voice."

Pausing to shake his head, "I can't do this again. I just cannot. So I am going to save you all the words you undoubtedly carefully crafted for this discussion. I need to admit that the time has now come. George, I have now celebrated the fiftieth year of my birth and the time has now come for me to acknowledge that I am a beaten man."

Now slumping into a chair at the Captain's table, "I am tired and I am weary of the energy it takes to hope any longer. I am tired of longing for what will never come. I cannot go on dreaming for what will never be. My ship of hope has run aground, and I need to abandon the ship of dreams I have been trying my best to navigate these many years. It has taken on water, and is listing to port; it is now time for me to abandon the shores of this land and settle not only my body, but my mind as well, in the land of those who have willingly taken me in."

Washington sat in silence and listened carefully as Benedict continued. "For reasons that are of little importance to you, or reasons that, to be honest, have little to do with my desire to return to this home, I am simply drained of all energy. I feel empty, and if the truth be told, I just don't care anymore. For my own sanity, I must move on with my life and waste no more time, and waste no more energy with the delusion of believing that it will ever be any different for me. It is over."

With reddened eyes, Benedict looked in Washington's direction. "You can go on doing the good works needed by this nation that you are building, and I will go on living the life given to me as a result of our good intentions. It is just too damn complicated for me to deal with anymore. It is over. I am done. If the truth is really to be told, my efforts were probably more self-serving than to become a true advantage to my children. Each of my older sons have adjusted reasonably well to their lives in Canada and England. And they are each living productive lives…in spite of their father's scarred reputation."

Now covering his face with both hands, "In time, the republic's memory of me will surely fade altogether, and I trust that our generation's abhorrence toward me will not be passed on to the next generation. In time, I suspect that my children may even be able to relocate to your country, if they should choose to do so. They may even be able to call this place home for the first time in their adult lives.

"That said, I do need to ask one favor of you. I no longer care what strangers, living or yet unborn, think of me. However, what still does matter to me is what my children will think of me once I am gone. I have just enough pride left to want my children and future generations of Arnolds to know the truth. I don't want my children to forever think of me as a scourge to this nation. So here is my proposition: I will forever leave these shores, never to return again. And for the rest of my life, I pledge that our secret will be kept safe. In return for my pledge of silence, I only ask one favor."

Benedict then made what was to become the final appeal he would ever make of the President. After a brief and frank discussion, and earnest negotiations of what Benedict was asking of him, the room fell silent. Benedict sat back in his chair with one eye closed and the other focused squarely upon his guest. "So, Mr. President, what do you think? Is this one small favor I ask of you worth a lifetime of my continued silence?"

Washington paced about Benedict's small cabin for a few moments. "Excuse me for just a moment, Benedict; there is something that I must first do."

Without waiting long enough to give Benedict time to react or answer, Washington left his cabin and walked up the steps to the deck's surface.

Surprised and confused by Washington's unexpected exit, Benedict sat quietly in his chair and waited. Listening carefully, he then heard the steps of someone leaving the ship and the steps of another walking down into the ship's hold. Benedict's instinct told him that something was not right with the situation about to confront him, and he quickly retrieved a pistol from a desk drawer. Loading its flash-pan with powder, he quickly moved to a far corner of the cabin, opposite its entrance door, and quietly waited in a deep shadow.

Washington stepped into the room and saw Benedict with his pistol drawn. "You may be old, my friend, but your instincts still serve you well. However, there is now no need for that, and I must apologize for my action. I agree to your terms, Benedict. I can't begin to explain how glad I am that you understand my situation and the troubles that would face me and this nation if the truth were ever to become known about our joint venture, yea, these many years ago."

"To be honest with you, Mr. Washington, I care less about your troubles than you might think. We did what we did for a reason, and we were successful in our efforts to win the war. As a result, I inherited my troubles, which you seem insensitive to or incapable of possibly understanding. And you inherited your troubles. Troubles which an objective eye might reasonably conclude were willingly accepted and even invited by you as a consequence of your claims to, and acquisition of, positions of power."

Slowly taking a small step closer to Washington from the corner of his cabin, Benedict leveled the muzzle of his flintlock pistol, placed more powder in its flash-pan and then pointed it directly at Washington's chest. "Do you remember the feeling of believing your life was about to end, Mr. Washington? Do you remember what it was like to expect that you were about to die and would never live to see another day?"

Pulling back and cocking his pistol's hammer, "Is your heart beating any faster now than it was a moment ago, Mr. Washington? Is your mouth drier than it was a few moments ago, Mr. Washington? Just how many beats do you think your heart has left in your lifetime? Fifty beats more? Perhaps as many as one hundred beats left in your lifetime? Are you counting them? Are your ears now ringing with the sound of fear, Mr. President? Do you remember that feeling of knowing your life was about to end? Do you remember my friend…Mr. President?"

Washington stood frozen in place as Benedict pointed his pistol at him. "Yes, I do remember, Benedict. Why do you ask?"

"Because, Mr. Washington, we should never forget that feeling. We should live each day as though it were to be our last." Lowering his pistol and, with a smirk, he added, "I think I owed that moment to you for whoever it was that you brought with you tonight, and for whatever reason you may have done so. I am just relieved to see that you still possess the nerves of a great oak, and didn't drop dead from fear."

Washington's shoulders slumped suddenly and, with a noticeable sigh of relief, he slowly sat down, shaking his head. "You bastard!" And then, after a moment's contemplation and recovery, he added, "Nonetheless, although a scoundrel, you are right, Benedict. I did have that coming, and yes, over the years I've discovered that getting old is not for the faint of heart. Had I been frail, I may have been dead before your bullet even struck if your threat was real, as I presumed it to be.

"As you've apparently detected, I am not as honorable as others believe me to be. And I did bring a trusted friend with me here tonight to be of assistance, should you and I not have been able to come to terms on the matter of your moving to these states. However, it is important for you to understand, and I am now being totally honest with you, Ben, I am indeed quite thankful that we could finally come to see eye-to-eye on at least some matters of importance," adding with a smile, "…at least those matters of importance to me."

Leaning back into his chair with his legs outstretched and his arms crossed, Washington concluded. "Now let's see if we can come up with something that will be acceptable to you, if not both of us. Once I am dead, and having no direct decedents to be concerned about, I am willing to risk whatever legacy I may have for the truth. And to tell you the God's honest truth, Ben, knowing that the truth concerning all of this will one day become known, I will be better able to face the end of my days with less regret than I would otherwise be able to do."

Nodding his head in agreement, "I, too, am relieved, George. And, I am pleased to hear that you have at least one person on this earth that you can call a trusted friend. I wish that I were as fortunate. There was once a time when I, too, had someone whom I could call upon as a trusted friend. But that appears to no longer be the case. Now, before you return to your isolated internment with the intriguing affairs of government and the struggles of your world order, let's get to work and see what we can come up with that will be acceptable to both of us."

CHAPTER 29

NEW YORK HARBOR –
MONDAY, OCTOBER, 24, 1791

"Richard, there has been a change in plans. I will be returning to St. John's by land once again, and not with you and the others aboard this ship. However, I am afraid that old Governor here will not likely tolerate another journey of such length. He needs a rest. I'll need to ask you to go back into the city and purchase a good steed for me that will be able to withstand the journey."

"Father, are you sure? What about you? Remember how much the trip took out of you when you and Governor took the land route to this place? Are you sure that you will be able to withstand such a journey across land as well? As I recollect, just yesterday you told me about the discomfort the trip from St. John's had on your *old bones.*"

Benedict smiled at his son. "Never mind that. I am quite sure I can make the trip in fine order. Now get me a good horse and then we can both depart this place."

Benedict's son did as asked, and Benedict began his journey north to St. John's. In consideration of his and George Washington's recent agreement and his determination to move away from the St. John's' community, Benedict understood that he needed to *personally* speak to Martin and Martha. He needed to let them know of the changes that were about to occur in his life, and, now that he has had somewhat more time to think about John, he also needed to discuss his thoughts about the role he would play in John's future. Paramount to his visit, he needed to inform them that he would soon be moving his home to England, where he would no longer be subject to the constant harassment directed his way by residents of the St. John's' community. However, not wanting to risk any misunderstanding of his intentions to move to another shore, Benedict wasn't going to entrust this communication to a post.

It took Benedict four days to travel from New York to Saratoga; the weather blessed him with clear, blue skies, but bone-chilling evenings. Not wanting to risk being recognized by any of the residents in the lower North River area, Benedict did not stop at any of the inns along the way. To minimize the risk of bumping into anyone who might know him, he camped his way north, as he did on many of his travels during the time of the Revolution. Although he had aged several years since he had last done so, it was gratifying for him to discover that he still had it within himself to forego the comforts of a warm room, a roof overhead, and hot meals during his journey. It was not an altogether unpleasant experience for him to live under the stars and once again witness firsthand all the beauty nature has to offer.

Upon arriving at the Van Derwerker Farm, Benedict found Martha feeding the chickens and gathering eggs. Although he approached the farm with some degree of anxiety, he was pleased to find that the reception he received this time was substantially better than the one he experienced during his last confusing arrival. When she first noticed Benedict's approach, Martha gave a big shout, "Hello, stranger," and waved excitedly. It almost seemed that Martha was actually glad to see Benedict again.

"Martha, I am sorry to keep popping in on you unannounced, but I have something I need to talk to you and Martin about. Is the old man here?"

"No, he and John are away for the day to help Sparker dig a new well. They left early this morning, but I expect them back before dark. Please come in and I'll fix you something to eat. Take your horse to the barn to get…wait a minute, this isn't Governor. What happened to Governor?"

"Nothing is wrong with Governor. He is fine. I just didn't want to subject him to another long trip in such a short period of time. Where did you say that Martin and John are? Who did you say that they were helping?"

"They went to help Alexander dig a new well at the inn. Seems that he needs a new one and wants to get it dug before the ground freezes."

"No, that is not who you said he was helping, you said something like *Sparker*. Who is Sparker?"

"Oh, Ben, I am sorry. Sparker is a nickname that some of us once used for Alexander. You may remember him; I believe you even met him when you stayed at his inn up the road a bit. I believe you stayed at his place during your first visit several years back before you found us here."

"Yes, I remember an innkeeper, but Martin told me that his name was Alex."

"I guess I am getting old and keep letting things from my past sneak up on me in some of the things I say. Now and then, I catch myself calling him *Sparker,* a name people around these parts gave to him after the battles at Saratoga. As the story goes, when the British were making their advance to Albany in '77, Alex traveled from the north to tell the General, I think it may have been either General Schuyler, whom he knew personally, or General Gates. He informed them that the British were about to descend upon this place on their way south to Albany."

Continuing with her story, Martha added, "It was his warning that *sparked* the generals into some form of action to get ready for the arrival of the British. After the battles, and after hearing what he did, some of us around here believed that Alex's action *set the sparks* for the gunshots that were fired in the battles here. That's when some of us gave him the nickname, *Spark*er. The truth be told, he didn't have much else to do with the fighting that went on here. But we all think that he was quite proud of his part in letting the generals know of the British's movement toward Saratoga…and the moniker some of us gave to him at the time."

Shaking her head and looking toward the heavens, "Most people in these parts have long since forgotten what we used to call him; like I said, sometimes my mind just slips backward now and then. It is tough getting old, Ben."

"Yes, Martha, some days are tougher than others. Some days I just can't remember much of anything – past or present. I don't think anyone ever told me what your innkeeper's last name is…"

"It is Bryan. Alexander Bryan. Why do you ask?"

"It is as I thought. Martha, the one thing I do remember rather clearly from my past is hearing the name you folks gave to your friendly innkeeper mentioned before. But I didn't hear it from you, Martin, or Theresa for that matter. And it wasn't Sparker that I heard him called. It was *Sparks*.

"I trust that nobody has said anything about me to your Alexander Bryan – either using my real name or Otis *McGurk*. Would I be correct in my expectations, Martha?"

"Yes, of course, Ben. Neither of us would have told anybody about you, or Otis."

Later that day, Martin and John returned after their day of digging, and like Martha, Martin, too, was noticeably happier to see their visitor than when he showed up on their doorstep during his previous visit. Nonetheless, still trying to figure this man out, and not yet understanding exactly who he was, or how he fit into his life, John was somewhat less than enthusiastic. He remained quiet and tenuous toward their mysterious visitor throughout the remainder of Benedict's visit.

Later that evening, while John was sleeping, Benedict explained to Martin and Martha the reason for his return visit.

"As if my life couldn't get any more complicated, I came back to tell you that there has been yet another change in my life. And I needed to tell you this personally so that there is no misunderstanding of what I am about to tell you. Although it has been my hope to one day return to this nation and live the remainder of my days among my countrymen, it is now clear that I will never be able to do so. And life for me in St. John's has become untenable as well."

Looking directly at Martha and Martin so as to better judge their reaction, Benedict sighed and continued. "As a consequence, I will soon be moving my home from St. John's to England. But I want you both to know that my decision to move at this time has absolutely nothing to do with John or the circumstances surrounding his birth. I am his father, and although it may take me some amount of time to figure everything out, I want you to know that I will do my utmost to provide for him.

"Right now, he has a life with you and obviously loves both of you, as he does his life here with you. Although I have only been a brief witness, your love and devotion to him is obvious as well. I need you to know that I would never, ever do anything to disrupt any of your lives any more than I already have. That is certainly not my intent."

Looking in the direction of the loft where John was sleeping, "Nonetheless, I am his father, and although I hardly know the little guy, he is my son. He has my blood in his veins and is, therefore, a part of me...and a part of Theresa as well. It is my desire to help provide for him, to the extent I can, without causing disruption in either his life or yours. We will just need to figure out how that can best be done as the days ahead unfold before us."

Now looking carefully at both Martin and Martha once again, "However, now that my future is settled, there is something more that I want to tell you. But, before I do so, I need your trust. I need your word that you will not share what I am about to tell you with any other. The two of you are the only people in this world that knew me well during the war and remained my friends after war's end. Over the years, you've demonstrated your interest in my well-being and your caring for me as a person; not for what I may or may not be able to do for you in return, but simply as friends. You may be the only true friends I have. There are others who call me their *friend*, but it is not the same. There are none, save the two of you, with whom I can confide my darkest secrets. And, to be honest with you, I need someone that I can talk to without reservation, and without fear or concern for what might be thought of me in return for my openness."

Hesitating before he continued, he looked into Martin's eyes. "You may remember, Martin, several years ago I told you that our bond of friendship was forged by respect for one another as simple human beings. And now our bond also includes love of family, as John is now our family connection. We are all related to the young lad, each in our own way. I know not what the future holds in store for any of us. And the secret that I am about to tell you, I may one day need you to share with John at an appropriate time, later in his life."

Benedict then began his tale by informing Martin and Martha that the person he first met with during his visit of '85, and then again during this trip, was none other than General George Washington, now President of the United States. Martin and his wife then spent the next two hours spellbound, as they learned of their friend's life as a double-agent, and his work with George Washington to provide information to him during the Revolution after he left West Point.

They listened as well to his frustration of not being able to return to the United States, and his firm commitment to Mr. Washington in maintaining their secret for these many years. They learned of Mr.

Washington's request of Benedict several years ago to stay away and not return to his homeland. They learned of Washington's concern over the possible disruption Benedict's return could have on Mr. Washington's efforts to establish a new government. They learned, as well, that Benedict's wife, Peggy, and their children were yet unaware of the true motives behind Benedict's actions during, as well as after, the war.

"It is important for you to understand that I've come to realize and accept the fact that the President absolutely needed to ask this of me. In the days leading up to my apparent defection, neither of us really understood how it would all unfold over the years. We were both just dealing with what we knew at the time and our mutually held belief that, if I was successful in joining the ranks of the British without being discovered as a spy, we just might be able to succeed in our efforts to defeat the British bastards."

After taking a sip of tea Martha had given him, Benedict shrugged his shoulders. "We quickly realized that if anyone were to hear of our collaborations during the war, his career as Commanding General of the Continental Army would come to an immediate end. When the war was over, he needed to continue his efforts to fight the political battles for influence and power as the leadership was being defined for the government to be established for this new nation. Therefore, my return again needed to be delayed. Now, as President, he has discovered that the battles for power and influence continue, and we both are of the opinion that this country would be better off, by far, with him at the helm rather than any of the others."

Martin interrupted, "What are you saying Ben?"

"I'm trying to explain. The success of the war, and the success of this country as a *unified* nation, rest squarely upon his shoulders. Without General Washington, the war would have been lost, and without him in a position of power now, I believe the country, as we know it, will not survive. It is his and my expectation that, if he were to be replaced now, the United States would soon become *divided* states in keeping with each state's diverse interests."

Looking toward Martha, "The President is able to do wonderful things because of who he is…or at least, who everyone believes him to be. That is the nature of power and politics…it is not necessarily what you are, or who you are, but what and who others believe you to be. For most people in this country, he is a god; he can do no evil. And, I count myself among those of this belief. Perhaps not a god, but at least nearly as important as far as the life of this country is concerned."

It was a long night for Martin and Martha, as well as their guest. Before the night was over, Benedict also recounted the problems he encountered during his first visit at the inn in Albany. He shocked them both with his belief that one of those involved in the attempt made upon his life then was none other than their friendly innkeeper, Alexander Bryan. He recounted the note he was given at the Albany inn and told them about the subsequent information he learned from George Washington who believes that the 'Brother Sparks' person mentioned in the note was the same man who provided Generals Gates and Schuyler with information about the pending arrival of the British troops at Saratoga several years ago.

Bending his head downward and raising his eyebrows to look toward Martin and Martha, "The President also told me that this 'Brother Sparks' fellow lives somewhere north of Albany…and his last name is 'Bryan.' Now who would you believe this Brother Sparks to be? Based upon what Martha told me earlier today, it must be your *Sparker*."

Smiling, Benedict added, "I don't hold any particular grudge against the man. He only knows what everyone else in this country was led to believe. I am a damned traitor and, based upon his understanding, his attempt to capture me during my first trip was an honorable effort. I am not worried about the man, either. He is a weasel. Nevertheless, you will need to be particularly careful in any dealings you, and John, may have with the man in the future."

Glancing once again toward the loft, "Who knows what he may do if he were to now discover that John is *my* son?"

Martin looked at Arnold. "Our Sparker is your 'Brother Sparks'? That meek, mild-mannered, and as you say, weasel-looking guy attempted to capture you? That is almost laughable, if it weren't true as you say."

Martin shook his head. "I can't believe that Alex would even be capable of becoming involved in such an elaborate plot as you described. However, now that I think back over the years, it would explain some of his unusual attentiveness given to us that seemed to begin sometime after your first visit. And I recall him bringing up your name, *Otis McGurk*, on occasion."

Looking toward Martha, "It simply struck me as just odd then, but it would now seem that he was perhaps attempting to catch us off guard in our response. He just doesn't strike me as anyone who could do such a thing as to attempt to capture and kill you. He just doesn't appear to have it in him. This man, who couldn't even dig a well for himself, made an attempt upon your life? It is so out of character with the man we know."

Benedict smiled. "Sometimes, it is the quiet, meek and unsuspecting individuals we need to be most cautious about." Puffing up his chest just a bit, "We burley types are obvious troublemakers. But it is the less obvious culprits that must be more carefully watched."

CHAPTER 30

TIME IN A BOTTLE – II

February 21, 1796
London
No. 15

Dear Martin:

It has been several months since my last letter and it is my sincere hope and expectation that you, Martha and John are all doing well during these cold and dreary winter months. The short, dark, and often overcast days of winter often take a toll on my spirit, and recent events have occurred within my family that places an additional weight upon my soul.

I write to let you know that I received execrable news regarding the death of my eldest child. With the heartfelt sorrow that a parent occasionally suffers, I recently learned that my son, my namesake, died from injuries received while engaged in a conflict with the Jamaican Maroon population on the northern side of the Jamaican isle. I've been informed that he received a leg wound (of all things) during a battle last October, and suffered the effects of an uncontrollable fever and illness to which he ultimately succumbed.

Martin, it is times like this that I truly long for your company. If only I could spend time at your and Martha's inviting fireside, to share in life's joys, and its trials and tribulations. It is at these times that I particularly miss your company, and your wise words of counsel.

As I continue to learn more information and accounts surrounding my son's death, I cannot help but think back to the wound I, too, received during the same month of the year as my son. I can't help but also wonder if God is taunting me with this miserable news. As you may recall, you and I received our wounds in the month of October and my son received his in October of last year. I am also reminded of my struggle for survival against infection and fever, and of my temptation to give way to death on more than one occasion. I have only you and Martha to thank for my survival at that time. I can only conclude that my son was apparently not in the presence of caring angels, as I was in your care. Had my son been so blessed, I am certain that he, too, would have survived. Yet, that was not to be, and he is now instead in the company of the true angels of this world: his mother, as well as his brother and sister who earlier completed their journeys to the Heavenly shores shortly after their births. Should my soul be forgiven for sins I have committed in my lifetime, I look forward to the day that my spirit can join them all as well. I am strangely comforted by the knowledge that my time will come, as it will for all others. I am likewise comforted by the knowledge that once I do depart this stage, as will another important player, the time will then surely come when my soul will be able to rest at last.

Unrelated altogether to my current tribulations, but more to my interest in departing this world, I do not believe that I have ever before shared the following bit of my history with you:

There was a time when I did attempt to hasten my departure from this stage in hopes that the news I have entrusted in the care of others could become known, sooner than later. Within a year of leaving your shores, I did have occasion of a meeting on the field of honor with the unsuspecting Earl of Lauderdale, who had publicly humiliated me in the House of Lords. I was prepared, at that time, to suffer this life no more. At the appointed time, I fired my weapon first but, with intent, my shot missed the poor fellow by several feet. It was my full expectation that once he saw smoke billow from my pistol, he

would return fire and hopefully hit his mark.
However, Providence once again intervened and
to my chagrin, the charlatan refused to return
fire; thus, my pitiful life continues.

In hindsight, I now understand my folly and
the reason for my survival of that duel. I have
since been able to consider John's future and,
with your understanding and agreement, we
have since begun plans for his joining my sons
in St. John's to work with them in our shipping
business. It is my hope that perhaps one day he,
too, may share in our business interests on the
North American continent and the West Indies.
My experience on that field of honor was just
another example of the intervention of
Providence in my life, and the hand of God in
shaping not only my life, but the lives of those
who will one day follow in my footsteps as well.

As if the news I bring to you isn't enough for me
to bear, at this time I also suffer from the effects
of gout. My dear Peggy tries her best to care for
me during my fits of disability. Martin, I was
once told by a very wise man... "Getting old is
not for the faint of heart." As I have aged, I
have found his counsel on this subject to be
indeed quite right.

I apologize for the melancholy tone of this letter and hope that you understand the basis for its emotion. Believe me, Martin, I know that the sun will one day shine again for me and my family; however, like your melancholy days several years before, my ability to appreciate the beauty of the morning sun just does not seem likely at this moment.

I will write again when my mood improves and once I've had an opportunity to better adjust to the news of late.

Until that time and the return of joy again in our lives, I am, Sir, &c.,

Lord Sheffield

May 30, 1796
Saratoga
No. 12

My Dear Friend:

We were saddened to hear the news of the recent death of your eldest child. Please accept our condolences for your loss.

As Martha and I read your letter, we could not help but to think back to the time you first shared information with Martha and me about your family while we were in Albany. We remembered how much your children meant to you then, and we likewise know how much each precious child means to you now. It is our sincere wish that the fog given by time will soon cover the sharpness of your vision of this tragedy, and you will one day be healed of the pain you now suffer as a result of the loss of your son.

As Martha and I have each dealt with similar losses over the years, the only bit of advice that we might now offer that may be of some solace is to suggest that, at least for the short term, try not to 'look directly' at your problem or your loss, but to look _beyond_ it. As I sit here and try to communicate this thought by words on paper, I've come to realize that it is difficult to explain to others. Allow me to just say that, as you attempt to adjust to your loss, try to _look ahead_ to the promises of what life will yet be, and not so much at what life will no longer be. If you can do this for the short term, I believe that you will come to understand that, as difficult as it is for us to accept, death is a natural part of life. And, as difficult as it will be for you to be without your son in the days ahead, his passing on to the next world is all a part of God's plan for him...and us. As you, Martha and I could only later understand, your *not* passing on in '77 and '78 when death was at your door, was part of His plan for you, this nation, as well as your family and ours. As we now believe this fact to be true, you must also believe that your son's passing is also part of His plan. Although we are not capable of understanding the reasons for His interventions in our lives when they become so obvious, it is this belief in His power that comforts us and keeps the dark days from clouding our vision of the true meaning of life, and of death.

You, of course, recall the loss of Theresa and John from our lives in '86, and the grief Martha and I experienced at our loss of their love and companionship. Like you now, we, too, didn't believe it possible, at that time, that we could be happy ever again. Nonetheless, our sorrow did in fact subside over time, and we knew it to be true when we one day caught ourselves smiling once again.

It is with this confidence in the power of our God that we know your day to smile will also come again.

Until that time, we remain your friends and confidants, et. C

Martin and Martha

April 28, 1799
Saratoga
No. 12

My Dear Friend:

I hope that this post finds its way to your location and finds you, your dear wife and family in good health and spirits.

I am pleased to inform you that in short order, John, now a strapping young man of 13, and I will be departing for St. John's. Your son, Richard, has informed us that he now has a place for John in his employ and is certain that John will benefit from the experience that he has planned for his development in the business of the trades.

Martha understands the value of the experience that you and your other sons have in store for John, but I fear that it will be somewhat difficult for her to adjust to a house with only me to look after. During our trip north and until my return, Martha will have the company of one of her brothers from Albany and his wife who will help her with the farm and keep her company. I expect that she will have little time to miss either John or me during our absence.

I look forward to my first trip so far north and the opportunity to meet your other sons who yet live in St. John's. One can only learn so much about another through letters, and I am anxious to meet your sons in person so that I can better judge your work as a father. Worry not, I will only tell them good things about you and will keep the things a son should never learn about their father to myself...

Thank you for your advice of travel, and your provision of the horses we will need to complete our journey. As you rightfully believed, the horses I have on the farm are better suited for short distant hauls and farm work; consequently, they are not likely to be able to make it to St. John's. Not to mention my return trip to Martha.

I will send you another post upon my return.

Until then, I remain your friend, et. C

Martin

CHAPTER 31

18 GLOUSTER PLACE, LONDON, ENGLAND
SUNDAY, JUNE 14, 1801

The mantel clock over the fireplace in Benedict Arnold's bedroom
struck six o'clock on a cloudy Sunday morning. Benedict's sister,
Hannah, opened his bedroom windows and outer shutters to allow
morning's light and the refreshing scent of crisp morning air to enter
his chamber. As she turned to look at her brother, a gentle breeze
fluttered in the curtains, at times parting them to allow even more light
into his darkened, gloom-stricken room. Benedict lay in his bed in a
semi-conscious state, his breathing labored.

Sadly studying her brother, she listened to his shallow breaths.
Hannah then turned to look at Peggy, who had been sitting with her
husband throughout the night. "My dear, it appears that he does not
have much longer. I will awaken the children." Shortly thereafter,
Peggy was joined at her husband's bedside by Hannah, and three of
Peggy and Benedict's children: Sophia, now 16 years of age; George, a
young man of 14; and his youngest son, William, who would turn 7 on
the 25th of this same month.

For a fleeting moment Benedict regained consciousness, looked to
his wife, and smiled ever so faintly. Undoubtedly knowing that his time
on this earth would soon come to an end, Benedict struggled with his
conscience for what was to be his last time.

"Peggy, my life's journey on this earth is about to end. I am tired
and the candle of my soul flickers dimly. Among my regrets is I only
now discover that all I really needed to do over these many years was
to simply allow myself to love more. *I should have been more understanding
and more compassionate toward my enemies, as well as those I've loved.*"

Slowly shaking his head from side to side, "I now understand. Despite our differing stations in life; despite whatever place on this earth we live, or the place we call home; despite which side of the battle line we may stand, and despite the time during which we walk in this world, I now understand that, despite all these differences, we are yet all the same. Regardless of the differences in the beliefs that I or others hold to be true, we are all, in the end, children of God. Nothing more; certainly nothing less."

Looking toward his children, "And I should have spent more time with those who made my life complete. I regret the missed opportunities I had to truly know others by my self-centered actions. My dear Peggy, before I leave you to face my God, I ask that you likewise view me and my life with understanding and compassion."

Reaching up with a troubled look, Benedict grabbed his wife's arm. "I fear that the journey my soul is about to take will not only be determined by the decisions I've made during my lifetime, but also, in some measure, by the understanding, compassion and forgiveness you, and untold others, hold for me after my life's journey is ended.

"Peggy, please. Please help me on with the blue one that I last wore at that dreadful bend in the river." Pointing in the direction of his feet, "It is in my trunk at my feet. My uniform…Help me put it on so that when I die, my soul may pass through its threads and know that, in my heart, I never truly abandoned the nation of my birth."

At first, neither Peggy nor the others surrounding Benedict appeared to understand what he was saying or what he wanted them to do for him. Their initial thoughts were that his words were those he sometime uttered while in delirium, passing into and out of consciousness. It wasn't until Hannah found and opened a trunk hidden under the foot of his bed that they saw the blue uniform to which he referred.

With visions blurred by tears, Peggy, Hannah and his three children all helped their struggling husband, brother and father don the old, moth-eaten and dusty blue uniform he once wore as an American General during the time of the Revolution.

Then, laying back onto his bed, with his back and head propped up by pillows, Benedict looked about the room to briefly study the faces of those he was about to leave behind. His glassy eyes looked into those of each member of his loving family. Looking first toward his children, William, Sophia and George, his eyes swelled with tears remembering the very first time he saw each of them shortly after their births, when their lives together first began.

Knowing that this was likely to be the last vision of his children, the thought occurred to him that their lives together have now come full circle. He had seen them into this world and they were now to see him leave them and the world behind. "Children, forgive this old and feeble man for the shortcomings I had as a father. Please know that any such shortcomings were not for the lack of love that I've held in my heart for each of you and your brothers who are not here with me at this time." Reaching up with his right hand to wipe a tear from young William's cheek: "Be strong, my son. This is the way of life. Unlike your older brother Ben, this is the way it should be – first the father, only then the son. Remember all that we've talked of and be strong for your mother and your Aunt Hannah."

Benedict then looked to Sophia and George. "I am so proud of my little girl, as I am with you, George, and all of your brothers. When you all witness life ahead, remember as well, to live your lives with understanding and compassion toward others. Let your brothers know of my love for them."

And then turning toward his wife, "…Peggy, please come close." Placing her head on Benedict's chest, Peggy listened carefully as Benedict whispered. "My dear Peggy, forgive me. Forgive me for my shortcomings as a man and husband. You are about to learn, when my testament is read after my death, that it lists the name of a boy whom you never knew to be my son. The young man, *John* as you know him, is in fact my son. A son who I love as dearly as the children who stand about me at this moment."

Peggy slowly lifted her head from his chest to look him in the eyes as he struggled to talk. "With this, please know that I've always loved you from the moment our eyes first met in Philadelphia, to this time. Forgive this weak-bodied man for his infidelity. Do not harbor any ill will toward the boy that should be rightfully directed toward me. His birth was the result of my indiscretion and is not a fault of his own doing. Like you in this matter, he is an innocent victim of my act. I knew his mother only once, and she died at his birth. He deserved better than me and what little I've been able to provide for his upbringing until now. Come closer still, my dear Peggy."

Peggy placed her left ear near Benedict's lips and listened carefully. She felt his breath on her ear as he faintly whispered: "At the bottom of my trunk is a Bible. Inside the Bible is an envelope sealed by my hand 10 years before. Once I am buried, open the envelope and share the information contained therein with our family, our friends and any others that you believe would be interested in knowing the truth…" Struggling, with all the energy he could muster, Benedict Arnold kissed the top of his wife's head, smiled at his sister and children and then, in his sixtieth year, closed his eyes for the final time.

"A son named *John*? Knowing *the truth*? The truth? What truth? What are you talking about, Benedict? Please tell me, what are you talking about?"

Peggy's questions were never heard. Benedict's life journey had ended; leaving his wife wondering, her questions unanswered, and the fate of his soul in her hands.

Hannah opened the glass-covered door of the mantel clock and, with her hand, stopped the pendulum's movement at exactly 6:30 o'clock. The silence of the clock's movement was deafening.

CHAPTER 32

LONDON, ENGLAND

Peggy was distraught; yet with the assistance of Benedict's sister and friends of the family called to their home, they prepared Benedict for his burial that would occur the following week. Removing his blue, tattered uniform and placing it back in his trunk, they then placed two white, thin, circular stones over the lids of his eyes and wrapped his jaw tight, keeping it closed as death laid claim to his body. Benedict's body was then wrapped in his white linen bed sheet.

During the week immediately following his funeral, Peggy Arnold was distracted from the loss of her life's companion by caring for their children and trying to come to terms with Benedict's accounts and estate left behind. When her husband's Last Will and Testament was read, it did what Benedict had said that it would. He provided not only for her, their children, the children of his first wife and his sister, but also for a boy named John.

It wasn't until hearing John's name mentioned in his Will that Peggy was also reminded of his final words. Something about an envelope Benedict said he placed within a Bible in his trunk. That evening, while alone in his room, she pulled his trunk from beneath the foot of his bed. Slowly opening its latches, Peggy lifted its lid and sorted through his clothing that Benedict had stored in his trunk, passing over his blue uniform and reached its bottom, where she did find a book.

Retrieving the book, she discovered that it was indeed a Bible as Benedict said it would be. Hesitating with the Bible in her hand, Peggy thought of his words, *the truth*, and his instruction to share the truth with their children, friends and others who would want to know the truth. The thought occurred to her that her husband had perhaps become religious when facing his death and wanted her to share in the truth given in the Bible. However, opening the Bible, she found hidden among the pages within the Book of John, a plain envelope sealed with Benedict's mark. The only markings on the front of the envelope, also in Benedict's hand, were the numbers, '*3:3.*'

Peggy moved to better light provided by the oil lamp burning brightly on Benedict's desk located next to his bedroom's fireplace. Breaking the envelope's seal, she opened and read the document within. She sat for several minutes, reading the document, time and time again.

While in its third reading, she sobbed. "You bastard! You bastard! How could you have done this to me? How could you have done this to our children? How could you? Why would you? You bastard! What you have done to me and my family for all these years? All these years...my mother...my father...our children...How could you, Benedict? How could you? Is this the way it has always been, for God's sake?" Dropping the document to the floor, Peggy laid her head on the table and wept.

After several minutes of torment, she composed herself and picked the document up from the floor to read it over one last time to see if there was something that she missed...something that would explain. There was nothing more.

"You were a spy for the Americans? *And for this, John André was hanged?*" In a fit of rage, she kicked Benedict's trunk on its side, spilling its contents onto the floor. "You kept the truth from me, your children and the world over for all these years and made me and our children live apart from our families and true friends for all these years? Is this *the truth* you uttered to me as your last word, for God's sake! Benedict, how could you? Our family suffered so...You showed no compassion to us. As far as I am concerned my dear husband, you, Mr. Washington and this document can all burn in Hell."

Picking up a candle from his bed's end table and walking to the fireplace with the document, Peggy held its corner over the candle's flame and tossed the burning paper into the fireplace. She watched intently as the flames danced over the document's curling pages, turning its words into ash. Grabbing his blue uniform from the floor; she tossed it, as well, into the fireplace where it smoldered briefly, and then burst into flames of yellow and green. "Mr. Washington, no one will ever know of this document or the pain and suffering my husband willingly brought to me and my family in his service to you. Benedict, you were a fool to believe that I would somehow understand and now right your wrong. May God forgive me for the hatred I now feel in my heart for both of you. If it were within my power, it would be my wish that you would both burn in hell along with the ashes of this document and this wretched uniform."

CHAPTER 33

<hr/>

MOUNT VERNON, VIRGINIA
SUNDAY, DECEMBER 29, 1799
(Eighteen Months Later)

Mrs. Martha Washington sat quietly in her dimly lit parlor; slowly sorting through her husband's personal effects. Looking tired and uncharacteristically disheveled, it was apparent that physical appearances mattered little to the former President's wife on this day. Sitting on the top of her desk, among the personal letters her husband had written to her from the beginning of their courtship, was a mahogany, hand-carved, wooden box with an engraved outline of an eagle with outstretched wings on its cover.

Ever since her husband's death 15 days before, Mrs. Washington struggled with what to do with the personal correspondence she and her husband shared over the years. Although a daunting task for any recently widowed woman, it was particularly so for the *'first widow'* of the first President. Martha understood that history would be interested in her husband's official records as the Commander-in-Chief of the Continental Army and as President.

However, it was her intention to keep his personal correspondence, particularly the correspondence shared between the two of them, separate and apart from the public documents that would be of interest to others. It was her and her husband's belief that their personal correspondence should be kept private and not subject to the scrutiny of any other. In keeping with this conviction, letters she believed to reflect his public life were placed in containers and given to others. Letters she believed to reflect his personal and private life were read one last time and then burned. Mrs. Washington was determined to prevent his, or her, private lives from falling into the hands of any other, at any point prior to, or after joining her husband at the gates of eternity.

With a gentle knock at the door, Billy Lee opened the door and leaned his head into the room announcing the arrival of Alexander Hamilton. Glancing up from her letters, Martha noticed for the first time that Billy Lee's hair had more gray then she ever noticed before. While thinking that the stress of her husband's passing must also weigh heavy upon his favorite servant as well, Mrs. Washington offered a caring smile and motioned that he should admit her invited guest into her chamber.

"Is there something that I can help you with, Mrs. Washington? I received a message just a few moments ago that you wished to see me." Alexander tried not to show his surprise at Mrs. Washington's unkempt and somewhat weary appearance.

"Yes, please sit down, Mr. Hamilton. I need to show you something that I discovered yesterday, and I don't quite know what to do with it. You have been my husband's most trusted advisor over the years, and I believe you cared for him, perhaps as much as I. Therefore, I want to share this with you to see what you know of it, and to seek your opinion regarding what you would suggest I do with it."

Martha Washington reached for the wooden box on top of her table and handed it to Alexander. "What an ornately carved box, Mrs. Washington; it is beautiful. The work of a highly skilled craftsman..."

"Yes, indeed, Mr. Hamilton, it is the work of a skilled craftsman. And its contents, I must say, would also appear to be crafted by an equally skilled artisan. It was given to me by my husband eight years ago, along with the instruction for me not to open the box until after his death. Although I was curious, naturally, I kept my pledge to him and only opened the box yesterday. At first I thought it might have been something personal he wanted me to have after he passed away, but I see now that it was not."

Trying to disguise her obvious disappointment, Mrs. Washington added with a cautious smile: "I was, as you might expect, somewhat disenchanted. But, then again, I long ago realized that sentiment was never one of my husband's strengths. And now that I realize that it wasn't a sentimental gift of the heart, I need to share its contents with you. I believe that he would expect me to do so. Please, open the box. I think you will agree that Mr. Washington would want you to be apprised of its contents."

Alexander opened the box to discover an unmarked envelope with a seal that had been broken but was still clearly recognizable as that of George Washington's. Looking at Mrs. Washington, "Do I have your permission to open the envelope?"

"Yes, of course, Mr. Hamilton. That is why I asked you to come here today. But before you do, please know that I was the one who broke the seal for the first time yesterday. The seal was placed on the envelope by my husband eight years ago."

Opening the envelope; Alexander carefully withdrew and unfolded the document within. After a brief study, he looked up at Mrs. Washington. "I've seen this document. Actually, I've seen an exact replica."

Waiving the now empty envelope in Mrs. Washington's direction, "Last year, I, too, was given an envelope by your husband. Like you, he gave me strict instructions not to open it until after his death. Your husband was cunning indeed, Mrs. Washington. When he gave me the envelope, he informed me that he reserved the right to request to see it at any point to check the seal he placed upon it."

Looking at the seal on the envelope Mrs. Washington had shown him: "A seal that was almost identical to this one. And true to his word, he did ask me to produce it on more than one occasion. If you look closely at the seal on your envelope, you can see that that the eagle's tail has all thirteen feathers. On the seal he used to secure the envelope he gave to me, I noticed that one of the feathers on the eagle's tail was missing…it only had twelve, not thirteen feathers.

Holding the seal close to the lantern on Mrs. Washington's table, "And I expect intentionally so. I believe that your husband had the seal used to secure my envelope crafted so that he could detect a forgery should I or any other attempt to create a duplicate. Who would ever notice that a single feather would be missing? No other casting of the seal could likely be made to replicate it. I believe that Mr. Washington may not have trusted me as much as he trusted you. He may have done it to ensnare me, or to test my trustworthiness."

Looking sheepishly at Alexander Hamilton, Martha Washington commented: "Apparently you did look closely enough at the seal to notice the missing feather, Mr. Hamilton. Perhaps he was correct in his concern regarding the trust he had placed in you. Why would you notice such a fine detail unless you had contemplated making a replica or some other skullduggery?"

Hamilton smiled with a faint blush of apparent embarrassment. "You have a point, Mrs. Washington. You do have a point there. I may have been tempted, but your husband's craftiness kept me honest. Nevertheless, I did read the copy given to me on the day following your husband's death. Now looking at the document he gave to you, I can attest that it is identical to the one he gave to me."

Shaking his head and smiling, "Your husband, may God rest his soul, was indeed a crafty gentleman, Mrs. Washington. You will note that it was written so that its reader would not suspect that a duplicate copy had been made. He did not tell me that he had given another copy to you. And, it appears he did not inform you that a duplicate copy had been given to me, either. I suspect that he gave copies to the two of us as a way to be assured that one of us would come forward with it after his death. Somehow he believed that he would be first to go, before either one of us."

Martha sighed. "Not an altogether unreasonable assumption considering the pressures and strain this country placed upon his shoulders as well as his soul…"

Looking at Mrs. Washington with a sympathetic smile, Alexander continued. "I kept the copy he had given to me for a day after I read it. Truthfully, as you may assume, I did not know what to do with it. And, then as I tried to sleep that night, I was restless. I kept thinking about your husband's legacy and what others would do with the information he entrusted to me…"

Glancing toward Mrs. Washington, "…and, now you, Mrs. Washington. I tossed and turned and kept thinking about all the good your husband has done in his lifetime. I kept thinking that all the good he has accomplished for this nation could be unraveled by the document entrusted into my care. The President built his entire public career on trust. His accomplishments during the time of the Revolution, his work on the formation of a new Confederation and a new world order for the public's good. He accomplished all this on a foundation of trust, honesty and courage.

"And now? What would happen if others who placed their trust in your husband were to now discover the information contained within this document? If, in fact, what is written here is even true – and there is no way for us to know for certain that it is true. Regardless of its truth, true or not, it would now tear his reputation to shreds. In doing so, his and our enemies would undoubtedly tear into shreds this young Republic as well, that he was instrumental in forming."

Walking to the cabinet where her husband had stored his liquor, Alexander asked: "May I?"

"Of course, Mr. Hamilton; how thoughtless of me not to offer. And if you wouldn't mind, please, just a small amount for me as well," adding with a smile and a twinkle in her eye that Alexander hadn't noticed until now, "I believe that two fingers will do nicely, thank you."

As Alexander poured each of them a drink, Mrs. Washington asked: "And just what did you do with the copy my husband entrusted into your care, Mr. Hamilton?"

Turning to look directly at Mrs. Washington, "I burned it.

"Even if what he stated was true, and as I said, there is no real way to verify the accuracy of what is written now, I believed that it was a matter between Mr. Washington and Mr. Arnold. If, in their wisdom, they chose to keep the matter a secret between themselves until now, so be it. I believe that Benedict Arnold is yet alive. The direction in this so-called *proclamation* clearly states that its contents are not to be made public until after neither man could talk about it, to either confirm or deny its content."

Looking away from Mrs. Washington and shaking his head, "If any of this is true, I expect that it may have been a pact negotiated between the two of them to ensure that neither man could embellish upon it, or to alter the truth to reflect better upon the sole survivor. If unveiled after the death of only one man, there would certainly be questions asked of the other. That is a God-given fact. There is no way of knowing what Mr. Arnold would now say if the document were to be revealed before he is dead.

Alexander looked directly into Mrs. Washington's dull brown eyes. "In spite of Mr. Washington's apparent trust in the man, I do not share the President's confidence in Mr. Arnold's honor. Although it may have been a pledge that they could, for good reason, keep, I simply could not trust myself with that pledge or the supposed knowledge contained in the document your husband entrusted into my care. So I burned it."

Brushing his hands quickly together as he spoke, he concluded, "I removed from my grasp the evidence of any such conspiracy the two of them may have had."

Alexander paced about the room for a moment and then continued with his thoughts. "Mrs. Washington, I do believe that your husband's legacy will be best served if your copy of this document remains private and never undergoes the scrutiny of the public eye."

As he spoke, Alexander swirled his brandy, remembering the evening spent with her husband in New York City several years before when they, too, drank brandy, perhaps in these very same snifters. He remembered the sickening feeling in his stomach when George Washington first confessed his and Benedict Arnold's plot to him that fateful night. The thought now occurred to him and he wondered how Martha Washington must be feeling at this moment. Alexander nonetheless kept this memory to himself.

For the first time in his life, he felt pity for this woman who just now realized, for what is very likely the first time in her life, that her husband may not have been as honest and open with her, as she had undoubtedly believed. As he pondered her circumstances, Alexander thought: *this would explain Mrs. Washington's dowdy appearance, in both dress and spirit.*

"I truly don't know, Mr. Hamilton. I, too, am concerned about what others will say or believe about my husband. And, I do agree that this document would damage my husband's reputation for certain. Although it has been my habit to honor my husband's wishes, I expect that he will forgive me in this instance. Although his life has ended, I think that we all know that his life's work goes on. Like you, I, too, believe that the country and my husband's legacy will be better served if this document never sees the light of day."

Without any additional hesitation, Mrs. Washington retrieved the document from Alexander Hamilton's hand and placed it in the fireplace among the letters her husband had written to her over the years. She then ignited the edges of the papers with a candle, setting them all aflame. Alexander Hamilton raised his glass toward the flaming documents. "To your privacy and your legacy, Mr. Washington. And to the preservation of the United States of America."

CHAPTER 34

VAN DERWERKER FARM
MONDAY, OCTOBER 26, 1807

At the young age of 13, Benedict Arnold's son, John, had moved from Saratoga to Upper Canada to live with his half-brothers, Richard and Henry, and to begin work in their shipping trade as arranged by Benedict before his death. However, unlike his father and brothers, John did not take to life upon the seas. Nor did he take a liking to the *"mundane,"* as he called it, day-to-day business affairs of the shipping trade. Thankfully for John, Benedict's Last Will and Testament provided land grants in Upper Canada for each of his children, to include John. Consequently, John eventually settled upon the twelve hundred acres of land bequeathed to him and became a moderately successful farmer. In doing so, he chose not to follow in the footsteps of his infamous father, but to live the life he learned to love from his Aunt Martha and Uncle Martin.

As the years came and went, John returned to Saratoga several times after moving to Canada. However, in the fall of 1807, just after his 21st birthday, John received a rather unusual letter from his uncle, asking that he visit Saratoga upon completion of his work on the year's harvest. John did as he was asked.

After supper on the second day of his visit, John joined his Uncle Marty at the fireplace for one of their customary *gatherings*. "I sure miss these fireside discussions we used to have when I was a boy, Uncle Marty. I remember the lessons learned while sitting right here and listening to you and Martha talk, and the stories you would share with each other and me. I want you to know that I plan on doing the same for my children when they get older, better able to understand and, perhaps, even appreciate a lesson or two from their *old* dad and mother."

After smiling at John's remark, Martin's mood turned serious. "Thank you for coming before the winter set in, John. I can't tell you just how glad I am to see you after all these years. It has been too long since our last visit, but I certainly understand that life on the farm does not leave one with much time for travels, or the luxury of not tending to your crops and animals."

"That is true, uncle. But, fortunately for Sarah and me, we have a tenant who is willing to do some of the work on our farm in return for us letting him settle on a piece of land down the road from where our farm is. He is quite able to take care of the animals and to help Sarah with some of the chores while I am away."

Joining Martin and John at the fireplace after cleaning up from their meal, Martha looked at the strapping young man and thought back to the early days of his living with them. "I just can't get over how you have grown over the years, John. A wife and two children! Glory be, how time does have a way of passing us by, and how things can change in what appears to be nothing more than a blink of an eye."

Looking at Martha with a scowl and a smile, Martin added: "Time goes faster for us, Martha, because we are old. What may seem like a month or two to us is in reality a full year for John and the rest of the world."

"Now don't pick on my auntie. It has been too long for me as well. I can't begin to tell you how much I've missed the two of you and your company. I have learned plenty of lessons about farming by the mistakes I've made over the years; mistakes that I am sure you would not have allowed me to make if I were working with you here, or if you were working with me in Canada. Are you sure you won't reconsider and move north to be with Sarah, me and the girls? I am certain that Sarah would appreciate your company, and I know that both of us could use your guidance at raising children. I keep telling Sarah how good a job you did with me, but she isn't so easily convinced."

Martha looked at her husband as she answered for the both of them. "Thank you for the thought, John, but this is our home. At this late stage in our lives, I expect that neither of us would be able to survive the adjustment to another home, let alone a home so far to our north. Winters are long enough here; I see no need to prolong them by moving northward."

Adding a few more logs to the fire, Martin settled back into his rocker and looked at John with a careful eye. "You are probably wondering why we asked you to come for a visit after all these years. I suspect that you know both of us well enough to understand that it was not for the lack of a reason."

"Well, it did cross my mind as an odd sort of request at this time of year, and frankly, I was afraid that something may have happened to one of you, or that you had some bad news you wanted to share with me in person. But, I can see that I was mistaken. I am, nonetheless, somewhat curious. Was there a reason why you wanted me to come now and not next spring or summer? Is everything all right with the two of you?"

Martin took the lead. "We are fine, John. But now that you are an adult and have reached the age of 21, and Martha and I are up in our years, the two of us thought that we should have a sit-down with you, in person to tell you something about your father."

John looked both confused and surprised. "My father? What do you mean? What is it that you want to tell me?"

Martha sat back to listen to her husband as he attempted to broach the subject of Benedict Arnold and what he had instructed them to do once both he and George Washington were dead. "Well, John, I am not exactly sure where to begin, so I am going to begin from the beginning, just to make sure we are all talking about the same things as we wander down this path we are about to take. As you recall, your mother lived with us when you were born. It seems that your mom and Benedict Arnold had an attraction to one another during one of his visits with us and lo, and behold, you were born. However, at that time, and as you now understand, your father was married to another and living alternately in St. John's and in London at the time…"

"…I recall the circumstances of my birth…" adding with a smile, "…and I've never liked it very much when anyone around me uses the word *bastard*."

"I am trying to be serious, John. But if you want to know the truth, I've never liked the use of that word by anyone either, regardless of what or whom they were talking about." Glancing in Martha's direction, "and I won't even begin to tell you what I think about the word *bitch*…"

Martha looked to Martin in return with a scowl and then with a smile as she patted her husband lovingly on the knee. "You are rambling, Martin. Perhaps it would be best if we just told John what we need to tell him directly, and not take the long way around at getting to the point."

Martin smiled again at John. "Women, always wanting to get right to the point…Nevertheless, your Aunt Martha is right and it would be easier if I just said what it is I have to say. I want to give you information about your father that he had given to us several years before his death. He gave us information that he wanted us to share with you when the time was right. By that, he meant, after he had passed on."

Looking at Martin, John commented: "My father, rest his soul, has been dead for several years now. Why did you wait until now to tell me whatever it is you want to share?"

"That is a fair question John, and one that Martha and I have discussed any number of times ourselves. I'll try to explain it better as I continue with what I have to tell you."

Martin stood up, walked to a desk and picked up a book. Returning to his rocker, Martin flipped through its pages to find an envelope that Benedict had placed within it several years before. Picking up the envelope, he checked the seal that Benedict had placed upon it, and showed John that it was still unbroken.

"Your father asked us to give the document within this envelope to you after both he and President Washington had died. Before he left us for the last time, he told us something about his past that he wanted you and his other children to know. As he explained it all to us, we were led to believe that both he and Mr. Washington had copies of this same document and that each would leave instruction with their families to read it only after they were both dead."

Martha interrupted her husband briefly. "John, have you been made aware of anything about your father's past by any other members of his family?"

"Well, I was told that he acted as a traitor during the Revolution and for that reason could no longer live in the United States. That is about it. But, before you go on much further, perhaps there is something more the two of you should know about me in this regard.

"When I was just a young boy and met my father for the first time, I heard you and him talking when you all thought I was asleep up in the loft. It embarrasses me now to tell you, but I didn't know who he was and I wanted to learn more about him. So, when you thought I was sleeping, I was actually listening to the three of you as you talked about me, my mother and something about my father's life."

"So you know about your father?" asked Martha.

"Well, sort of, but not really. I remember him and you talking about other people that I didn't know and saying things that I didn't understand. So I don't actually remember most of what you were talking about. But what I do remember is that hearing the three of you talk as you did led me to understand that he was a nice man and not the bad man that everyone else apparently thought that he was."

Martin looked up from staring at the flames in the fireplace. "He was a nice man, John."

"Yes, I've since come to learn that for myself over the years, but when I was listening as a young boy, I remember thinking that there was something soothing and comforting about him. It was obvious that you all cared about me and what might happen to me and I was somehow comforted when I listened to the three of you talk. I felt loved. Seeing this book, it does bring back images of that time and recollections about a *secret* document that he placed in the book. I remember him getting up and going to my mother's cabin and bringing back the book. I saw him place the envelope within the book and then hand the book to Uncle Marty. And now, here it is again…the same book and the same document."

Martin looked up at John. "Yes. The same book and the same document placed within it by your father. After listening to us then, do you now know what it was that your father did during the Revolution and the agreement he had with Mr. Washington?"

"Well, not really. I was able to understand that he did something bad for the country and began working for the British. I know that after the war, he had met with someone, but at the time, I had never heard of President Washington and I didn't know who it was that he had met with until I was much older. I also remember something about a pact or something secret. But that is about it. Is there something more that you think I should now know about my father?"

Martin and Martha looked at one another, neither knowing quite what to say.

However, before either of them could say anything, John stood up, pensively paced about the room and spoke up again. "To tell you the truth, I am not sure I need to know, or necessarily want to know, anything more about my father than I already know. He was a kind man. A loving father and husband who provided for his family as best he could. And he was your friend. What more can a son ask for than to be surrounded by people who love him and to learn that he has a loving, kind and thoughtful father?"

"What about others and what they think of your father and his actions during the Revolution? Doesn't it matter to you what others now think of your father?"

"Well, I know that he was a man of controversy for others, but not for me. I don't know why I should care now what others, who are strangers to me, think of my father. I see that to be of little importance to how I think of my father and what I remember of him."

Martin looked at Martha and then John. "That may very well be, John, but your father asked us to give this document to you. Frankly, based upon what he told us at the time, it would appear that there were other copies of this same document. And, based upon what your father told us back in '91, we expected that either your father's family in London or the family of Mr. Washington's would have made it public by now. We waited for years after Mr. Washington's and your father's deaths, thinking that the families of one or the other would somehow make the information contained within this document known."

Looking into John's eyes, Martha added: "But to the best of our knowledge, neither did. We waited and even read some of the newspapers coming out of Albany to see if there was any word about your father and Mr. Washington. But there was none..."

Martin then added: "So Martha and I then needed to decide what we should do with the copy we had. On one hand, it is clear from what your father said to us, it was his intention that the information entrusted into our care should become known after he and the President both died. And it has apparently not happened as planned. Knowing what we do, and after thinking about what your father had asked us to do more recently, we decided that we would do exactly what your father asked of us. We are giving the document to you. We are leaving it in your hands, and after reading it, perhaps you can then best decide what should be done with it."

"Are you telling me that neither of you have seen the document? How can you be sure what it says if you haven't read it? Perhaps it's not what you think it is after all."

"To be honest with you, John, neither Martha nor I doubted what your father told us. And he told us that the content of the document would explain his actions during the Revolution. He told us that he wanted his children to know of his actions. I can remember our discussions with your father about this as clearly as though it were only yesterday:"

> 'I know that, to her credit, Theresa once argued against keeping family secrets. And I would agree. But what I am going to ask of you is to just keep it secret for a little while, but not forever. I don't know if that will make it any easier for you, but it won't be like you could not share the information for the rest of your lives. Just for the rest of my life – however long that might end up being. I have given my bond to another to maintain the information I am about to share secret until the day I die, and I am going to ask the same of you. But before I commit you to this act of secrecy, I need to ask for your permission to do so.'

"While listening to your father, I even remember your Aunt Martha and I looking at one another with raised eyebrows and then each of us turning in unison to look at your father. I told him:"

> 'Ben, we don't have a clue what the hell you are talking about. So, it wouldn't be difficult for either of us to keep your secret. We wouldn't begin to know how to

explain what you just said, even if we were of a mind to do so.'

Martha chuckled, "Your father then laughed and said, that we didn't know what he was talking about because he hadn't told us anything yet."

Martha then added to Martin's memory of their conversation with John's father. "I remember telling your father:"

> 'You are right about that, Ben, but if I understand your question to us if, in fact, there was a question hidden among the words you used, you are asking us if it is all right for you to tell us something that we cannot share with anyone else, except possibly John, and then only after you die...if we don't die first that is. Is that what you are asking us?'

"And then I think that your Uncle Marty was somewhat insulted by your father's next comment:"

> 'And I thought that Martin was the smarter of the two of you...yes, that is it, Martha. Before I actually commit you to something, I would like your permission to do so. It isn't something terrible, and it is something that I would like John to know about me when he grows up and, as I had promised to another, only after I die. Are you willing and able to do this for me Martha? How about you, Martin? Can the two of you keep a secret that cannot be shared with any other for a lifetime...for my lifetime?'

"I also remember your uncle telling your father that we would agree to keep secret whatever it was that he wanted to tell us:"

> 'I can't speak for Martha, Ben, but not knowing what it is that you would have asked of us would kill me if I

didn't agree to it. So I am going to say okay, just to find out what the hell it is that you are obviously dying to tell us...not dying in the real sense of the word, if you get my meaning.'

Martha added: "We all laughed and agreed that we would do our utmost to do whatever it was that your father was about to ask of us. You see, John, we had the utmost respect for your father and believed that he would not ask us to do anything that would jeopardize either of us, or you."

Martin then recounted what it was that Benedict asked of them:

'I have a document that I would like to give you and ask that you keep it in a safe place where no other will ever find it inadvertently. Mr. Washington and I have agreed that we would see to it that it is made public after both of us are no longer of this world. The intent is to have the content made public after we are both gone and no longer subject to question on this matter. For me, I don't really care any longer what people, other than the two of you and my family, think of me. However, it is important for me to know that, once I die, my children will then truly know me as the man I am and not the man the world over understands me to be. For that reason, I ask that you take possession of this document and, after both Mr. Washington and I are dead, give it to John to read so that he, too, will then know who his father really was, as a man.'

Martha then added: "After telling us that, your father then stood up, took a candle from our table and left the room."

Martin chuckled a bit, adding: "Martha and I both thought that he needed to use the necessary in a hurry, but after a few moments, your father returned to us, carrying a book that he had taken from your mother's cabin out back. He then told us:"

> 'Here. I am going to put the document within these pages. Sometimes the most obvious places are the least noticed. Keep this book on a shelf or in your bookcase with other books and when the time comes, all you will need to do is to hand the book to John and ask that he read the document I've placed in here on this day for him.'

After sharing their story, Martin closed the book with the envelope once again hidden within its pages, and handed it to John. "So, John, we have now kept our promise of 16 years to your father. You now have in your hands the information that your father asked us to deliver to you *at an appropriate time*. Now that you've reached the 21st year of life, this seems like as good a time as any other."

Looking from her husband to John, Martha added: "What you do with the information is now up to you."

CHAPTER 35

SARATOGA
FRIDAY, DECEMBER 16, 1831

It has been 24 years since John's visit when Martin and Martha gave him information about his father. John had long ago returned to his home, along with the book that Martin and Martha had given to him as his father had asked them to do. John was a good soul. He stayed in contact with his aunt and uncle over the years by letter and saw them less frequently as the years passed them all by. There were more letters in the beginning; fewer and fewer letters as time progressed and the demands for John's time were to be shared with others in his life.

Martha and Martin had not heard from John in over a year and in mid-December of the year, 1831, they received a package sent to them by John's wife, Sarah. Opening the package, they found a book, *Meditations and Contemplations* by James Hervey and the following letter:

November 8, 1831
St. John's

My dear Uncle Martin and Aunt Martha:

It is with sorrow that I write to tell you that John passed away last month from complications stemming from his struggles with consumption over the last several months. He went to his Heavenly home on October 22nd.

The children and I are attempting to adjust, as best we can, to our loss. I know and regret that the news I bring to you now will bring sadness to your hearts as well. For that I am regretful, but I know that you would want to know what happened to John.

I can't begin to tell you how much the two of you meant to my husband. I fondly remember all the stories he used to tell me, and our children, about his early life on your farm in Saratoga. Although he was not able to do so in his lifetime, he had hoped to bring one or more of the children to you for a visit, so that they could meet you and see where their father grew up and first learned how to work on a farm. Regrettably, there was always work to be done on the farm, which left very little time for any travels.

You will also see that I've sent a book to you that, before he passed away, John instructed me to return to you. My John told me that you had given it to him during one of his visits in the distant past and that, if anything should ever happen to him, I was to send the book back to you. I regret having to fulfill this wish of his, hoping the day would never come.

I send, as well, my love and gratitude to you for raising such a wonderful man. The lessons you *taught him so well of not only farming, but how to be a loving, caring human being has been equally shared by him with me and our children as well. For that I will be forever in your debt.*

With Regret and Sorrow, I remain,

Sarah Arnold

After reading the letter to her husband, and with the book in her lap, Martha wiped the tears from her eyes and looked up at Martin. "Our poor John. He was too young. I can't possibly imagine how Sarah is going to manage the farm and raise their seven children. It is so sad, Martin."

Martin sat quietly in his rocker for several minutes as though consumed in thought about the letter, and the book Sarah had returned to them. "We are all that is left, Martha. How is it that we lived to be so old? Why is it I live on at 87, when all of my friends and all of my family, except for you, my dear Martha, have departed this world before me?" Hesitating for a moment, Martin turned to his loving wife and, motioning toward the book with his head, he asked: "Is *it* still there?"

Martha opened the book and thumbed through its pages. Looking up, she then nodded her head that it was. Pulling the envelope from the book, she handed it to Martin, who inspected it carefully. Although his vision was now blurred with age, he was able to see that the seal placed on the envelope by Benedict Arnold over 40 years before was still intact. "Well, Martha, it seems that John was true to his word as well. The seal has not been broken, and it would seem that he didn't need to know anything more about his father than he already knew. Now it appears that nobody will ever know."

Martin then looked up from the envelope at Martha with a smile: "That is, unless…"

"Oh Martin, what can we do now? Who would ever believe anything that either of us *old-timers* have to say about anything, let alone something about Benedict Arnold and President Washington? They would believe us to be out of our minds, which would not be a far stretch of anybody's imagination nowadays. Everyone would just think us to be blathering old fools, living our lives in the past, and not relating very well to the present."

"But we have the document, Martha. It is right here in my hand. We can give it to someone who can tell others about it. Others can then learn about Benedict and know that he really wasn't a traitor."

"Well, perhaps we could, Martin, but *should* we? Benedict didn't ask us to do anything of the sort. We did what he asked us to do. We gave the document to John; by doing so, gave John the opportunity to learn more about his father. But he chose not to. That was his choice to make and not ours. We did what Benedict asked. But he never said anything about you or me telling anyone else. He didn't, Martin."

"I suppose you are right, Martha, but what would be the harm in doing so now? Someone out there may care about learning the truth about Ben. And others might like to learn more about our President and what he did to our poor Ben."

"Martin, if neither Ben nor Mr. Washington could see to it that the truths become known, do you really believe that we would be able to do so now, after all these years?"

"I suppose you are right, Martha, but I don't see the harm in trying either."

"Martin, you are starting to repeat yourself again. Just stop and think for a moment. You are 87 years of age and I am 83. If either of us were to now try to let others know about our Ben, can you just imagine the ruckus others would make around here? Can you imagine what others would likely now say about us? I don't know about you, my friend, but at my age, I don't believe that I have it in me to deal with the troubles that we may have if we were to give this document, and whatever it says, to someone else. I just want to be able to get up in the morning, breathe the fresh air, spend time alone with my husband, and go to bed at the end of the day in the warmth of his arms."

"In whose arms, Martha?"

"Why yours, you old fool. I love falling to sleep while lying next to you and feeling your warmth and feeling your breath. If not just to make sure that you are still alive and haven't left me alone to get myself up in the morning."

Both Martin and Martha laughed, until their thoughts again turned to John and the *gift* he had returned into their care.

"Well, Martin, why don't we just do nothing for now. Let's just put the document back in the book, and put the book away for now. Someday, something may come to us as to what we should do."

"That is probably best, Martha. Although I am not sure how many *somedays* I have left, until we are sure of what to do, I expect that it is best to do nothing. That is easy for me to do. I am getting pretty damn good at doing nothing anymore."

CHAPTER 36

SARATOGA
SUNDAY, DECEMBER 11, 1841

On Saturday, December 10, 1841, just 10 days after celebrating his 97th birthday, Martin's journey in this world ended. Martha, now in her 89th year, was left behind in the care of dedicated friends and neighbors. Once it became apparent that Martin and Martha were no longer able to care for the farm, its crops, its animals, or to a lesser extent, themselves, they made arrangements for a neighbor to step in to manage the farm and to provide care for them in their declining years. In return, Martin and Martha agreed to leave the farm to their neighbor and his family in their Last Will and Testament. Neither the Van Derwerkers nor their neighbor realized at the time just how long this caring arrangement would last. But last it did. The Van Derwerkers and their neighbor each maintained their lifetime commitment one to another.

Therefore, when Martin and Martha were both in their 70s, they moved out of the larger home and into the cabin where Theresa and her first son, John, had once lived. They had long ago discovered that, in their advanced years, life had become simpler in many ways. At some unknown point in time, they each realized that neither was any longer afraid of death, or of those who had since passed on from this world into the next. This former distraction no longer clouded their vision or their enjoyment of the days yet remaining in their lives. For this bit of wisdom, gained late in life, they were eternally thankful. Consequently, it didn't take Martin or Martha any time at all to become comfortable with being in the cabin they had once shunned for years on end. They even refurbished and kept many of the same furnishings that Theresa had used while she was yet alive.

On the day of his death, Martin's body was moved from his and Martha's cabin to the main house, where he was prepared for burial and lovingly placed in a pine casket one of their neighbors had made several days before…just in case.

Now alone for the first time in her life, Martha sat in her well-worn rocking chair, sipping tea and looking about the room she once shared with her life's companion. Sitting quietly, Martha studied the furnishings, mostly made by the hands of her husband. She considered as well the items she, Martin, and Theresa had carefully placed about the room on tables, desk tops, and shelves. Items that provided earthly links to memories of days-gone-by, and turned the otherwise stark, wooden room into a home, chockfull of life's memories.

Martha gently rocked as she recalled the many good, and the few not-so-good, memories created in this very room over the years with her loving family and friends. Looking about the room, Martha's face grimaced when her eyes confronted the still barren fireplace mantel. Void of any mementos of life, it remained as it had been since Benedict's last visit, more than 50 years before. Over the years, the empty space on this altar-like mantel served as a reminder, not of life, but of death. For Martha, the mantel's empty space reminded her of the equally empty space left in her life by those who have gone before – a space that has grown even larger and darker now that her Marty was no longer by her side.

To help fend off the chill in the room, Martha covered her lap with the quilt Theresa had once started, but was never quite able to finish before she died. Gently stroking its fabric and feeling Theresa's delicate needlework, Martha remembered that, unknown to either her or Martin at the time, Benedict had once removed the quilt from Theresa's cabin and took it with him to St. John's. She remembered Benedict later telling her that, on the evening he learned of Theresa and John's death, he spent the entire night in the cabin *talking* to Theresa and John…at least talking to them in his mind.

She remembered Benedict telling the story to her and Martin about that evening spent alone in this very room. She remembered the serious look on his face, and the equally confused look on Martin's face, when Benedict told them that while here that evening, John *told* him to smash the ship so his little brother would not try to sail it and possibly suffer his same fate. Benedict bewildered Martin even more by telling them that Theresa also *told* him that she had intended to give the quilt to Martha as a surprise so she could keep warm during the cold winter nights.

"So you took it home and asked your sister to finish it for Theresa…and for me."

Holding her head steady, but looking upward with her eyes, "Thank you, Benedict. Thank you for finishing Theresa's quilt for me. She never did tell me for whom the quilt was being made. I just assumed that she was making it for herself and John."

Studying the crafted quilt once again, "I only knew that it was taking forever for Theresa to finish, and she was never able to do so before she died. You took it home, asked your sister to finish it for me, and then brought it back. What a lovely gesture. I never suspected that she was making the quilt for me. Thank you, Ben, and thank you, Theresa. It has indeed kept me warm on many a cold winter's night. And, I expect that I will need it even more, now that my Marty is no longer here with me." With a deep sigh she slowly nodded, "I will likely need this now, more than ever before, during the long and cold winter days ahead."

Continuing to talk to herself, Martha looked about the room for other memories of her and Martin's past together. While admiring the furnishings, her eyes came upon a bookshelf located in a darkened corner of the room. Martha slowly got up from her rocker and shuffled to the bookshelf to retrieve a book: *Meditations and Contemplations*. The same book Benedict had once retrieved from this same cabin and had given to her and Martin with a document hidden among its pages. The same book she and her husband had, in turn, given to Benedict's son, John, as they were once asked to do. And, as fate would have it, the same book that was returned to them upon John's death.

Rocking next to the fireplace, she firmly held the book next to her chest with frail, trembling hands. Martha raised her eyes upward and asked: "Now what, Ben? Everyone is gone except me. What do you want me to do with this book and the secrets it yet holds? Do you want me to just leave it alone in the chance that someone will one day discover it and then know of your deeds?" Closing both eyes and raising her head upward even more, Martha asked again: "So tell me, Ben, just what should this old lady do with such a book as this?"

Several minutes passed before Martha looked downward, opened the book to find the envelope, still hidden among its pages. Holding the envelope in her hands for several more minutes, Martha then broke its waxen seal and withdrew the document Benedict had entrusted into her and Martin's care more than 50 years before. Noting that the paper was brittle and the ink on its pages had faded, Martha smiled and offered the comment: "…not unlike me and my vision…" Nevertheless, leaning close to the light given by the burning fire, Martha took a deep breath and, after these many wondering years, finally read the document Benedict had left behind.

October 23, 1791
New York City

To Whom It May Concern:

This proclamation, drawn by my hand on this date, attests to the agreement that Major General Benedict Arnold and I entered into <u>prior</u> to his separation from the American ranks to engage those of the British Army.

After war's end, and fearing personal retribution from others should the truth concerning Mr. Arnold's apparent defection become known during our lifetimes, this document also serves to confirm and attest to the agreement reached between Mr. Benedict Arnold and me on this date. It is hereby agreed that the pronouncement of the information contained herein shall not be made public until after Mr. Arnold and I are both deceased.

Let it be known: Prior to September 23, 1780, Major General Benedict Arnold and I agreed that he would make way into the camp of the British Army in an effort to obtain intelligence concerning their military campaign on this continent from the highest levels of their command.

Let it be known: It was never Major General Benedict Arnold's or my intention to turn over the fortifications at West Point. It can be confirmed by others present and who may still be living at the time of our deaths, that leading up to September 23, 1780, my movements were orchestrated to ensure that I would arrive in time to refortify that installation and prevent its loss to any British force that might advance to it.

Let it be known: The negotiations between Major General Arnold and the British intelligence officers during the year preceding the General's movement to the British lines were made known to me as major developments in his progress to leave our ranks occurred.

Let it be known: Although Mr. Arnold wished to return to this nation at war's end, and assume his rightful place among the victors of war, I requested that he not do so for fear of the aforementioned retributions, and to prevent possible disruption to my ability to assist in the formation of a meaningful government and, subsequent to my election, effectively serve as the President of the United States of America.

Therefore: By the powers bestowed upon me as the President of the United States, I hereby pardon Mr. Benedict Arnold of any and all supposed acts of deception and defection as perceived by others in his attempts to obtain intelligence for use by me as the Commanding General of the Continental Army of the United States of America in service to this nation.

By this act, I hereby restore Benedict Arnold's rightful claim of due respect for himself, his heirs and future generations of descendants. Thought to be a traitor by everyone, save me, during his lifetime, let it be known from the reading of this proclamation that Mr. Benedict Arnold's actions were in keeping with the highest traditions of service and honor.

Your most humble and obedient servant,

George Washington

President of the United States of America

After reading the words printed on parchment at long last, Martha sat in her rocker for a number of minutes, staring at the flames of the fireplace while still gently stroking the fabric of the quilt carefully folded on her lap. "Well, isn't this something? Did you hear that, Martin? So this is what we've been clinging to for all these years? Now what am I to do? So Mr. Arnold, what would you like me to do with it now? Tell me, Ben, what should I do?"

CHAPTER 37

SARATOGA
MONDAY, DECEMBER 12, 1841

L arge crystalline flakes of snow gently fell from the heavens above as the few remaining members of Martha and Martin's family and friends gathered to bury their friend.

Immediately following a brief funeral service given by their pastor, Martha gingerly approached Martin's spartan casket. "You were always such a simple man, my dear husband. A friend of ours asked that I give you a gift to take with you."

With a smile on her now deeply wrinkled face, Martha then leaned toward her husband and whispered: "He told me that you would likely know what to do with it…"

With Benedict's cherished document once again hidden among its pages, Martha carefully placed the book under her husband's right hand; then softly kissed her husband's forehead, bidding him good-bye for the final time. Slowly stepping back, Martha watched and listened as the cover to her husband's casket was carefully nailed into place. The sound of the hammer's strike on the head of each iron nail rang heavy in her ears. For Martha, it was a deafening sound that she would never forget.

Once the remains of her life's companion and the book containing the document their friend had entrusted into their care a lifetime ago were secured, Martha slowly led the bent procession of aging mourners up a slight hill leading to the location Martin, himself, had selected for his burial. From within the branches of a towering pine near the freshly dug rectangle into which Martin was about to be placed, a solitary crow welcomed these momentary guests.

Following a final graveside prayer, Martha added: "I loved you more than you will ever know, Marty. But, just so you don't forget, I will see you soon and tell you so myself." Then, out of the corner of her eye, Martha noticed a gathering of five crows, silently watching from a perch within a nearby, leaf-barren tree. Listening carefully, she once again heard the distinctive call of a solitary crow echo in her ears. Tears gently rolled down each creviced cheek as Martha looked first in the direction of this gathering of black feathered mourners, and then to the heavens above. And then, with family and friends straining to hear, Martha smiled and softly whispered: "I will see you all very soon."

It would appear that time is as relative on earth as it is in heaven. Six years after Martin's life journey ended, Martha's did as well. The sole remaining individual ever to learn of Benedict Arnold's quest to have the truth be told died peacefully in her sleep on Friday, March 10, 1848 – just 7 days after quietly celebrating her 96th birthday. While attending to Martha's earthly needs as she lay on her deathbed, her friends listened attentively as she incomprehensibly mumbled, over and over again in her delirium: "Martin... Theresa... John.... John... Ben.... George... pardon... Martin... George... pardon... Ben... Martin... John... Ben... John... book... pardon... George..." Over, and over again until she could be heard no more.

After she breathed her last, Martha's caretakers looked to one another and asked: "Who do you suppose Ben and George might have been?"

EPILOGUE

A nd, so it ended. As portrayed in this telling of Benedict Arnold's life's journey, only seven mortals of this world ever learned the motives for his actions during and after the days of the Revolution. An eighth, John Sage Arnold, had an opportunity to discover more about his father, but chose, instead, to know his father from his heart; caring not what others ever thought about this man of history. For John, Benedict Arnold was simply a father, a man who loved his family, his friends, and apparently, his country. Nothing more and nothing less…

16. *Fact* – On February 18, 1781, just four months after Benedict Arnold's movement to the British ranks, Alexander Hamilton did indeed write Philip Schuyler a letter in which he stated: "…With this key you will easily unlock the present mystery. At the end of the war I may say many things to you concerning which I shall impose upon myself 'till then an inviolable silence.'"

17. *Fact* – Within 1 year of Benedict Arnold's movement to the British ranks, the war for independence all but ended with the American victory at Yorktown.

18. *Fact* – George Washington died on Saturday, December 14, 1799, taking secrets to his grave.

19. *Fact* – Benedict Arnold died on Sunday, June 14, 1801, taking secrets to his grave.

20. *Fact* – Martha Washington died on Saturday, May 22, 1802, taking secrets to her grave.

21. *Fact* – Peggy Shippen-Arnold died on Friday, August 24, 1804, taking secrets to her grave.

22. *Fact* – Alexander Hamilton died on Wednesday, July 11, 1804, taking secrets to his grave.

23. *Fact* – Martin Van Derwerker died on Saturday, December 10, 1844, taking secrets to his grave.

24. *Fact* – Martha Van Derwerker died on Friday, March 10, 1848, taking secrets to her grave.

25. *Fact* – Everyone takes secrets to the grave.

Another fact worthy of note: Martin and Martha Van Derwerker were real people who lived during the time of the Revolution. Their remains are interred in a cemetery, now overgrown with dense trees, brush and undergrowth, located just outside Saratoga Springs, New York, in the Township now named Northumberland.

I first learned of Martin and Martha in a now tattered and dog-eared copy of a branch of my family tree, handed down by my late Grandmother, Esther Martin, daughter of Sara Van Derwerker-Peterson. It had been researched and written by another Van Derwerker ancestor, J.B. Van Derwerker, who served as the Saratoga County Historian in the 1930s. While thumbing through its pages, I discovered the name *Martin* Van Derwerker, who, it was noted, fought at the Battle of Saratoga during the American Revolution. What caught my attention was his first name. It was the same as my last. Although knowing full well that his first and my last names were nothing more than coincidence, I was nonetheless drawn to this man and wondered about him, his family and their lives.

As described on the Historical Marker alongside the road leading to the cemetery, the land in which Martin, Martha, and 144 other Brownville Hamlet residents are interred was donated to his community by Martin Van Derwerker.

In addition, as given in the story you just read, Martin and Martha did, in fact, live to the ripe-old ages of 97 and 96 respectively, when the life expectancy in rural communities of the United States was less than 50 years of age. Even by today's standards, for any individual to live as long as Martin and Martha is a remarkable achievement. The fact that *both* did so during the era of the Revolution gave me pause to wonder: *what was it that kept Martin and Martha going all those years?*

So, that is how my journey started, ultimately leading me to spend six years of my life writing this story I now share with you.

Benedict Arnold: Legacy Lost (A Ghost's Story)

While reading background information and piecing the puzzle surrounding Benedict Arnold's life and the life and times of Martin and Martha Van Derwerker together, I described my early writing to a friend who asked me two questions: *What have I learned by my work? And, where did my thoughts and ideas for this story come from?*

In answer to the first question asked of me, I offered the following:

> *I've learned that, in some inexplicable way, by looking to my past and connecting with those who have gone before, I've also become connected to others, who, as I look ahead, will live in the future and will one day glance back at my generation and ask... really, who were these people?*

In response to the second question, and, keeping in mind that *this is a ghost's story*, the answer to this question is one secret that I am likely to take with me into *my eternity*. I will take the answer to this question to my grave, along with two other, yet unanswered questions I have asked of myself, time and time again since I first began to write this account of Benedict Arnold's life's story:

Why it is that one man's legacy must die so that another's might live?

And finally:

What if?

"The heart has reasons the mind knows nothing about."
Blaise Pascal

ABOUT THE AUTHOR

Will Martin is an independent psychohistorian living in Saratoga Springs, NY, and dedicated to exploring the life and times of the American Revolutionary Era.

During the first chapter of his life's trilogy, titled *"Growth and Education,"* the author was born and raised in Jamestown, NY, a blue-collar community in western New York where he attended public schools. Coming of age in the late '60s, the author served a tour of duty in Vietnam, during which time he joined a reconnaissance platoon and received a purple heart and silver star. The author attended college in the tumultuous times of the early 70's; graduating with a degree in Psychology.

As the author began to seriously consider the fog covered shroud that blocked a clear vision of the final chapter of his trilogy, which others call *"retirement,"* he was blessed with a discovery of yet another passion: creative writing. With the same effect of an epiphany, the author learned that endorphins are not exclusively reserved for long-distance runners. For those who can fully appreciate the meaning of this statement, he looks forward to joining your world.

As a beginning to his newfound passion, the author dedicated a portion of the last six years of his life writing his first manuscript, *Benedict Arnold: Legacy Lost (A Ghost's Story)*. While doing so, he discovered an era that he knew little of, and now wants to know more about.

Consequently, the author now knows what he will spend the rest of his life doing: researching the lives of early American characters of history, and developing more works of historical fiction to uncover other untapped history mysteries.